SAILING FOR GRACE

JOSEPH BAUER

RUNNING WILD

SAILING FOR GRACE

Edited by Lisa Diane Kastner

Published in North America and Europe by Running Wild Press. Visit Running Wild Press at www.runningwildpress.com, Educators, librarians, book clubs (as well as the eternally curious), go to www.runningwildpress.com.

Paperback ISBN: 978-1-960018-51-9
eBook ISBN: 978-1-960018-50-2

Library of Congress Control Number: 1-960018-51-5

ALSO BY JOSEPH BAUER

The Accidental Patriot

The Patriot's Angels

Too True to Be Good

For Sister Hope Greener, SSJ, founder of Providence House in Cleveland, Ohio, where she translated her love of vulnerable children into their care and well-being.

"In the little world in which children have their existence, whosoever brings them up, there is nothing so finely perceived and so finely felt as injustice."

Charles Dickens

PART I

1

You couldn't say that Will Goodbow was one of those people who didn't know what he had until he'd lost it. He'd known it all along.

It made losing Grace all the harder for him; harder than losing anything before. Harder, he thought, than anything he could ever lose again. But now, after all that had happened, he understood that when a loss was deep enough, it could hollow down through his lungs and gut and lie sleeping in his soul like a troubled guest. Once awakened, it could take him places he never imagined.

Besides, he had promised her.

"I want you to do this, Will Goodbow," she'd said. Her eyes, those beautiful eyes, seemed larger as her face shrank around them. The disease was taking everything it could take. Every day a little more. Relentlessly. Even the elastic band of the knit cap she wore to cover her hairless head was loosening. It slipped down nearer one ear as she turned to him from her bed. Only a few days before, when they sailed together on their yacht, *The Sails of Grace*, the cap had stayed put.

"I understand what you want," Will said.

"But you haven't said you will *do* it."

It was true. He hadn't. He had his reasons. For one, he didn't *want* to do it. He didn't share Grace's passion for the whole issue; in truth not genuinely for any part of the problem. He wouldn't know *how* to do it even if he did care about it the way she did. He wasn't a lawyer; he knew nothing of the process or the rules or if it was even legally possible for *anyone* to do what Grace asked. *Hell, I've never even been to the place,* he told himself.

Of course, he could just lie to her. Assure her he would do what she asked and, knowing him as she did, believing in him as she did, loving him as she did, she would accept his word. Take him off the hook. He'd read that it happened often in families: untruths to the dying, assurances of hope unfounded, palliative deception. He knew he could do that and be done with it, just move on. But knowing he *could* assuage her falsely only underscored his conflict, because more than anything, more even than his hope that she would stop insisting on this thing from him, he did not want to deceive her, could not. She was not the perfect wife. Who could be? She was more perfect, Will judged, than anyone or anything else in his life, so much more perfect than himself. What did he owe such a love when it was ending? When life was leaving? Whatever else, surely he owed honesty, Will Goodbow thought.

He searched for safe ground. "I promise you I will look into it," he said.

It wasn't enough. She raised her chest from the bed and looked into his eyes, fiercely.

"*No,* Will Goodbow! You will not '*look into it!*'" Grace said. "This is not a *business* prospect." If it can be said that contempt can be uttered gently, she had succeeded. If barely. "Don't give me '*look into it,*' Will Goodbow!'"

Will rose from his chair next to her and turned away. He moved his large hands from his hips to his pockets, and back again. Finally, he turned back to her.

"You know that if I say I will do it, Grace, if I say that to *you*, I will really *have* to do it," Will said. "Especially now."

He did not look away, though he wanted to. His eyes were locked on hers. Each knew the depth of the other's pleading. Each nearly seventy-years old, they'd been together nearly forty. When he had loved that long, he knew these things.

"Of course, I know that," she said. "Why else would I want you to promise it? And I know it will be impossible to help all of them. But *some* of them, Will. You must help *some* of them! Promise it to me. Promise me you will help some of them, Will. Promise me now. Promise my soul. Because there has never been anything that you really tried to do that you couldn't do. That you didn't do."

Will moved to her and held her face in his hands.

"Oh, Grace," he said. "My good, good Grace. I promise you. I promise you I *will* do it. I will do it for as many as I can."

The doorbell rang, announcing the young man's arrival from home hospice.

* * *

She died the next night. Will was at her side. She did not speak again about his promise. She knew she needn't.

2

Burp Lebeau was not an easy man to know. He was, they said, an acquired taste, and few truly knew the crusty old local legend of the sailing town. Certainly, no one knew him the way Will Goodbow knew him.

Such different men in most every respect, it was hard to pair them in a person's mind. Goodbow was the mega-wealthy owner of diverse businesses, a staple of the Newport upper crust. Lebeau was the sun-browned sailor of Cajun roots who piloted yachts for the rich locals in the fair months and shined and repaired them in the others. Goodbow's expansive home sat high above the harbor, a marvel of New England architecture. Lebeau had lived for thirty years in a small detached carriage house of a Newport mansion where domestic servants had resided a hundred years earlier. In terms monetary, in terms educational, Will Goodbow and Burp Lebeau were, as the sailor had once put it in the vernacular he understood best, "oceans apart." But if you searched for two grown men with as deep affection for each other as these men, you'd be hard pressed to find them in all of Rhode Island.

Burp struck a stark figure, as men of the sea often will. Though average height, just under six feet, he was so thin below the waist that he looked shorter. His feet—often bare—were rough-hewn and chafed, his fingers and knuckles permanently swollen at the ends of his muscular arms. He'd lost so many caps to wave and wind that he'd given up wearing them decades ago. His face and nearly hairless scalp showed it, the leathery skin creased in deep wild lines.

The old captain had seen Goodbow just once since Grace's death. It was at her funeral in the small church near the shore north of Newport, where Burp sat in the last row. He'd arrived early to be sure of a place in a rear pew, to be inconspicuous during the service, and to have time alone in the little chapel to think about Grace and pray for her before it started. But when Goodbow walked in with his son and daughter-in-law behind the rolling casket, the new widower saw Burp immediately and stopped, motioning him to step out of the back pew and join them in the walk forward. The old sailor did not like to call attention to himself; his first impulse was to resist and wave his friend on. But when he saw the sadness in Goodbow's eyes and his gesture towards the casket as if to say, "for Grace," he rose without protest and stepped in behind the three family members, taking a seat in the front pew next to his friend.

Since Burp had first learned of Grace's illness—from Grace herself on a week-long sail to the Florida Keys a year earlier—he'd been asking himself whether he knew her even better than he knew her husband, as close as he and Will were. Though he'd considered the question many times, he never came to a sure answer. He could only conclude that he loved them both. But when Grace's end neared, he worried that his feelings about Will might change when she died or, worse, that Will might feel differently about him. Over all the years, Burp had rarely been with one of them and not the other. *Surely, it would not be the same without Grace,* he feared. But when she *did* pass, his first sensation was that nothing seemed to have changed after all. If anything—and strangely to him—he felt *closer* to Will than ever. Perhaps, he thought, it was the new sharing between the two of them. The sharing of the loss of Grace.

His feeling was punctuated when he saw Grace and Will's son at the market two days after his mother's death.

"Ben," the old sailor said. "How is your father?"

The son was thirty-five years old and already prospering in Newport real estate, independent of his father's Goodbow Companies. It had been Grace's suggestion that her son not come into his father's business.

"Why not?" Will had asked her. "It's common. Sons come in all the time."

"And look what happens with most of them," Grace said. "They end up somewhere between pampered brat and resentful child, always either giving orders or taking them. Always trying to live up to dad, never quite making the grade. Ben can find his own way. He's a beautiful boy."

Grace was right, Goodbow now considered. It was more satisfying to be an adviser than a boss, he found, and he came to see that working together would have altered his relationship with his son, fundamentally. Besides, it was gratifying in its own way to watch his son succeed without him, not to mention the troubles of suspicion and envy that were avoided in the ranks of the Goodbow Companies where talented others needn't fear a family successor likely to block their own ascents. Nepotism, and perhaps worse, the perception of it, was a pernicious influence, one his companies were spared.

In Ben's encounter with Lebeau in the market, the son was not offended or surprised that the sea man had asked about his father instead of extending sympathy for his own loss of his mother.

"He's low, Burp. He's not talking very much. He's not calling anybody to tell them."

"Oh."

"But I am glad he called you, Burp. I know he at least called you. He told me he did. Right after he called me, he said."

"He knows I loved your mother."

"She loved you."

Burp simply nodded.

"I'll tell dad I saw you," the son said. "He'll be glad."

"Do that. Good. And tell him that if he'd like to take out *The Sails of Grace*, we could. Just the two of us, if he wants."

But weeks passed without word from his friend. Every few days Lebeau went to the large vessel's slip to check its moorings. Each time he went below to see that everything in the galley and baths were in order—and to look for any signs that Goodbow had visited *The Sails of Grace*. There never were. The old sailor's doubts returned. Goodbow was never away from the big boat for more than a few days, if only to sit on the deck and read or lounge below with his whiskey. Maybe Grace's death *had* changed things. He took a job piloting Tom Brewster's family to Bar Harbor, Maine, resigned to the belief that it could be a long time before Goodbow re-emerged in his life like the old times, if he ever did.

But when Lebeau returned with the Brewsters and brought their boat into Newport Harbor, he saw *The Sails of Grace* parked at its slip and Goodbow hailing him from her deck.

"Burp!" Goodbow shouted.

"Will!"

"Taking on Tom Brewster now, are you?" Brewster divided his time between Newport and Boston where he was a senior partner in a prominent law firm. He and Goodbow had been friends for years in the sailing community.

"Took his crew up to Maine." Burp called back.

"I don't like that!" Goodbow shouted.

"Why not?" came the return.

"Because I can't afford to pay you what he pays you!"

"Like hell! You're rich as God and cheap as dirt, Will Goodbow."

"Come over here when you're tied in. Maybe I can work you down."

Goodbow had returned from sorrow, Lebeau thought. It pleased the old captain. In his joy, he was clueless as to where his friend would soon journey.

3

"Remember Grace's favorite port?" Goodbow asked Lebeau as the old captain stepped onto the deck of *The Sails of Grace* and took Will's outstretched hand. "Her favorite bay to put in?"

"Sure. It was Charleston. Charleston, for sure."

"I'd like to sail down there for a couple nights. I've got some reading and thinking to do. It would be a good place. Could you do it?"

"When?"

"As soon as you can. Tomorrow? The day after?"

"Day after will work."

Goodbow held a sheaf of papers at least an inch thick between the flaps of a tattered manila folder. Burp saw that he'd obviously been studying them; the pages were disheveled, a few hanging nearly halfway out of the folder, others with corners turned over. A thick rubber band surrounded them.

"Working on a new deal?" Burp asked, nodding toward the papers.

"Of a sort, I guess."

"I thought you were going to slow down on your business stuff?"

"I thought I was too. But I guess some things have happened."

Burp regretted his comment. *Everything* had happened, he knew. Everything for his friend. "Been below?" he quickly asked.

"Yeah. I see you kept the liquor cabinet stocked."

"And untouched."

"Well, let's do something about that," Goodbow said. He stepped toward the stairs to the galley below. "That sun will be down eventually. I need to tell you about something."

* * *

The two men sat and talked for hours. Neither showed any concern for time, other places to be, or matters to attend. Just the two of them sat on the comfortable sofas below the deck of the massive yacht. One or the other rose occasionally to pour a little more whiskey, infallibly offering service to the other when he did. Neither ever declined. Looking back later, many months later, Lebeau wondered what might have happened had he listened differently, responded differently to what Goodbow told him that late afternoon and evening.

"You know how upset Grace was about all the problems down there," Goodbow said.

"The border, you mean? The thing with Mexico?"

"Yeah."

"Sure, I know. Before it was even that big in the news, she was talking about it," Burp said. "Can't say, though, I agreed so much with her."

"Me either," Goodbow said.

"I think she'd just let *anybody* get in."

"She would."

"But that was Grace's heart, Will. Bigger than the sea."

Lebeau thought his comment might have saddened Goodbow. After all, she'd been gone only a month or so. Maybe it was not his place to say tender things about her. And it did seem to hit Goodbow. He smiled in a way that wrinkled his eyes and pulled his cheeks up, the way some do to stem emotion or buy time before speaking. But it was not too long before he responded to Lebeau.

"She was involved in a lot of causes, you know. Over the years, a lot of things. Seems like there was always something," Goodbow said. "Even way back. The draft dodgers who went to Canada during Vietnam, remember that?"

"I do. Sure, I do. It was our own generation."

"She thought it was terrible that a lot of people didn't want them back."

"You were one of 'those people,' as I recall," Burp said. "You were pretty hardnosed about it." Goodbow looked up from his drink with a you-had-to-remind-me look. "I mean, you didn't think they should get off Scott-free," Burp said. "I agreed with you. I didn't either."

"You had your reasons. You'd served, Burp."

"You'd of too if your number'd been pulled. Wouldn't you?"

"I think so. At least I told myself so when I disagreed with Grace about it."

"That was a long time ago."

"Yeah, but then came the thing about the Syrian refugees a few years ago. The Trump campaign, the Muslim ban and all of that. Grace went wild over that too. Passionate, really. She organized letters to Trump saying he should let in as many as the Germans were. Millions of them!"

"I remember," Lebeau said.

"She wanted me to sign one of those letters," Goodbow said.

"Did you?"

"No, I refused. She was angry, really angry. Wouldn't talk to me for days. But then she came around. Said it was all about forgiveness. That if she thought it was wrong of me not to welcome those people, it was wrong of her too not to forgive me for what I believed."

"Sounds like Grace."

"I'm surprised she didn't try to get you to do it. To sign a letter to Trump."

"She did."

"Really!" Will was sincerely surprised. "Did *you* do it?"

"I did. Yes, I did."

"She never told me that!"

"Sounds like Grace too."

"Did you ask her not to tell me?"

"You don't ask a person like Grace *not* to say something. There was a lot of fire in that little package. So, I didn't, no. But I knew you were having a row with her about it, and *she* knew *I* knew you were. I assumed she'd probably tell you, but now when I think about it, it's just like her not to. She didn't want to stir up anything between you and me."

"You're probably right, Burp. She never encouraged anger or hard feelings, did she?"

"No, she didn't. She was a fighter, like I said, but she was gentle about it, mostly. She fought her own battles. Didn't make people take sides."

The old sailor saw his friend react to his assessment, raising his wide brow and tilting his head, as if in mild doubt. He reached for the bottle on the galley counter. "Well, in the end, Burp, I'm afraid she did. Goddamnit, I'm afraid she did."

Lebeau was taken aback. He sat up straight and rigid and looked at his friend, seriously.

"What the hell are you talking about?"

"She made me promise to fight her battle."

"Battle with who?"

"The system. The government. What it's doing."

"What it's doing about *what?*"

"The people coming in, trying to come in. The families, the parents and their children."

"At the border?"

Goodbow nodded, sighed and slumped to his sofa seat, smiling weakly and raising his glass to the old sailor, as if toasting a resignation. He leaned forward and told Lebeau everything. How she began talking about it long before she died. "Well, really," he said, "it was a couple of months before, but it was so hard then for us, it seemed long. It was the separation of the children from their parents that bothered her the most," he told Lebeau. "Sometimes I thought it was killing her as much as the cancer was."

"She got after you on this after she'd given up on getting better?"

"After we both had. She said she knew she couldn't keep fighting. She needed *me* to do it. I didn't want to. I told her I didn't. She was letting go of life, but she wouldn't let go of this. 'You have to promise me you'll go there yourself,' she told me. *Me! Myself!* 'You have to get these children back with their parents.' Now, how in the hell am I going to do that?"

"You had no idea how to do it?"

"Of course not."

"And you told her you didn't know how?"

"Of course."

"And you still promised her?"

"I did."

"*All* of them back together?"

"No, not all of them. Even she knew that could never happen. But at least some of them. As many as I could."

Lebeau reached for his friend's arm and held it, saying nothing.

"Aren't you going to ask me if I meant it?" Goodbow asked after a silence.

"Will, Will, Will . . ." Burp said, then stopped. He looked Goodbow in the eye. "You know I don't need to."

It was not that it was unusual for the two of them to talk of serious matters. Many times they had. But usually, Grace was present as an equal or even gently leading with her brilliance, her humanity, her modesty. But Lebeau appreciated, even in the moment, that speaking at length and deeply *with* Grace was not at all the same as talking *about* Grace. Looking back, the old sailor saw—he feared too late—that his role as Will's friend had become something quite different—and upsettingly new—in listening to Goodbow without Grace listening too. *Should I say something for Grace? He says she said this, but did she really mean it the way he thinks she did? She was a dying woman! Was her judgment compromised? To ask this—demand it of Will—seems ironically selfish of Grace. Because selfish was the last thing Grace was.*

Thinking back on it much later, Burp Lebeau knew that he had felt these doubts even as Goodbow told him that day on *The Sails of Grace* what he had promised and how he would begin his work to fulfill his vow. He knew he had not expressed his doubts to his friend; not challenged him to consider the risks more carefully; or tried to explain the possibilities of Grace's desire and the unreasonableness of her insistence. Instead, he had looked and listened as Will showed him what he had learned from his sheaf of papers, his research on conditions in the Rio Grande Valley; the immigration laws and the rules of asylum.

In Burp's sailor's mind, when you knew you should have done something but didn't, you couldn't go back and undo it. It was overboard. Irretrievable. And even more unsettling, you could not undo the events that followed *because* you didn't. Old sailors, Burp Lebeau concluded, took the workings of their silence to their own graves, with the silence itself, as if to the bottom of the unvisitable sea.

They sailed for Charleston the next morning.

4

There wasn't a non-stop to El Paso, even from Boston, so Goodbow flew from Providence through Atlanta *and* Houston to reach the Texas border city. He couldn't remember when he'd last made two stops or spent eight hours to get anywhere on an airplane that didn't cross an ocean. But in a way it seemed fitting, he thought, to begin his quest with at least some measure of inconvenience, modest as it was. Work his way into this thing, he reasoned, this mission so preposterously different than anything he'd ever attempted. Get used to the aberration of it all, one small step at a time.

Some things he felt he needn't forego in making good on his ill-reasoned promise to Grace; he flew first class.

He could have chosen a place other than El Paso to begin his education about the "crisis at the border," as Trump had monikered it when the issue first flared just in time to fuel his presidential campaign in 2016. His famous "rapists and criminals" rhetoric, describing an "invasion" of "illegal immigrants" had met, at first, with cries of foul from some Americans: it wasn't really a crisis, many initially retorted.

But by late 2018 and certainly mid-year 2019, pretty much everyone had dropped objection to the term "crisis." The national debate turned instead to what *kind* of crisis it was and how the nation's values—if there were such things—should address it.

Trump's repeated characterization of the migrants struggling to reach American soil as bad people pouring illegally across his mostly wall-less border played well to those who believed that the crisis was indeed one of national security, threatening the citizenry's fundamental safety. But others saw the crisis more as a humanitarian issue, a moral challenge to the national soul. A few, a precious few like Grace Goodbow, made the hard effort to parse and understand the dilemma more carefully, more accurately than the leader of the free world, the public at large, or even her husband. The people presenting themselves in groups at the border may have been acting *inconveniently* for a free society reluctant to ingest large new numbers of non-white members, but they were not acting *illegally*. Each one of them had the *right* under American law—not to mention international norms of decency—to present themselves and their children (legally) at the border, or anywhere inside the country, seeking refugee status and apply—at least apply—for asylum in the country of the red-white-and-blue banner, the country of broad fields and farms, the country of honest policemen, freedom, and hope.

Goodbow did not think of himself as favoring one side or the other of the debate; indeed, as he thought about it, he realized he did not fully appreciate either Grace's passion or the reality of the problem to any degree. But he had to start somewhere, and El Paso seemed as good a place as any, especially because the contact to whom he was referred by the staffer from Human Rights First was stationed there.

"You're from *where?*" the organization's employee had

asked, in seeming puzzlement, when she took his call to the New York City phone number he'd culled from its website.

"Newport, Rhode Island."

"And *why* do you want to go to the southern border?"

"To learn about the place. Learn about the problems. See it firsthand," he'd said.

"You're writing a book or something, are you?"

"No."

"You're not trying to sell something to the government? Temporary buildings or something?"

"No."

"If you are, we'll have to check you out before we can help you. Reporters are always trying to use us. Right-wing, left-wing, all kinds of crazies. And businesses trying to make money down there. You wouldn't believe how many people say they make a great tin building or waterless toilet."

"I assure you; I am just a citizen. I only want to understand what is happening down there. And see if I can help. I've read that you help the people coming across. Help them with asylum."

"We do, but how could *you* help?" she asked. "Are you a *lawyer*?" Suddenly her voice was energized. Goodbow thought it'd been a long time since he'd heard anyone speak with enthusiasm about lawyers. "We *need* lawyers! As many as we can get! But I have to tell you, it's all *pro bono*. We can't pay you."

He felt mildly guilty correcting her misimpression. He told her no, he wasn't a lawyer, but that for the first time in his life he wished he was because it would make him more useful. He told her he was comfortable financially (a huge understatement), no longer working much (a smaller one), and that he needed to get involved at the border because he had to in order to keep his word.

"Keep your *word?*" the woman asked.

"It's a long story," he said. "And private, if you understand. But I want to go down there and I thought you could give me a contact. Someone I could meet, someone who could show me around, show me how it all works down there. Someone who is helping these people."

There was silence on the line. He wondered if he should have just said, *Yes, I am a lawyer! Boy, can I help Human Rights First! And pro bono is my middle name!* But finally he said instead, "I would be pleased to make a donation in return for your help. In fact, I will make the donation in any event. Right now. I know your work is important. But I would be grateful if you could connect me with someone and tell them I'm coming."

He was still cynical enough to wonder whether she would ask "how much?" But she didn't.

"It's Mr. *Goodbow*, is it?" she said. "G-O-O-D-B-O-E?"

"B-O-W. Will Goodbow."

"Got it. Take this name down. Lane Williams. He's been with Human Rights First a long time. He's not a lawyer either, but he's our liaison in El Paso with the CBP. We have a little office near the CBP station at the entry point. He gets along with pretty much everybody."

"CBP?"

"You *are* green. Customs and Border Patrol."

"Of course."

* * *

She gave Goodbow a cell number for Lane Williams and took Goodbow's, which she said she would pass on to her colleague with instruction that a donor would be contacting him for a "look around" the border.

She took his credit card number too, for a donation of one-thousand dollars.

He'd made his first step, small as it was. He made the next when he called Lane Williams the following morning, a little nervous as to how the aid worker would react to orders from the home office. But Williams was as pleasant as a maître's de greeting a regular at a fine dining establishment.

"Yes, yes, Mr. Goodbow," he said on answering. "I'm happy to hear from you so soon."

Will was relieved. "This is kind of you, Mr. Williams. Very kind."

"Lane. Call me Lane. And I should be thanking *you*. We need benefactors. Believe me, we need benefactors. We need people to understand what is really going on down here. When are you coming?"

"I'd like to come as soon as you can have me."

"I have to go to Hidalgo tomorrow, but any day after that will be fine. Say, Thursday? I could greet you Thursday. Or is that too soon?"

"No," Goodbow said. "Thursday is good. I'll get down there tomorrow night and meet you Thursday morning."

"Very well. But it is not so easy to find a place to stay here."

"Really? El Paso is a big town now, I thought. There must be a lot of hotels."

"There are, but they're always jammed nowadays. With all the news, the press people are flooding in all the time. There's a joke going around that the Marriott lines are longer than the asylum lines!"

"You're kidding me."

"Only a little. All the decent places are booked. We keep a standing reservation at the Fine Sombrero Motor Inn a few blocks down the street. Right on the border, on the US side. So that people from headquarters can come down. Or special volunteers."

"Well, I don't want to take it if you have . . .."

"No, no," Williams said. "It's open tomorrow night, and for the next three after. But I should tell you, it's not a great place." He paused. "But you'll be safe there."

"I'm sure it will be fine."

"All right then. I'll hold it for you. How many nights?"

"All four."

"You'll have a car?"

"Sure. I'll come to your office Thursday morning. Nine-thirty okay?"

Two days later when the Newporter tooled his rental sedan to the curb in front of the small Human Rights First sign he saw immediately that the little room inside was dark. *Did he have the time difference right,* he asked himself. At first, it seemed surprisingly quiet on the morning streets at the border. Only a few people could be seen in any direction, most in tan, hatless uniforms. *Maybe I'm early,* he thought. He looked through the door, searching for a wall clock. There was one. *Yes, I am on time. He must be running late.*

The slanting sun was streaming heat to his unshaded side of the street. Across the two lanes he saw a steel bench beside a turning red-and-white barber pole, the kind that used to be ubiquitous on main streets everywhere. And it rested in the shade. A good place to wait for Lane Williams. Even a somehow comforting place, he thought, on his first day in this new, strange, dusty place where he could collect his ideas on what to say to the aid worker. Enough but not too much about what the hell he was doing there. But Goodbow never reached his place of temporary rest and contemplation. He came closer to finding his eternal one.

He was in the center of the road when the screaming police SUV whirled from a corner a hundred feet to his right. A bulky rescue truck bounded behind it, horns and sirens blaring. He froze like an animal in the suddenness and sound of the moment; he wasn't sure whether to lunge forward, back, left or right. He sensed only that diving to the pavement—his impulse—was the poorest choice. He shot upright and still, pulling his shoulders and feet in as if an elevator door were closing toward him and by thinning his broad frame he might somehow avoid impact. Whether his paralysis was born of fear, shock, or, in the circumstances, just utter lack of good options, it likely saved his life. The police car squealed sharply left, narrowly missed Goodbow's right shoulder and sailed over the curb before regaining control. The medical van behind it veered to the right, passed even nearer his other shoulder. A gust of moving air buffeted off the vehicle's high flat side and knocked him off balance. He turned to see the truck bouncing along the sidewalk, barely reducing speed with only the driver-side tires in the street, before drawing back and resuming its pursuit.

Goodbow straightened himself and turned to watch the speeding vehicles. Only then did he see the apparent object of the commotion. A block ahead two jeeps with Red Cross markings were parked angularly, effectively barricading the street in front of a low cement building. A line of slim horizontal windows ran across the building. Atop it from a high pole, an American flag hung limp in the windless morning air. A CPB station, he surmised. The police and emergency squad squealed to a stop near the jeeps and their occupants streamed out. He stepped quickly to the sidewalk and ran toward the commotion.

Later he would think back on what he saw that first morning at the border and wonder: *Was this Providence? Mere chance? Was it meant to steel him for what lay ahead, or frighten him away from his nascent purpose? This, in his very first hour in the place.*

He reached the black iron gate and peered in. His view was

brief. He'd barely steadied his feet when the gate burst open from its center and a uniformed burly border patrol officer rushed toward him. The officer raised his arms, then waved them together aggressively down and to the side like a football referee signaling a catch out of bounds. Goodbow instantly moved to the side. Behind the officer streamed a gurney carrying a young girl, flanked by other border agents, medical workers fore and aft, and others trailing behind whose purpose Goodbow couldn't surmise. But he could see a man crying frantically beside a woman who was more composed, both walking quickly behind the stretcher with a man in a khaki, but civilian, suit.

"Are you a doctor!" the first officer barked at Goodbow.

"No."

"Then get the fuck out of the way!"

"What's happening?"

"I *said* 'Get the fuck out of the way.'"

Goodbow moved further to the side and watched as the EMTs hurried the gurney into the rear of the rescue vehicle. The El Paso police cruiser pulled in front of the truck, apparently preparing to escort it from the scene. He heard the iron gate clang shut and turned to see that the crying man and the stoic woman were still inside with the man in the suit. They were looking into his eyes. He was talking to them in Spanish, raising his left hand in front of his chest and using his right to take the fingers of the left hand one at a time, speaking in an unexcited tone, as if explaining something. *First this, then this, then this,* Goodbow imagined. Then the woman covered her face in her hands and the man bent over, broken, crying even more loudly. The man in the suit raised him up and embraced him and then the woman embraced the crying man too.

Goodbow moved back in front of the gate so that he could watch more clearly. Two uniformed agents appeared beside the crying man and the woman and talked to the civilian in the summer suit.

"Manny," he heard the civilian say to one of the officers. "It would be good to let him settle down a little. He understands now what is happening. He will get ahold of himself. He just needs to settle down a little before you take them."

The man he called Manny took the other officer a few steps away and spoke to him. The second officer stood with his legs spread apart and his arms folded as he listened to Manny, appearing to require convincing. But after a minute, the two officers turned back to the civilian. Goodbow could not hear what was said, but the agents walked casually away and motioned to a bench about thirty feet down the fence on the Mexican side. The man, the woman, and the civilian in the summer suit walked slowly to it and sat.

"Hey!" Goodbow recognized the voice of the officer he'd first encountered and turned to see his approach.

"I'm sorry, I didn't mean to be in your way."

"Are you press?"

"No."

"NGO?"

"What's that?"

"Aid group. Aid worker."

"No."

"Then what the hell are you doing here?"

I've been wondering that myself, Goodbow thought, but was sensible enough not to say it.

"I'm just looking around. As a citizen. Trying to understand this."

"You from around here? You don't sound like it."

"Rhode Island. Newport."

"You came all the way from Rhode Island to 'look around?'"

"Well, I promised someone I would."

"You promised." The buttons on the short-sleeved shirt of the big officer looked about to burst. *Why do they always look like that?* Will thought. The agent leaned back and put his hands on his hips. "Well, that's a new one. I'll give you that."

"What was that all about just now?"

"Kid coming in was sick."

"That girl?"

"Yeah. Came in with a flock, like they all do."

"Flock?"

"Families, a bunch of families together. Usually from Central America, not Mexico. This bunch was from Honduras."

"And the girl was that sick?"

"This one, I guess, was."

"What do you mean, *this* one?"

"We can't always tell whether they're sick or just bullshitting. To get across, you know. We're not goddamned doctors. How can we tell? So, we hold them in there until we can get a doctor to check them."

"You don't have doctors all the time?"

"Fuck no. This girl was in there since the middle of the night. By the time the doctor got here, he took one look at her and told us to get her to the hospital. Looked at us as if we were crazy or something. Hell, it's not *our* call!"

"The man who was crying, and the woman. The girl's parents?"

"Yeah."

"They didn't leave with her."

"Hell no."

"Why not?"

"If that worked, they'd *all* be getting sick."

On the state of his knowledge, Goodbow could see his

point. *Perverse incentive* they called it in economics. He knew the term, the concept: an incentive to do wrong or take corrupt advantage in a system that was otherwise beneficial, efficient, even humanitarian. The risk of opportunism, greed, even outright evil by a few trumped an idea or regulation that was good for the many.

"That's sad," Goodbow said.

"There's a lot of sad down here. A ton of sad. But it does make you think," the officer said.

"What do you mean?"

"These people are coming up here *knowing* it's a bitch to get in anymore. They're not stupid. They're informed. There are agencies in their own countries telling them what they'll be up against. And still they come. Thousands of miles, most of them. I mean, it must be *really* bad for them down there to put themselves into *this* mess. I mean *crazy* bad."

"From crazy bad to crazy sad," Goodbow said.

"Yeah, and I don't know which is worse."

The gate opened and the man in the summer suit and the border officer he'd called Manny came out together. "Okay, Lane," Goodbow heard the officer say. "I'll let you know where they are after processing. And where the child is, if they move her."

"Appreciate it, Manny. And if you get more like this, please do call me."

Manny nodded, joined the larger officer Goodbow had met outside the gate, and disappeared into the concrete building.

"Mr. Williams?" Goodbow called to the civilian. "Lane Williams?"

"Yes, that's me." He looked at his wristwatch and turned his head toward his small office down the block.

"I'm the appointment you're late for." Goodbow walked to him, smiling, and extended his hand. "Will Goodbow."

5

The little office of Human Rights First used to be a dry-cleaning store. It was narrow at the street front with floor to ceiling glass flooding morning light into the small anterior space that served as Lane William's office. Steel gray four-drawer filing cabinets lined the three walls that were not glass. Lane's desk was a simple wood table in the center of the front space. A three-bulb globe light grasped the ceiling over the table. The fixture appeared fairly new. Three rows of long surface-mounted fluorescent light holders striped the ceiling, tubeless and disconnected. The stubs of red and black wires protruded from their ends, wrapped in black plastic tape. When clouds slipped in front of the sun, the office light dropped noticeably.

"Little dim in here, isn't it?" Goodbow asked as Lane draped his suit jacket over the swivel chair behind the table and sat down. "Why not use the fluorescents up there?"

Lane Williams leaned back, as if surprised by the question. "Odd," he said. "You're the first person that ever asked that."

He called to the young staffer who emerged from the back room. "Shelly, anybody ever asked that before?"

"Not to me," she said. She was pretty and slim, Goodbow judged not yet thirty. "Not even the fire inspector," she said. "Which *I* thought was odd. The wires hanging out and all."

"That's what I thought," Lane said. "First damn time. But I'll grant you, Mr. Goodbow, it's not a bad question. I had them replaced by the regular bulbs. They throw softer light, more natural. Warmer. Those fluorescents made everything seem hard in here. Institutional, if you know what I mean. Now, I'm not kidding myself. This little place isn't going to be homey to anybody. Probably shouldn't be even. But when we have the asylees in here, 'specially with their little kids, they're frightened. Anxious. Worried what happens next. We don't like it to feel like a factory to them. Or a police station. Do we, Shelly?"

"No, we don't, Lane," she chimed in, dutifully. "Which is why I keep saying we should get some of these hard chairs out of here and bring in a couch."

"Noted," Lane answered. "Actually, more than noted. That's a good idea. We should ask Sr. Hope Annie if maybe she has an extra couch at her respite center. Or if she could scrape one up for us."

"Fine," Shelly said. "You want me to call her?"

"No, I'm probably going to see her today anyway. Mr. Goodbow here is a benefactor from Rhode Island. He wants to have a look around. I'm taking him over to meet Sister."

Shelly looked at Goodbow. "If you want to understand what happens here, Sr. Hope Annie can show you a lot," she said. Then she looked to Lane. "But she's not around today. I know it. She's over in Clint. There are some nuns over there setting up something like she did here at the El Paso station. She's meeting with them there. If I were you, I'd take him to Manny Angeles today."

"Manny's on my list too," Lane said.

Shelly gave a thumbs up to Lane and disappeared into the rear room.

"What's back there?" Goodbow asked, nodding to the back area.

"Supplies. Mostly clothing, dry and canned food too. We don't have the quantities that Sr. Hope Annie keeps at her respite center; we don't need as much. She's got families sleeping over there. The people come here just for help on process, so we can prepare them for what's coming before they go to a place we find for them. But it's surprising the state they're in when they walk in from the border station. Some of them haven't eaten in a couple days. Some of the kids' clothes are worn through. We give them their emergency needs right here, when we can."

Goodbow dragged a chair to the front of the table and sat; Lane retrieved a cigarette from his jacket pocket. Goodbow noticed the "No Smoking" sign on the wall near the door. "Where do we begin?" the NGO manager said.

"Maybe with how you got involved down here," Goodbow asked.

"I was going to ask the same thing about you."

"It's not easy for me to talk about."

Lane offered a puzzled look. "You have a family member caught up in this?"

Goodbow seemed startled at the suggestion.

"It's not that unusual," Lane said. "You'd be surprised how many families have a son or daughter marry an undocumented person and the whole family gets to feeling like it's living in the shadows. Especially when the couple has children. They worry the illegal will be found and deported. What does the rest of the family do then? Even the grandparents worry they may be in trouble. You know, for harboring the illegal son or daughter-in-law."

"No, that's not my situation. Happily."

"Then what brings you here? I doubt you're looking for a second career."

"I made a promise."

Lane Williams drew on his cigarette and rocked in his swivel chair. "A promise?"

"To my wife. My late wife. When she was dying."

There was a long pause, broken by a ringing phone. Lane Williams ignored the ringing, his eyes fixed on Goodbow's. The two of them overheard Shelly in the backroom answer on the fourth ring.

"Well, I'm sorry for your loss." Goodbow felt the man's sincerity. "This was recently?"

"Yes. A few months ago."

"And what did you promise to do?"

"To bring parents back to their children. When they've been separated down here. Or take children back to their parents, I suppose."

"There's a problem with that."

"What do you mean?"

"The United States government."

"Mr. Williams, I knew that before I came down here."

"But do you *really* know the problem, Mr. Goodbow?"

"I know it will be difficult, if that's what you mean."

"No, what I mean is there is no way to do that. No legal way."

"*No* legal way?"

"None anymore, once they're denied asylum. In the old days, the Texas Rangers and the border enforcement officers had some discretion to work with charity groups and churches. Humanitarian exceptions, they called them. But that's long gone. All that's left is illegal ways, all dangerous. I certainly would not encourage any of those."

"Smuggling, you mean," Goodbow asked.

"Right. Some crazy things are tried. Tremendous risks. Stupid risks. You've got desperate people and money-grubbing thugs packing them into dumpsters, all manner of things. A lot of them end up dead. You don't look like a smuggler."

"I suppose not."

Lane rose and reached for a coffee pot sitting atop a file cabinet. He looked at Goodbow, invitingly. "You?" he asked. Goodbow shook his head, no.

"So, how did it get this way?" Goodbow asked. "The kids and the parents; separating them. Or has it always been like this?"

"Oh, no. It really only became a problem around 2015. Got a lot worse in the years after that. Before then, the vast majority of migrants coming in down here were adult male Mexicans coming alone, and money was the biggest reason they wanted into America. To work, to make money and send it back to their families in Mexico."

"Doesn't sound like asylum," Goodbow said. "They were running *to* something; not *from* something."

"You don't sound too sympathetic."

"I'm not. I'm not for 'open borders' where just anybody and everybody gets in."

"You think a lot of people *are* for that?"

"I think my wife was."

"Well, do you see that the 'open borders' question is separate from the problem of the children and the separated parents?"

"I'm not sure I do. That's what I came here to learn."

"Because you promised your 'open borders' wife."

"Because I loved her."

Lane leaned back and lit another cigarette, considering the situation. The conversation had taken an awkward path. *I'm an immigration aid worker, not a grief counselor!*, he thought. *How to handle this large, old widower from Rhode Island so committed to his late wife, yet so ambivalent, at best, to her values? But he's serious about this. Down here from the comforts of his wealth. And he's not in active mourning, I don't think. He knows what he is doing, what he is trying to do. Maybe the best thing is to help him learn what happens and what does not, introduce him to the right people here and hope that he'll eventually see what he cannot do, hope that he will stay out of trouble and go back to Rhode Island.*

"You asked how it got to be this way," Lane finally said. "How it came to be that so many families were separated upon entry."

"Yes, I don't understand it."

"I want to help you understand it. It's not a pretty story. I can take you to others who know it too, probably better than I do. The human side of it, and its history."

"I would like that."

"But you must understand that I do not want to encourage you to do something foolish, or illegal, or dangerous. That is important to me. And to my employer. We are helping down here. We are doing what we can to lessen the suffering. But if it is found that we are encouraging illegal entry, that will be very bad for Human Rights First."

"I understand. And I am grateful. I only want information so that I can decide what is possible."

"All right, then. Shelly says that Sr. Hope Annie Rivers is out of town today. Shelly must be right, because she is always right. But I can give you the nun's phone number. She has a small house not far from the border, near her respite center. She's rarely gone overnight, in case there are problems at the center and she needs to go back there. You can probably reach her tonight at home." Lane wrote the nun's cell phone number on a post-it note, taking care that it was legible. He handed it across the table to Goodbow. "And now I can take you to Officer Manny Angeles at the border station."

"I think I saw you with him this morning near the gate," Goodbow said. "When you were talking to the parents of the sick girl."

"Yes, that was him."

"You seem to get on well with him."

"I do, and with many of the other officers too. Most of them are very good men and women. They want to do the right thing. But they must follow the law. As I must; as *you* must, Mr. Goodbow."

"We've covered that."

"Good. Let's go see Manny. The afternoons are hard for him. He has to deal with all of the families that have been brought inside in the morning. As the hours go by, there is anxiety for everybody. But I can at least introduce you and ask him if he will meet with us at the Four Amigos after his shift."

"The Four Amigos?"

"It's a bar a few blocks from the patrol station. A favorite of the officers. And myself."

"Isn't it usually the *Three* Amigos?"

"Already taken. About six times."

6

Nothing that Goodbow heard from Lane Williams and CBP officer Manny Angeles that afternoon at the Four Amigos made him feel more comfortable with what he was doing at the border or lessened his anxiety about what might lie ahead if he continued his quest. But he learned. Did he learn. Looking back later on their long talk, he considered that it had been a veritable seminar on the reality of migrant parents and children and the practices, policies and laws that governed their treatment. The cost of his education? He bought the beer.

Manny came through the door, greeted the bartender with a wave, only minutes after Goodbow and Lane Williams arrived. The exterior was made of tired stucco, but Goodbow approved of the inside. A long bar ran almost from the front door to the rear wall on the right side. A chandelier with brightly colored glass shades hung from a shiplap ceiling that was very high over the bar and slanted down to about ten feet at the opposite wall. The flooring was dark wide plank pine, unevenly varnished but clean.

"How long has it been now, Manny?" asked Lane Williams to open their talk. They sat at a table at the front window. "You and I working together down here."

"Six, seven years, I think." As they talked, other uniformed officers streamed in, most took seats at the long scarred bar top.

"Things have changed a lot, haven't they?"

"Some ways yes, some ways not," answered Manny.

"How do mean?" asked Goodbow, leaning towards the officer.

"The border is like the river that makes it. It ebbs and flows. Sometimes it is low and clear and seems safe. Then it gets high and muddy and dangerous. But I'm not talking about changes in weather. It's changes in politics."

"And changes in politics make for changes in who's coming across, or trying to," Lane said. "And how many of them."

"If you'd asked me four years ago who was wanting in, I'd have said single males, working age, almost all of them Mexicans. Only a few families tried to get in together. And not hordes of single men. The flow was pretty manageable, especially once the Mexican economy got a little better and they could find work there."

"But you have to understand, Will," Lane said. "Manny's talking about the people trying to get in under the rules. The numbers were manageable for those people, at least at the points of entry, like El Paso here. But you have to remember that there are two completely separate streams of people to deal with. Going way back—and still now—there is a whole different set of people trying to get in illicitly. Coming across the river in boats, even swimming, or being smuggled in trucks at San Diego."

"Why do they do that? Why don't they go to the ports of entry like the others? Just get processed under the rules?"

Lane and Manny smiled at each other, as if amused and deciding who would answer Goodbow's question. Lane nodded demurral to Manny.

"For a few different reasons," Manny explained. "Remember, I'm still talking about a few years ago, when most were Mexicans. And you need to know that most of these people did it the right way, not by trying to sneak in. And for years, the number of illegal attempts had been falling. To the point that in some years more immigrants were *leaving* the US than trying to come in illegally."

"Hell, I never heard that," said Goodbow.

"The public is misinformed about a lot of what is really the truth down here and what *has* been the truth down here. But I don't mean to say the illegal crossings are not real. They're very real. They're a very real problem."

"I interrupted you," Goodbow said. "Go back to where you were. The reasons anybody would try to cross that way when there is a legal way to do it."

"Well, some of them know there *isn't* a legal way for *them.* Because they have criminal records or are even on the run from Mexican authorities. They know they will never be cleared at the point of entry when they are processed."

"These are the rapists and murderers that Trump talked about?"

"Some were. There's no denying there were some like that. But I don't know any agent who would say it was the majority of them. Most would say it was a small fraction."

"What's a 'small fraction'?"

"Two percent, I'd say. Maybe less," Manny said. "If you include the drug movers, maybe more."

"I'd say way less than that," said Lane Williams. "If you're talking violent criminals. But I'll admit I'm biased. I'm trying to help these people." Manny Angeles looked skeptical, but didn't engage his friend.

"So why do the others try it?"

"Some of them know the US puts limits on the numbers of legal immigrants that will be allowed in each year. They think their chances are poor of getting in before the limit is hit. Especially after the Trump stuff and the talk about 'the wall.' A lot of them said to themselves, 'The US is against us. Why would they let us in if we get in that line? They will just turn us back.' And it's hard to argue with their reasoning."

"So they come across the desert and try to sneak in?" Goodbow said. "They don't go to the El Paso station or any of the others?"

"Right," Manny said. "Or they come first to the legal entry and see the waiting lines and give up. Head down the border and cross the river at night. And if they do make it across the border they are vulnerable to thugs—including American thugs—who say they can smuggle them into the heartland."

"For every penny they've got," Lane said.

"Or even worse. Some of these people, some of these *Americans*, are human traffickers. I'm not kidding you."

"Sex traffickers?"

"That and other things," Manny said. "Even the men and boys can be trafficked as low-cost workers, damn near slave labor. But to these people, in their situation, they think that at least they'll be 'in.' At least for a while."

Goodbow took out a notebook and a pen. "Do you mind?" he asked. "This is a lot to take in. I'd like to make some notes."

Manny and Lane left the table to use the restroom in the rear. By the time they returned, the Four Amigos was pulsing with noisy patrons and the smell of Mexican food wafted in the air. Goodbow looked at his watch. Nearly six. The pitcher of beer in the center of the table was drained, only remnants of foam streaked its sides. "Another?" Goodbow asked as the two sat down.

"I'd say it's time for margheritas," Lane said.

"A specialty of the house?"

"Specialty? It would be hard to say that," Manny said. "Everyplace has them. But, yes, they are very good."

"Well 'when in Rome,'" Goodbow said, waving to a waitress. The new pitcher arrived in moments.

"But the families thing," Goodbow said. "The parents and the children. You haven't mentioned them. When did that all start?"

"Like Manny said, until a few years ago it wasn't common to have a whole family show up at the entries. In fact, more families avoided the entries and tried to cross illegally, thinking they'd never get in together at the processing stations. But there *were* some families in the lines."

"What happened to them?"

"Back in George W.'s terms, and Obama's too, we had the discretion to process them as a family unit," Manny said. "Keep them together during processing, while we did all the background checks on the parents."

"And after processing?"

"Unless we found something bad about them, we'd release them with instructions on how to obtain legal status under the asylum laws through the immigration court."

"You released them together?"

"Sure, usually to a group like Sr. Hope Annie's. We'd work with Lane and his staff to find transition places for them."

"But parents were separated from their children way before Trump, weren't they?" Goodbow asked. "Especially under Obama."

"It's true that some were. But under the Bush and Obama

policies, the CBP officers had the authority to do that only when we believed the children were in danger with those parents, or believed they weren't really their parents at all. So it happened, but not often. We'd detain the parents and get the kids over to someone like Sr. Hope Annie, or Lane would. Sometimes we got it wrong—they really were the parents. Or it turned out the first information on a criminal rap sheet in Mexico was incorrect. Lane and other NGOs sometimes could find better information from local authorities down there."

"Or the patience to keep looking for it," said Lane, smiling slightly.

"Granted," said Manny.

"And to their credit, the CBP and ICE would reunite the parents with the children if the thing got cleared up," Lane said.

"Also true," Manny said.

"So what changed?" asked Goodbow, still making notes. "How did it get to be that more families were being separated? What was behind the change?"

"Seven words," said Lane. "The 'Northern Triangle countries, asylum, and politics.' I know it's seven words, don't bother counting. I've given this speech before."

"The countries are Honduras, El Salvador, and Guatemala," Manny said. "The Northern Triangle Countries of Central America. Those three countries fell into states of chaos. Near total breakdown of law and order. Rampant police corruption. Violent crime all over. In real terms, war zones. Whole populations unsafe from gangs, rape, robbery, bloodshed. No organized government either willing or able to protect everyday life. The state of things we've seen before, maybe, in the middle of Africa. War lords ruling with sheer terror and people fleeing for their lives. Or more recently, in Syria or the Sudan. But you can't walk from Africa or Syria or the Sudan to an American border. And, at first, we didn't think people could do it from those Central American countries either. Well, they did."

The pitcher of margheritas was three-fourth's gone. "Another?" Goodbow asked.

"Why not?" said Lane Williams. Then, "Manny, can you follow Will back to The Fine Sombrero? You know, in case he needs a good word if he's pulled over?"

"Of course," Manny said. The re-order was made.

"I'm still paying," Goodbow said.

"We have good memories," Manny said, raising his near-empty glass. "For such acts of kindness. Especially when they're picking up the tab!"

"You were saying?" Goodbow said.

"Yes," Manny continued. "They came all that distance. Walking a thousand, twelve hundred miles, sometimes more. Through the whole length and terrain of Mexico. From the bottom to the northern border of that big country. All the way to us."

"In caravans."

"Yes. Sometimes in the thousands. Often, more than half of them children, even young ones."

"It was big news," Goodbow said.

"And big politics," Manny said. "It was almost a perfect storm. Trump's campaign in 2016 was a lot about immigrants. The country was worried about it. Not only in the border states; all over the country. Some Syrian refugees from the civil war there had been permitted in and resettled to northern states. Not in any big numbers like in Germany and other places in Europe, but enough to be noticed and talked about. It worried some people. People, good people, wondered, 'What's happening? What's happening to America'?"

"I was one of them," said Goodbow.

"Everyone saw these throngs moving up to our border," Manny said. "Some things were said that were not true. Like there were Muslim terrorists among them from the Middle East."

"Not a single one was found," Lane Williams said.

"But people were afraid," Manny said. "Americans were afraid. Again, these were not bad Americans; not bad people. What were they to think? They see the crowds on TV and cable news and politicians are working them up. 'Imagine my town,' they think. 'What if all of those people come streaming in *here*, not speaking English and wanting us to take care of them!' I'm not talking about Americans living near the border; they know better than that, they've lived with migrants their whole lives. They're not afraid. I'm talking about Kansas, Nebraska, Georgia—everyplace else. 'This is an invasion!' they think. They see the news and the hysteria, but they don't see people like Sr. Hope Annie and all the others working to resettle these people and helping them make their way into work and life in this country."

"Should we order something to eat?" Goodbow asked. "Before I'm broke?"

"Yeah, right," Lane Williams said, amused. "But no, I've got to leave before long. My wife expects me home for dinner."

"Same here," said Manny.

"Okay, then," Goodbow said. "But before you go, tell me how the parents and children came to be separated in such larger numbers?"

"When the caravans started coming from those other countries," Manny said. "Politics was a big part of it. The administration wanted that wall and the money for it; Congress was balking. Trump wanted to look tough. And his first attorney general, Jeff Sessions, was a fervent anti-immigration guy. He sincerely believed we had to stop these groups from coming in, stop them from trying to come up."

"I agreed with him," Goodbow said. "On what I knew. Or what I thought I knew."

"The thinking was 'deterrence,'" Lane Williams said. "Which had never been the thinking before, when families were separated only to protect the kids. But under the new administration, it wasn't long before the idea was: if we separate these parents and kids, and they know we're going to do that, they won't keep coming up. Just to avoid being separated, they won't come up."

"When was this, exactly?"

"It started a few months before it got that much attention," Manny said. "DHS and the Department of Justice did a 'zero tolerance' pilot thing for four months in early 2018. We at the BPC were told we no longer had the discretion to separate or not separate. It was 'detain and separate everyone' if they are not in 'legally.'"

"Who's 'in legally?'" Goodbow asked.

"They're legal if they came in under a visa or if they successfully applied for asylum to a US asylum officer."

"Which really means most of the families are illegal because of course they don't have visas and the only way to apply for asylum is to have somebody there that you can apply to," Lane Williams said. "And there was no set up to do that for these numbers of people. It was like forcing big crowds through a keyhole at the designated entry point. Completely unmanageable."

"It was pretty weird," Manny said. "We were telling them they'd be detained and separated unless they had entered legally, while we were making it pretty much impossible for most of them to *be* legal."

"Reminds me of 'Catch 22,'" Goodbow said.

"Not far off," Manny said. "About 2,500 children were separated from their parents in that pilot phase. In those first couple of months in 2018. These were families that gave up waiting on the Mexican side. They'd been huddled in the heat for weeks, some of them. Parents get desperate. They get it in their heads that *anything* will be better than what they have, if they can get across. And they find ways. And then they're arrested. They can still file for asylum down the road, when a filing officer is available. But for now, they're in the country illegally and so we arrest them and detain the children separately from the parents. We agents were not happy about it—who wants to take kids from their parents? But those were the orders. And at first, there wasn't a huge outcry from the public. So, in May 2018, Sessions and the Department of Justice issued a formal 'zero tolerance' family separation policy. Another 3,000 children are separated. By then, most of the kids separated in the initial phase had already been resettled into families that would take them; all across the country, but mostly in Texas and the Upper Midwest."

"Who finds these families?"

"People like Sr. Hope Annie," Lane Williams said. Mostly religious organizations. The Catholic Bishops Council and the Lutheran Family Relief group are the biggest ones. DHS works with them; releases the children to their custody."

"And what happens to the parents?"

"Different things," said Manny.

"What do you mean?"

"Some get to court and make their case for asylum, and get it granted. But it's the exception, not the rule."

"Percentage wise?" Goodbow asked.

"In a few years it got as high as thirty percent of the applications were granted," Lane Williams said. "But lately it's been less. In some immigration courts, the grant rate is as low as ten percent."

"But at least some of the separated parents are eventually granted asylum?" Goodbow asked. "How do they get back to their children?"

"The agencies who resettled their children try to reunite them. They usually can, even if it takes months to do it," the man from Human Rights First said. "But most of the separated parents don't get granted asylum. Some of the judges are more sympathetic than others. Some of the parents don't present themselves well, especially if they don't have a volunteer lawyer, which many don't. So those parents are 'subject to removal.' Which means they can be deported back to their home country. And all of them were when the 'zero tolerance' policy was put in place. Some were taken back to those countries on Mexican buses. Others just fended for themselves."

"And their children are somewhere in the US?"

"Right."

"What a mess," said Goodbow, as the two others rose from the table.

"That's just what it is, sir," Manny said. "I'm even sorry I had to explain it to you."

"Well, I asked for it."

"Maybe you should meet my wife, Maria," Manny said, as Lane Williams moved to the door. "She knows things and has her own perspective. She's with the Red Cross, assigned to the border to assist with humanitarian needs. She works a lot with the parents that are deported. Tries to help them any way she can. Maybe you could come to our home tomorrow night for dinner? It is not far away. You can learn more."

"I would love to. That's very kind."

He handed Goodbow a drink napkin on which he had

written his address. "Where will you eat tonight?" he asked the visitor.

"I thought either here at the Four Amigos or at my motel, The Fine Sombrero. Which do you recommend?"

Manny smiled as he shook Goodbow's hand goodbye but curled his brow as if neither option was overly appealing.

"Pick your poison," he said.

7

Why would a woman, on nothing more than a phone call the night before from a stranger staying at the dilapidated Fine Sombrero Motor Inn, wheel her station wagon to its entrance precisely on time to collect him as he'd asked? If the question were put to Sr. Hope Annie Rivers, her answer would be as quick and sure as the knife of the trained chef to the chicken's bone: faith. And, as it were, a little advance background research too.

"Is this Sr. Hope?" Goodbow had asked when she'd answered his call the evening before.

"It's Hope *Annie*," she'd replied. She had just kicked off her dusty loafers in front of the small microwave oven in which her TV dinner sizzled. Her little house was filled with the hot night air, swirled by a pedestal rotating fan sitting awkwardly in the center of the main room.

"Excuse me?" Goodbow was confused.

"Hope *Annie*. My name is Sr. Hope Annie. And who are you?"

"My name is Goodbow, Sister. Will Goodbow. Lane

Williams and Manny Angeles told me about you. They suggested I meet you."

"Lane and Manny," she'd said. "Lane and Manny." There was a lilt in her voice.

"You know them, then."

"Of course, I know them. What did they say about me?"

"That you've been working with the families coming across the border. That you know what you are doing. That you can get people to do things."

"They are good men, Lane and Manny."

"Yes, they seem it. I met Lane this morning. His organization in New York put me in touch with him. I saw some of what he does, and he took me later to meet Officer Angeles."

"Did you see what happened at the entry this morning?" she'd asked.

"The sick girl?"

"Yes."

"Yes, I was there when they rushed her out. I heard the commotion and went there from Lane's office. I didn't make a good impression, I'm afraid."

"With Manny?"

"No, with another border patrol agent. Big guy."

"Sanchez, maybe," Hope Annie said.

"That was his name, I think."

"He is rougher than Manny, but he is not a bad man. There is good in him too. There is good in most of them. I see it. But some people expect too much of them. Their work is hard. A lot of times, they are not able to do what they really want to do for the people coming to the entry stations."

"I could see that with Manny, and I guess with the other guard too."

"Both are good men, and so is Lane Williams. But Manny, Manny is very special. His name fits him."

"Manny?"

"*Angeles*. Manny Angeles is an angel. And he is brave. I say to him that his name should be Gabriel, because he is strong and brave and protects the children. So is his wife, Maria. Have you met her?"

"No, but I expect to soon. Manny invited me to his home for dinner, tomorrow night."

"Good. You must meet her too. If Manny is an angel, Maria is his wings. Thank God for both of them. They are special gifts to us. But what are you doing meeting all these people? Why do you want to meet me?"

"Because Manny told me you help the people, Sr. Hope."

"Hope *Annie*."

"I'm sorry, Sister. Sr. Hope Annie." Goodbow paused. "Manny said you help them."

The nun retrieved her heated dinner from the microwave and set it on the painted table in the little clean kitchen, but she did not sit down. As she stepped for dinnerware, she told her caller about her history at the border. How she had been teaching migrant children in the valley for many years until the numbers of asylum seekers had swelled to bursting and her superior had visited the places of entry. It was three years ago, she told Goodbow. Her superior in the order was younger—a fair bit younger—but saw in Hope Annie the qualities suited to a new mission. Others could be found to teach in the schools, she'd told her charge. But daily work with the refugees required a tenderness and a toughness at the same time, with both the families and the officials. The order arranged for a small warehouse on the American side, useable as an operations center. There were places for beds, improvised bathrooms and even a small examining room that volunteer doctors came to daily. Living quarters for herself were also secured, the tiny bungalow a few miles into the city in which she'd taken Will Goodbow's phone call.

"We help them as much as we can. We do what God wants us to do. Are you a reporter?"

"Everyone asks me that. No, I'm not writing anything. I'm not a newsman. I'm just trying to understand the problems down here. The problems for the parents and the children. And Manny said you work with the children. The children who are alone."

"Yes. They are the *little* angels. We care for them for God. Like the little girl today. Her name is Gloria. Seven years old. She was very ill. The infection in her foot was spreading through her whole little body. But in the hospital, she is getting better. She will come to stay at our center soon."

"Her parents will come to your center too?" Goodbow asked.

"That is not so easy. That is not so good. But we do care for their parents too, when we can."

"What do you mean, 'when you can?'"

"When their parents have not been sent back. When they've only been detained here."

"But when the parents are turned away, you can't find them?"

"No. Hardly ever."

"What about the parents this morning?"

"Lane Williams and Manny are working on it. But it is not easy. The rules are confusing. Those parents may be lucky, because of Lane and Manny. They know where the parents are being held and will probably know where they are sent if they are deported. Many others are not lucky."

"I don't understand."

"We tell the border people, we tell them on both sides, 'Tell us where the parents are and maybe we can get them to their children. We have found places for their children.' But they say the parents cannot come in and cannot come back. They are gone from the border, they tell us. Deported. Sent back. They say even *they* don't know where they are!"

"Maybe I can help you find them," Goodbow said. "The parents. Maybe there is a way. I don't know, but maybe. Maybe if I can meet the right people. Can you take me with you tomorrow on your work, so that I can learn?"

"Where are you staying?"

"At the Fine Sombrero."

"The Fine Sombrero? Then you are learning about this place already. It is very unclean there."

"I've noticed."

"Yes, I will pick you up at the front door at seven o'clock in the morning. Is that too early?"

It was, as Goodbow normally slept till at least eight. But he told Sr. Hope Annie, "No, that is good."

"Okay. Wear light clothing. By ten, it will be a hundred degrees. At least."

He was waiting in a worn chair across from the manager's counter when she drove up in a dusty Chevrolet Malibu station wagon that Goodbow guessed to be at least ten-years old. The man from New England thought she might get out to look him over and be sure of him, but she just leaned out from the driver's window. "It's me. Get in," was all she said. He walked around the front of the car and climbed into the front seat. An empty paper beverage cup sat on the passenger seat that the portly nun flipped limberly to the back bench without comment. He saw a lit cigarette propped in the console's ash tray.

"How did you know it was me?" Goodbow asked.

"Do you think I am stupid?" she said. "I called Manny and he described you. And told me, yes, he and Lane told you about me." She reached for the cigarette, pinched it between her lips, and threw the shift lever to the drive slot, eying traffic on the street.

"You smoke," Goodbow said. "I'm surprised."

"Why?" she shot back, seemingly incredulous. "Don't *you* smoke?"

"No. I never did."

"Do you drink?"

"Yes, I do."

"Well, I don't drink. So we're even."

"Even on what?"

"Sin."

She turned sharply right into the street and sped ahead, tires squealing.

"I didn't mean to offend you," Goodbow said. "I just didn't expect a nun to smoke, is all. I'm not difficult about smoking. My wife Grace smoked. It never upset me."

"And I am not difficult about drinking. So, we should get along fine."

For the first time she looked at him and smiled.

8

They drove first to the respite center. A broad plastic sign stretched above the entrance and was its most modern and colorful trait: Place of Angels Respite Center, it read in bright blue italic letters against a yellow background. Wing-like white swirls, similar to the Nike sports logo, underscored the name.

"You like angels, I see," Goodbow said as they pulled in.

"Angels mean hope and protection. Everyone likes an angel."

"I guess they do. You could have called it 'Angels of Hope.' It would be fitting."

"And it would be vain."

"Then how about 'Angels Who Smoke?'"

She responded by jerking the car to a decidedly abrupt stop in the parking area and plunging her second cigarette butt into the console's ashtray. "So, now you will meet some real angels," she said.

She walked him through every room in the converted warehouse, pointing out its purpose. Even to Goodbow, most were obvious. Two of the rooms were much larger than all the others. One of them was in the front of the center. Other nuns and a few volunteers sat at tables greeting children and offering them cold beverages. There were far fewer parents. They were offered coffee. The nuns and their staff all wore smiles and seemed cheerful, and so did some of the younger children. A few parents were there; they appeared apprehensive. The other large room was in the rear of the building, plainly a sort of community dormitory with a dozen or more rows of mattresses and cots, sheets and thin blankets folded and resting neatly on them. Down one hall there was a laundry room already filled early in the morning with volunteers operating the machines. Across the hall, Goodbow heard showers running. A young boy ran out into the hall wet, naked, and giggling until a woman's arm snatched him like an umbrella handle and returned him behind the door.

There was little opportunity for Goodbow to talk to Sr. Hope Annie during the tour. It seemed that every third step she was approached urgently with some need or other, some question or other. Often, she didn't even break stride while delivering her answers, usually in Spanish, which Goodbow could not understand. The short nun repeated her instructions to him in English. "Yes, there is more cereal. Look behind the diapers in the smaller storage room" . . . "The broken washing machine will be fixed this afternoon, don't put too many sheets in the other ones, that is what happened to the broken one" . . . "Dr. Menendez will see everyone who needs him, he will not leave until he does."

* * *

Goodbow was moved by what he saw, but happy to now sit alone with the nun at the quiet café a few blocks from the center.

"Iced coffee?" he asked her as a waiter approached. She nodded and he ordered two.

"I can see already that you are brave," the nun said. Goodbow was puzzled.

"How?"

"You're not worried about the ice."

"Should I be?"

"I don't think so. But if I am wrong, you will be the first to know."

"Seriously, Sister."

She grinned and her eyes lit up. "Oh, I am just kidding you. This is the American side of the border. El Paso city water. All is fine on this side."

"I'm glad to know that."

"Though I have seen a few ice trucks coming over from the other side," she said, leaning toward him, mischief in her eyes. "They were delivering farther down the street though. I think."

"I can see you are a handful," Goodbow said.

"A sense of humor is important down here," she said. Some days it is all that gets you through."

"How long have you been doing your work?"

"Three years now, if you mean the respite center. But for many years before that I worked from a distance, teaching the migrant children who settled in the Rio Grande Valley. If you could call it settled."

"What do you mean?"

"Many of the children were only here when their parents were allowed in for seasonal work in the fields."

"On the temporary work visas?"

"Yes. Really, all of those families, or nearly all, got here that way. And most followed the law and went back when the visa expired. Then most of them were back again the next season. It was difficult on the children, on their schooling. It seemed you could never get too far with any subject before they had to leave and go back to Mexico."

"I can see that would be hard."

"And hard on the mothers and fathers. They wanted their children to be educated. They wanted them to have friends. But if they stayed instead of going back at the end of the visa, they were then undocumented. They were so called 'illegals.'"

"Poor options."

"*Worse* than poor! They faced a terrible choice. And so some of them decided to stay and take the chance of being caught."

"By ICE?"

"Yes, mainly. But until the last few years, there wasn't too much enforcement. ICE was not looking hard for them, unless one of the parents did something wrong, something criminal. Which was not often. But anytime you have enough people, there will be a bad apple or two. And then there is a lot of publicity about those few. Not so much down here, but in the rest of country people think that everyone who stayed is bad. Dangerous. This president has added a lot to that."

"I'd rather stay away from politics, Sister."

"Well, you can't hide behind it, either. You can't ignore facts because politics are being played."

"I didn't say that," Goodbow said, a little defensively.

"What did you mean then? Why do you want to 'stay away from politics?' I am not trying to be difficult with you; I am just being honest. It comes with being a nun."

It took Goodbow aback. *She sounds like Grace!* he thought. *Warm, caring, smart. And challenging.*

"I guess I mean that a lot of people want to blame Trump

for everything that is sad. It's not like he created the immigration problem. I can't say I agree with what he's done about it, and I don't like his rhetoric at all. But he has done some other things well for the country."

Sr. Hope Annie turned away, in thought. She took three sips of her iced coffee.

"Maybe you are right. Maybe we should stay away from politics." She smiled. "I believe there is good in everyone, except the very, very few that are pure evil. I do not think Mr. Trump is one of *those.* I don't think he is as bad as he talks. But you, Mr. Goodbow, I know for sure there is more goodness in you than anything else."

"Thank you."

"That's why I warned you about the ice!"

9

"It isn't true," Manny Angeles said. The border agent rustled in his chair in the small front room of his and Maria's house where he sat across from Goodbow that night.

"What isn't true?" Goodbow asked.

"That we don't know where the parents are. That they can't be located."

Goodbow startled at the statement. If true, it might change everything. Until now, he could see no clear way to fulfill his promise to Grace. He had made some progress, to be sure. Through the devotion and guile of Sr. Hope Annie, he could discover the whereabouts of some of the separated children living in American homes that had taken them in. But how could he reunite them with unfindable parents?

"What are you talking about?" he asked.

"The government is lying," Manny said. "It keeps saying we have lost track of the parents that were sent back. But that's not true. Not for many of them. Our consulates have lists."

"Why would the government say this? It makes no sense to me," Goodbow said.

"Really?" Manny looked disbelieving. "It's politics, Mr. Goodbow. The president doesn't want them back. All the publicity. Think how it would look. He would be humiliated by the media and called a liar too."

"He is called a liar all the time anyway. He doesn't seem to mind it. Neither do his supporters."

"No, but his base does not want these people back either. He cannot look weak to them. He has called these parents criminals and invaders. His people think they are scum. From 'shithole' countries. He cannot bring them back into his great America now, even if it is to return them to their children. He will never do it."

"How did the consulates get these lists?"

"When we took children from parents at the point of entry, we always had an interview record for each family. Just a few pages, but we always had the parents write in the section for their address in their home country. Almost all of them did, even if it was only the name of a small village. These sheets were compiled in the border station. Many of the parents were sent into Mexico to camps, but the Mexicans don't want them either, so often they were transported back to their home countries. The transporters would take our lists and turn them over to the American consulates."

"Why make the lists at all?" Goodbow asked.

"Some people at DHS didn't want us to," Manny said. "But we agents thought we needed to. To prove that we had them taken back and that they got there. We didn't want to be accused of anything."

Maria Angeles came down the stairs in a clean dress. Her long black hair was still wet from washing. Goodbow thought she looked beautiful, radiant.

"How do you know the consulates still have the lists? That they kept them," Goodbow asked Manny.

Maria stepped to her husband and kissed his cheek, then turned to Goodbow, answering for her husband. "Oh, they have them," she said. "We know they do. We have even seen some of them."

"*We?* You mean the Red Cross?"

"Yes. And myself. Myself, I have seen one of these lists. In Honduras. We press the consulate officials to keep them because we need them to get supplies to these people. Some of the officials don't like this, but most of them are good people and they are fine with it. They have been there many years, some of them, they know the people are good. They know the people are in danger all the time. When I was in Honduras, I learned it was some of the consulate officials who helped the people get into a caravan in the first place. Gave them things to help them on their way. Food, soap, blankets. Even notes to show the Americans at the border saying they were not criminals."

"Maria, do you remember the names of the people at the consulate who were helpful?"

"I remember them all, Mr. Goodbow. But there is one with the most courage."

Will Goodbow looked seriously into Maria's eyes. He did not want to press her to name the official in Honduras by asking her directly. He hoped she would offer it on her own. Instead, she looked to her husband with you-don't-need-to-hear-this eyes.

"Manny, why don't you go to the kitchen?" Maria said. "So I can have a moment with our guest." Manny rose and left the room, silently.

"You understand, Manny has to be careful," she said to Goodbow. "The department knows I am with the Red Cross. He thinks they watch him because of me. He is probably right. So, I have to be careful too, careful about what I tell him and others. I cannot even talk to the press without approval."

"I understand," Goodbow said.

"I am not sure you do. If I tell you who to talk to at the American Embassy in Honduras, you can never say to anyone that I did. Not to the official, not to anyone. It cannot come back to me, because if it comes back to me, it will come back to Manny. He would be fired, or worse."

"I understand."

"You must promise me."

Another promise, Goodbow thought. Another he knew he must make.

"I promise you, Maria. I promise you for Manny too. I will never use either of your names."

"Well, then," Maria said. "The man is Leary Deen. I am not sure that is his real first name, but that is what they call him at the embassy. He was a teacher in New York before entering the foreign service. He has been posted in Central America for many years. I don't know how long in Honduras, but at least quite a few. I could tell by how many people knew him on the streets. Liked him. Leary Deen is a brave man."

"He is the ambassador?"

"No, he is on the ambassador's staff. The embassy has departments. Some to serve Americans living in Honduras or visiting. Others to serve local Hondurans. Leary works in the Consulate for Visas and Migration. His department is in the embassy building. On the first floor."

* * *

Over their simple supper, the three of them talked about the conditions for the children on the American side of the border and the news reports that the Mexican police were becoming more aggressive with the families waiting on their side of the border at the places of legal entry. Will told the couple about Grace and her struggle, and about her devotion to the cause of the parents and the children. But he did not tell them she had induced his promise to come to the border.

As he left the house to return to the Fine Sombrero, Maria stepped out with him into the darkness.

"Do you think I am not brave because I do not want you to tell Leary Deen about me? Because I have made you promise not to?"

Goodbow's impulse was to embrace her, but he did not. He put his hands into his pockets and looked into her eyes.

"No, I don't think that," he said. "I think you are a loyal and caring wife. I had one too."

10

In his room that night at The Fine Sombrero Motor Inn, Goodbow studied maps of Honduras on his laptop computer screen. He had always thought of the country as positioned on the Caribbean side of the descending Central American land mass. And the maps showed him that it mostly was. But he was surprised to learn that a deep indentation at the southwestern edge of the country reached the Gulf of Fonseca, a quiet inlet of the Pacific Ocean. Small islands were nestled in the narrow gulf, some of them uninhabited. The Google satellite maps showed that only one of the islands, Isle de Tigre, was developed to any extent, featuring a town called Amapala. He did a Google search: *Lodging in Amapala.* His brow lifted at the results. There actually were a couple of hotels there. And kayaks and small sailboats to rent. Even several *Trip Advisor* postings about the city and the hotels. "If you're backpacking in Honduras, Amapala is for you!" one read.

Why that little section of the country on the Pacific caught his eye, he couldn't say. He knew the US embassy must be in Tegucigalpa, the capitol city in the southcentral mountains. He turned his attention to it and street maps showing the embassy and hotels nearby. It was nearly ten o'clock when he called Lane Williams.

"Do you know a man named Leary Deen?" he asked.

"I know who he is, but I really don't know him," Lane answered. "He's with the State Department."

"In Honduras?"

"Right. Rough place."

"I gather."

"What do you want with this man Deen?"

"I've heard he has information on returned parents. Returned without their children."

"Who told you that?"

"I can't say."

"*Can't?* Or *won't?*"

"Both."

"So what do you want from me?"

"I just hoped you knew him. Could introduce me to him; vouch for me. But I'll just go down there and introduce myself."

"To Tegucigalpa?"

"Yes."

"Goodbow, you're going too far with this."

"How else am I going to find some of these parents?"

"If I knew, I would tell you. But getting yourself into trouble down there won't help anybody."

"What kind of trouble?"

"The worst kind. The kind where you disappear. It's dangerous, Goodbow. Especially for someone like you. Big, old, American on your own? You'll be a Butterball turkey the day before Thanksgiving."

"It can't be that bad," Goodbow said.

"Trust me, it can be. You can't trust law enforcement. They

don't even have it. You get one street off the mark, it could be a disaster."

"I'll manage."

"No, you have to take somebody with you. We have a guy who does escort security for us when we need it and, believe me, you do. He's retired military. He did uniformed security at US embassies in some tough places. Like Libya and Somalia. And then Honduras. You have to go with him. He'll make sure nothing happens to you. He'll know his way around Tegucigalpa."

"I want to pay for him."

"You'll have to; we can't. This guy takes jobs from a bunch of NGOs. You'll have to coordinate with him on your schedule. Take this down."

Goodbow grabbed the notepad and pen from the bed stand.

"His name is Huff Langley. L-a-n-g-l-e-y."

"Huff?"

"Family name, I guess. He grew up in south Boston. Here's his cell number."

Goodbow looked at his watch. He was tired, but a drink sounded good. The bar would still be open, probably manned by the motel manager as he had found before when the hour was late.

* * *

"Your bourbon, sir?" the manager said as Goodbow strode to the bar top.

"Thank you, Rico. Yes. Neat." The manager slid a generous pour across the wood counter. "I'm glad you're here, Rico. I know I am scheduled to check-out tomorrow." Rico nodded. "I wonder if I could extend my stay. Some things have come up." Rico looked concerned. "Is that possible?" Goodbow asked.

"For how long?"

"I'm not sure. I expect to be away a day or two and then return. I'd like to know I'll still have the room. Could I book it for a week?"

Rico looked more concerned.

"You want to hold the room for a whole week?"

"I can pay in advance. For the whole time. I know you fill up. Whatever rate you think is fair. Will that work?"

Instead of answering immediately, Rico reached gently for Goodbow's glass, poured more bourbon into it, and a separate shot for himself.

"Of course, Mr. Goodbow. That will be fine. I'll take care of it right away. Same card?"

11

He hadn't asked Huff Langley for a description when he'd contacted him and arranged his escort, but it turned out Goodbow didn't need one. The ex-marine's deep voice and pronounced Boston accent were unmistakable, even at three forty-five in the morning when he called Goodbow's room from the lobby two days later.

"Huff Langley," he said as he extended his large hand to his new client. "Not much of a crowd here at the old Fine Sombrero, eh?"

"Not at this goddamned hour," Goodbow said.

"Well, you must have checked the flights, didn't you?"

"Yeah," Goodbow said. "After you told me we'd be going on a flight leaving El Paso at five in the morning!"

"So you know why we have to do it this way."

Goodbow did, and nodded approvingly, as much as one can approve of such an uncivilized departure time. There was one —*one*—commercial flight from El Paso to Tegucigalpa with a single stop in Houston and a total duration of less than 6 hours.

It left El Paso at 5 a.m. The *next best* alternative was twenty—*twenty*—hours spread across four connections.

"I've never heard of such a lousy schedule," Goodbow said.

"Well, there's not a lot of demand for Tegus," Huff said, using the local moniker for the Honduran capitol, phonetically pronounced 'Tay-goose.' "The flight we pick up in Houston is one of the only direct flights from anywhere. And it'll be just half-full. Mostly government people going back and forth, a few coffee or tobacco importers."

"You've done this route before?"

"Oh, yeah. I did two years at the embassy there."

"When you were in uniform?"

"Yeah. I'd done two tours in Iraq and then they detailed me to State Department security. First in the Middle East, then to Central America. Nicaragua; El Salvador. Finally, Tegus. All of us marines protected the facility. But me, they put me on a lot of personal security, especially in Honduras. Whenever the ambassador left the embassy, I went with her."

"Why you? Doesn't the State Department have its own personal security people?"

"They do." Huff smiled. "But sometimes there's nothing like a marine. And I suppose my size helped."

He *was* a mountain of a man, Goodbow considered. Taller than himself, Goodbow judged him at least six-foot five, broad, and muscular.

"Did Lane Williams tell you why I'm going down there?"

"To see Leary Deen at the embassy, is all he said."

"You know him?"

"Leary? Sure. Good guy. A little nerdy, but he's got guts. Works hard down there." The marine looked at his watch. "C'mon," he said. "We need to get a move on."

"At this hour? What's the hurry?"

"Because I have to check a bag. For this." He pulled a black handgun from a belt holster and showed it to Goodbow.

"You can do that?"

"*I* can. TSA's cleared me. I've got the same status as an air marshal; except I can't carry on board."

"This all seems a little much."

"Wait till we're down there. You might change your mind." Huff saw alarm in Goodbow's brow. "If it makes you feel better, I haven't fired this thing in years," he said. "But I've never been down there when I didn't put my hand on it." It wasn't much of an assurance.

It was too early for coffee in the motel lobby; Goodbow saw no sign of life behind the desk or in the back office. He trudged behind Huff Langley to his car parked at the door.

"Can we grab coffee someplace? Is anything open now?" he asked the ex-marine.

"I've got you some in the car," Huff called back. "Marine made. The best. I've gotta have coffee before I do anything. Figured you'd be the same."

Such a simple thing; morning coffee. Goodbow felt almost embarrassed to feel so strongly grateful for Huff's gesture. "If you don't drink it all on the way, bring it in with you," Huff said. "There won't be anything in the airport either, till we get on the plane."

Huff's advice became moot. Goodbow drained his tall cup as Huff pulled into the airport entrance. The concourse was as quiet as expected. Huff spoke quickly to a TSA agent; they plainly were acquainted. The agent took Huff's small leather satchel readily and handed it off to a baggage handler. "Get it on the plane to Tegus," Huff said to him. "Gate 3. And mark it like you always do so security brings it out to me down there, will you?"

"Sure," the agent said. "Your usual sidearm, Huff?" he

asked, writing on a clipboard. "Your Sig Sauer 226?" Huff nodded, and he and Goodbow moved quickly through the sparse line.

Daybreak was just arriving as Goodbow looked down from his seat and saw the Rio Grande passing beneath him. He was leaving his country. He shivered. He sensed a passage underway. He thought of Grace. He smiled.

PART II

12

Six hours later, as the lightly filled Airbus 326 descended in its final approach to Tegucigalpa, Goodbow looked out from his window seat at the mountains encircling the city. He would have preferred the aisle seat—he always requested one, even in first class—but Huff had told him that on the leg to Tegus he needed the aisle seat himself.

"For your legs?" Goodbow had asked as they boarded in Houston.

"No," he'd answered. "For *your* back."

"Really? I think that's a little much, isn't it?"

Huff looked at him, a bit sternly. "Can I call you 'Will?'" he asked.

"Of course."

"Let's not argue about protocol, okay, Will? It's just the way this is done. Stateside, it was okay with me. But not now. I have a job to do. When I'm on the aisle, the only way to you is through me. You never know who could be on this plane, or who might get on when we land down there."

"Well, I just like to hang my legs out, is all."

"What the fuck, Will. It's first class. You've got enough room. Just climb in there."

You know, buddy, I'm paying for this, don't you? Goodbow had thought. But he was sensible enough to react only with a look of protest. On the whole, the big marine really had been considerate enough, he reasoned; bringing the pre-dawn coffee and all. He had silently taken his seat at the window.

Now, as the plane prepared to land and banked steeply, almost too steeply for Goodbow's comfort, he looked out below. "Beautiful terrain," Will said.

"It is," Huff said. "This is all part of the central highlands of Honduras. Three-fourths of the whole country is mountainous, and nearly the entire population is in this central section of them. There are plenty of rivers and the valley floors between the mountains are flat. Tegus sits at about 3,200 feet, but the other floors are mostly higher."

"How large is Tegus?"

"A million people."

"Are there states in the country?"

"The whole country is about the size of the State of Georgia. Divided into sections, sort of. Regions. But they call them 'Departments.' Eighteen of them. And about 300 municipalities scattered throughout them."

"Is there a national government running them?"

"Not like you'd expect." Huff said. "Very little central control keeping anything together, anyone together. No broad institutions. Kind of no national identity. They have these 'departments', but as far as I can see they're not much more than lines on a map. When there's a problem, well, 'it's not my department,' if you know what I mean."

"Is this why there's the crime, the gangs?" Goodbow asked.

"I'd say so. The criminals and gangs are mostly left alone to do what they want. At least in their own colonia."

"Colonia?"

"Neighborhood."

"The 'good' thugs stick pretty much to petty crimes, mostly theft and hold-ups. But the 'bad' thugs are into really terrible shit. You don't want to know."

"I don't think I do."

"There are a few things I do need you to know, though. For both of our sake," Huff said. The aircraft wheels bounced unevenly and the brake thrusts bellowed. Goodbow looked at him with a questioning brow.

"First, you don't speak Spanish, do you?"

"No."

"Good. Don't talk to anybody on the street who says anything to you in Spanish. Don't look at them in the eye. Just say 'English, English.' They'll almost always leave you alone, because hardly any of them speak English, and it's not worth they're trouble."

"What would they be saying to me in Spanish anyway?"

"Give me your wallet."

"I see."

"And we need to dress well; business clothes. But don't wear a watch and never hold your cell phone. Cell phones are the number one bait for muggers. That, and jewelry. Take a look at the women you see. Most of the local women don't wear any. No bracelets, no necklaces. Not even earrings. And not because they don't have such things. It's because if they wear them on the streets, they won't have them for long."

"Why business dress? So we don't look like tourists?"

"Tourists?" Huff seemed amused. "Will, there aren't any tourists. Or hardly any." Huff rose from his seat but motioned to Goodbow to stay in his. The ex-marine stood in the aisle and

looked carefully to the back of the plane; none of the passengers moved aggressively toward the front. He nodded to Goodbow and the old industrialist brought himself, stiffly, to his feet.

"Most of the Americans down here are living here. Working here. A lot of them are teachers or people working for NGOs. They tend to live in a couple of the better colonias. They don't feel too unsafe in their own colonia, but when they venture out, even in the most public areas, like around the Embassy, they're prime targets for hassling or worse. But if you're dressed in a suit or wear a good jacket, they think you're probably with the US Embassy or that you're FBI or DEA."

"Those guys are down here?"

"In numbers. To some of the citizens, their presence is the closest thing to law and order here."

If, in telling all this to his client, it was Huff Langley's purpose to heighten Will's senses and accept the need—even urgency—for caution, he succeeded. As the two men stepped off the plane and into the jetway to the concourse, Goodbow followed the marine as instructed, one step behind and said to him, in the tone one might use to his doctor when rolling down his sleeve after a flu shot; uncomfortable but appreciative: "Thank you." He thought the big marine might offer to lug his carry-on bag—after all, he was much younger—but Huff didn't. *Maybe he wants both hands free,* Goodbow thought. For the first time, a sensation of something odd came into him. Not fear exactly, but a step toward it. Not anxiety really, but not pleasurable expectation either, as you might feel shuffling into a stadium gate before a football game. Physically, he noticed that his ears felt warm and his vision unusually sharp. At the threshold into the undecorated, brightly lit concourse he saw a man in a security uniform holding the leather satchel Huff had given to the TSA officer in Houston.

A photo identification card was looped to the satchel, and the man checked it against Huff's face. Without saying anything he handed the bag to him. Huff pointed to a steel gray bench a few feet away and led Goodbow to it. He dropped the satchel on the bench, removed the black handgun and slid it, effortlessly it seemed to Will, into the stiff holster clip near his right pants pocket.

As they stepped into the early afternoon sunlight, Goodbow looked at his watch as he dutifully removed it and put it into his pocket. "At least we're on schedule," he said.

"Which isn't great," Huff said.

Huff Langley knew that most kidnappings of American and European businessmen in Mexico and Central America happened at either airports or center-city ATM machines. The ATM takings were for the low-end kidnappers. You didn't have to pay anything to find your prey. All you did was wait long enough in a getaway car parked near a dimly lit machine. But for the high-end kidnappers, airport transportation stands were the way to go. Eastern European criminal hackers made a meal out of finding passenger lists in airline computer systems and selling them on the deep web to Central American syndicates who brokered them to nattily attired criminals waiting in shiny Lincolns and Mercedes with forged Uber stickers as the executives stepped out of the terminal. Many a man had escaped a planned taking by arriving a half hour early; he was gone before he "disappeared."

"Why do you say that?" Goodbow asked.

"Never mind."

"Well, looks like there are plenty of options here for a ride downtown," Goodbow said. At least a dozen sedans and an equal cluster of battered-up taxis were parked at an island one narrow lane away from the curb.

"We're not looking for an *option*," Huff said. He pulled a

photo from his suit coat breast pocket. "We're looking for this guy."

He showed the picture to Goodbow. It looked like a passport photo of a young handsome man, except that there was an additional image in profile.

"You arranged for this?" Goodbow asked.

"You object?"

"Of course, not."

"Good. Because you're paying for it."

Huff explained that the US Embassy staff were provided a vetted transport service when moving around the area on official business. Following the 1976 kidnapping of the American businessman William Niehous in Caracas—a shocking event at the time that many believed had precipitated a cottage industry in executive takings—embassies paid much more attention to the safety of its own people and to Americans visiting as part of government or sanctioned NGO operations. Goodbow vaguely remembered the Niehous case.

"The guy from Toledo?"

"Yeah. Bill Niehous. Family man. Rising executive at the Owens-Illinois Company, about forty. He was running the company's operations in Venezuela, living here with his family. He was targeted. Leftist political thugs took him from his home. Came in through the front door in police uniforms, drugged him and dragged him away. That was before most companies had kidnapping insurance too. Poor guy was held in the jungle, chained up, for three years and four months. Everybody except his family gave him up for dead, including the State Department. A couple of farmers found him by accident, and he escaped. Unbelievable story. And, thank God, the guy came out of all that normal. Lived a happy life back at his company, and in retirement. Died in 2013 at 82."

In the months ahead, Goodbow would remember Huff's story about William Niehous many times.

"But I'm not here on government business," Goodbow said. "How come I get this treatment?"

"Call it alumni courtesy. I still have street cred with them. I called Leary Deen and asked him to take care of it; he sent me the driver's ID."

"Oh."

"But since they didn't invite you down here, you're still going to be paying for it."

"Yeah, yeah. I said fine."

"Here he comes."

It was funny, Goodbow thought, how a photo of only a face could lead your mind to fill in the rest of a person's body so wildly wrong. The picture showed a man with abundant thick black hair, high cheekbones, wide-set eyes and a pronounced chin. In Goodbow's brain, he prepared for a large, muscular fellow, probably overweight, someone like Jay Leno. But the young man who trotted toward them from the taxi bay might have weighed, Goodbow judged, a hundred-thirty pounds if he were wearing climbing boots and winter clothing. He couldn't have been taller than five feet-four in his slim frame. An ID badge flapped from a lanyard around his neck: "Affiliate, US Embassy," it said above the man's mug shot.

"Sergeant Langley?" he asked.

"That would be me."

"Bid Morrell. You have my picture?" Then he looked at Will. "Mr. Goodbow?"

"Yes, thank you," Will said, extending his hand.

"Our car is right over there," the driver pointed to a white Toyota Camry at the end of the line of sedans across the lane. "Leary Deen is expecting you."

When the three of them reached the car Huff stepped first

to its trunk, then quickly to the front end, examining the license plates.

"No embassy plates?" he asked.

"It's a rental car. The whole fleet is in for service." Huff saw then the small *Avis* decal on the corner of the windshield.

"A *rental?*" Huff said. "Why don't you just paint bullseyes on the damn doors?"

"I know it's not great," the driver said.

"Well, at least there's three of us," Huff said. Goodbow blanched, visibly.

"What does *that* mean?" he asked Huff. "Am *I* supposed to do something?"

"Yeah. You're supposed to look big."

"I am big."

"And not too old."

"That's harder."

Bid Morrell climbed in behind the wheel and Huff opened the rear door on the passenger side. "Get in, Will," the marine said. "This side. Sit behind me. Not behind Bid." Goodbow hesitated and Huff read the question in his eyes. "They always go for the driver's side," Huff said. "So, just stay behind me."

"You sure know how to make me nervous."

"Let's just hope I'm being overly cautious."

But it turned out he wasn't. They had traveled only a few miles when a battered red pick-up truck emerged suddenly from a narrow street to their right and braked to a stop in front of them, blocking their passage. As the embassy driver screeched to a halt to avoid collision, a bicycle rider appeared at his window, apparently coming from a different direction. From his back seat, Goodbow saw a hammer smash through Bid's window, grazing the driver's face and cutting his ear. A plume of tinted glass shards spewed in, rebounding against the inside of the windshield and Huff's passenger window.

Goodbow sat frozen in the back seat; he thought only to cover his face with his hands.

Huff barked to Bid: "Lock it when I get out!" He leaped from the car.

Goodbow watched as the marine streaked around the rear of the car toward the attacker, standing at the driver's door one hand on his hammer, the other on Bid's collar. The bicycle's handlebars and wheels splayed askew on the pavement. Looking back on the frenzy, Goodbow would wonder if it was his fear in the moment, or just the truth of how it all happened that made the images seem to rifle past in fast-forward. Huff's amazing speed to the attacker; the blur of the marine's repeated blows to the man's hammer-holding arm; the weapon falling and seemingly even before it reached the ground, Huff's devastating two-fisted left-sided swing, like a slugger swinging an invisible bat, that snapped the assailant's jaw violently back and to the side as he fell in a lump atop the bicycle.

Huff raced toward the pick-up truck, pulling his sidearm from his belt holster. He fired two shots in rapid succession deliberately above the truck's roof and glared into the cab, as if daring the driver, sitting alone, to open his door or show a weapon. The driver did neither. Instead, he turned the truck sharply left into the other lane, toward the first assailant, now staggering to his feet, hindered by the wheels and chain of the bicycle. Huff pranced back to the original attacker. *My God, he's fast on his feet,* Goodbow thought. He watched Huff pull the man viciously to the bed of the truck and hurl him into it. Off the truck sped with both assailants.

"You two okay?" Huff asked, leaning into the glassless driver's window of the white Camry.

"He's bleeding," Goodbow said.

"Is it bad?" Huff asked the small driver.

"I don't think so."

"Will, you're not hurt?"

"I'm just shaken up. You were really something. My God."

Huff retired his handgun to its holster clip and Goodbow saw the perspiration pooling in the front of his shirt beneath his suit jacket as he got back into the car. He looked calmly at Bid.

"Get us to the embassy," he said.

13

"I'm sorry you were welcomed so rudely to Honduras, Mr. Goodbow."

Leary Deen's office on the first floor of the embassy was brightly lit and modernly furnished, but it was windowless. In fact, the entire ground floor of the massive building was encased in corrugated gray concrete interrupted only by a steel reinforced plexiglass entrance and a dozen emergency exits around the perimeter that opened only from the interior.

"I apologize also for the view. But I guess you know already that windows are sometimes misused in this place." Leary smiled. Goodbow didn't. "However," Leary said, "the coffee is good, indeed. Would you like some?"

"That would be kind."

"Sugar? We think it brings out the richness."

"On your recommendation."

While Leary fetched the coffee from the hall, Goodbow looked carefully around his tidy office. Bookshelves filled one wall from floor to ceiling and he stepped to examine them. Some of the books looked to be legal treatises, and many were government publications from the Department of State or DHS. But most of the books were literature, principally American. Grace had been an avid reader; Goodbow thought that if she were here at this moment she'd be standing at the racks perusing the titles, and would probably even use the step stool in the corner to see more closely the volumes at the top. The twentieth century appeared well-covered. Hemmingway, Fitzgerald, Steinbeck, McCullers, Roth, Bellow, Updike, Conroy, Irving. All of them were there, and others.

"Quite a literary collection," he said to Leary Deen when Leary reappeared with two coffee cups resting uneasily on saucers, spoons tinkling on them. He left his office door open.

"I was an English teacher in Brooklyn," the diplomat said. "The school system had an 'enrichment program' if you'd had enough years in. Teaching abroad. I signed up for Honduras. That's how I wound up here."

"You enjoyed teaching here?"

"Very much. I was supposed to be here for one school year, but I talked them into letting me stay another. I've never married; my parents were still healthy, no one was needing me to go back."

"And then?"

"The New York system drew the line when I asked for another extension. By then, I'd met a lot of the Americans down here. Quite a few were attached one way or another to the State Department. Or so they said."

"That sounds a little odd."

"Well, in these countries you never really know who's in the State Department or who's in the CIA, military intelligence, or even some other agency. It's a given that you don't press anybody. But after a while, it gets to be pretty obvious."

"How so?"

"Well, like me. I've got my name on the door and it's the

department we call the Consulate for Immigration and Visas. The people in the building see what my activities are. What I'm actually doing week to week. I'm here when I'm supposed to be; I'm always doing something with either Americans in-country with crime or travel problems, or local Hondurans looking to immigrate or get travel visas to the US."

"So that means you are who you say you are?"

"Right. But there are people with funny titles in departments nobody seems to know anything about. Like 'Needs Analyst' in the 'Cultural Development Department.' And maybe the guy or woman with that title seems to be gone for weeks at a time. Where are they? What are they doing? Nobody knows and you learn not to ask too much about it."

"Seems mysterious."

"You do have to get used to it. It takes a while. You have to accept and trust that you're part of a bigger thing and that bigger thing is a good thing. It helps when you see the quality of the leaders."

"The ambassadors?"

"Them, and the senior career people too. When you've had any amount of time at all with them, you can just tell they're good people. They're not political, they're not partisans. They are dedicated to foreign service for our country. All they want is for America to be understood as a place that wants the best for everybody in a damn complicated world where we can't do everything but *have* to do some things. You get to trust these foreign service professionals and understand that you yourself are not going to know everything that has to go on. You have to accept that whatever *is* going on, there are reasons for it that good people have signed off on."

"Hopefully."

"Yes, hopefully. People are not perfect. There will always

be some mistakes; there will always be a bad actor here and there."

"And when you run into one of those?"

"You use channels. You use the process. You speak up."

"That works?"

"It has for me." Leary Deen paused and placed his cup back on its saucer, then tilted his head and looked across at Goodbow with a small smile that conveyed kindness and a desire to change the subject.

"So, we were asked to host you by Lane Williams of Human Rights First," Deen said.

"Yes, from El Paso."

"They say Lane is a fine man. He has been here many times, though I'm not sure I personally ever met him. The NGOs are an important part of our work in the foreign services. There are many things we could never do without them. People like Human Rights First and the Red Cross."

"Yes, the Red Cross, too. I've . . ." Goodbow caught himself. He nearly mentioned Maria Angeles and how he had met her with her husband, Manny, the US border agent. But he remembered his promise. "I've heard the Red Cross is active down here," he recovered.

"We try to open doors for them," Leary said. "Help them understand the local conditions. Help them get aid safely to the colonias—the neighborhoods—that need it. Those two groups, Lane's and the Red Cross, have been especially interested in the problems at the US border and the asylum seekers. Since Lane arranged for your visit, I assume it has something to do with that?"

"Well, it does, yes."

"What in particular?"

"The parents and the children."

"Which parents and children?"

"The separated ones."

The consulate official seemed surprised by the path the conversation was taking. He rose from his chair, gestured to Goodbow to stay in his own with a motion that said, "Fine, fine, all is fine." He walked to the office door and closed it gently.

"Lane assured me you were not a reporter."

"I'm not."

"And at age seventy, if you don't mind my saying it, I doubt you're looking for a job."

"Correct again."

"Then what is it about the separated parents and children that interests you?"

This guy even has the diction of an English teacher! Goodbow thought, trying to formulate a cogent and still truthful response that would not violate his promise to Maria Angeles by implicating her or her husband. A half minute lapsed; Goodbow sipped his coffee to buy contemplation.

"This sounds unusual, I know," he finally answered. "In the last few months, I've become interested—very interested—in the removal of children from their parents at the US southern border. It was not something I ever wanted to be involved in. To be honest, I never agreed with the liberal politics that is so much against it, so upset by it. But then something happened to me." Suddenly, Goodbow stopped. The pause was awkward for both men.

"So, something happened," Leary Deen said. "*What* happened?"

"My wife died."

"My word. I'm sorry," Leary said. Then he asked Goodbow something that some might have judged, at best, as abrupt and insensitive. But even as he heard it then, and more so later when his mind came back to that first time together in the windowless office, Goodbow took Leary Deen's question not as forward, tin-eared, or regrettable in any sense, but instead as a tender, human gesture between men who hardly knew each other. Who knew they were talking about important things. "What was her name?" he asked.

"Grace. Her name was Grace."

"Lovely name."

Goodbow nodded.

"And her passing? When did it happen?"

"A few months ago."

"Was Grace a Honduran?"

"No."

"But her passing brought you here? How? To Honduras of all places."

"I said it is hard to understand. I hardly understand it myself."

"You said it had to do with the separated parents and children. But that happened at the US border, not here."

"I've been there too."

"I know because you met with Lane Williams there. But he didn't explain why you wanted to come here to meet me. He didn't say it had something to do with your wife."

"Grace was very taken with the problem of the parents and their children. She couldn't understand how our country could do it. Separate them. It was immoral, she thought. In her last months she devoted herself to it. She wrote letters to senators and the president, to bishops too, sending them money to help, even though she didn't know how it could help or what could be done by anybody." Goodbow rose and walked to the bookcases.

"And then she died?" Leary said.

"Yes, but before she did—just before she did—she asked me to get involved in this."

"She *asked* you?"

"She asked me to promise her. Promise her that I would. After she died."

"And you've been trying to keep your promise?"

"Yes."

"Lane told me you came all the way from Rhode Island."

"Yes."

"You can afford to just drop everything in your life and try to do this for Grace?"

"I am a man of means."

"But maybe not the kind of means you'll need for this thing."

"I told Grace that. I don't know how all the money in the world can do what she made me promise."

Leary Deen was moved by the big old industrialist standing in his office. Moved by his circumstance, struck by the unusualness of the whole conversation. He had seen strange things, had met many anxious people in his foreign service; observed sickness and violence and pain and yearning. But the complicated yearning of this man Goodbow was somehow different altogether. And perplexing.

"But I have to ask again," Leary said. "Why are you here? What is it that you think I can do for you? The children were taken from their parents up there, not here."

"But some of the parents were brought back here."

"How do you know that?" Leary's tone was not defiant or aggressive. It was flat, objective.

"I can't tell you. People could get in trouble. I promised I would not identify them."

"You make a lot of promises."

"Lately, I have."

"Surely, Lane Williams didn't tell you that. Human Rights First has had nothing to do with the sending back of anyone."

"I told you I cannot say how I know some parents were

brought here. But I have been working with a nun up there—she didn't tell me either, she has no idea where the parents are—but she told me the border agents say they don't even know where the parents are whose children were taken and kept in the States. That our government doesn't know!"

"And you doubt this?"

"I do. I don't think it is true. At least for some of the parents. I think the whereabouts of some of them is known."

Goodbow knew the moment—the next critical moment in his journey, the outcome of which would either give it hope or dash it brutally—had arrived in Leary Deen's windowless office. He did not expect what was next said.

"I enjoy Honduran cigars," Leary said. "Maybe you do too?"

"I do, actually," Goodbow said. The mere mention made him think of the deck of *The Sails of Grace* and Burp Lebeau, and long cigars together on the deck while Grace read books below.

"Excellent." Leary waved his arms toward the walls and looked furtively at the ceiling. "As you can see, we can't smoke in here. But we have a courtyard off the cafeteria." He opened a drawer in a credenza behind his desk and thumbed through some files. He extracted a sheet of paper and inspected it, then tucked it in his jacket and stood up. "Let's go outside and enjoy a good cigar. I have one for you too."

* * *

When they reached a small iron table at the corner of the courtyard furthest from the dining hall, Leary looked at Goodbow earnestly. "I didn't think we should keep talking in there," he said. "It's an embassy, after all."

"You think your office is bugged?"

"No. But you can never be sure. Normally, I don't give a damn if anyone can hear. I'm not talking about anything that matters in that way. But you reached a question that might."

"Might what?"

"Matter."

"About the parents?"

"About their whereabouts."

"So it's true? We do know where they are?"

"'We' is a big word," Deen said. "I wouldn't take it very far. I really don't know how many people in the government know, or how high up it goes. It may not go up at all."

"But *you* know?"

"I know where some are. Some. For sure, I only know where twelve are. Six mothers and the six fathers. Yesterday, I knew of only ten parents. Those were brought back here a year ago. The sixth set arrived only this morning. They were stopped in El Paso, but their daughter was taken from them. She was ill when the family got to the border. The US agents took the child into the US to a hospital."

"Leary," it was the first time Goodbow had used the consulate man's name. "Will you tell me who they are? Will you help me find them?"

"What will you do with them if I do?"

Goodbow drew on his cigar and savored it before answering. "It might be better if you don't know that," he said.

Leary Deen smiled. "Two hours here and you are already talking like a diplomat," he said. "Yes, Goodbow, I will help you find them. They are nearby, here in Tegus." He pulled out the paper he had taken from his cadenza drawer. "These are their names." Goodbow looked at the names, all typewritten on government letterhead except the last two names, added in handwriting.

"Who gave you this list?" Goodbow asked.

"The driver who brought them to the Honduran border gave it to an official there. He passed it on to me. He said a US border patrol agent told him to do that. It had the first ten names. But the names of the last parents, the ones who came today, I added myself."

"This is very helpful, Leary," Goodbow said. "Thank you. May I keep this?"

"Yes. But you need to know that the addresses are unreliable; they move from house to house, finding any place they can to stay. I don't have any address yet for the new parents who returned today. All of them are very afraid. The gangs target people who try to get to America. To punish them and discourage others."

"Do you have a way to contact them?" Goodbow asked.

"Only two of them have cell phones, as far as I know. They act as the contacts for the rest."

"I'll need a few days to do some things," Goodbow said. "To talk to some people before I contact them. Before I meet them."

"Okay."

"I'll stay in the city and call you. Maybe you can take me to them on the weekend?"

"There is a church they know in one of the colonias and I know the priest there. It can be arranged. I will try to set it up for Sunday after the service. It will not seem strange for them to be going to the church on a Sunday, so I do not think they will be too afraid to go. If the priest thinks it is safe, I think they will come to meet you, to hear whatever it is you want to tell them."

"Which I think it's best you not know."

"I am not sure," Leary said. "If I can help them, I want to. I will not be afraid to hear what you have to say to them."

Maria Angeles was right about this man, Goodbow thought. *He is a brave man.*

"You are helping them by helping me," he told Leary. "I

don't know what more you can do for them. I'm not even sure what I can do for them. But if you learn what I'm planning you may not be able to help others. Others like them."

"Perhaps you should worry a little more about yourself, Mr. Goodbow."

* * *

Huff Langley was waiting just inside the embassy entrance when Leary Deen escorted Goodbow to him. For the first time since leaving Newport, the old industrialist felt a spring in his step, a sense of optimism. The consulate official had been more than he could have hoped for. He turned to Deen and thanked him, pumping his hand.

"Just one other thing," Goodbow asked him. "How did you know that I am seventy years old?"

Deen smiled, wanly. "Oh, one of those fellows upstairs in the Cultural Development Department sent me down a copy of your passport. As a courtesy, you know. But I suppose it's a good thing you asked."

"Why is that?"

"Because now you know that somebody besides me knows you came here."

14

The Hotel de Maya Plaza was surely not the standard to which Goodbow was accustomed, but it had its virtues. It was only two short blocks from the embassy, reasonably clean and, he saw, heavily guarded by national police in military style uniforms. They were changing guard as he and Huff Langley climbed the steps to its entrance about four o'clock. The decision to stay over in Tegus was spontaneous so they had no reservation. Goodbow worried this might be a problem but Huff viewed it as a security advantage. He told Goodbow that even if he had known they would be extending their stay in the capital, he would have insisted that no advanced booking be made. It was better, he said, that they were not anticipated.

"I hate reservations," he'd told the Rhode Islander. "Most times when a hotel guest gets hit up it's because the thugs got a tip from inside that he'd be there."

As a further precaution, Huff did the talking at the registration desk and booked a suite on the top floor with two queen beds under his own name, identification and credit card. "You don't mind the family way, do you?" he'd asked Will before he stepped to the reception clerk.

"No, but it's not on account of the money, is it?"

"No, it's not about the money. It's just a lot better this way. If you want your own room, we'd have to have connected rooms, and we'd have to move to another hotel tomorrow, because a room would be under your name tonight."

"Oh, brother," Goodbow had said. After the violent incident on the way in from the airport he wasn't inclined to question Huff Langley's judgment. But when he heard Huff answer "One night, just one night" to the clerk's question, he moved up to the marine and pulled him aside.

"I thought you said we wouldn't have to move tomorrow?"

"We won't," Huff said quietly. "I'll extend it in the morning. As far as this guy needs to know, we're staying only one night." He waved Goodbow back to his place to the side. *There's more to this escort work than I imagined,* he thought.

Once inside the room, Huff looked it over closely, even removing the drawers from the bathroom cabinet to be sure there was no access panel or hole in the wall behind it. He pointed to the electronic safe sitting on the closet shelf. "Don't use this damn thing," he said. "Oldest trick in the book. You might as well leave your stuff in the hallway." Goodbow nodded, appreciatively.

"I could use a nap," he told Huff. "It's been a long day already."

"I figured. Go right ahead. I've got a book to read. I'll sit outside the door so you can close the shades. A drink when you get up?"

"You read my mind."

"Lane Williams told me you enjoy a drink."

"How did that come up?"

"I asked him. I always ask that. There's nothing worse than guarding a drunk."

"Well, I'm not."

"He said you weren't. Don't be touchy. Take your nap."

* * *

Will slept longer than he'd expected. When he woke he saw lights from outside peeking through the curtains; it was already dark. He fished into his pants pocket for his watch where it had rested since he'd removed it in the rental car at the airport that afternoon. Six-thirty. He rinsed his face in the bathroom and heard two knocks at the room door. Huff walked into the room. "I heard you get up."

"Are we late for happy hour?" Goodbow asked the marine.

"It runs late down here," Huff said. "Everything does."

It must have come to him, Goodbow thought, as things sometimes do, in that space between sleep and wakefulness. When ideas and thoughts slip quietly into the mind. He realized that he didn't know what, if anything, Huff Langley knew about his intentions or his purpose for being in Tegucigalpa. It was strange, he thought, that the escort had asked him nothing about them. The question needed to be addressed. He would be making phone calls that evening from the room. For certain to Sr. Hope Annie and Maria Angeles; maybe to others. It would be awkward in the extreme to have those conversations—and Huff overhearing them—without understanding what the marine knew and didn't know; what he wanted to know and didn't want to know.

They sat at a low table in the lobby bar of the Hotel de Maya Plaza in downsized upholstered chairs trimmed in shiny chrome. Service was immediate. Huff Langley ordered a premium tequila unfamiliar to Will; Goodbow a Bushmills Irish Whiskey on the rocks.

"I'll bet there's not much call for that down here," Huff said. "Surprised they have it."

"You're so careful and prepared, I'm surprised you didn't check out the spirits list before you picked this place."

"For myself, I didn't have to. I've stayed here before. I knew they had my favorite. I could have checked for you but that's special recon. It's extra. And I know you're tight with money."

"Speaking of what you know, Huff, did Lane Williams tell you anything about why I wanted to come here, to Honduras?" The big-bodied escort had said or done nothing in their time together that caused Goodbow to doubt his word but, still, the industrialist leaned over the table and watched Huff's eyes carefully to measure his answer.

"Just that you were going to see Leary Deen," Huff said. "He didn't say why, and I didn't ask."

"Nothing else?"

"That you were a donor. A nice guy. Older."

"Nothing else?"

"Well, I guess he mentioned you were a little unusual. Seemed worried about you getting around by yourself down here." Huff sipped his tequila and straightened up in his armchair. "And he said you were loaded. Owned a bunch of companies."

"Nothing about my wife or certain border agents, or a nun?"

"No. None of that. Why are you asking me all this?"

"I just think it's strange you'd be guarding a guy on a trip here without knowing anything about why he's making it, that's all. Don't be upset with me."

Huff slid back and seemed to be relaxed by Goodbow's comment. He smiled at his old client.

"It's not that I don't wonder about things. I can see you're greener than hell for an old ..." He halted. "For a guy your age and experience. I can see why Lane called me to take you. And I don't figure you're here on business because I know Leary Deen and business is not Leary Deen's thing. But it's not my job to know this stuff, and sure as hell not my job to ask people about it. Half the time they're government types carrying secrets—or maybe money—and they're not supposed to talk about it. I only ask the agency the practical things I need to know to do my job. Like the person's age, health, allergies."

"And whether he's a drunk."

"Right. Or, her."

"Her?"

"You never know. I had a woman on an aid mission once. A conference in the interior of Guatemala. Some of the others at the thing had security too, and the guards are all standing outside this tent while the closing reception is going on in there. Hooping, hollering, steel drums. After a couple hours we hear a crash inside the tent and shouting—foul, *foul* language. We rush in and my woman is in the thick of it. Throwing shit and totally intoxicated! I had to carry her over my shoulders to the jeep."

"Crazy."

"Best part: she was a goddamned minister! Methodist. It was a religious conference! Now, that one really tested my discretion. But I never said a word." Huff flipped the bar menu to Goodbow's side of the table. "Take a look. We can get the dinner menu too." He looked across the lobby to the dark street outside. "We're battened down for the night."

"Good," Will said. "I'd like to eat early because I have some calls to make from the room."

"So, that's why you want to know what I know. Which is nothing."

"Right. I think what you overhear will make you wonder a lot more than you already are wondering."

"Well, you're not going to arrange to kill somebody, are you?"

"Of course not."

"Then there's no problem."

"What do you mean?"

"I thought you were a businessman! Didn't you read the fine print?"

"Fine print on what?"

"On the goddamned protection agreement."

Goodbow set down his whiskey glass and retrieved a folded document from his suit breast pocket. "This thing?" He waved it in front of Huff Langley.

"Yeah. Look at the bottom part. Right above our signatures. Look under the light here." He shoved the tiny table lamp toward Goodbow.

The penultimate paragraph was legalese of the highest, mind-numbing order. It read in bold type:

32. The Security Professional engaged under this Agreement, his employer, and any other person involved in retaining Client, understand, commit and agree to hold absolutely confidential any and all information gained, facts learned, or conversations overheard pertaining in any way, directly or indirectly, to the activities of Client (or anyone Client meets, contacts, or mentions) during the period of service, including the identity of such persons, the nature, howsoever general, of the conversations, or the place or places where such occurred, except for, and only except for,

activities of violence against persons or discussions of same.

"See," said Huff Langley. "No problem. I see nothing, I hear nothing."

For once, Goodbow thought, he needn't make another promise, at least tonight.

15

While Goodbow was learning in Tegucigalpa that day, and planning his next steps, Sr. Hope Annie did her best in El Paso. She was worried about Goodbow. Lane Williams had called about the little girl, Gloria, and had told her the industrialist had traveled to Honduras to meet Leary Deen.

"To *Tegus*?" she exclaimed to Williams. "Does he know what he's doing?"

"I discouraged him, but he insisted. He said he had a tip that Leary Deen might know the whereabouts of some of the separated parents."

"Who told him that?"

"He wouldn't tell me. Said he had promised to keep him, or her—or whoever—out of it. But, you know, it may be true. Do you know Leary Deen?"

"The man at the embassy there? Yes. He came up when we opened the respite center. I think the State Department made him come to look it over—make sure we were on the level and authorized to house detainees. But I could see he has a good heart. He said, like me, he'd been a schoolteacher. He was very good with the children he met."

"He is a good man," Lane Williams said. "He never holds anything from us that he can possibly share. Sometimes, things he probably shouldn't. Manny says he gets pretty close to the line. Manny says he trusts him. He argued inside the government against the zero tolerance policy, and I know he has given some of the asylum seekers letters to show to the border agents and the judges, saying the person is not a criminal in Honduras and that the family is in danger in their colonia."

"But did Goodbow go alone?" Sr. Hope Annie asked.

"No, he's not *that* crazy. Or at least, I'm not. I sent a guard with him. Huff Langley."

"That big marine?"

"Yes. You know him?"

"When a Congresswoman visited our center he was her security. I'm glad you sent him with Goodbow."

"They were going to come right back." Lane did not know about Goodbow's change of plans. "I expect to hear from them later tonight, probably when they land in Houston. Huff will take care of him, don't worry."

"And what about little Gloria?" the nun asked. "You said that's why you called."

"Gloria is getting better. The cut on her foot was very bad and the doctors say the infection was building for a long time. But the antibiotics are taking hold."

"When can she come here to us?" Sr. Hope Annie sounded like a hopeful grandmother anticipating a grandchild's visit.

"Not for another day or two, at least," Lane said, then paused. "But when she does come, she is going to be needing you a lot, Sister."

"Oh, no. Are you telling me? . . ." But, in truth, Sr. Hope Annie knew what she was about to hear.

"Her parents were denied entry, without detention. They were sent back. Manny did his best, but their asylum request was sent to another office for immediate removal assessment. Manny couldn't stop it. And the other office summarily ordered them back. I'd have never known if Manny hadn't found out and called me."

Sr. Hope Annie and Lane Williams both understood—and loathed—the new rule the administration had put into effect to deal with the overcrowding of the normal asylum application process. So called "catch and release" with a future hearing before an immigration judge was no longer being used. Nor were most asylees being detained to await a hearing in future months. Instead, under the new process many were almost immediately interviewed by special border agents who were authorized to grant temporary asylum status—which the agents almost never did—or summarily reject their application and order them removed—sent back across the border, normally with no assistance to get back to their home country. It was the fate of the great majority.

"Oh, dear," the nun said. "So little Gloria's parents are gone."

"Well, they've been removed. But there is one small good thing. I was able to get them escorted back to Honduras on a Mexican bus and I sent notice to Leary Deen at the embassy. I told him about Gloria in the hospital. Human Rights First subsidized their bus trip to Tegus, which is where they came from. I've never sent special word to an individual at the embassy before, but after Goodbow said the guy may have some knowledge of other parents, I thought maybe he could keep an eye on Gloria's parents too."

"Well, let us hope so," said Sr. Hope Annie, lighting a cigarette on her end of the call.

"Hope and pray, Sister," said Lane Williams.

16

In Goodbow's mind, pieces of a plan were coming together. Surely not a plan in any ordered, describable sense that he could yet write down on paper. But pieces of one with a vague outline, elements still more figment than fact, swirling and floating in his broad brain like molecules and atoms awaiting a catalyst to bond, combine, become—if he could will it—action.

Some of the components were coming into view. There was Sr. Hope Annie; her brave spirit; her connections with other nuns and ministers working in the cause; her general knowledge of the whereabouts of children placed across the US in foster homes by faith organizations. He'd called her from The Hotel de Maya and told her what he'd learned at the embassy, that he hoped to meet a dozen parents on Sunday. The Sister had only hours before heard from Lane Williams that Goodbow had traveled to Honduras under the protection of Huff Langley. The nun was astounded to hear his news and nearly gushed with joy. She told him what Lane Williams told her about the removal of the parents of the little girl, Gloria, and how Lane Williams had made sure that Leary Deen knew about them.

"They must be the parents who came back here today," Goodbow told her. "He said their child had been taken into an American hospital."

"Lord Jesus in heaven!" she gasped. "This is a great gift! Such a great gift, Goodbow!"

"Do not be too excited, Sr. Hope Annie," he'd said. "It is good to learn where some of the parents are, but that is not the same as returning them to their children, or Gloria's back to her. I still have no ideas on that." The fiery nun spoke so loudly that Goodbow held his phone away from his ear.

"But you are thinking? You are thinking, right?" she asked.

"Yes, but nothing has come to me yet."

"Well, it will come. The Lord will make it come. Why else would he have sent you to help them?"

"It was Grace who sent me."

"What is the difference? To me, there is no difference. You, your wife, Lane, Manny, Maria, Leary Deen, even little angel Gloria! Everything is of a piece. Oh, this is such a gift!"

"You have such faith, Sister. I don't think I have such faith."

"I think you do, and you just don't know it. It will come to you."

"And if it doesn't?"

"Then use mine," she'd said.

And there was Leary Deen; his dedication and savvy; his willingness to bring Goodbow to the parents he knew of in the dangerous capitol, risking his own standing at the embassy. He'd already called Goodbow barely an hour after the two had parted at the embassy.

"I reached one set of the parents," he'd reported. "Juan and Juliana Rodriguez. Of course, they were very excited. They are going to reach the others and come to the church Sunday morning. Juan will call me when he's spoken to them all. But they are very happy to hear that you will meet them. I told them they must tell no one. They understood. And I told them this does not mean there is a way to get them to their children. Only that you are trying to find a way, if one is possible."

"This is good, Leary. Thank you."

"We must be careful not to give them too much hope, Goodbow," Deen had said. "It could be false hope."

Goodbow knew the foreign service officer was right. But he'd replied, "Let's have faith."

"You sound like Sr. Hope Annie."

Goodbow knew Deen was right about that too.

And now there was the ex-marine, Huff Langley, sent to him by Lane Williams. How fortuitous that a man with such an understanding of this Central American country, so strange and uncomfortable to Goodbow, would accompany him, protect him, and teach him about the unusual features and terrain of the place. He'd sat in the hotel room chair and listened to Goodbow's calls.

"I take it that's the nun you mentioned," he said when Goodbow finished his call to her. Goodbow nodded. "Sounds like a firecracker."

"Totally committed," Will said.

"What's her name?"

"Sr. Hope Annie."

"My God, I've met her. She started the place for families in El Paso."

"That's her."

"I think people like her are like marines in battle," Huff said. "Believe they can do anything."

"Maybe having a cause does that to you."

"I suppose that's right," Huff said. "When you think about it, there's a pretty fine line between a cause and a duty. You feel either one strongly enough, you'll charge up that hill no matter what."

Huff Langley could not have known, as even Goodbow did not know then, that what he next told the industrialist would shape indelibly everything that happened after.

"I think if you ever want to get those parents out of Honduras," he said, "you should get them out of Tegus first. Get them someplace safer. Someplace where they can stay in one place for a while. This city is no place for them, especially since they tried to go to the US and had to come back. They're targets now for the gangs, more than ever. They hate the people who try to get away from them."

The marine went to the desk in the hotel room, opened the thin advertising magazine resting on it, and switched on the desk lamp. He thumbed the pages until he found a map of Tegus and, on its back side, a map of the whole country. "Look at this," he said. Goodbow loped over to the desk and lowered his big frame into the swivel chair.

"Here's where we are," Huff said, putting a thick finger on the larger letters marking Tegucigalpa. He moved his finger in a radius around the capitol city. "This is all tough territory. I've been all through it. I wouldn't recommend any of it for them."

Goodbow leaned over the map and saw the long coast along the Caribbean to the northeast of the country. "What about this area?" he asked.

"Better than here, but it's a long way. And not very secluded." The marine slid his finger in the opposite direction, to the most southwestern niche of the country, the narrow bay of the Pacific Ocean that Goodbow himself had noticed when he studied a map of Honduras before meeting with Lane Williams in El Paso. "This place," Huff said. "It's quiet. It's safe. No big towns, no gangs."

"You've been there?"

"A couple of times. To Amapala. Quaint little town on the Isle de Tigre."

"In the Gulf of Fonseca."

"Your eyes are pretty good for an old dude."

"I saw it once before when I googled Honduras."

"It's a nice place. I took a girl down there."

"A couple times," Goodbow said.

"Well, not the same girl."

"Oh, really."

"The first one didn't like the beach. It's jet black. Dead black sand. Volcanic ash, really. So hot in the day you can't walk on it. But it's good for boats."

"Boats?"

"Sailboats, mainly."

"Really?"

"Yeah, there's even a marina. It was small, but some pretty big sailboats were there. I doubt they were owned by locals. Maybe your nun can find another nun they could stay with in the cathedral there. Or, there are a couple of hotels. We could take the parents there and they'd be safe until you come up with something."

And at that moment, it came to Goodbow. A tingle ran up his spine and down again. A catalyst had arrived, he knew. Thoughts and people and places were firing and re-firing in his brain as if electrified, bonding one to another in a plan he could see now for the first time. Yes, a catalyst had arrived.

Its name was Burp Lebeau.

17

Goodbow tried to sleep on the drive from Tegus to Amapala, but it was no use. It wasn't that he was too alert; to the contrary, he was near exhaustion, sleeping little since his arrival in Honduras with Huff Langley on the unreasonably early flight two days earlier. It was the roads.

The embassy vehicle fleet was back from maintenance and Huff had secured a comfortable Grand Cherokee—*with* government plates—for the three-hour drive to the black beaches of the Gulf of Fonseca. Goodbow was surprised that most of the route was one expressway or another, with portions of them reasonably well-maintained. But in many other sections, the roads were so pitted with large potholes that the ex-marine had to weave, it seemed incessantly, to avoid them. That is, when he *could* avoid them. Every three or four minutes, an unpredictable tire would pound into one and Goodbow's head would bounce, just as unpredictably, off his headrest. He knew he shouldn't be irritated, but eventually couldn't help himself.

"For Pete's sake, Huff, do you have to do that?" he said, in a disapproving tone.

"There's no fucking way to miss them all, Will!"

"Can't you drive slower? That would seem to help."

"And take a lot longer to get there? That would mean we'd be driving back in the dark! You think *this* is bad? Your old false teeth would never fit again."

"I don't have false teeth."

"Stop your complaining or you will."

But Huff didn't say it in true anger, Goodbow knew. And it had been the industrialist's idea to make the drive to Amapala in the first place. The meeting with the parents at the Tegus church was two days away and sightseeing didn't seem appetizing. Besides, Goodbow thought, it would be wise to scout out the coastal area and gain a feel for the place. He was especially intrigued by Huff's mention of the sailing marina there. Perhaps he could even make a contact for Sr. Hope Annie; someone she could work with or refer to her network of sisters, someone who could help find housing for the parents as they waited for next steps if he could finalize them.

As he and Huff approached the furthest reaches of the country's southwest and descended the high hills toward the quiet bay, Goodbow's heart quickened. Huff stopped the SUV at water's edge. The bay laid expansively before them, lapping up against the black sand that stretched out hundreds of feet to meet it. They got out of the car and stepped in front of it.

"They say it was Columbus who sailed to the coast on the other side of the country and named it Honduras. Spanish for 'deep'. Because the water in the Gulf of Mexico was so deep off its shore."

"We missed high tide," Goodbow said.

"Looks like it, yeah."

"Is that the island you talked about?" Goodbow pointed to the land mass out in the bay.

"Yeah, that's Isle de Tigre. There are others between it and the Pacific, but it's the biggest, and the easiest to reach. There's a causeway to it over there." Huff pointed to a low bridge stretching to the island. "It's just three-kilometers to get there," he said.

"I don't see any marina," Goodbow said.

"It's on the other side of the island."

"Amapala is the village on the island?"

"Yeah. You can see the old church spire." Goodbow squinted. "That's Amapala," Huff said. "The marina sets on its edge, facing the Pacific."

"Let's go there," Goodbow said. "I want to see the landings."

"We're not going for a goddamned boat ride, are we?"

"Not today."

"Because I didn't arrange for any boat."

"You won't need to, Huff."

"What does that mean?"

"It means if I needed a boat, I wouldn't need to arrange for one. I have my own."

Huff thought the comment odd. He'd overheard his charge's phone calls the night before to the nun in El Paso and to Lane Williams, and his conversation with Leary Deen when he'd called Goodbow from the embassy to confirm the Sunday meeting with the parents. And he'd noticed the old industrialist's interest when he'd mentioned the quiet region on the Pacific coast that they were now visiting. But nothing had been said by Goodbow about boats. When they buckled up in the car, the marine turned to his passenger with a look of puzzlement.

"What?" Goodbow asked.

"Tell me about this boat. Your boat. How does that fit in to this?"

"I'm not sure it does, but it may."

"What kind of boat?"

"A sailboat. A sailing yacht, really."

"Yacht?"

"Yes, a yacht. Suitable for the ocean."

"So a real fancy thing?"

"I guess people would say that."

"How big is it?"

"Thirty-two meters."

"Meters, not feet?"

"Meters."

"Like a hundred feet long."

"Just about a hundred and six feet, actually."

"For just you and your wife."

"Usually. Plus the captain. Sometimes a crew. It sleeps twelve, plus the captain."

"You don't sail it yourself? You always have a captain?"

"Yes. I'm not a good sailor, myself. There's a lot to it. You're out there for days, weeks, months even. And there's a lot of automated controls. Besides, he's my friend."

"The captain?"

"Yes. Like a brother."

"So, more than a friend?"

"Yes. And to Grace too. She loved him too."

"Does this captain know you're down here?"

"He knows I went to El Paso. He doesn't know I'm down here in Honduras."

Huff finally turned on the ignition and put the car in gear, without looking away from his client. "Why do I think he's going to find out pretty soon," he said.

They drove the causeway to the island, to the old little town of Amapala and parked at its outskirts, walking from there toward its center. The narrow streets were a mixture of ancient stones, irregularly shaped, and gravel, winding between low, tidy, very old buildings. The colors of the town were striking to Goodbow: much yellow, reminiscent of old Florida, to which generous amounts of bright tones of blue and green were added. But all of the buildings were much less modern than even the oldest of Florida's, with few windows and roofs made uneven by markedly different materials used to cover them. He was surprised by the people—more than he expected—walking the skinny sidewalks in front of the shops leading to the town center where the church and its tower stood in a plaza ringed with bright flowers. It was early afternoon; the sun hung high and left the plaza almost entirely unshaded. The air blowing in from the Pacific bay was pleasant, matching the disposition of the locals who stepped with upright gaits, many hatless, and looked about with smiles and frequent gestures of acknowledgement to their fellows. Very unlike what he'd observed on the tense avenues of Tegus where everyone seemed to stride rigidly, heads down as if eschewing contact, all manner of hats pulled to the brow.

He and Huff walked to the marina behind the church. From Huff's description he had hoped for more, especially larger sailing crafts. But he knew he shouldn't be surprised that the boats moored were all modest and numbered less than ten. He judged the broadest beam of any to be five meters at most and none with a stern to bow length exceeding twenty meters. Only one had dual masts. He saw immediately that all the boats were suited only for recreational sailing in the bay waters; none would be safe on the ocean for any distance, even under the expert command of Burp Lebeau.

"How do these compare with yours?" Huff asked.

"They don't," he said. "I don't see a fueling station. Do you?"

"What do you need fuel for? These are sailboats."

"Big cruisers and sailing yachts coming in here would expect fuel. Diesel."

"Then they must not come. There's no fuel station."

Goodbow took out his notepad and made an entry: *fill in Panama.*

The tide was still moving out. He took Huff to the longest of the three piers and they stepped to its end. The water was clear.

"Six-feet deep now, you think?" he asked the marine.

"I'd say so. Maybe a little deeper." Goodbow made another note: *six feet at mid tide.*

"So what do you think?" asked Huff.

"About what?"

"Whether the parents would be better off here until you figure something out. You could put them in the little hotel over there." Huff pointed down the street past the church.

"I think it's a good idea, Huff. Can you help me get them here, if they're willing?"

"I'm in this far."

"You're a good man."

"You're growing on me too."

They reached the Grand Cherokee. "So have you figured the rest out? After you get them here?"

"Getting there," Goodbow said.

* * *

The drive back to Tegus was, in truth, not much different than the ride down. Rough as hell. But this time it was more comfortable for the old industrialist. Maybe it was a feeling that progress was made in Amapala; a sense that perhaps this was, after all, something more than a fool's errand. Maybe it was simply pure exhaustion.

He slept most of the way.

18

"Dad, really? A *burner* phone?" Ben Goodbow was sincerely surprised by his father's call from Tegus, and not a little concerned. "What do you know about burner phones?"

"Nothing. But my friend Huff recommends it."

"Huff?"

"Huff Langley. He's a former marine that works security for people in Central America."

"A bodyguard?"

"He calls it escort service. The man at Human Rights First found him for me."

"Oh, God, dad. This is getting worse," Ben said. "How long have you been down there? You said you were going to Texas. How'd you wind up in Honduras?"

"Ben, relax. I'm not getting you into this. I won't do that."

"Except you want me to buy you a burner phone."

"Well, not for me. It's for Burp Lebeau. I need you to take it to him. He won't be expecting it. But I won't be back for a while, and I need him to have it so that I can call him."

"Burp *has* a phone."

"Huff says he shouldn't use it when I call him. Or if he calls me. Huff knows these things."

"For Pete's sake, dad."

"I'd ask Burp to buy it himself, but I guess the things are kind of pricey. I'd wire him the money, but I guess that's not a good idea."

"According to Huff," Ben said.

"Yeah. He says money can always be tracked."

Ben noticed his father's calm, certain tone. He sounded as composed as he might while making a reservation with a familiar travel agent. *How far is he going with this thing? I should have resisted more when he told me about his promise to mom,* his son thought.

"Well, it's been a few days since I bought a burner phone, dad. But I assume they come in all kinds."

"What'd you mean?"

"Like how long they stay active, how many calls you can make on them, that kind of thing."

"Make sure it will work for a long time."

"*How* long?"

"At least a few months."

"When I get it, should I call you with its number?"

"No. For a while, Ben, I don't think it's a good idea to be calling each other. Here's the number for the Hotel de Maya in Tegucigalpa." Goodbow recited the number. "When you get the number for Burp's phone, just call the hotel and leave a message for me with it."

Ben sighed on his end of the line. It distressed Goodbow to hear it. It wasn't anger that the father felt; indeed, nearly its opposite: sadness and empathy, wrapped in a ribbon of conflict. He had gone to El Paso ambivalent and skeptical. But each day he sensed his footing gaining sureness, his commitment to his promise to Grace deepening further. But now he heard the strain and concern in his son's voice, and it pained him to hear it. He worried he was hurting his son, not so much by enlisting his help for Burp Lebeau's cell phone, as by giving him reason —good reason, he knew—to fear for his father's well-being. It was not something a father should do. In that moment with his son still on the line, stirred by an impulse he could not control and wouldn't want to even if he could, his mind went to Grace with his dilemma. *Grace, oh Grace, is this the right thing?*

But there was only the slightest pause before Ben seemed to answer the question he'd put to Grace in his own soul.

"You're doing the right thing, dad," his son said. "I understand why you're doing it. I'll take care of the phone for Burp. Just be careful, will you."

"I will, son."

"Stay close to Huff."

"I will, son."

But the son sounded unconvinced. "I mean, real close," he said.

19

When the embassy staffer wheeled the mail cart into Leary Deen's office and lobbed the morning delivery onto his desktop, Leary's eye went immediately to the orange envelope protruding from one corner of the banded bundle. The interagency envelopes were color coded. He was accustomed to receiving mainly blue envelopes, the State Department color, or the occasional yellow, from the Department of Defense, usually in regard to some military delegation or embassy reception. But orange envelopes were rare. It designated the Department of Homeland Security. He drew it first from the stack. *TIME SENSITIVE*, large letters declared. Well, he thought, at least it wasn't marked "classified."

Leary didn't know why communiques from DHS put him on edge. Or, maybe he did and simply preferred not to acknowledge it. His heart always raced at the sight of an orange envelope, and it did that morning. It didn't slow when he saw the letterhead above the brief handwritten note inside: Breen Edwards, Secretary.

Breen Edwards! Breen Edwards never contacts me! And a personal note?

If he could understand his inner feelings more clearly, Leary would know that one of the reasons he received requests from DHS with trepidation was that he didn't much like its chief, cabinet member Breen Edwards. Physically, Edwards was a towering man, good looking by any account, with thick silver hair, a deep voice and distinguished flair. To Leary Deen everything about him said, *this man is in charge.* To the modest, unassuming diplomat in the consulate for immigration and visitor affairs, Breen Edward's bearing alone was enough to hinder affection. But it was more than that to the soul of Leary Deen. The cabinet member's policies and—even more—the earnestness with which he pursued and enforced them, irked Leary.

The embassy man knew that his judgment of Breen Edwards might be too harsh; many other foreign service officers that Leary liked and admired did not share his view of the DHS head.

"You act, Leary, like he has the same job as we do," one colleague had said to him over lunch when Leary was critical of Edwards' immigration views. "Breen Edwards' job is to prevent harm to the 'homeland'. He says that's why he promotes what he does. A lot of people around here agree with him."

"Separating parents from their children prevents harm to the homeland?"

"You isolate out that one thing, Leary, and harp on it," his colleague said. "It's a lot more complicated than that one thing. The whole immigration issue is a lot bigger. Do you really think anyone *wants* to take children from their parents? But maybe in the big picture—the biggest picture—you have to sometimes."

Leary Deen understood that his colleague had a point, at least in the 'national mind,' if one could say there was such a thing. If you believed fundamentally, as most did, that the borders could not be freely open to all, per force there had to be limits. Limits meant numbers. And if the numbers were flowing over the limits, you needed—the reasoning went—to do something to reduce the numbers, reduce the demand, discourage the numbers from continuing to grow unmanageably. In the national mind, deterrence was an acceptable strategy. What could be done to make them *not want* to come to the border?

Leary Deen's problem (or was it a virtue?) was that he didn't believe the national mind was duly informed, that in fact it was often *mis*-informed, and that—at least in recent years—dismissive of American traditions of refuge. It particularly upset him that to the man on the street there was little if any difference between people wanting to live in the US because it would be better to live there, and people wanting to live in the US because, in their own minds, they were not going to live at all if they didn't. To Leary, for the former group, coming to the US was a choice. Often a rational, reasonable choice, but still a choice. And a choice that rational, reasonable immigration policy could address. But for the latter, including the hundreds of thousands fleeing the Northern Triangle Countries, choice had nothing to do with it. It was "get out" or live in terror of harm to yourself or your children—or worse. And to Leary, a whole other set of values and national needs were implicated by the straights of these people. There were still rational and reasonable responses that could address their dire needs. But to Leary, deterrence was not one them, at least not deterrence achieved by the separation of parents and children at the US border.

He read the note from Breen Edwards three times. Its tone was sterile, but its effect on Leary profound. He made himself a cup of coffee, closed his door and sat for ten minutes in silent concentration. Then he reached to his suit jacket for his cell phone and called Goodbow, who had just finished breakfast with Huff Langley. There was no small talk; were no pleasantries.

"Listen to this," Leary said abruptly. "I received a handwritten note in this morning's overnight from Washington. It's from the Secretary of DHS."

"DHS?"

"Department of Homeland Security."

"Oh."

"This is what it says:

'Have been advised that you received an American businessman,

Wilton Goodbow, this week in Tegucigalpa. Please report any requests

made to you by direct reply with copy to Office 319 in your building. No emails.

Breen Edwards.'

"That's it?" Goodbow asked.

"Yes."

"Just that?" Goodbow asked again.

"That's it."

"What is 'Office 319 in your building?' CIA?"

"No, I wish it were," Leary said. "Or even DEA."

"Then who is it?"

"It's the FBI station here."

Silence came over the line. Both men were puzzled.

"Do you have any idea why Breen Edwards would ever have any interest in you?" Leary asked.

"No. I hardly know who he is."

"Have you been a big donor to the President? Maybe they're looking after you."

"No, I've never given him anything. But, I haven't been completely against him. Not like Grace was."

"Her letters to the President. You said she wrote letters. More than one?"

"Oh, yeah. She kept writing until she got an answer. Which she didn't like so she wrote more."

"Well, that could be it," said Leary. "Sometimes the Secret Service gets its antennae up if they think somebody might be a crank. They might have put her name into a database."

"You're kidding. They thought Grace was a threat?"

"Sounds extreme, but you never know. After the killings in El Paso, tensions have stayed high. Everybody is still on edge. Trump has kept the immigration thing hot, hot, hot. And if your wife was put on a watch list, your passport would have tripped it when you flew to Honduras."

Goodbow remembered how the embassy official had been delivered a copy of his passport before he had arrived for his meeting. But Leary Deen had seemed to laugh that off; this seemed different. Goodbow inquired why.

"You told me someone from upstairs had sent down a copy of my passport, before I came to see you. That didn't worry you, did it?"

"No, because I assumed it was done because I had listed you two days earlier on the guest log, when Lane Williams asked me to host you. It's a standard security measure. And it didn't come from Office 319. It came the way they always do, from building security." Goodbow noticed that Leary's cadence had slowed, as if his words were interspersed with thoughts. His tone was somewhere between reflective and serious.

"Does this change things for you, Leary?" Goodbow asked.

For me? Leary Deen thought. *For me? I just told this man that he is about to be of interest to the FBI and he asks if this changes things for me?*

"What do you mean, Goodbow?"

"Can you still take me to the parents on Sunday?"

"Of course, I can," said Leary Deen.

"How will you answer that note?"

"I don't know," said Leary Deen. "I have a hard choice to make."

"Don't get yourself in trouble."

"There may be a way I can handle it without being dishonest."

"A diplomat's skills?"

"Something like that," Leary Deen said. "But whatever I do, don't worry; I will take you to the parents on Sunday. In the meantime, stay close to Huff."

"I'm hearing that from everybody," Goodbow said.

20

Goodbow and Huff Langley each welcomed the rain that fell Saturday morning on the city of Tegucigalpa. But for different reasons. The old businessman wanted relief from the beating Honduran sun that had prevailed since their arrival. Huff was pleased to see the streets of the downtown district less filled. He could get his charge out for a walk without undue risk. He saw that Goodbow needed exercise; he'd been pacing in the hotel room and more quiet than usual. Every few minutes he would pick up his notebook from the desk and flip its pages, make a new entry, then pace again.

Huff drew the curtain, only a little, and peered down to the street. "It's letting up some," he said. Goodbow was so preoccupied that he didn't register the marine's question.

"What?"

"I said the rain is letting up. How about a walk?"

"I'm thinking," Goodbow said.

"Yeah, and you're driving me crazy."

"I said, I'm thinking."

"Well, you can walk and think at the same time, can't you?"

Goodbow stepped to the window and looked out, confirming the conditions. "I guess a walk does sound good."

They had walked two blocks before anything was said. Every hundred steps or so, Huff would pause so that the older man moved ahead of him; then he quickly glided next to Goodbow on the opposite side. "Why do you keep doing that?" Goodbow finally asked.

"Just a healthy habit," Huff said.

"Well, it's irritating."

"It's also irritating to any thugs watching us. They can't be sure where I'll be if they try to take us."

Four days ago, Huff's concerns would have struck the New Englander as overdone. But, again, the assault on the rental car as they drove into the city disabused him of any skepticism now.

"I understand, Huff. I'm sorry. I'm glad you're here. I'm glad you're so careful."

"You seem upset today," Huff said. "Quiet. What's going on?"

"I have to call my friend, the captain. I have to call him today, before we meet the parents tomorrow."

"About the boat," Huff surmised.

"Yes."

"You want him to sail it down here."

"Yes."

"You think he'll say no."

"No, just the opposite."

"Oh."

"He won't say no. Because he's my friend and he loved Grace. He won't say no, and I'll be dragging him into this with me."

"Well, isn't that what real friends do?"

"What?"

"Get dragged," Huff said.

"What are you talking about?"

"Dragging. And friends."

Goodbow stopped and turned to his guard. "You've lost me," he said.

"Never been in combat, have you?" Huff said, without condescendence.

"No, I haven't. I never served. My captain friend did, though. In Vietnam."

"Even so, you've been in fights, you've been in struggles. Not in a war, I get that. But in your business, for sure in your family. You've fought with people you love, people you care about. When everything seemed to be on the line."

"A few times, sure. But I'm still lost."

"If you'd ever been under fire in a war, you'd understand. Sometimes you drag somebody, Will. And sometimes you *get* dragged. Your friend will know this."

"You make it sound like getting dragged into something is some kind of duty. How can that be?"

"Because sometimes it is. That guy I drag back to cover behind a building needs to keep himself alive too. To live another day. To be there for somebody else. Maybe, even for *me*. If he can. For the common purpose. And because it's just the right goddamned thing to do."

Ever vigilant, the large marine paused and looked in every direction. Only a few people were on the streets, mostly older citizens in hats, carrying small umbrellas; nothing threatening to his eye.

"What's this captain's name?"

"I can't tell you that."

"Why not?"

"Because you might have to tell it to someone else. Like the FBI. I can't put him—or you—in that position."

"Well, you said this captain loved your wife," Huff continued. "And you sure loved her, that's fucking clear. Look at what you're doing down here! It's crazy! But maybe that's your common purpose with the captain. Or will be, once you ask him. To do this for Grace."

Goodbow looked up into the eyes of his guard. Like Burp Lebeau, Huff was so unlike himself. So different in skills, experience, ambitions. He'd known Burp, it seemed to him, his whole life; this man Huff Langley for four days. Yet somehow, some way, the three of them now were connecting in common purpose none of them had sought.

"I think I see now what you mean," Goodbow said.

The rain had stopped, and the air had lightened. The door of a food market opened just ahead of them and the breeze carried a sweet ripe smell of produce and dairy to them. A small man in a spotless white apron, obviously just donned, pulled a broad wooden wagon on cranky iron wheels out to the sidewalk. It took all his strength to move the heavy cart laden with brilliant red tomatoes and shiny watermelons. He was leaning backward so severely as he pulled that Goodbow feared he would catapult into the street should the wheels lock or his grip dislodge.

"Now, there," Huff Langley said, looking at the market worker. "There's a man who knows how to drag."

* * *

Back in Newport, a typical morning fog was beginning to burn off the surface of the quiet bay when Burp Lebeau boarded *The Sails of Grace* with his thermos of coffee. He checked the mooring latches; all were secure. He'd been thinking about Goodbow every day, really every part of every day, since his friend had left for Texas. He was anxious. Ben Goodbow's visit to his carriage house quarters the night before to deliver him the new cell phone hadn't helped.

"I really don't want to get into it," Goodbow's son had answered when he'd asked him what the phone was for. "But I told him I would get it to you, and I have." The son wouldn't come inside to talk further, despite Burp's urging.

"Is he still in El Paso?" Burp had asked.

"No. He went from there to Honduras."

"Why the hell did he go there?"

"He got a lead about the embassy down there. About some of the parents whose children were taken at the border."

"Is he safe?"

The younger Goodbow saw the worry in the sailor's eyes.

"He has a guard, but that's all I know. A guy named Langley. Huff Langley. Ex-marine that escorts people to Central America for the government and the non-profits along the border."

"He's not giving it up, is he?" Burp said, unsmiling.

"Doesn't seem like it."

"He can be as stubborn as your mother."

"Tell me about it."

"What do you want me to do?"

Goodbow's son knew it was an important question. The old sailor was his only real way to influence his father. But Ben was torn too; he owed Grace too. If he worked to dissuade his father, was he disloyal to her? Standing at Burp's door, he could almost see his mother leaning against the trusted captain.

"One side of me wants you to talk him out of all of this," he said. "Another side wants me to help mom get what she wanted."

"You can't know that you could make a difference in how he thinks, anyway," Burp said. "No matter how hard you tried. And the same for me. I think he has to decide for himself."

"I don't know what he's going to call you about. He's still grieving, I think. Who knows if his head is right yet? But it's not my place to tell you what to do, Burp. I'm just glad he has a friend like you. And that goddamned marine with him." The sailor and the son embraced, and Ben left.

Now, he went to the helm and opened the cabinet below the large wheel where the maps were stored. At his suggestion, Goodbow printed a new copy every year of the global navigation guide published by the National Oceanic and Atmospheric Administration. The NOAA document ran over four-hundred pages in the three-ring binder they'd prepared, a veritable mariner's encyclopedia of nautical geography. Hardly any Americans knew it even existed, but for men and women of the world's seas, it was indispensable. It mapped every navigable port on every ocean and sea of the globe complete with the distance between each in nautical miles, estimated sailing speeds according to prevailing wind data, and details about water depth, mooring facilities, even fueling information. He'd told Goodbow that every ocean-going vessel should carry the guide and that the merchant marine industry relied on it as a bible.

"This thing is incredible," Goodbow had said when he'd first seen it. "It must cost a fortune to compile and keep current. Our government publishes it, but *anybody* can have it? I wonder if it's part of the foreign aid budget," he'd said.

Lebeau used the guide's index to thumb through to the Caribbean. He remembered sailing off the long coast of Honduras decades ago. He tried to recall the voyage and running his finger down the map lines brought the memories back to him. It wasn't an excursion for Grace and Will Goodbow, he remembered. It was more an instructional trip than anything else. An insurance company executive from Providence had purchased a twenty-four-meter yacht and docked it at Newport Bay. He hired Lebeau to teach him how to sail it. The man's thought was to sail north to Newfoundland, but Burp dissuaded him. Not preferable for a novice, he'd told the customer; the North Atlantic was too unpredictable, even in reasonable weather, and a full crew would be required. The Mexican coast in the Gulf, mooring in Belize, was a better choice. And it had been. The boat owner, about Burp's age, learned well from him and his lean crew. By the time they departed Belize, the owner asked if Lebeau and crew could extend the voyage a few days, long enough to sail south along the Caribbean side of Honduras, with himself at the helm, more or less unassisted.

Now, the old sailor recalled with a smile that he had even brought up that trip to the Goodbows years later on one of their longer sails together. "You know, I had a customer once who took the helm himself for three days," he'd called out to Will, lounging on the deck next to Grace. "Gave me a nice rest. Got to sit back and watch the beach go by." Will peered at him over his sunglasses; Grace did too. "Why haven't you ever done that?" the captain asked.

"Did he pay you as much as I do?"

"No."

"Then you have your answer."

The burner phone came alive so loudly in the Velcro-ed pocket of his wind shirt that it jarred Lebeau; his elbow knocked the map binder from the helm console as he drew out the phone.

"Will," he said.

"Where are you, Burp?"

"On *Grace*."

"How is she?"

"Beautiful as ever."

"I'm in Honduras."

"I know. Ben told me when he brought me this fucking spy phone."

"That was Huff's idea."

"Heard about him too."

"He knows what he's doing," Goodbow said.

"Oh, I'm sure *he* knows what he's doing. I'm just not so sure you do."

"I'm not sure either. That's why I called. Will you hear me out?"

"I haven't thrown this thing into the sea, have I? Sure. I'll listen."

"But you have to tell me first that you won't do anything you don't really want to, just because *I* want you to. I don't want to do that to you. It's dangerous. You could get in a lot of trouble. It's probably not legal."

"Probably?"

"Okay. It's *not* legal. At least that's what people tell me. But it may still be *right*."

"I'm listening."

Goodbow talked for a solid twenty minutes. Like a priest sitting silently through a long, anguished confession, Lebeau never interrupted, except that every minute or so he uttered a gravelly "a-huh" merely to signal that he was still on the line. Goodbow told him about Lane Williams and the little girl, Gloria, that he saw rushed away on a gurney on his first morning in El Paso. He told him about fiery Sr. Hope Annie and her center, and her network of nuns finding temporary homes for migrant children separated from their parents. Without naming the Red Cross worker Maria Angeles or her husband Manny, he told him about the city of Tegus and why he'd gone there on a tip from sources at the border in El Paso; how he'd promised his sources that he would not tell the government what they had told him about the government's knowledge of the whereabouts of some of the returned parents. He told him about Leary Deen and Huff Langley, how he liked them very much and that especially Deen was taking great personal risk because he worked at the embassy and the FBI knew Deen was communicating with him in the country. He told him Deen had identified six sets of parents, including little girl Gloria's, who'd been returned without their children to Tegus where they lived in daily fear of the gangs who targeted Hondurans who had tried to immigrate to the US. He told him he was meeting with the twelve parents the next day at a church in the Honduran capital; and that Leary Deen and a catholic priest were arranging it.

"And me?" asked Burp. "Where do I fit in?"

"Have you ever heard of a port called Amapala?"

"Spell it."

Goodbow did.

"I don't think so," Burp said. He knew he hadn't seen it on the map he'd just looked at. "Is it in Honduras? On the Caribbean coastline?"

"Honduras, but on the Pacific side," Goodbow said. "There's a little slice of Honduras on that side, just north of Panama."

"As in 'just north of the Panama Canal?'"

"I think you see where I'm going," Goodbow said.

"Or where *I'm* going, you mean."

"If you sailed *Grace* through the Gulf and down the Caribbean, you could cut through the Canal to the Pacific. Then north to the Gulf of Fonseca. Amapala sits on the Isle de Tigre about sixty kilometers into that gulf."

"Why there?"

"It's where I can get the parents to wait for you. Where they would be safe. Huff and I can get them there; it's three hours by land from Tegus. They could board with you there in

Amapala. I went there with Huff to look it over. There's mooring there."

"For a boat as big as *Grace*?"

"I think you could manage it. There's no diesel there, though. You'd need to fuel up somewhere else."

"You realize I can't bring a crew," Lebeau said. "It can't get out I'm doing this, and I wouldn't want to get anyone else involved."

"I know. There's no room on *Grace* anyway."

"And I can't sail these people back to Newport, you know. I'd never get through the Canal with them aboard. Every room is combed there."

"Oh no," Goodbow said. "Not back to Newport with them aboard. You'd sail them north to a landing in California."

"Where in California?"

"I don't know yet. But there are options. One of the bays where I've already got slip rights, where you've docked before. One not close to a coast guard station. You yourself never leave the boat and the parents never hear your name. Not from me and not from you. You have to be only 'Captain' to them. You have my word on this, and I need yours. If this comes back on me, so be it. But not you, Burp. I can't have that."

"Kind of you," Burp said, dryly. "But if I *can* get them that far, where do the parents go from there? And what do I do then?"

"Sister Hope and her nuns will take them right from the boat and drive them to their kids, probably in Texas, but maybe farther north in the US. You take *Grace* home by any route you want. You could pick up a crew for the sail home, if you want to."

"That nun has balls."

"Like a brass monkey's."

"And when does this all happen? When would I leave Newport?"

"If the parents say yes, just as soon as you could. I'll know tomorrow if they want to do it."

The line went quiet. Lebeau stooped down and retrieved the map binder; the rings had not dislodged.

"Burp? You still there?"

"Let me call you back," the sailor said.

"Oh. You want to think it over," Goodbow said. Burp detected the trace of disappointment in Goodbow's voice.

"No, Goddamnit. I don't want to *think* it over. You know what happens when I think things over. I get sensible. I just want to study these maps and chart a course; figure out how long it will take me to get to this lovely port of Amapala. I'll call you when I know. It will take a while to get it right. That's a lot of sea."

"Well, maybe you should think it all over. Think it over for both of us."

Sunlight glinted off the chrome bow rails. The fog was fully dispatched over the rippling bay. A horn sounded in the starboard distance. The smell of the sea swept into the helm of the boat and over his face. Burp felt the hairs on his neck stand up.

"Like I said," he said, "I'll call you when I know. In a few days."

21

On Sunday morning, Huff Langley waited at the hotel entrance for Leary Deen while Goodbow sat in the breakfast room, studying the names of the parents. He wanted to memorize them before the meeting.

It was a carryover from his business days. He always tried to remember names and to know them in advance when he could. It was not that he wished to convey false warmth or premature familiarity. In fact, he never used first names in addressing anyone until and unless they insisted, and sometimes not even then. To Goodbow, it was simply a matter of respect. A man's name was part of his dignity; it was not to be taken lightly, its availability not to be presumed.

Grace was unlike him in this way, he knew. She greeted everyone by first name—if she knew it—even on first meeting. But Grace exuded a natural warmth and ease that made it nearly impossible to receive anything she said as forward or insincerely delivered. For her, it was almost as if last names were mere necessary appendages to the given names that really mattered. They'd discussed it once.

"A given name is the only name a person has that is chosen for them," she'd said. "The surname is compulsory. But the given name is the first expression of love in the life of a person."

"Even in my case?" he'd asked her. "Wilton? Seems like an odd way to express love."

"It's unusual," she'd allowed. "But it was a family name and people did that more often in those days."

"It was my great-grandmother's maiden name."

"Well, your parents must have loved her very much to want your name to remind them of her."

"She died young. Long before I was born."

"Well, people don't stop loving someone when they die," Grace had said. "Sometimes they may love them even more. Because they miss them and remember them."

When she had said that years earlier, he wasn't sure he believed it. He did now.

The Honduran surnames were a challenge to him. He was pleased there were only six of them to learn. The first was easy: Rodriguez. The others not so much: Mejia. Alvadaro. Sanchez. Cruz. Carrasco. On a new page in his notebook he made a list of the names in alphabetical order and committed them to memory.

* * *

The cathedral he'd seen in Amapala was made of lovely stone and well-maintained. A grass apron surrounded it bearing abundant florals. Goodbow expected something similar in the Tegus neighborhood to which Leary Deen drove them. But it was nothing like it. St. Antonio's Church was built of modest brick and stucco and slivered between taller buildings on a busy avenue. There were no stained-glass windows on the front of the building, and only a single step up from the sidewalk to the church's entrance. Goodbow wouldn't have judged it a place of worship at all but for the large copper bell cantilevered from the roof line below a simple white cross. Even on Sunday morning, the street was congested with cars and vans jammed to every curb space.

"I can drop you here at the front and find a place to park," Leary Deen said, stopping the embassy car at the church entrance. Goodbow unbuckled his seat belt and slid to the door of the back seat where he sat next to Huff. But the ex-marine reached to Goodbow's knee and restrained him.

"No, Leary," Huff said. "Let's stay together. Find a place."

Leary turned to his passengers in the back seat. "Really, Huff, you're here to take care of Goodbow. I can watch myself."

"It's not you," Huff Langley said. "It's the car. I need to know where it is in case there's a problem."

If diplomats knew anything, it was when to concede an unwinnable argument. Leary Deen pulled around the next corner and found a curb slot a block and a half up. When the three of them stepped out of the car, Leary handed Huff the keys without waiting to be asked.

"The Mass will be in Spanish, but Father Lopez's English is very good," Leary said as they stood at the church entrance. "We should let him translate for the parents, instead of me. They will trust him. I told him we would sit in the back when we arrived. Mass is underway now. When it is over, he'll walk to the rear to send off the parishioners. Our parents will stay behind."

Only one sign hung on the door into the vestibule. It was the standard NO FIREARMS symbol in red, black and white. Goodbow looked at Huff and the marine buttoned his sport jacket so that his sidearm would remain concealed.

Goodbow had attended only a few Masses over the years, each at the wedding of a friend's child. He'd been struck by the pageantry and music, and the order of things; how every utterance from the altar received an immediate and knowing response from the pews and how the routine of it all seemed somehow to imbue an air of comfort. In little St. Antonio's there was no organ or other musical instruments, no overt pageantry; even Father Lopez's vestments were minimal, only a thin ivory alb and a simple blue stole that hung from his neck to his belt. But still the routine was there, the voices of the people exchanging with Father Lopez's, a harmony of its own, a cadence, Goodbow sensed, of solace and hope.

The priest was very tall and concerningly thin, with serious dark eyes that warmed, if only for a moment, when he infrequently smiled. He recognized Leary Deen standing in the rear pew and the two of them traded silent nods.

"Go in peace," the priest said at the end of the service and then walked quickly from the altar to the rear, without looking at the three of them standing in the last pew. People flowed into the aisle and followed him to the doors. But Goodbow saw that the men and women straddling the center aisle in the second row did not file into the aisle like everyone else. There were twelve of them in all; they stood in their pew rigidly, looking straight ahead, as if at attention.

When all of the regular churchgoers had received his goodbyes, the lanky priest pulled the heavy entrance doors shut. Goodbow heard the thud of a locking bar. Huff Langley nodded in approval. Father Lopez returned to the front of the sanctuary and spoke quietly to the group of parents.

"What is he saying to them?" Goodbow asked Leary Deen.

"Probably assuring them that they don't have to do this. And that they are not in trouble."

"He seems very serious."

"He's not a jovial man. But he is sincere."

The priest gestured the parents into the aisle and stepped

ahead of them toward Goodbow, Leary Deen, and Huff Langley. The three of them moved to the aisle to greet them.

"Let us go into the vestibule, Mr. Deen," said Father Lopez. "The light is better there."

It was, but barely. A single light globe hung above from a tarnished chain. In Spanish, the priest introduced each of the parents and Goodbow's eyes darted from each pair to the names on his written list. He immediately recognized the mother and father he had seen at the border station in El Paso talking to Lane Williams. That morning at the gate, the father had crumbled in grief as his daughter was wheeled away on the stretcher; the mother was stunned and numb. How differently they looked now. The father stood erect and tall; his wife's eyes were animated, excited.

"Can you tell these people about your guests and why they asked to meet them?"

"Of course," Deen said, in Spanish. "Thank you for helping bring them." The priest nodded, seriously. Leary motioned to Goodbow. "It is Mr. Goodbow who asked to meet them." He pointed with an open hand to Huff. "Mr. Langley is here to accompany Mr. Goodbow." Deen saw puzzlement in the parents' faces. "To keep Mr. Goodbow safe. As an American, in a new place." The parents nodded, understanding the words of Leary Deen that he himself mostly could not. "Mr. Goodbow does not speak Spanish, so he has asked me to explain why he is here. We wonder, Father, if you would translate for him what the parents have to say? And their questions. We assume they will have many."

"If they wish me to," the priest said.

"But the first thing is that they should understand that none of this is official government business," Deen said. "Neither American nor Honduran. No one has authorized us."

"I have told them you are from the US consulate," the

priest said, in English. "Obviously, this worries them even though I have told them not to be afraid. They did not want to come until I told them it was about their children. Of course, I could not explain how it was about their children, because I don't know. But I said you were a good man and that I trusted you."

"Thank you, Father."

"But I still must ask," Father Lopez said, still in English. "Does anyone else know they are here to meet Mr. Goodbow?"

"No. No one in Honduras. Only myself and Mr. Langley. And Mr. Langley is a private citizen. He was a US soldier, but no longer."

The thin priest moved to face the parents and spoke to them in a quiet voice. Several of the parents spoke too. It seemed to Goodbow that they talked three times as long as the priest's exchange with Leary Deen had lasted. Finally the priest turned back to the three Americans.

"Okay," he said. "They understand you are not speaking for the government and want to know more," he said, in English.

"Very well," said Leary.

"But they want Mr. Goodbow to speak for himself," the priest said. His tone was insistent.

Goodbow visually reacted. The priest's statement chilled him. A change of plans in a strange place. He had assumed Leary Deen would make them comfortable; he was experienced in dealing with the local people, he knew their customs and manners. Now, Goodbow knew—with not a little trepidation—that he would have to explain the nascent plan himself.

"Mr. Rodriguez speaks English well," the priest said, motioning one of the parents to step forward. "And he is trusted by the others. They want him to translate what Mr. Goodbow says. With my help, as needed. But they want to hear it from

Mr. Goodbow since it is he who wanted to meet them about their children."

Leary looked to Goodbow for his agreement; the old New Englander nodded. "All right, then," Leary said.

So Goodbow described his plan to twelve puzzled faces. How he had found them through Leary Deen and how he wanted to take them to their children in the US, if he could learn where the children were. He had ways of doing that, he told them, mainly with the help of Catholic nuns who were working with families at the border and finding places for the children across the US when their parents were turned back.

"So, you don't know where our children are now?" the parents asked.

"No."

"You have no idea?"

"Not yet. Except for Gloria. Gloria Carrasco. Because she only just arrived in the United States and is still in El Paso under the care of a nun. She is out of the hospital and well."

He saw Gloria's parents beam. Much later, when he repeated the meeting in his mind, he remembered that in the moment the sight of their elation and hope in their eyes did not bring to *him* anything like elation. It brought fear and anxiousness. Doubt. *What am I doing? What am I doing to these people?*

"But you think you can find the rest of our children?"

"If you give me their names, I think I can."

"But he cannot promise it," Leary Deen interjected. The parents looked at Father Lopez, who was reactionless. "There is no one who can promise that," Leary said. He looked at the Carrascos. "And he cannot guarantee that you will make it to Gloria, even. Only that he will try. But I can say it is likely all of the other children are near to each other because they all came into the US at about the same time, and all of you, except the

Carrascos, were turned back at about the same time. I received your names on a single list. Except for Gloria's parents, who were added only a few days ago."

"If we go with you, how do we get there? And where would we go if you don't know where our children are?" Juan Rodriguez spoke in English, then raised his hand to stop Goodbow from answering until he translated the questions to the other parents.

"You won't leave your country until we have found your children," Goodbow said. "But while we are finding them, we need to keep you together and safe so that we can leave at the right moment. And from the right place." Goodbow saw the parents' serious eyes moving between his own and the priest's as he answered.

"Right place in Honduras?" Juan said.

"Yes."

"But it is dangerous for us in this country. That is why we left with our children the first time."

"I know."

"And we cannot stay together here. It would be easier for the gangs to find us in one place. They hate us because we tried to leave. They find out these things. We have scattered since we came back. To different colonias."

"I know. Mr. Deen told us that. We think you should leave Tegus and wait somewhere safer in Honduras."

"Where could it be safe?"

"In Amapala."

"Amapala?" Juan seemed puzzled. "Where is Amapala?"

Father Lopez stepped between Goodbow and the parents and spoke to them. It was the first time he used his hands to gesture; he seemed to be drawing as if on a whiteboard. The priest turned to Goodbow. "I told them about Amapala. Most of them do not know it. I told them where it is in the southwest, on the Isle de Tigre where the beaches are black. I told them I have been there, and it is not like Tegus. I told them there is a famous church there."

"Thank you, Father."

"Of course, they wonder why they would go there to wait, as it is the wrong direction to America. I wonder too. But, go on. Tell them more."

"Because you would be safe there and because it is by the sea," Goodbow said. "It is the only part of your country that touches the Pacific." Juan's brows raised. *What does the sea have to do with this?*

"You will not go to America by land. You will go by sea."

"By *sea*?"

"You will get on a sailboat in Amapala. Then up the Pacific to a place to be arranged in California."

Even Father Lopez seemed confounded. "They will be safe at sea?" he asked, but not in a tone of protest or overreaction.

"They will travel the sea in my boat," Goodbow said. "It is a large boat. It can hold them all out of sight, with room for provisions. It is suitable for long journeys. It is a sailboat, but it has motors too."

"And you would drive this boat?" Juan said.

"No. I would not know how to sail such a distance. I am not really a sailor, myself."

"It is your boat, but you don't know how to drive it?" Juan asked.

"It is not unusual, Juan," Father Lopez said gently. "When people like Mr. Goodbow have large sailboats like his, others sail them for them. They have a captain for that."

"So, your captain will take us?"

"Yes."

"What is his name?"

"I cannot say his name."

"Why not?"

"Because I promised him I would not. Because this is dangerous for him. He could go to prison if he is found out."

"You are asking them to trust their lives to a man who's name they will not know?" the priest asked. But he did not ask it in Spanish; only Juan understood the question.

"They know *my* name," Goodbow said. "If they will trust me, they can trust him. I have known him almost my whole life. It is a great risk he is taking for me and for them. There is no need for both of us to be punished if we are discovered."

"But you can assure us," the priest said. "That your captain does not work for your government either?"

"He does not. He was a soldier once, long ago. For forty years he has been only a sailing captain. He is my age, but very healthy and strong. He will keep them safe on the boat."

"He will steer the boat alone?" Juan asked. "Such a large boat?"

"It's not 'steering,' really," Goodbow said. "But it *is* a big boat. For such a journey he would normally have a crew to help him. But, yes, he will captain the boat alone. Other sailors could not be involved. And besides, there would be no room for them. With all of you. He can manage the boat alone, but it will make the trip longer as he will have to anchor at night so he can sleep."

"We know that others have tried to go in boats to America," Juan said. "Many have drowned. Many have been caught. How will we not be seen? How will we not be arrested?"

"They did not go in boats like this one. My boat is not a fishing boat or a commercial ship. It is not the kind of boat that would be used to smuggle anything. Not drugs, not people. It is a fancy boat used for pleasure. It does not go fast like a speedboat. Even if the navy sees it, they will not believe it is carrying people seeking asylum. It has rooms below the deck for sleeping and eating and staying out of view. When you are in sight of land or other ships, only the captain will be above deck. Only he will be seen."

"But won't the border police be there when we land in America?" Juan asked.

Leary Deen and Huff Langley wondered the same thing. And Goodbow worried about it too, more than any other part of the plan.

"That is a problem," Goodbow said. "We will need a place to come ashore in America where there is no US Coast Guard checkpoint, at least at the time. Which rules out the big ports and the larger cities and anyplace where a border patrol station is near. It has to be a place where you can be met by the nuns who will take you on the next part of your trip. Driving you overland to where your children are living in the US, wherever that is. But we intend to find a small harbor where boats like mine are usual. Where the captain and the boat will not draw attention."

"And not be searched?" Juan asked.

"That is the hope."

There was a pause as Mrs. Carrasco whispered to Juan. "She asks about Gloria," Juan translated. "Where will she be? How will her parents be brought to her?"

"The sisters will take Gloria soon to one of the homes where the other children are already staying," Goodbow said. "She will be together with them when all of you arrive."

"If we do make it there, won't someone know we are in America?" Juan asked. "That we are back with our children? Won't we be arrested and sent away again, back here?"

"It will be known," Leary Deen said. "It will come out. Maybe very soon. But you will go with papers asking for asylum under the American law. I will make sure you have them. Father Lopez has said he will give you letters—we call them affidavits—stating that it is not safe for you to be in Honduras because you are now political enemies of the gangs." The priest nodded, unsmiling. "You do not have to ask for asylum at the US border or at any official place. That is not the law. You can ask for it anywhere on American soil. There are people in the US that can help you take your papers to the government. Even get you lawyers, which I know they will try to do. But again, you must remember there are no guarantees."

"When could all of this happen?" the priest asked. He had said nothing in a long time. "If they wish to try it?"

"If they agree to try this, the captain will start sailing from the American east coast very soon," Goodbow said. "The sisters will start looking for the children as soon as they have their names. All of the parents should go to Amapala as soon as I can arrange a place for them to stay. There are two hotels there. They will not need any money. It will probably take the captain at least two weeks to get the boat to Amapala. Once they are onboard, it will be another week or so sailing north to California."

"So, we may see our children again in three or four weeks?" Juan asked.

"Maybe a little longer. There is always the weather."

Juan called the priest and the other eleven parents to the side of the vestibule. They spoke softly for ten minutes. Juan seemed to do most of the talking; as far as Goodbow could see, the priest said nothing. No voices were raised; there was no apparent arguing. Two by two, the parents stepped to a table against the wall where Juan moved aside the pamphlets stacked upon it. On the back of one of them, he printed carefully the names of their children next to the names of their parents, handing up the list to each pair for confirmation. They walked back as a group, the priest in the rear.

"It was not that long ago that we left our children," Juan

said. "Not that long since we have seen them. But it seems like years. Four weeks or so more doesn't seem bad at all. Especially if there is hope. We want to try it. We all want to try it. These are the names of all of the children, next to the names of their parents." The Honduran handed the list to the old New England industrialist. "We all wonder," Juan said. "Does the boat have a name?"

"Yes," Goodbow said. *"The Sails of Grace."*

Juan translated the name to the others.

"It is a good name," Juan said to Goodbow.

Will looked at all of the parents, at Father Lopez, and then again at the parents.

"The boat was named for my wife. You will be sailing for her," he said.

Father Lopez struck a puzzled look, silently imploring Goodbow to explain. But Goodbow didn't.

* * *

At the hotel bar that evening Huff told Goodbow that the expressions of the parents as he spoke to them—slowly, in a deep tone—were of neither disbelief nor cynicism; more confoundment tinged with hopefulness; the look of persons wanting to believe but worrying it was foolish to do so. "And the priest," Huff told him, "the priest really helped."

"How?" Goodbow said. "He hardly said anything."

"Oh, he said plenty. Just not with words. He stood off to the side where all of them could see his face clearly. He kept his eyes only on you, Will. He never looked over at them the whole time you explained it. But they kept looking at *him*. He kept that solemn face of his."

"He never did smile, did he?"

"Not that I saw," Huff said. "But he sure nodded a lot. And

always up and down. When the parents saw him nod, they nodded too. Like a signal. I almost think it's why the Father didn't want to translate."

"You think he wanted only to listen? And either approve or disapprove?"

"I think so. And he approved."

"Well, a smile would have been nice too."

"Believe me, Goodbow. He gave you something better than a smile."

"You sound like I should be grateful."

"Aren't you?"

"I'm really not sure."

"Why not?" Huff asked. Goodbow sipped his bourbon. Unsmiling, he looked back at the marine.

"Because now there's no turning back," he said.

PART III

22

Goodbow knew the die was cast.

The meeting with the parents at St. Antonio's Church made his promise irretractable. The parents' loss of their children, alone so far from them in conditions they could not imagine, had brought them desperation and indescribable sorrow that he, with his improbable, wildish plan had salved. Yes, the man from New England knew, in mind and in soul, that the events were now in motion, the wheels were turning, the gears were meshing. And he knew that with each revolution, the inevitability of their direction—the path of his and the parents' journey—was more deeply engraved, his commitment further cemented, its reversal impossible.

Goodbow's first feelings after the meeting at St. Antonio's were a mixture of self-doubt and anxiety. And why not? From the beginning, his whole mission had been undeniably Quixotic, and he knew it. He was not a self-deluded man; he never had been. He had not achieved his station in life through imprudence or unreasoned risks. Grace had been the dreamer in his life, he the sure-footed one. It was the ying and yang of their relationship and they both had known it. "You are the consummate pragmatic," Grace had once said to him. "And I love you for it. Just don't get *too* boring."

But now her death and the promise she'd elicited had placed him into her shoes, into her soul. He could not expect the experience to be comfortable. How could it be? Everything about it was counter to his intuitions. And so he was surprised that when his initial emotions after the meeting receded they were replaced by an odd feeling of near exhilaration. Not the exhilaration sparked by a sudden sporting accomplishment, or the kind that attaches to supreme confidence that an urgent need will indeed be satisfied, as when one emerges from a fearful storm into clearing weather. For Goodbow, it was more a sense of exhilarating *relief*, howsoever temporary it might be. Relief that accompanied an appreciation, deep in his being, that he had come this far. This far for Grace.

But it was very temporary. When he stepped out of the shower the next morning, he was startled to see Huff standing in the middle of the room, his suitcase packed and sitting on his bed. He and Goodbow had discussed their departure plans the night before. Goodbow thought it was settled. They would go to the embassy in the morning to see if Leary Deen could help with the vehicles needed to move the parents to Amapala, assuming he and Huff could arrange for their lodging there in the next day or two. Then Goodbow would work the phone from their hotel room, speaking to Sr. Hope Annie, and probably other nuns in her network. He'd already called her to report the names of the parents' children so she could ply her channels to locate them. He was anxious to learn of her progress. He and Huff weren't supposed to be going anywhere just yet.

"We have to leave," Huff said. "Leary Deen just called me.

From the embassy kitchen because he couldn't use the phone in his own office."

"My word. What happened?"

"When he walked into the building this morning, FBI agents were already standing in his office, waiting for him. He saw them through the blinds and headed down to the kitchen to call us. He wants us out of Tegus on the first flight we can catch. Before they can question you here."

"Right now?"

"Right now."

"Won't they stop us at the airport?"

"They might. But there's a flight that leaves in ninety minutes. If we get moving, we can make it. Unfortunately, it's not to Houston. It's to Los Angeles. But who gives a shit? I told Leary to tell them we've been staying here at the de Maya Plaza."

"Why would you do that? Won't they come for me?"

"They would probably figure you're here anyway. They know you have money and it's the nicest hotel near the embassy. My guess is they'll call the hotel to see if I'm still registered." Goodbow remembered that Huff had taken the room in his own name. "They'll be told that I am. That we're both still here."

"How."

"Because I just arranged it while you were in the shower. For five hundred bucks the desk manager was helpful. As far as the hotel knows, we're here until Thursday and that's what they'll say if asked. If the FBI thinks we're still in town they may not send somebody to the airport. They have a small force here, only a few agents. I had to pay in advance for the extra days, plus the five-hundred grease payment. I'll be expensing it to you, of course. But the guy did throw in a ride to the airport. He's meeting us at the back-alley door in five minutes."

"I'm beginning to feel like an ATM machine."

"Don't let it run out of cash."

* * *

At the same moment, Leary Deen returned casually to his office on the first floor of the embassy, holding a scone atop a napkin. "Good morning, agents," he said, showing no apprehension. "I was expecting you, but not so early. I would have brought more scones. I stopped down to the kitchen for this one."

He didn't know the agents and, surprisingly, they didn't offer their names or introduce themselves. He stepped close and looked at the identification badges hanging from their lanyards.

"Agents Robert Everett and Myles Burlacher," Deen said. Though it had disquieted him that the two had not offered their names, Leary didn't show it. "I'm Leary Deen."

"Yes, we know."

He set the pastry on his desk and shook hands with each of them. "I hope you've not been waiting long." As he sat down, he opened the top drawer of the desk and withdrew a small plate. Before closing the drawer he pulled his cell phone from his jacket pocket and placed it in the drawer. "Let me turn this thing off," he said. He tapped the audio recording icon on the phone, silenced the ringer, and closed the drawer, but not all the way.

"Breen Edwards is interested in what you know about a man named Wilton Goodbow."

No small talk? These guys go right to the point, don't they? Deen thought. "Passport control says he came into the country five days ago," Berlacher, the younger of the two, said.

"He did come here, yes," Deen said. "Last Thursday." *Don't appear defensive. Nothing out of the usual.*

"What for? Why did he come to see you?"

"It was an arranged visit from an NGO stateside. I get quite a few of them."

"Which NGO?"

Deen turned pages on a desk calendar, unnecessarily. "Yes, Human Rights First. That's what I thought." He turned back the calendar pages.

"They sent him down here?"

"He doesn't work for Human Rights First. He's a donor, I was told. They asked me to receive him, help him understand Honduras a bit, the situation here."

"When did they arrange this appointment?"

"A day or two before he came."

"Did he come alone?"

"No. A security guard came with him." Deen noticed that the agents exchanged eye contact and nodded, almost indiscernibly. *Ah, good thing I didn't say he was alone. They already knew about Huff Langley.* "I met them both in the lobby, but only the donor came to my office."

"Wilton Goodbow."

"Yes, but he introduced himself as Will."

"And did you know the security guy?"

"Oh, yes. Huff Langley. He served at the embassy here on the protection detail for several years. When he was a marine sergeant."

"Now he's a private citizen?"

"Yes. Makes his living escorting officials and NGO people to and from the States. A very nice living, I gather. He's one of our own civilian contractors too."

"Is he political?"

"Huff Langley?"

"Yeah."

"No, I don't think so. Good guy, no nonsense. He took the ambassador around a lot when he was stationed here. She never put up with politics from anyone."

"What about Wilton Goodbow? Did he seem political?"

"I was only with him a short time when we met here." *When we met here. Technically, the truth.* "But I didn't sense he was much of a political activist. A nice man, a little unusual, I guess." *Show some candor. Don't make them drag everything out of you.*

"Unusual in what way?"

"Naïve, maybe? I mean for such a wealthy man. He didn't seem to appreciate the danger down here."

"And just what did he want from you? What did you talk about?"

Okay, here comes the hard part. Just stay relaxed. "What the Human Rights First people told me when they set it up. He was a donor looking to understand what he was helping with, their work here with immigrants. I suppose to be sure they were legitimate. The generous have to be careful, I guess."

"Anything more specific?"

"Yes, I remember we discussed how the Red Cross and Human Rights First help resettle parents and children. How difficult it is for everybody."

"Did he ask you if you knew where any parents are that were returned from the US border?"

The sixty-four-thousand-dollar question. "Yes. I told him I knew there were a few somewhere here in the city, but that I didn't know where they were living, that I thought they move around all of the time." *Still, technically true. They didn't ask if I gave names to Goodbow.*

"Did you know his wife is a political activist? She is

complaining a lot about the problems at the border, about government policy."

"Not anymore."

"What do you mean? She organized letters to the president and to Breen Edwards."

"Mrs. Goodbow is dead," Deen said. He could see the agents were startled.

"How do you know that?"

"Her husband told me. I think her death has stirred him to be generous, or maybe more generous. In her memory, maybe. He seemed to miss her very much. And he seems to be a man of great means."

"Anything else you want to tell us?"

"Yes. He and I smoked a cigar together in the courtyard before he left. I offered it to him." *There will be tape!* "You know how Americans like a real Cuban."

"Anything else?" The two agents had never taken seats; they leaned against the wall. Now they assumed upright footing; they were about to leave, Deen hoped.

"Well, Langley did mention that they were staying at the Hotel de Maya Plaza. They were going to spend some time going around the country. Staying a while."

"Thanks, sir," the younger agent said as the two moved to the door. "That should do it for us."

Only then did Leary Deen notice that his ear lobes were burning, that he was perspiring at his collar. "No problem," he said, affably. "I hope I have pastry for you next time." *Heaven help me if there is a 'next time.'*

When the door closed behind them he opened the drawer and stopped the recording. *In case they say I lied!* But he knew he hadn't lied. Somehow, he hadn't. A good diplomat was Leary Deen.

23

Burp Lebeau knew the course from Newport to the Pacific coast of Honduras would be complicated, but he was surprised by just how tedious it would be as he charted it aboard the boat deep into the evening after the call from his friend. The mere distance was daunting; at least twenty-five hundred nautical miles. With lucky winds along the US east coast he could make good time on the first leg of the journey. Sailing at light weight, *Grace* could maintain a southwest bearing at 30 knots or so, easily, about 35 miles per hour. But winds in the Gulf of Mexico were often slack, and almost never as strong as the Atlantic's. He expected the craft's twin diesel engines would be useful there, but even at full throttle they could push *Grace* at just 18 knots; less into a headwind.

He considered hauling *Grace* overland to Corpus Christi to shorten the voyage in both miles and time. But that, or any other overland alternative, was precluded for the same reason that the long journey from Newport Bay was so hard: he had to do it alone. He could sail *Grace* without a crew or involving anyone else, for as long and as far as it took. It would be brutal and lonely, and probably dangerous if bad weather hit, but he knew he could sail her alone. But he could never trailer her alone or put her back in the water without a team. Even Clark Kent could not do that.

His eyes burned with fatigue as he checked and rechecked his daily charts, matching them to the drawings and calculations in the NOAA manual. In the end, he concluded that a twelve day estimate for the sail from Newport to Amapala was reasonable, assuming no weather so severe as to require mooring. Reasonable, that is, if you could call eighteen hours a day at the helm for ten straight days reasonable.

He decided to re-confirm his calculations in the morning when his mind was fresh, before calling Goodbow back. He stepped off *Grace* about midnight, exhausted, utterly spent.

And he hadn't sailed a mile.

24

As tired as the old captain was in Newport, Sr. Hope Annie was at that very moment afire with energy in her little kitchen in El Paso, two time zones ahead. It was not that late, about ten o'clock, and she was a night owl anyway, accustomed to working in the evenings. There was usually paperwork for the state and federal agencies and never enough time to complete it during the busy hours at the center. And even when there wasn't paperwork to do, the cooling night air refreshed and motivated her. Often, she'd move the tall oscillating fan to the back screen door off the kitchen, turn the lights on bright inside, and sit outside the door with a book, her bare feet soothed by the cool concrete slab beneath her. Her reading tastes were polar: salty romance novels and scholarly biographies, especially of American presidents. A pile of each were stacked neatly at the end of her kitchen countertop.

Her favorite president wasn't the first Catholic one, John F. Kennedy, though she admired him. It was Thomas Jefferson. She was drawn to the Virginian's brand of personal religiosity and private spirituality; his insistence on unfettered religious freedom for the individual, tolerance of all beliefs, and his disdain for rules devised by any man to govern the soul of another. One of her fellow nuns once challenged her. How could she hold a man in such regard who kept slaves and took one of them as an illicit concubine?

"That's why I trust him," Sr. Hope Annie had said. "Flawed almost to perfection. If only he smoked!"

On this evening, the nun's energy was inspired not by satisfying reading, but excitement. Her new friend Goodbow had called Sunday afternoon from Honduras to report that—yes!—he had located some of the parents. He'd given her the names of their children, and she'd written them down carefully, fifteen in all. She recognized nine of the names immediately as angels who had passed through the respite center months earlier, and little Gloria who was living there now, awaiting her own foster home. She was so happy on the phone that she could barely contain herself.

"This is miraculous!" she'd exclaimed. "Miraculous, Goodbow!" Her joy was so elevated that it jarred Goodbow.

"I think you should settle down, Sister," he'd said.

"Why?" she shot back. "Can't your friend bring the boat? Won't he do it?"

"No, no. He is willing. But there are many things that could go wrong. We can't be sure of anything."

"We can be sure of God's will," Sr. Hope Annie said.

"Well, I can't argue with that," Goodbow had replied. "But I can't say that I know what it is."

"Faith, Goodbow! I told you, *faith!*"

"I guess it is time to borrow some of yours," Goodbow said.

"It comes interest-free. Take it."

"You still believe you can find the children?"

"Yes."

"How?"

"Faith, and a lot of good sisters. Many of these children stayed with us at the center. We will have records of where they were placed. But the ones I recognize—I know they were taken in by families in Minnesota."

"Minnesota? I thought most of the children were in Texas."

"In the beginning—when the separations first started—almost all of them were. But there got to be so many, we could not find enough foster homes there. We used our sisters up North, and the Lutherans. There are clusters of foster homes there. Most are in the smaller towns. I told you, my sisters and I can take the parents to them if your captain can bring them to us."

"That's why we shouldn't be too excited," Goodbow had said. "Not yet. The parents want to do it, but it will not be easy to get them out safely. It may be even harder to get them *in* safely. And it will take time. The captain is charting his course, but he must sail alone, and it is a great distance."

"How will you get the parents to the ship?"

"I will need your help, Sister."

"In Honduras?" she asked.

"Yes."

"We have sisters in Tegus, but there is no river there for your captain. And it is very dangerous."

"I've learned. Huff Langley says he knows you."

"Yes, I know the marine. I am glad he is with you."

"He showed me a place a hundred and fifty miles southwest of Tegus on a bay out to the Pacific. Amapala. Have you heard of it?"

"Yes. I've never been there, but some of the sisters have. It has a famous cathedral."

"And a small port. It's much quieter and safer than Tegus. Can you find sisters to take the parents from Tegus to Amapala?"

"When?"

"As soon as you can. There are inns there where they can stay and wait for the boat. I can pay for the rooms. The sisters could stay with them. That would be best. They may have to wait there for weeks; I am not sure. But they are in danger if they stay in Tegus. They shouldn't wait there. They have to move around all the time to avoid the gangs. We need to know where they are and that they can leave at the right time."

"Then I will go to Tegus myself," Sr. Hope Annie said. "The sisters there may be able to help me drive them to Amapala. I can make arrangements at the center and leave for Tegus in a few days. But how do we find the parents in the big city? So that we can take them out?"

"I don't know, yet," Goodbow had told her. "Leary Deen may be able to help, but I'm not sure. And maybe Huff can escort you, but I haven't asked him yet."

"Oh, the marine would be good. Yes, that would be good."

"And I need to tell you that Leary is concerned. He's been great, he's been brave. But he is worried. The embassy is watching him. They know I came to meet him. The FBI there wants to talk to him. They may find out everything. They may find out about you."

"Let them."

"But we have to be cautious. And not get our hopes up too much."

"Hope goes up and down," she said. "But faith, *real* faith, doesn't go down. Keep your faith, Goodbow. Call when you know more. In the meantime, I will prepare things in Tegus."

"You do inspire me," Will said.

"Goodness has brought you to us. Goodness will guide us," Sr. Hope Annie said.

"Grace brought me to you."

"That's what I said, didn't I?"

Thank you, Lord, for that woman, he thought as the call ended.

A day later, she moved the fan to the screen door when her phone rang. It was an outdated iPhone that Lane Williams had given her a year ago—a dinosaur, he'd called it—when she accepted it with delight. She expected the call was from her sister ally in Tegus calling with a report. She was looking for cars large enough to transport the parents out of the city. But it was Goodbow again, with news not altogether promising.

"I am in Los Angeles," he said. His tone was strained. "It's been a long day and I'm tired. Is this too late to call?"

"No. But why are you in Los Angeles?"

"Huff and I had to hurry out of Tegus. Leary Deen warned us. Told us to leave before the FBI could question me. They were questioning him. So we took the first plane leaving Honduras."

"What about Leary? Is he okay?"

"Yes. Somehow he was able to tell them the truth without disclosing the plan. At least for now. But it changes things. They will be looking for me."

"You are not stopping, though, are you?" Her tone conveyed not doubt, but presumption.

"No. I am not giving up," he said. He could tell she was drawing on a cigarette.

"Good. Then you didn't call again just for more inspiration."

"No, Sister. I called to say that we are going to have to be even more careful than we thought. I guess you could say, I'm 'on the run'. I hope to get back to El Paso, and I will stay in touch with you. But I can't keep calling you this way. For your sake or mine. Or for the parents and their children."

"What do you mean? I don't know what you are getting at," the nun said.

"Sister. Have you ever heard of a burner phone?"

"A *what?*"

25

Goodbow and Huff Langley sat down in their room at the LAX airport hotel with bourbon on the rocks that Huff fetched from the lobby bar while Goodbow was on the phone with Sr. Hope Annie.

"Got you a double. Didn't think you'd mind," Huff said as he handed Goodbow's to him.

"Looks like you've got a triple in yours," Goodbow said.

"Didn't think you'd mind that either."

"Though I *am* paying for it."

"Naturally."

"Do you think I got wealthy being this generous all my life?"

"Actually, yes. You don't seem like the stingy type. I doubt you've ever been cheap."

"Well, it would be nice if you stopped trying to prove it all the time," Goodbow said, but he clinked Huff's tumbler after saying it.

In truth, the old industrialist's appreciation of the former marine was deepening each day. Obviously, he could not have asked for more in terms of his personal safety under Huff's careful watch. But the sergeant was also practical and knowledgeable—Goodbow would never have found Amapala without him—and even more, as Goodbow came to see, a clever, modest, and even funny companion. Which was one reason the turn of events that brought them precipitously to Los Angeles concerned him. Would Huff Langley leave him now? Before the FBI interest emerged, the two had discussed the marine's continuing with him in Honduras, the possibility that the two of them would personally travel with the parents from Tegus to the small port town; get them situated there with nuns to look over them, then return to the US. That idea was out of the question now, at least for Goodbow. Huff had not said no to the original proposition, but he hadn't committed himself either. Even if he had committed, Goodbow knew he could not morally hold him to it in the new circumstances. It was one thing to agree to help in a humanitarian endeavor with an NGO donor and some nuns. Exposing yourself to the spotlight of the FBI and Breen Edwards was quite another.

What to do now? Sr. Hope Annie had just told him—he knew sincerely—that she would go to Tegus herself and lead the parents to their waiting place. And he—imprudently—had raised to her the possibility of Huff accompanying her to protect them all. Goodbow knew, sitting with the marine in the airport hotel room, that he could not keep this from him for long. Really not any longer at all. He had to talk to him *now*. And he admitted to himself, without pride in the fact, that it was, after all, probably a good thing that his companion had ordered the triple bourbon for himself.

"Huff," he asked. "What do you want to do from here? Now that we are back in the States."

"What do you mean?"

"We're back from Central America," Goodbow said. "I don't think I can go back. With the FBI thing, you know."

"Good to hear you say that. You shouldn't. You definitely shouldn't."

"The FBI may look for me here. In the US."

"If Breen Edwards pushes, they probably will. More than probably."

"I know you can't protect me from them."

"I'm glad to hear you say that, too. You're right. I can't."

"I talked to the nun from El Paso."

"Hope Annie."

"Yeah. She remembers you."

"What did she say?"

"She wants to go to Tegus for me. To take the parents to Amapala."

"She 'wants' to, or you think she *will* if you press her?"

"No, she wants to." Goodbow reached for his drink; so did Huff Langley. "But I did mention that maybe you could go with her."

"Oh you did, did you? When you talked to her just now?"

"Yes. I know I shouldn't have. She surprised me by saying she wanted to go. I really just wanted her to be sure and be careful. She's already sending out her network to find where these kids have been placed in families. She's strong willed. When I told her we'd had to leave and so I couldn't move the parents myself, she right away said she would go to Tegus and shepherd them. But it's too dangerous. I know that now. So I said maybe you could go back too and watch them. Help them get there. Maybe stay until the captain shows up with the boat."

"Did you promise her?"

"No, I only said 'maybe,'" Goodbow said, truthfully. "And I told her I hadn't even asked you." He quickly added, "But she liked the idea a lot. Said that would be very good."

Huff Langley shook his head from side to side and sat in silence, unsmiling. A minute passed before he rose and started for the door, glass still in hand. Goodbow's heart began to sink. When the marine reached the doorknob he turned back and faced his client.

"I'm going down for another. But before I drink too much, I should give you my answer."

"Oh. Right now? What is it?"

"I'll do it."

Goodbow bolted upright in his chair, energized. "You're sure?"

"I *said*, I'll do it."

"Then I have another request," Will said.

Huff stared at Goodbow, as if daring. "What now?" he asked.

"Bring me another one too. I want to celebrate."

26

It was one of those things he sensed but didn't fully realize when it began.

When Goodbow talked late into the evening with Huff Langley in the Los Angeles airport hotel room, he must have known that what Huff advised would mean loneliness and anxiety. Probably fear. It wasn't that he didn't listen carefully to what the ex-marine said; it wasn't that he doubted the truth or practicality of what Huff described. But in the moment, sitting above the LAX runways sipping his bourbon, waiting for Burp to call with his chart plan, the reality of what Huff proposed for him—the life he would live over the next few weeks—didn't truly seep in. Maybe it was the rush he felt from their successful escape from Tegucigalpa. Maybe it was the faith of Sr. Hope Annie, infecting him—momentarily—with a sense of unearned well-being, unwise confidence that all was well in the world.

But now he had come back down to earth. And heading to a part of it he had never visited: northernmost Nevada in a rental car secured for him by Huff at the airport. It was all new to him, but he didn't encounter its newness the way he and Grace had greeted so many ports and sea towns in their journeys. They had favorite moorings and dockside eateries up and down both US coasts, and some much more distant. They made it a point to return to them. But they especially looked forward to new destinations, and Burp did too, often suggesting an out of the way inlet that even he in his vast experience on the sea had never sailed. The excitement of anticipation in such travels had been palpable to all three of them.

This was different. Yes, there was anticipation. But excitement or pleasure? His physical senses were heightened, to be sure, to an uncomfortable degree of hyper-alertness. But Goodbow didn't feel anything that he could call excitement or pleasurable anticipation. Instead, he felt anxiousness and apprehension. And worse, deep loneliness.

"You have to assume they will be looking for you when they find out we've left the hotel in Tegus," Huff had told him.

"I thought I'd go back to El Paso. Lane Williams can get me back into The Fine Sombrero. It was all right there," Goodbow had said.

"Bad idea. They'll know you flew to Honduras from El Paso. And they probably know about Lane Williams by now. Leary Deen had to tell them something about how you came to him."

"I suppose you're right."

"I *am* right," Langley said. "You need to keep moving for a while. I can rent a car under my name and you can drive it out of California. Maybe go north where there's not so much attention to the border problems. Lay low until your captain gets the people up the west coast. Manage the thing by phone. I'd suggest Nevada."

"Nevada? That's not north."

"It's more north than you think. Nevada borders Oregon up there."

"I never knew that."

"Just keep driving; don't stay in any big cities along the way, and don't get pulled over. The furthest Nevada county is Humboldt. It's a big, quiet county. Borders Oregon to the north and Idaho to the northeast."

"Your geography is impressive," Goodbow said.

"The only decent size town in Humboldt County is Winnemucca."

"How do you know these things?" Goodbow asked in amazement.

"One of my marine buddies was from Winnemucca. We went to Vegas on a leave and he took me up to see his folks there. Sleepy and pretty. Sits below the Santa Rosa Range of the Sierra Nevada Mountains."

"Won't I seem like an odd stranger?"

"People come in and out of town all the time for the views and the weather. You won't stick out there."

* * *

At the rental car center, Goodbow reached for a road atlas, but Huff stopped him on the way to the cashier and purchased it on his own credit card. Goodbow nodded, understanding. As they walked outside to the rental car aisles, Huff warned him about using his credit cards on his trip.

"We have to assume they'll know soon that we flew to LA. So you may as well use an ATM here. But get as much cash as you can. How many ATM cards and accounts can you tap?"

"A few. They may have different daily limits."

"Use 'em all to the max."

Goodbow was able to withdraw twenty-five hundred dollars.

"That's it?" Huff asked when he saw the money. "You'll have to pay in cash for everything!"

"I'll make it do."

But the marine fished out his wallet and handed over all of his own cash to Goodbow. Nearly another thousand. "No worries; I can get more for myself."

"You're going to need a spreadsheet for all these additional expenses."

Huff started to roll his eyes but restrained himself. "No worries," he said again. "I keep 'em all on an app."

The marine chose a rental company that permitted the renter to choose the vehicle of his or her liking from a long row of candidates and shapes. Goodbow eyed a sleek, low-slung Lincoln in forest green that reminded him of the hull trim on *The Sails of Grace.*

"Sorry, no can do," Huff said, pointing instead to a big-wheeled, high seated white Land Rover three spaces down with a California plate. They walked to its rear.

"I don't like it," Goodbow said. "Look how high the thing is. That's for a young person. I'd need a running start to jump into it!"

"You'll manage. The height is one reason it's right. You'll be looking down on vehicles in your mirrors. Easier to recognize a police cruiser way back there; to back down on your speed. Plus there's another one over there just like it."

"What's that got to do with it?" Goodbow asked in puzzlement. But Langley didn't answer and Goodbow confined his protest to a disgruntled look.

Huff went inside the building with the keys to finalize the papers. Goodbow waited at the trunk, looking at the oversized tires, skeptically. In a few minutes Huff returned, looking relaxed and matter of fact. Without prior announcement, he looked calmly in each direction and darted two spaces to the nearly identical white Land Rover he had mentioned. He squatted at its back bumper with a Swiss Army knife and in less than a minute removed its Nevada license plate. He stepped quickly back to Goodbow, waiting at the original Land Rover with fearful eyes. "Keep an eye out," Huff said, then removed the Land Rover's plate and substituted the other. "Keep watching," he said, and then completed the switch on the car next to the post.

"I am very concerned about what you just did, Huff," Goodbow said as they climbed into the Land Rover and left the lot.

"Well, you're right about one thing. It's what *I* did. Not you."

"But if I get stopped, the plate won't match what's on these rental papers," Goodbow said, putting them into the glove box. Huff was at the wheel; they were to drive back to the hotel and separate ways from there.

"You mean the rental papers that will have them looking for *that* plate, and not *this* one? For *that* car and not yours? That's why I keep saying, *don't* get pulled over. And let's hope the poor bastard who rents that other one doesn't either."

Goodbow rode silently until they reached the driveway into the hotel.

"I'm in over my head," he said finally.

"I think you are, too," said the ex-marine. "And when you're in over your head, it's time to start thinking about saving your neck."

* * *

It was an eighteen-hour drive from Los Angeles to Winnemucca, assuming legal speed and no construction or accident delays. Goodbow's first thought was to complete the trip to the edge of the Oregon border with just one overnight stop. It would conserve his cash. But he'd never before driven an SUV or a jeep (he couldn't decide if the boxy Land Rover was one or the other) and Huff Langley's admonition on speed had registered. He lingered in the right lane below the speed limit and passed only the slowest moving trucks. Huff had urged him to get out of California as soon as possible, so he headed only a little north and mostly east toward Las Vegas on I-15. By the time he reached Vegas, he'd been driving nearly six hours. Fatigue was setting in. If he stopped soon for the night, he would have at least twelve hours still ahead of him to his destination in the shadow of the mountains. Unwise to tackle in a single day, he knew. He concluded there was no point in trying. He would take an extra day to get to Winnemucca.

He couldn't remember when he had last driven this long. His eyes were heavy, and it was tempting to pull off the interstate at one of the numerous motels on the outskirts of Las Vegas. But Huff had been clear in his warning to avoid large cities, so he turned north on Highway 95 to the little town of Beatty near Death Valley National Park. He saw the updated, attractive sign for the Old Tombstone Motel, incongruent with the pitted gravel parking lot and the weathered plastic chairs sitting two-by-two outside each room door. Everything was relative, he knew. It was no Fine Sombrero Motor Inn, but it would have to do.

27

He had just returned to his room with fast food when Burp Lebeau called at last with his own travel plan. Goodbow's loneliness receded at the mere sound of his friend's voice. But his first words to Burp were cautionary.

"You're calling on the burner phone, aren't you?" he asked.

"Yeah. Like you told me."

"Because it might be easy to forget," Goodbow said. "You might call on your own phone out of force of habit."

The old captain went straight to the point. "Thirteen days," he said. "Thirteen days to Amapala, pushing hard. I charted it in twelve but added one extra for weather. And that assumes only two days to make the Panama crossing, which is 'iffy.'"

"Is there bad weather forecast?"

"Something ugly out in the Atlantic, but it's three-hundred miles east of Bermuda, moving southwest. If I leave right away I can beat it. Once I make the turn into the Gulf at Miami, it should be smooth. But I won't be able to do all the usual prep on *Grace*."

"What do you mean?"

"Whenever we sail her this far I take apart the helm before we leave. Tighten and grease the chains to the rudder gears. It's a full day job to do it right."

Goodbow remembered watching Burp do it once a few years ago. The disassembly alone was tiresome; the matrix of chains and sprockets leading to the forty-inch helm wheel in the steering console was formidable.

"Have you felt anything funny at the wheel lately? When we took her down to Charleston Harbor?"

"No, it seemed fine. But it wasn't turning a heavy load. It was just the two of us on board and not a lot of provisions."

"Well, you'll be alone until Amapala. You'll have a load of provisions for them, but it won't be *that* heavy."

"Yeah," Burp said. "I think it will hold up. I'll pack the tools in case there's a problem. I can work on the chains at sea, so long as she's anchored, and the water isn't too rough. I'd rather do that than sail in the storm that's coming down. I'll leave at first light."

"Are you set with food and water until you reach the Gulf?" Goodbow asked.

"I'm set with food and more than water."

"I assumed."

"And I added three bottles of tequila to the liquor case. I figure it's these folks' preference. To settle their nerves."

"Probably a good assumption," Goodbow said.

"Where are you now?" Burp asked. "Are you back in the States?"

"I'm in Nevada."

"Nevada?"

"Long story. But I'm fine."

"How long?"

"Long."

"Why the hell Nevada?"

"Remember the guy I told you about at the US embassy in Honduras?"

"Larry somebody."

"Leary. *Leer-ee.* Leary Deen. Somehow the FBI found out I was down there to see him, and it was some kind of red flag. They questioned him and they wanted to find me. He told the marine and me to leave before they could. Huff didn't think I should go back to El Paso because they knew I came from there. And the first flight out was to Los Angeles, so that's where we went. He rented me a car at the airport and suggested I go to Nevada. Make my way up to a little city in the northern part of the state."

"So, Will Goodbow is a goddamned fugitive."

"Well, not officially. As far as I know, there's no warrant for me or anything. I haven't done anything illegal, anyway."

"Not yet."

"Not yet," Goodbow chimed.

"Well to me, this is sounding more and more like spy shit," said the old sailor. But his tone was more of fascination than disapproval.

"I'm just lying low. Kind of 'on the road.' Managing the plan from inland, working by phone with the nuns and Huff Langley."

"The marine isn't with you?"

"No. The guy's a saint," Goodbow said. "He's headed back to Tegucigalpa with the nun from El Paso. She needs his protection a lot more than me now. They're going to get the parents in the city and drive them over to Amapala. To wait for you and *Grace*. But really, the less anyone knows about the others the better. But you and I, let's talk every day."

"Good. Make it late in the day. We can have a drink together, in a way," Burp said. His raspy laugh as he said it made Goodbow smile. "Just that I'll have a hell of a better view," Burp said.

"I don't know. You'd be surprised at the beauty out here. It's desert, but it's mountains too. You should try it sometime."

"No," Burp said. "I'll stick with the sea."

28

Sr. Hope Annie rarely wore her full habit anymore. It reflected no disobedience on her part; since her departure from the classroom in the valley, its donning was discretionary except at formal functions of the order, which were few. She reserved it for special circumstances, such as when greeting an incoming sister at the airport whom she assumed would be similarly garbed or a day like this one when she hoped it would aid a special purpose. She had learned that clerical trappings sometimes produced a certain deference in public settings; a social acceptance almost nearing privilege. And—counter-intuitively—fewer questions, her hope this day.

"I'd like to buy a pre-paid cell phone," she said to the young saleswoman at Mobile Planet, clad in a short tight skirt and high-heeled pumps.

"You mean a burner phone, Sister?" the woman said.

"Is that what they call them?" Hope Annie asked, in her most innocent tone. "They don't catch on fire do they?"

"Oh, no!" the woman laughed. "It's just what we call them! Because they're very basic. They're not smart or anything. No internet. No email. You throw them out when you've used them up, or you buy more time if you still want to use it."

"Yes, that's what I want. I just want to make and receive calls."

"But a burner is not really very economical, when you think about it," the woman said. "And they're so temporary. I could set you up with a smart phone on a monthly plan for the same money."

"But then I'd have to keep paying for it, right?"

"For the smart phone, yes."

"No, no. I have a regular phone, right on the wall. That's what I use most of the time."

"A *landline?*" The young woman seemed incredulous.

"I guess so, if that's what you call it. It works fine. But I need a phone to take with me on a little trip. Not for that long. Nothing fancy."

"Oh, where are you going?"

The nun smiled. *Didn't she get the memo? No questions!*

"A pleasure trip."

"Oh! I wish I could go on a pleasure trip!"

"I need it to work for three weeks," Sr. Hope Annie said.

"I have one for fourteen days; the next one is for a month. Unlimited calling."

"Will it work across the border?"

"Oh, a *fancy* trip!" The young woman's eyes lit up. "Lucky you! The international use, though. That's extra."

"Okay. Give me a month's worth."

"What countries?"

"What?"

"Where are you going? What countries do you need it for?"

"Does that make a difference?"

"Oh, yes! Europe is ridiculous! But Mexico and stuff, it's not too bad."

"I'll take the 'Mexico and stuff'. What does that cover?"

"Mexico and Central America."

"That's fine."

"But not Brazil or Argentina."

"I understand. Fine."

It came to ninety-three dollars, which the nun paid in cash.

"Have a nice trip, Sister!" she heard the young woman call as she walked to the door. "Come back for a smart phone sometime!"

"I'll pray for one," the nun said.

On the walk to her car she spotted a bench in the shade. She knew she had not been entirely truthful. She hadn't used the wall-mounted phone in her kitchen in months; hardly ever since Lane Williams had blessed her with the iPhone. She should do penance, she thought. But she sat down in the shade and smoked a cigarette, before calling Goodbow to report her new phone number.

29

Agents Everett and Burlacher were slightly more polite when the manager came out to see them at the registration desk of the Hotel Maya de Plaza than they had been to Leary Deen is his office a day earlier. They introduced themselves.

Huff Langley had been right with his hunch that the agents would not go to the Tegus airport if they believed Goodbow was still in the city, that they would come to the hotel first to find him. But as it happened, they afforded the industrialist a small measure of additional breathing room by waiting until the next day to go to the Maya de Plaza. Burlacher had been inclined to go to the hotel straight from the embassy after their interview of Leary Deen. But Everett reminded him that the DEA had intercepted a drug shipment north of the city and wanted the agents to join them for an inventory of the goods that noon.

"At least let's call the hotel and see if they're registered," Myles Burlacher said. And as Huff foresaw, the agents received the answer Huff paid for. The room registered to Huff Langley and his guest, an older man from America, was occupied and departure was not scheduled for three more days.

Weeks later, Goodbow would wonder how things would have been so very different had the agents only gone to the hotel or the airport immediately.

"Yes, agents," the hotel manager said when they arrived at the Maya de Plaza the next day. "Is there a problem of some kind?"

"We don't know," Burlacher said. "We're looking for a guest. Wilton Goodbow. G-O-O-D-B-O-W. Is he still here? And another—H. P. Langley. L-A-N-G-L-E-Y."

The manager stepped down the line of computer screens and made a long series of entries; then even more. Finally, he stepped back in front of the agents.

"We have had no one registered under the name Goodbow. But there is a H. Langley here and the notes say he has been staying with a guest, an older gentleman. They are both Americans. They arrived five days ago and are staying another two nights."

"Can you call up to the room? See if they're in?"

"Of course."

The manager reported that there was no answer. "But I am not surprised," he said. "There is a note that no housekeeping would be needed until tomorrow. The gentlemen were going to do some touring."

The two agents looked at each other. Neither showed alarm. The report jived with what the consulate official had told them.

"Leave these cards for them," Burlacher said. The manager fingered the cards, surprised at the thin card stock. He expected something more formidable. "Have them call us as soon as they return, okay?" Everett said.

"Surely. I will have your cards taken to their room right away. With a note."

30

The *Sails of Grace* glided past Norfolk as the sun set over Burp's starboard horizon on his first day. He had hoped to reach the Outer Banks by nightfall, but the southeast wind was disappointing. He could barely reach thirty knots all day, and when dusk brought even less wind he lowered the sails and switched to the diesel engines at full bore for the last ninety-minutes, anchoring a few miles downcoast from the naval yards. It was unusual to run the twin diesels so hard for that long, so before climbing to the deck with his whiskey he opened the transom hatch below aft and inspected the engine fasteners. All tight.

He turned up the volume on the marine radio and sat atop the deck, sipping his liquor and listening. He enjoyed the unclassified chatter from the naval and coast guard vessels and was amused when one transmission mentioned *Grace*. "*New sails in south. Big private. A beauty. Stationary, in irons only.*" The expression meant that none of the boat's sails were hoisted; and since the craft wasn't moving it was presumed moored for the night. He wondered whether the transmission would trigger interest for a look-see, and it did. A half hour later a shiny red and white coast guard cruiser streamed past, a few hundred yards from his portside. Three crewmen stood at its rail and waved. It was returned by a rough-hewn hand holding a whiskey glass.

It would be a quiet night at sea, he was certain. But he thirsted for news on the weather far out in the Atlantic. He moved the radio dial to the weather advisory frequency and went below to fix dinner while he waited for the report due on the hour.

Goodbow called just as the heat came up on his skillet and he lobbed in a generous mound of butter.

"I've got my drink, Burp," Goodbow said when he answered. "You?"

"Wild Turkey. One cube only. But one of those nice big ones."

"Your favorite. Been a good day, I'm guessing."

"Just fine, until now. You called when I'm cooking."

"What's on the menu?" He knew how much Burp enjoyed cooking on board.

"Scallops. Pan searing them in butter and garlic. Nice big mothers." He turned off the burner. "Where you now?"

"No man's land. Middle of Nevada. I should make it to Winnemucca tomorrow."

"How you feeling?"

"A little nervous. Lonely. You?"

"Hungry. For my goddamned scallops."

"Not nervous?"

"No."

"Still want to do this?"

"We've been through that."

"I know, but I want to be sure you know you don't have to."

"I've never done a goddamned thing in my life that I didn't

want to do. Besides, this is kind of interesting. Kind of fun, even. How many old yacht captains get a chance to run from the law?"

"Well, I hope it doesn't come to that."

"It won't. It won't."

"Why are you so sure?"

"Because this is Grace we're talking about."

"Which Grace do you mean?"

"Either. Both. *Grace* is Grace."

"Maybe you're right, Burp."

"Did you tell the gutsy nun about her? About Grace? What you promised her?"

"Sure."

"Well, I'll bet she'd say the same thing. *Grace* is Grace."

"I think she already has."

The call ended. If the Atlantic weather report came over the radio, Burp didn't hear it. He knew it really didn't matter anyway. The scallops were lush and full of the flavor of the sea. Whatever the coming weather, he was raising sails at first light.

31

Huff Langley recognized her immediately when she strode into Lane Williams's office with a cigarette hanging off her lips. He had met her only once before but the little nun with the pretty face was unmistakable. She was not wearing her full habit, but as a sign of courtesy, she wore its head piece. The piece's white wimple stretched across her hairline at her forehead, the light blue fabric coif covered her hair, and a veil of the same cloth draped in the rear to the top of her shoulders.

"Please, Sister," Lane Williams said, waving at her cigarette even before the door had closed behind her. She threw her head up in apology, caught the door athletically with her back foot, and flicked the cigarette, still lit, to the pavement outside.

"Sorry, Lane," Sr. Hope Annie said. "There's no smoking in here! I never remember that, do I?"

"Rarely," said Williams. "It's just the rules, is all. I don't like it either." He was himself a pack-a-day smoker, often out of rule even in his own office.

"Oh, there are always rules," she said amiably. "And some

of them we follow." She looked to the ex-marine, who had risen when she entered as if greeting an officer. "I remember you," she said. "Sergeant Huff, right?"

"Yes, Sister. Huff Langley." She could see he was amused by her cigarette.

"You think my smoking is odd?" she asked.

"A little, yes."

"You don't smoke?"

"No."

"But I'll bet you drink!"

"I do, yes. Maybe more than I should."

"Aha! Another Goodbow! He is the same way!"

"We did enjoy some together on our trip."

"You came with Mr. Deen when the respite center opened."

"Yes. I was still a marine then. At the embassy. How is the center doing?"

"Filled. Busy. There are more families and children every day. It would be better if it were not so filled and not so busy. But what can you do?"

"Well," said Lane Williams. "I don't think this will let up anytime soon. The families need you. Personally, I am sure more of them would be turned away if you were not there to take them temporarily. You are a Godsend."

"I am only the sent part."

"Whatever. But when I called Leary Deen to see if he was notified about the parents of the little girl Gloria—the Carrascos—he told me that you and Mr. Goodbow were up to something. He wouldn't tell me what. Only that Gloria's parents were back in Tegus; that he'd added them to the list of the other parents."

"Did you tell him that Gloria is well now? That she is staying with us at the center?"

"Yes. I'm sure he will get word of that to her parents, if he can."

"The girl is an angel! So sweet and kind to everyone. She shows off her healing foot to the other children. All of the boys want to look at it."

"I'm happy about that, Sister. But I called you and Huff so that we could talk privately. Together."

Lane Williams sat down at his table desk. The nun and the marine sat across from him in plain wooden side chairs.

"You sound so serious, Lane," the sister said. "Like something is wrong."

"There may be. It depends on what you are doing. What are you cooking up with Goodbow?" The NGO manager was indeed less affable than usual.

"It does not involve you," Sr. Hope Annie said.

"If you are trying what I fear you're trying, the government might not see it that way."

"Why is that?" she asked.

"Because I helped Goodbow go to Tegucigalpa. I arranged for Huff to guard him."

"So?" the nun adjusted her skirt and leaned back in her chair. "He is a citizen who wanted to learn. He made a gift to your organization and you contacted the embassy for him. What is wrong with that?"

"Nothing. But now he says he is going back there." He looked at the marine.

"Goodbow is going back?" The nun asked, startled.

"No. Huff is. Huff says *he* is going back. And not with Goodbow. With *you*!"

"So?"

"Huff won't tell me *why* you two are going or what you are planning to do down there," Williams said. He looked at Huff for confirmation, but the marine simply raised his brow, a facial "no comment."

"Huff says his contract with Goodbow prevents him from talking about it. Everything is totally confidential, he tells me," Williams said. At this, Huff Langley nodded, affirmatively. "Well, I don't have to be Einstein to have my suspicions," Lane Williams said. "You know that I am sympathetic to the problems of the migrants. All I do is work to help them."

"I know that, Lane," the nun said. She leaned forward and looked at him earnestly. "You have comforted many, helped many. You have helped me."

"Always working within the law," Williams said. "Doing what I could do, what my organization could do—*within the law*."

"So, what are you saying to us?"

"I'm saying that if you think you can go down there and bring parents back up through Mexico to their children here, you're making a terrible mistake."

"I can honestly say we are not going to do that."

"You'll never make it. You'll get caught, and somebody will probably go to prison for it."

"I told you, we are not going to do that. It would be too dangerous. And the Mexican police are cooperating with the US government now. We would never make it, even if we tried."

"But you still won't tell me what you are planning?" If there is such a thing as affectionate frustration, it was the tone he asked with. "Don't tell me you have a contract with Goodbow too?"

"No. But I have one with God. It has very strict terms."

Lane Williams was skilled in difficult conversations; he knew when it was wise to keep probing and when it was time to yield to exasperation. He walked to the door, opened it, and kicked a rubber door stop beneath it. He walked back to his chair and pulled a pack of cigarettes from the sport jacket draped on it.

"I think I need a cigarette," he said. "The hell with the rules."

"Don't worry, Lane," said the nun, drawing out her own. She leaned over the table and Williams lit her cigarette, then his own. "You will not be involved in anything," she said. "And as you say, it is best for you that way, and your organization."

Then she asked him for paper and pen. On it she wrote the number for her new burner phone. "If you want to reach me, though, I have a new phone."

"You lost the one I gave you?"

She didn't answer, only handed him the paper.

"Just use this one," she said with a kind smile. "It's better for everyone."

32

It was not that Leary Deen wanted "out" from Goodbow's plan. He knew he was already into it up to his teeth. He wanted to aid the old man from Rhode Island in any way he legally could. He wanted the families to be reunited. But now he worried that he himself might cause the plan's failure, unless he acted with great care.

He could not come under more scrutiny, if there was any way to avoid it. Not so much for his own sake, but for Goodbow and the families. For the success of the plan. He had told the truth to the FBI. But their questions next time might be more precise. He knew he must not learn anything more. Not from Goodbow; not from anyone. If he did, he would probably have to disclose it, with horrible consequences. He wished harm to no one, and his continuing participation risked them all.

He surely could not assist in the transport of the parents to Amapala. That would be far too much involvement to ever explain away and, if he himself was followed by the FBI, expose the whole venture before the parents even were afloat.

Besides, he didn't even know where they were staying in Tegus, awaiting word. Only Father Lopez did.

Deen was confident that Huff Langley was savvy enough to know not to call him at the embassy. The marine had strong evasion skills and he understood the means and methods of law enforcement. But he worried that Goodbow—wherever he was—would not be so disciplined. Goodbow probably *would* call him, he knew. Such a call would be discovered and the investigation given more urgency. No, Deen decided, he must contact Goodbow first.

At lunchtime he walked up the busy avenue and climbed into a taxi a few blocks away.

"Train station," he said to the driver in English. He never spoke Spanish on the streets, for the same reasons Huff Langley had instructed Goodbow before their arrival in Tegus. And for good measure, he displayed his US Embassy credentials on his chest for the driver to see.

The train station in Tegus, like all of them in the country, was furnished with pay phones. He found a bank of them mounted to pillars in the center of the terminal and poured in a handful of coins.

"Yes?" Goodbow said.

"It's Leary. Leary Deen."

"Oh, I'm glad you called, I was just . . ."

"Don't say anything, just listen."

"Are you all right?" Goodbow was concerned. Maybe the session with the FBI had not gone well.

"I'm fine. But just listen. Don't even tell me where you are, Goodbow."

"Okay."

"I can't hear anything I don't already know about your plan. Anything I know, I may have to tell. Probably *will* have to tell."

"I understand."

"So no dates, no new places, no new people. Nothing I don't already know."

"Got it."

"I want to help you with the parents, but I can't call them anymore."

"But then . . ."

"Just listen. Father Lopez should be your contact, not me. I think he will agree, but I can't promise that. But *him,* I *can* call. I can tell him you will be calling him. I'll have to say again to him that this is not government business. And this time, I really should tell him it's risky, dangerous, even for him. He has himself and his people to care for."

Goodbow nodded silently on the other end of the line. He had just risen from his first night's sleep in Winnemucca.

"But if the priest is willing to do it, he could work with the nuns you told me about. He could get them to the parents."

"The nun won't be . . ." Goodbow was trying to tell him that Huff Langley would be with her for the transport of the parents, that the nun would not be alone in the country.

"Please!" Leary interrupted. *"Don't tell me anything!"*

"Sorry," Goodbow said. "It's hard for me not to tell you things. But I understand why you don't want to hear them."

"Just take down this number for Father Lopez." Deen recited it twice. "His first name is Ambrose. He's up early for morning Mass. Confessions are late afternoon. Are you Catholic?"

"No. Should I tell him I am?"

As tense as he was, Deen couldn't suppress a laugh. "You don't lie to a priest, Will. In your case, I don't think you lie to anybody."

"Well, lately I'm doing a lot of things I don't think I do."

"Well, maybe he will make you a Catholic. Just remember not to call *me.* Good luck." Deen hung up.

The abruptness of his call and the consulate official's stressful voice shook Goodbow. His hand trembled a bit as he set his phone down on the room desk. His stomach tinged nervously. He stepped outside to look at the snowcapped mountains above the town, hoping that the natural beauty would calm him, as looking at vast water always seemed to. But it didn't.

I'm dragging people into this now, he thought, gazing at the range. *What am I getting them into? What I am getting them into, Grace? . . . . Grace?*

33

Breen Edwards was not pleased. The public protests from humanitarians against the family separation policy had not abated even when the practice was largely stopped by the public outcry. Where are the children? Where are the parents? What is being done to re-unite them? They were questions that seemed reasonable to many. But the answers to them were complex, nuanced, and in the end, politically embarrassing.

Several thousand children had been scattered across the country. Some of them were in their second or even third foster home or—worse, if not fortunate enough to receive the help of someone like Sister Hope Annie—housed in HHS detention facilities that resembled juvenile prisons. Documentation of their whereabouts was sometimes inconsistent or incomplete. Their parents were also far flung. Some waited in tenements across the border, pawns in the running argument between the US and Mexico as to who shouldered responsibility for their well-being. Others had made their way, assisted or unassisted by the Mexican government and NGOs, to their countries of origin, usually Guatemala or Honduras. The paper trail in many of their cases had disappeared like rabbit tracks in melting snow. Scores were unaccounted for. How could you reunite children and parents when you couldn't find and identify them? And, in Breen Edward's case, didn't much want to, at least in public view. Not because he was heartless; not because he wished to prolong the sadness and longing of any of the parents and their children. It was something different.

To the DHS chief, every reunification meant another agonizing news cycle filled with political criticism, heart-wrenching visual images, and emotional media coverage. The families were magnets for public empathy and, conversely, scorn for the policies that had separated them in the first place. The media—in Breen Edward's eyes, the biased, irresponsible, liberal media—had one overreaching objective, and it wasn't in truth the welfare of the migrant families. It was embarrassment of the administration with an eye to its destruction. He wished the families could be reunited as much as the gushing liberals did. Their separations had never been his idea. He knew and resented that the media rarely if ever acknowledged that some of them had happened well before Trump's election, even before the masses were streaming to the border. He chafed at the one-sided political manipulation and judgment that the grandstanding media created with each one.

"Just get the thing cleaned up quietly," he instructed his deputies. "Find these families before somebody else does."

Somebody like Wilton Goodbow. The news from the FBI in Tegucigalpa that Grace Goodbow was deceased did not assuage his suspicions of the Rhode Islander. It heightened them. Her recent death was confirmed, but it all seemed to him too coincidental. The woman's last emotional, pleading letter to the president had preceded her passing by only two weeks. And now her wealthy husband was snooping around the border and had even traveled to Honduras. Honduras! Who does that? And a majority of the separated parents and children were from that country. A man of means could make a lot of mischief.

"What do you mean, you couldn't find him?" he barked at Agent Musbacher, who'd drawn the short straw and had to report in that Goodbow had evaded questioning in Tegucigalpa.

"He'd left the hotel when we went back there."

"You believed he was still in the country when you went there the first time?"

"There was no reason not to believe it. The manager was honest. He didn't know he was gone. Neither did the embassy man. Goodbow fooled everybody. He and his guard flew to Los Angeles. We know that from passport control. They could be there now; they could be anywhere."

"Well, find them," Breen Edwards said. "Especially Goodbow. How hard can that be? An old guy like that."

"It will take resources," Musbacher said. "Obviously, we can't do it from down here."

"Let me think about it. I'll call the director. Be prepared to brief a US team."

Edwards looked again at the copies of Goodbow's passport on his desk and his wife Grace's next to it. She looked slight and attractive in her photo, wide set eyes below a high forehead. He looked large, broad faced with thick silver hair, a bit unusually long. Formidable.

Something's not right here. Something is not right.

34

"*Hola.*" Father Lopez answered his chiming phone.

"It's Will Goodbow, Father. The American."

"Oh, yes. Leary Deen said you would be calling. From the US. That you had to get out of Honduras. But I did not expect it so soon."

"What did he tell you?" Goodbow asked.

"Only what he had said before. When you came to the church. That what you are doing is not government business. Not approved by it. By your government or mine."

"Just that?"

"And that if I did whatever it was you were going to ask, I should understand the risks. As he put it, he didn't want to either 'encourage me or discourage' me." Silence came over the line; the priest expected his caller would say something next. But Goodbow didn't. Finally, the priest spoke himself. "I am glad you called, though," he said.

"I am glad you will speak with me," Goodbow said.

"We can speak," Father Lopez said. "But there are different ways one can speak to a priest. One way has its advantages."

"Oh?"

"Perhaps you could speak to me in confession. Would you like to make a confession? It is the least understood sacrament."

"I'm not a Catholic."

"I didn't ask if you were a Catholic. I asked if you would like to confess to me. Are you troubled about what you are doing? Worried that it is wrong? Worried that others could be harmed by your actions?"

"I am, but I don't intend that."

"Ah," the priest said. "These are the subjects of confession. Actions and intentions. Many come to me not knowing whether they have sinned or not sinned. But troubled that they *may* have. Or that they *might.* Sometimes they ask, 'If I do this, if I do that, am I sinning?" We talk about it. They learn, and I learn. I learn much. Many things. But what I learn in a confession, I never say to anyone else. No one. *Ever.* It is a sacred vow. And it is respected, thank God. That is why I said it has its advantages."

"For the penitent or for the priest?"

"Usually, for the penitent," the priest said. "But in this case, maybe for both." The priest moved to the windows in his small office and closed the blinds, darkening the lightless room. More fitting, he reasoned.

"Did Leary Deen suggest this to you?" Goodbow asked.

"No. He is not a Catholic either. One of the few in Tegus who isn't. But let's begin your confession. After all, you have already answered the first question."

"What is that?"

"How long has it been since you made your last one?" The priest, so somber when Goodbow had met him in person, laughed loudly. "The next question is, 'What is troubling you, son?' But in your case, since you are older than me, I will just leave that last word out. So, what is troubling you? Why did you come to speak to me? Go ahead. Speak to me."

"I have a plan to remove parents from your country and return them to their children in the United States where they were taken from them."

"Do you know if that is unlawful?"

"I have a pretty good idea."

"Do you intend to harm them? The parents? The children?"

"Of course not."

"Will you profit from this plan? Are you doing it for money? Money for yourself or someone else?"

"No."

"Then why are you doing it?"

"Because I promised my wife I would do it. Before she died. I didn't want to do it. I didn't really even care about any of this."

"But now you do care?"

"I am still not sure it is right, but somehow I do care now. I have seen things I didn't know. I didn't lead a life that showed them to me. People like the nun from Texas. Like Leary Deen. Like Huff Langley. Like the little girl, Gloria."

"The girl with the cut foot?"

"Yes. The Carrasco's daughter."

"Maybe someone was showing you all of this in the life you led, but you didn't know it. Maybe because it was not time for you to know it; not time for you to see it."

"Who was showing me? God? I am not a religious man."

"What has religion got to do with it? God does not need religion to show right from wrong, or good from evil. And people do not either. Was your wife religious?"

"Not really."

"*See?* And yet she saw right from wrong. And I can tell she saw much good. She saw good in you. And she showed you these things, even if you did not want to see them at first. I think she was a blessing to you."

"That she was."

"When one receives a blessing, one should share it."

"If it can be shared, I guess so."

"Every blessing can be shared, Goodbow," the priest said. "That is part of the reason it is a blessing! So, what should we speak about to help you share this blessing? What is it that you came to me for?"

"The nun in Texas. Her name is Sr. Hope Annie. She wants to come to Tegus with Huff Langley to take the parents that I met to Amapala. To wait there for my boat. But Leary Deen cannot help me anymore. He can't bring the parents to the nun and Langley. He would if he could, but he thinks he will be stopped, and then everything would be stopped."

"So you need someone to do that. To bring the parents to the nun and the guard."

"Or arrange a place in Tegus where they can pick up the parents."

"What was your wife's name?"

The question seemed out of place.

"Grace." Goodbow answered.

"That figures," Father Lopez said, then paused as he crossed himself. "You and Grace came to the right confessional. Sometimes, God's will and man's laws collide. Do not be troubled in your heart. I have heard you and you are forgiven, Mr. Goodbow. You are forgiven by God. Absolved. And, yes, I will bring the parents to my church to meet the nun and the guard. Call me with the time that I am to have them there."

Goodbow felt relief sweep over him.

"I cannot thank you enough," he said. "Is there some penance I must do?"

"Yes," the priest said. "Succeed."

"Succeed? That doesn't sound like penance."

"Maybe it doesn't. But if you succeed, I fear penance will come with it."

Goodbow would never forget what the priest said. "I'll call soon. Or, Sr. Hope Annie will."

"Okay, but understand. I have given you *God's* absolution. I cannot speak for lesser authorities."

"I know. I wish you could, but I understand."

"And one other thing," said the slender priest. "Do not make the time between four and six in the afternoon. I hear confessions then."

35

Leary Deen was right in his assessment of Huff Langley's instincts. The ex-marine *was* savvy. As soon as he'd committed to escorting Sr. Hope Annie to Tegucigalpa and to help in moving the parents safely to Amapala, he knew it must happen as quickly as possible, and that an indirect route was preferable. Within days the FBI likely would know that he and Goodbow had flown to Los Angeles; perhaps they knew already. If a decision was made by the government to pursue Goodbow, he himself would be sought too. It would be difficult to re-enter Honduras if he was wanted for questioning; he'd be put on a no-fly or red flag list in short order. And the only practical way to get there was by air. There were no functional passenger train systems across borders in Central America; and travel by bus was out of the question. They would be riding for three days.

Sr. Hope Annie nodded agreeably as he explained this to her when they had left Lane Williams' office.

"Goodbow called me last night," she said. "He talked to the priest you met with the parents. He said he will bring them to the same church. We just have to tell him when we're coming."

"Then we should leave right away," he said.

"Now?"

"Tonight," said Huff. "We can fly direct to Panama on American Airlines. An hour layover there and if we're lucky we'll catch a non-stop from Panama City to Tegus on Copa Airlines. That flight is under two hours. We'll make arrangements with the priest when we arrive in Honduras, tomorrow morning. Can you leave that quickly?"

"There is another sister who can cover for me at the center. I don't need to say where I am going. I make a lot of trips. It will not seem strange."

"Is your passport current?"

"Yes."

"Wear your full habit."

"Isn't this headpiece enough?"

"No, I want the full megillah."

"You do?"

"Yes."

"It will look terrible on you."

"Very funny. Just wear it."

Only two hours later, Langley picked her up at her small house near the respite center. Sr. Hope Annie bounced out the front door with a large suitcase, garbed as instructed in full habit—with one exception. She drew the line at the shoes. The order's standard issue shoes were heavy, stubby black leather; hot, clumsy and uncomfortable. All of the nuns complained about them. The boxy shoes lined their closet floors, neat and shiny from lack of use. But few chose the replacement that Sr. Hope Annie preferred. Black Converse brand basketball shoes with high tops and white laces. It may simply have been the natural inclination of a soldier to look at the boots of another—

in combat you could usually tell a lot about a soldier from the condition of his boots—but Huff Langley noticed the athletic sneakers immediately.

"What's with those?" he said, pointing to her feet.

"My shoes?" She feigned amazement at the question.

"Yes! *Those* fucking things." He pointed to them again.

"What's wrong with them?"

"Do nuns really wear them?"

"This one does. And watch your damned language."

"The idea is to *not* draw attention."

"I'll keep the skirt low. The shoes will be barely noticeable."

"And for Pete's sake, don't smoke in the airports down there, even though they still let you."

"Even if they didn't, I still would," she said. "Clergy have to have *some* privileges." Huff glared at her but took the suitcase from her hand. "But if you say it is that important, I won't," she said. "*Sergeant.*"

An hour later they boarded for Panama.

36

It still seemed odd to Goodbow that he could be in Nevada and also, generally speaking, nearly at the edge of the Pacific Northwest. The night air was crisp—an understatement—and the days sunny and dry under the mountains. A downright comfortable place, he concluded. And it was a plus that the Mountain View Lodge and Resort was a considerable step up from the earlier motor inns. He took a spacious room on the second floor of the main lodge, a well-maintained structure in the log cabin motif.

He was an experienced traveler but not this kind of traveler. His contentment in Winnemucca surprised him. Sailing was solitary and ever so nomadic. Grace and he and Burp Lebeau rarely moored in any port for more than a night. The whole appeal to them of sailing was the motion and the sea, the rustling of the silk and the clatter of the fittings, the intimacy of the hours in many of which not a word was uttered. How different this was, he thought, from anywhere he'd been, and mostly because he was taking root. Taking root in Winnemucca.

The more he drove the white Land Rover, the more he regretted having judged it harshly in the LAX rental aisle. He'd grown to like his high perch behind its wheel and the large vehicle's sturdy handling on the imperfect roads he explored outside of town. He was bounding along a gravel byway at the foot of the mountain range when Sr. Hope Annie had called in the morning after she and Langley had arrived safely—and unaccosted—in Tegucigalpa. He pulled to the grassy shoulder to speak with her. There was good news on the locations of the children in the US; she had confirmed them.

"They're all in a town called Breckenridge," she'd told him. "The Lutherans up there found families to take them in for the time being."

"Breckenridge, Colorado?" He'd heard of the ski town in the mountains west of Denver, not far from Vail. His son Ben had been there.

"No. Minnesota. Breckenridge, Minnesota."

"I've never heard of it."

"Well, the people there probably never heard of Winnemucca, Nevada, either," the nun said.

"Fair point."

"It's a couple hours northwest of Minneapolis on the North Dakota border, not very far from the Canadian border. It actually has an interesting history. The children are staying there with four families from the same church."

"Do the families know about this?" Goodbow asked.

"Not yet."

"Shouldn't we tell them?"

"Huff says we should wait. He thinks it's too early. Word might get out."

"And you?"

"I agree with him," she said. "At least until the parents are on your boat, and maybe not even then. The children will be very excited. It would be terrible to disappoint them."

"What about little Gloria?"

"I'm getting her up there to join the others. Lane Williams is getting the paperwork approved through HHS."

"Health and Human Services?"

"Yes, they are in charge of placing separated children. Lane's group works with them all the time."

"But you didn't tell Lane what we're doing, did you?"

"No. He tried to get it out of me and Huff, but we didn't tell him."

"Good. He's done enough. Will his office take the girl up there?"

"No. Maria Angeles is driving her in a Red Cross car."

"Maria?" Goodbow was surprised.

"Yes, she was happy to."

"What does *she* know?" Goodbow asked, concerned.

"I don't think anything."

"Did you mention me to her?"

"No, but she brought you up. Asked about you. She's very fond of you. Said Manny is too."

"And what did you say?"

"That everybody likes Goodbow. That was it. I didn't tell her anything about Huff or Leary Deen or your trip to see him. I just said that little Gloria had come across the border because she needed the hospital, and that her parents had been turned back. She said she knew that. And I said that Lane and I had found a home for her with other children in Minnesota. She remembered some had gone there. She was happy for Gloria."

"Well, be sure she doesn't learn anything more. I'd hate to see her get caught up in this," he said. He knew the nun still did not know that it was Maria who had sent him to the Central

American embassy and Leary Deen, or of his promise to her never to disclose her name as his source.

"I won't. I understand."

"Have you called Father Lopez yet?" he asked.

"We're calling him today. To see if he can bring the parents to the church tomorrow. I've already reached the Franciscan sisters near Amapala. They have rooms in their convent. We won't need the hotels. Huff is renting two vans."

"How are the two of you getting along?"

"All right. He's stubborn."

"He knows what he is doing, Sister."

"He took out two rooms at the Holiday Inn, but he is staying with me in my room!"

"He has his reasons. He doesn't want the hotel to know he's staying with a nun. Everyone would talk about it."

"Well, he is very free with your money."

"I've noticed. I think it's his nature. But I'd appreciate it if you don't take after him."

She laughed, almost girlishly. "I don't think there is much chance of that!" she said. "I would make a lousy marine!"

"Some might disagree, Sister."

"Where is the captain? Where is the boat?"

"Crossing the Gulf of Mexico."

"On schedule?"

"So far."

"When will he reach Amapala?"

"In a week or so. But it depends on how long it takes him to get through the Panama Canal."

"He can't just drive through it?"

"No, you don't just drive through the Panama Canal. There's a whole process. Paperwork and inspections. Fees and certificates. You have to wait your turn. Then they tie you to something like a barge and guide you through the locks. You have to hire trained people to manage the lines. It's only three or four hours once you start through, but it can take days to get the arrangements confirmed and the helpers on board. Most sailors allow four or five days for the whole thing. But trust me, he'll make it."

"Your captain must love you very much to do this for you."

"He loved Grace very much too."

"Still, this is much to ask of him."

"I know. I worried about that. But he wanted to do it. I think he's finding it exciting, even. In some way."

"I can understand that. I see it in Huff too, though I think he must have seen much excitement before this. And yet he seems very committed to you. It is not just a job to him."

"Maybe it's *because* of what he has seen. It's not for the money I'm sure. He has plenty of work. He wouldn't have to do this."

"Well, faith works in strange ways," said Sr. Hope Annie.

"Faith. You always come back to faith, don't you?"

"No," she said. "But it always comes back to me."

37

The piers near the Caribbean side of the Canal entrance were lined with all manner of yachts and commercial ships when Burp Lebeau approached the Panama coast on his eighth day at sea. He knew there would be few options for mooring, but the degree of congestion still surprised him. He'd have to be patient and wait for a slip to open. There was no way around it.

A transit permit was mandatory and available only on shore at the office of the Panama Canal Authority. The paperwork was formidable, and it had been three years since he'd last made the crossing. A dozen consultants—transit agents, as they were known, operated out of small storefronts at the shore, greeting boat owners and offering their assistance, well worth the typical fee of about two hundred dollars. For that stipend, the agents walked sailors through the fee and measurement procedures (the ultimate crossing fee was a function of precise vessel length), secured a time slot for the actual crossing, and found "line handlers" required by the Authority for the passage. Yes, it was wise to retain one, the old captain decided.

The usual wait for a confirmed crossing time was three to four days. But an adroit agent with the right connections could sometimes acquire an expedited reservation, lopping the wait time in half. But the first need was getting ashore. Burp anchored three-hundred yards off the piers and stood at the rail watching the parked crafts, looking for any sign of departure so that he could take its place. After an hour, he lifted anchor and edged *The Sails of Grace* in closer to the piers. Other boats were appearing behind him; he wanted to establish his priority. It was only another hour before he was rewarded.

The feeling ashore was festive; market-like. Under colorful canopies, transit lines were offered for sale or rent, and men were available for hire as the handlers to manage them as a boat descended the locks in the crossing to the Pacific. And of course, food and beverage abounded. Boat owners, many of them young, free-spirited, and adventurous, swirled among the agents' stands and the vendors' huts that flanked the strikingly formal façade of the Citibank branch. The bank was to the Canal Authority what the heart is to blood, what the brain is to memory. All transactions and fees pumped through it.

"Where's your crew?" the rugged transit agent asked as he came aboard with Burp to measure *Grace* stem to stern.

"You're looking at it," Burp answered.

"You're sailing this thing alone?"

"For now."

"You're crazier than these kids!"

"I've got the sea miles to work by myself. And *Grace* can almost sail herself."

"Grace?"

"The boat. *The Sails of Grace.*"

"Oh. Yeah."

"She's outfitted to the hilt with pneumatics and electronics.

Even automated furling booms to raise and move the mainsails and jibs."

"I see," the agent said, admiring the instrument panels on the helm console.

"That doesn't change the crossing fee, does it?"

"No. All that counts is the length. Let's tape it out. I have to take in a preliminary measurement when I apply for the crossing permit. But they won't trust that. A certified guy from the PCA will come on board later and do the official measurement and then the actual fee is computed. I'll sign up the line handlers and you pay for them with the fee at the bank. For a boat this long, you're required to have four of them on board and food and water for them during the crossing. Sometimes there are screw-ups and they're on your boat all damn day. The bank sends the money through and then the PCA will issue your ticket with a crossing date and time."

"What can you do to get me a quick slot?"

"In the old days, we used to be able to 'grease the skids', if you know what I mean. But the PCA nowadays is straight arrow. I know the head dispatcher pretty well, though. If you're willing to go real early, I can probably get you a slot day after tomorrow. The young people don't like the early times. Hard partiers, you know?"

"How early?"

"Why? Are you a hard partier?"

"When I want to be."

"Dawn."

"Done."

38

Father Lopez answered the heavy knock on the steel rear door of his church to find Sr. Hope Annie standing with a smile and Huff Langley towering behind her without one. The street behind the church was little more than a one-way alley; the two passenger vans that the marine had rented were pulled up over the curb, even then leaving barely enough room for a small vehicle to pass, much less a police cruiser.

"Come in," the priest said.

"We should go immediately," Huff said, before Sr. Hope Annie could answer. "We don't want to be seen."

"Come in," the priest said again. "You must be blessed with the parents first. They are right here waiting."

"No, really . . ." the marine started to protest until an elbow emerged abruptly from the nun's habit and landed in his ribs, accompanied by an unkind look.

"Of course, Father," she said, pulling Huff with her into the rear sacristy.

The parents stood together in pairs, each holding large-handled travel duffels of canvas or old leather. They looked apprehensive, alert. Sr. Hope Annie greeted them in Spanish and moved her smiling eyes across each of their faces, pausing slightly as she looked at each mother and father. "I am Sr. Hope Annie. Did Father Lopez tell you? I am from America and this man and I are going to help you try to get there. To your children."

"You have found them?" Juan Rodriguez asked? "You know where they are?"

"Yes," the nun said. "They are safe. They are with families in America. And we are going to take you to them, if we can. First to Amapala to wait for Mr. Goodbow's boat. His captain will sail you to America. And then I will meet you there and take you to your little angels. With God's help."

The tall priest stepped in front of the line of parents and placed his right hand on the head of each. He did the same to Sr. Hope Annie but stopped when he came to Huff. He looked into the marine's eyes. "I would like to bless you too," he said. "If that is all right." Huff nodded unenthusiastically and the priest placed his hand on his head. Then he stepped back and extended his hands high and wide with open palms.

"God in heaven," he said in Spanish. "Bless these travelers in the name of St. Christopher, patron of journeys, and keep them safe in their passage. May Mother Mary, a loving mother herself, guide them and their captain on the sea. Protect them and their protectors and protect their children—your children—whom they journey to join."

He made the sign of the cross and the parents and Sr. Hope Annie replicated it; Huff made an awkward semblance of the gesture.

"We really must leave now," Huff said.

"Yes. Yes," the priest said.

Sr. Hope Annie embraced the priest and led the parents

out behind Huff and into the vans. Some of the parents were surprised by the seat belts. A few had ever ridden only in buses and needed help fastening in.

They were anxious. They were quiet. They were leaving Tegucigalpa.

39

Who could blame Will Goodbow for never having heard of Breckenridge, Minnesota? After all, he was not an amateur presidential historian like Sr. Hope Annie. And who would think that a community of just thirty-six hundred persons surrounded by sunflower fields as far as the eye could roam would have a curious place both in the history of the American promise and Goodbow's quest to fulfill his own? But it did.

He found the town marked in the smallest print in his spiral-bound road atlas and quickly googled a driving map to it from his waiting place in northern Nevada. At first, he winced. It was fourteen-hundred thirty-six miles away; the fastest route a twenty-two-hour drive across Idaho, Wyoming, Montana and North Dakota. *Ughh. Four frick'n days!* But as the old New Englander looked for more information on the small burg in the Upper Midwest, his interest was piqued.

"Est. 1857," read the notation in the *Compilation of the Villages and Settlements of Minnesota* that he found online. *Just before the Civil War,* he thought. Goodbow was by no means an aficionado of Civil War history, but he knew enough to realize that talk of secession, and the issue of slavery undergirding it, had roiled the American conscience in the years leading up to the Civil War. He was surprised to read in the *Compilation* that though a state could not be further north than Minnesota, the town of Breckenridge was named just before the War Between the States after the newly elected 14th Vice-President of the United States, John Cabell Breckinridge of—no, not Minnesota—but Kentucky! Odd, Goodbow thought. And it got odder from there.

An interesting and complicated figure, John Cabell Breckinridge probably warranted more attention in American history than he'd received, Goodbow concluded as he read on. The Kentuckian was a fixture in the pre-Civil War federal government from an early age, serving prominently in the House of Representatives where he was regarded for his oratory, intellect and—not incidentally—dashing good looks. Breckinridge knew well and liked the Illinois legislator, Abraham Lincoln, his equal in neither handsome appearance nor resonant speaking voice, whom he had first met in 1849 in Lexington when the lanky lawyer married Breckinridge's own cousin, Mary Todd. When he took office as James Buchanan's vice-president the same year as the small Minnesota community approvingly adopted his name (misspelling it), he became the youngest vice-president in United States history, barely a year beyond the Constitutional minimum of thirty-five; a distinction he still holds.

But, as Goodbow learned, other less noble distinctions earned in the next decade of his life made the Minnesota town founders' choice of his name a case of local consternation, embarrassment, and at best, poor timing.

Congressman and then Vice-President Breckinridge did not urge the secession of the southern states over the issue of slavery or its debated expansion into additional states of the union. He hoped secession would not happen. But he was outspoken in the right of the southern states to decide to leave the union if it came to it. He was considered by the Democratic Party as a candidate for the presidency in 1856, but did not actively seek the nomination, which eventually went to Buchanan over challenger Stephen Douglas of Illinois. But four years later, when the democrats could not agree initially on a candidate at their deadlocked convention in Charleston, South Carolina, the Southern Democrats broke from the national party, formed their own, and nominated Breckinridge as their candidate, making him one of three challengers to Lincoln on the 1860 ballot. The other two were Douglas as the formal Democratic candidate and John Bell of Tennessee, running under the banner of the Constitution Union Party.

Goodbow was surprised to read that while Breckinridge carried neither Minnesota or his home state of Kentucky, he actually garnered the second most electoral votes in the 1860 presidential election; had no candidate earned an electoral vote majority and the decision had been sent to the House of Representatives, it is quite possible that John Cabell Breckinridge would have become America's 16th president instead of Honest Abe.

In truth, Breckinridge never believed he would defeat Lincoln. And under election laws of the day, he was able to run in that same 1860 election for an open seat in the U.S. Senate from Kentucky. He won that race; Vice President Breckinridge became Senator Breckinridge. The small community in Minnesota retained a prominent, if somewhat diminished, namesake.

Lincoln's election ignited the brewing southern fervor for secession, and even willingness for war to achieve it. Officially, Kentucky chose neutrality in the war, and asked both Union and Confederate forces to stay off its soil. But Breckinridge decided he could not be loyal to southern life and also abide neutrality. *Still a sitting United States Senator*, he joined with Jefferson Davis and the Confederate cause as an important general and battlefield commander for the South. This made him the first elected official of the United States government to bear arms against his own country and, as a result, the first and only US senator to be expelled from Congress for treason. By the end of the war he was serving as Secretary of War for the Confederates and a principal advisor to Davis at confederacy headquarters in Richmond.

After the surrender at Appomattox, confederate leaders, including Jefferson Davis, were rounded up and arrested. But Brenkinridge escaped arrest by fleeing from Florida (*by sail-boat,* Goodbow noted with amusement), first to Cuba, then England, and eventually Canada, where he lived in exile for nearly four years. He returned only when he was assured that the Christmas Day presidential pardon granted to all confederates by President Andrew Johnson in his final days in office legally applied to him too as a fugitive living outside of the country when it was granted.

These ignominious "firsts" must have been an awkward burden on the shoulders of the good people of little Breckenridge, Minnesota. Goodbow could find no record, though, of recrimination against the town fathers for their choice of name, or any serious consideration of changing it. He put it down to virtuous Lutheran tolerance. Perhaps, he considered, the same inclination that opened the Minnesotan's homes a century and a half later to the migrant children from Honduras living there now.

He studied again the road atlas and his google map search. The internet map displayed three routes from Winnemucca to Breckenridge. Two claimed nearly the identical distance in miles and estimated driving times. But the third option displayed a much longer time to destination. The faster routes followed interstate expressways for the bulk of the drive; the longer zig zagged through mountainous terrain in Wyoming and Montana. He chose to defer his decision for the moment. Burp Lebeau was still days from Amapala; Sister Hope and Huff had only just arrived there with the parents to await the captain. His choice of route was not pressing. For the time being, he was comfortable and secure in Winnemucca.

Until his cell phone rang.

40

Much later, Leary Deen would look back and admit that it was probably never realistic to think his telephone contacts with Goodbow and Father Lopez would go forever unconnected by the FBI. Still he regretted his most obvious error: he had never told the priest not to call *him* at his embassy office.

Deen had been careful to dial Goodbow and the priest only from the train station pay phone and, before that, Huff Langley from the embassy's basement kitchen. He'd assumed that since Breen Edwards had sent the FBI to him, his office phone would be at least logged for incoming and outgoing calls, if not tapped for listening and recording. So when he answered Father Lopez's call, fear flew into him.

"They have left," the priest said in his first sentence. "They left yesterday."

"We should not discuss this, Father," Deen said.

"Why not?"

"We just shouldn't."

"But you said it is not government business."

"It isn't, but some people might not see it that way."

"I just wanted you to know that they are on their way. So that you could tell Mr. Goodbow."

Oh, God, thought Deen. *He used his name!*

"Father," he said, as calmly as he could. "I am sorry, but I have to hang up now. It would be best if you didn't call again."

He walked at a casual gait until he was out of the embassy, then as briskly as he could to the nearest taxi stand. This time he rode to the inter-city bus terminal. It was further than the train station and seedier, but he did not want to go back to the same place to call Goodbow; besides, embassy personnel never traveled by bus except for local transportation. It was unlikely he would be seen there by anyone who knew him.

"Is this Will Goodbow?" he asked when Goodbow picked up his call.

"Leary?"

"Yes. I'm calling from a pay phone at the Tegus bus station. Did you know the parents are on the way to Amapala?"

"Huff and the nun already called me. They made it there. They're okay."

"Well, the priest just called me at the embassy."

"So?"

"I wish he hadn't. I didn't want to know anything more. And I should have told him not to call me there."

"You sound worried. Is it that big a deal? A priest calls the embassy. A lot of people call the embassy, don't they?"

"They don't mention your name when they do."

"*My* name?"

"Yeah. The name that the FBI is interested in. The name they came to see me about. He said he called to tell me they were on their way 'so I could tell *Mr. Goodbow.*' He used your name!"

"You think they bugged your phone?"

"It sure wouldn't surprise me. That's why I'm calling. To make sure *you* don't call me. I don't know what the hell their capabilities are. If you call me, they may be able to figure out where you are. Wherever the hell that is, which I don't want to know. And be sure you don't call Father Lopez. They're probably going to be talking to him soon, now that he called me. And if he doesn't tell them what they want to hear, they may track his phone too."

"His phone! He's not even an American."

"That makes it easier for them. I wish he was an American, for all our sakes. Trust me."

"You keep talking about *them*," Goodbow said. "Like it's *us* versus *them*."

"Anymore, I'm not sure '*what*' is; not sure what '*they*' is," Leary said. "It's laws, it's morals, it's what you can live with."

"I'm beginning to think they're not all the same," Goodbow said. "They don't always line up."

"But one thing is always the same."

"What?" asked Goodbow. "What is always the same?"

"The truth. And you need to know I will tell it. If it comes to that."

"I want you to, Leary. Grace would want you to."

"Then don't call me," Leary Deen said. "And don't call the priest. Wherever you are, be careful. Wherever you're going, get there fast."

As he returned the phone to its hook in the Tegus bus terminal, the consulate official looked furtively around the station lobby. He saw no one that he recognized, and no one seemed to be looking at him. But his nerves were un-soothed; his heart raced as he strode out for a taxi. *This is not going to end well.*

Two-thousand miles north, the man from Rhode Island, the widower on a mission, moved once again to his motel room window and gazed at the mountains. This time, their majesty did enter him. He wouldn't call it a sensory pleasure of the kind when welcomed flavors reached the tongue, but it was a kind of pleasure nonetheless; a special satisfaction, a peacefulness. He felt as if he was standing on the deck of *The Sails of Grace,* turning gently, evenly into a sunset ahead. He was alone but he was not afraid. His sins had been forgiven.

41

Leary Deen caught a break.

The FBI agents in Tegucigalpa had suggested that Bureau resources in California be enlisted to pursue Goodbow and Langley. The local agents wanted to remain in Tegus and follow leads in Honduras, including ones they hoped to elicit from the embassy official, Leary Deen. But Breen Edwards believed that bringing in new agents would waste time and there was no reason to think Leary Deen could offer more; everything he'd said in his first interview had checked out. With the Bureau director's consent, he dispatched Myles Burlacher and Robert Everett to the States to track down the "persons of interest."

But as they say, every action provokes an opposite and equal *re*action. And this reaction portended anguish for Will Goodbow, holed-up in northern Nevada.

"Look at this," Everett said to his partner on the flight to Los Angeles. He passed his laptop computer to him. "This month's phone data in and out of the embassy. Look at incoming call number 1438."

"Okay, I see it," Burlacher said.

"The area code. 401. That's the Rhode Island area code. The only one in the whole state."

"You think it's Goodbow's phone?"

"Who's else would it be?"

"The call's not to Leary Deen's office."

"That's because they all come into the central line; the log doesn't show the extension they're transferred to." Burlacher checked his notes of the Deen interview. "The date is about right. Deen said Goodbow called him to confirm his visit a day or so before he came to the embassy."

"So, we have a cell phone number that might be this guy's. What can we do with it? There's nothing we have to get a warrant on it or to get more from the phone company. No judge will do it."

"We don't need a warrant to trace his cell tower pings."

"True. But we'd need support from the technology section. I suppose we could get it."

"And what about a FISA warrant? With that, we could listen in on him."

"FISA? That's a terrorism or foreign government thing. There's no terrorist threat here, and no foreign government involvement. Honduras didn't bring Goodbow down."

"You know that, and I know that," Burlacher said. "But do you think it will matter to Breen Edwards?"

* * *

Myles Burlacher was right. It didn't matter to Breen Edwards. The DHS chief took the call from the agents when they landed at LAX.

"Maybe you can't call it terrorism, but it's sure as hell a matter of national security," he said to the agents. "Do the

FISA application right away. Put in there that you've briefed me and that I consider it a matter of national homeland security. I'm in charge of the goddamned stuff. We have the husband of a harasser of the president travelling to Central America, meeting with our consulate, and doing who knows what else."

"There's red tape, you know."

"I know that."

"The FISA court rules fast, but DOJ has to jump through a lot of hoops to clear the application before it's filed with the judges. Especially after the Carter Page and Russia shit."

"I'll take care of that with the attorney general. He'll see it my way."

42

On the night of his thirteenth day at sea, Burp Lebeau angled *Grace* into the quiet waters of the Gulf of Fonseca and approached the Isle de Tigre and its town of Ampala fifty kilometers from the Pacific. The breeze was light in the evening air; the tall sails could muster only about fifteen knots and Lebeau refrained from using the diesel engines for want of attracting attention by their noise. Using the number Goodbow had given, he spoke for the first time with Sr. Hope Annie and her protector Huff Langley that morning from the ocean. He was nearing the gulf and could reach them by mid-day, he told them.

"No," the nun said. "Sergeant Huff says not in daylight."

"Why not?" he asked. "I'll be able to dock more easily. It will be near high-tide, just beginning to recede."

"No, Huff says no. Not until night. Here, you talk to him." She passed her burner phone to the marine.

"Captain," he said. "There's probably never been a boat like yours to sail in here. The masts will be seen all over. The whole town will come out. Believe me, darkness is the best. I can be on the docks with a lantern."

"Low tide will be at ten-thirty," Burp said. "The keel will be near bottom then, even with no one aboard. It has to be earlier," Burp said. "Or well after two in the morning, when the tide comes in."

"The people will be tired then. It'll be dark by eight-thirty. Can we say nine?"

Burp was uncomfortable. He had checked his notes for the information Goodbow had given him about the water depth at the moorings. He had planned to guide *Grace* into the longest dock available and tether her securely for the boarding. But he needed at least mid-tide depth to do that, unless the tide was higher than usual, and he knew from his tide chart that on this day it was not. He would have to adjust his docking maneuver.

"Take your lantern to the longest dock. I'll pull to the end of it, not the side. I'll use the fore and aft anchors to steady her. I'll throw you ropes to tie to the dock, and a boarding plank. Have everyone on the dock with you."

"Okay."

"But if the water is just too low, I'll have to take her back out and wait. If she goes aground, we'll be in trouble for a long time. And we could have damage."

"Understood."

"Nine o'clock, then."

That night as he sailed in, his console depth gauge relieved him somewhat; the bay was deeper than he had expected and without extreme variations. Still, he studied it intensely. The sky was clear and star-filled, a crescent moon hung high on his port side. When *Grace* glided silently past the two-kilometer buoy in the center of the channel he saw the light flickering ahead, slightly starboard. The water depth was still more than ample; he prayed it would stay that way. He extended the electronic anchor riggings so that he could lower the weights when ready. They rolled out humming from the front and back of the boat and stopped in unison with a thud. He flashed the bow lights, but only them, and only twice, and proceeded in darkness toward the lantern.

The lights of the town shed enough glimmer to the shore that when he was a half mile from the moorings he could see the silhouettes of the people lined up on the dock behind Huff Langley and the nun. The cathedral spire rose high from the hill behind them.

"I don't hear anything," Sr. Hope Annie whispered to Huff at the end of the dock.

"It's a sailboat," Huff said.

"Shouldn't we see it by now?"

Before Huff could answer, the large vessel emerged before them under the starlight. The nun and some of the parents standing behind her gasped audibly at its size and magnificence. The main sails seemed to tower to heaven and bluish light glinted off the shiny masts. Burp trimmed the large sails and adjusted the smaller jibs. Eighteen-feet, read the depth gauge, but he could see the water had dropped a good two feet below the dock surface ahead. *Close. But maybe outboard motors have hollowed the bottom there. That happens at docks, Grace. That would be good, Grace. Take it gently, Grace.*

He angled to the right so that he could approach the dock on a straight line, limping the sails to reduce his speed to just a knot or two, and finally to pure glide. Before *Grace*'s bow had reached the end of the pier he slowly lowered the aft anchor and when it settled, the vessel now abutting the pier, the fore anchor too. There was no pressure from the keel; it had not hit bottom, that he knew. But how much above the bottom did it rest? He judged it must be slight.

"Here you go!" he called, hurling the thick ropes to Huff.

The marine wound them around the wooden posts at each end of the dock, then reached for the aluminum landing ramp that Burp extended to him. "Be careful with them," the captain said. "The damn thing is pretty skinny. Pull up the side rails and make sure they lock in. I'm going to turn on the lights below."

"Better if you didn't, Captain," Huff said.

"Well, I'm going to. The steps to get down there are narrow and steep. Somebody'll break their neck. I'll cut them when we move away."

Huff considered pressing his case, but a captain is a captain, he concluded. He looked up the hill to the town and all across the mooring area at the shore. He saw no one or any moving lights. He motioned to Sr. Hope Annie and handed her the lantern. He lodged the rear end of the boarding ramp into a slot on the wooden dock and planted his weight on the front edge where it rose to the deck of the large boat. The nun, in full habit and her basketball sneakers, walked the parents one-by-one up the ramp and onto the deck, kissing each one as she turned to fetch the next. She took Juan Rodriguez first and introduced him to the captain.

"Juan speaks English," she told him. "Very well. He can help you speak to the others."

"We're loading the ark, 'eh Sister?" Lebeau said with a smile. *She's pretty.*

"They *are* coming in pairs," she replied. "I am not to know your name, Goodbow told us. No one is to know your name. So I will assume it is Noah. Saint of the seas."

"Is he a saint?"

"No, I just made it up. But he should be. Where would we be without him? Where would these people be without you?"

"Well, I hope I am as good a weather forecaster as he was."

She held out the lantern to see as much of the side of the craft as it could illuminate.

"Where is Grace's name?" she asked.

"On the bow transom. And on the port side."

"This is not the port side?"

"Tonight it isn't."

The nun was puzzled.

"Port is the left side from the wheel. Starboard is the right. When we set sail and turn around, you'll see it."

"Good," she said. "I want to see the name on the boat."

And minutes later, she did. The parents were below and out of sight. Only the wiry old captain could be seen, standing at the helm wheel as he spun the vessel out with the front bibs and a single main sail. The lantern's beam and the dim moonlight were just enough to see the large italicized lettering. *The Sails of Grace.*

"She is a beauty, isn't she?" said Huff Langley as the captain and his passengers slipped into darkness.

"Yes," she said. "And so is he."

43

An hour later, Sr. Hope Annie reached Goodbow. He'd heard from Burp in the afternoon and knew his captain friend expected to make the rendezvous in Amapala that evening. The old New Englander was anxious for news.

"They are all on the ship with your captain," the nun said. "Huff wanted him to wait until dark, and he did."

"The water was deep enough to dock *Grace?*" Burp had told him that he wanted to sail in before the tide had receded very much.

"I guess not the regular way," she said. "He didn't pull up to the long side of the pier. He pulled up to the front of it, sideways. He is handsome for an old man."

"You never called *me* handsome."

"I've never had cause."

"He watched his language? Sailors, you know."

"We both did."

"You sound very happy."

"Oh, I am very happy. The parents are very happy."

"And Huff?"

"Still stubborn. But I think happy too. He says we have to leave very soon. We are driving to Tegus in the morning, straight to the airport."

"Through Panama again?"

"I don't think so. He said, 'That bridge is burned.' What does that mean?"

"I don't know, but it's probably not good."

"He said we will fly to San Diego. Because you told him the captain will land the boat there."

"That's the plan. At a yacht club there."

"I asked him if we should go back separately, but he said no. He said it is better together, maybe we could help each other. What do you think that means?"

"I don't know, but I agree. I do not want you to be alone down there. I told you he knows what he is doing. We should trust him. But once he gets you to San Diego, I am going to insist he get out of this. He has done so much already. They are surely looking for him. You'll be safe in the US without him, won't you?"

"Sure, Goodbow. And what are they going to do to a nun, anyway? Even one who smokes!"

"And you have the other sisters ready? For the drive to Minnesota?"

"Yes. The Dominicans are sending a sister with a fourteen-passenger van from their house in Bakersfield. They are putting new tires on it, even. They are just waiting to hear from me."

"God love them."

"Oh, you don't have to ask him that," the nun said. "He does."

44

Agents Burlacher and Everett did what agents should do when looking for information at airport car rental counters. They began at the largest companies and worked their way down.

"Is Avis still number two?" Everett asked his partner.

"I don't know," Burlacher said. "But I'm pretty sure Hertz is still number one."

It didn't really matter. Huff Langley had chosen a brand well down the list for the rental he'd made for Goodbow's use. It took the FBI agents three hours to make their way to the end of the line.

"Hello, sirs," the perky counter clerk said. "Thank you for waiting."

"Actually," Burlacher said, "We didn't wait. We cut in." He gestured appreciatively to the customers behind them and raised his FBI badge to the clerk.

"Oh, then. What can I help you with? Do you need a car?"

"Not yet. We need information."

"Sure. What information?"

"We need to know if you have an outstanding rental for either an H. Langley or a Wilton Goodbow."

"How do you spell those?"

"L-A-N-G-L-E-Y and G-O-O-D-B-O-W."

The clerk pecked at his keyboard and squinted.

"Not this week," he said.

"Check last week."

"Just a second; I have to clear this screen." The customer next in line squirmed audibly; Everett turned and sent him a condescending glance. "Oh, here's something, yes," the reservationist said. "There's an outstanding rental to a Hufford Langley. Texas driver's license. Eight days ago."

"When is it due back?"

"It's not."

"What do you mean, it's not?"

"It was rented on our 'touring program'. For long-term rentals. There's no set return date or location."

"Then how do you know what to charge?"

"We charge the credit card for sixty days, and the customer authorizes us to charge it again if the car isn't returned before then. Every week after sixty days, we charge another week on the card. An open-ended thing. We don't do it unless the card has a high enough credit limit and there's no expiration coming up. The customer can bring the car back here or drop it at any of our locations. The final charges are settled then. Of course, there's a premium rate. For the flexibility, you know. Though, this guy got a discount. Former military."

"What car did Mr. Langley take? We need the details."

The clerk studied his computer screen. "A current year Land Rover all terrain. Nice vehicle. White. Nearly new."

"Is everything on your screen there? VIN? License plate?"

"Yeah, it's right here."

"Print it out for us, will you?"

"Sure."

"What about the other man? Wilton Goodbow. Anything for him?"

"I don't see anything for him."

"Check again."

The clerk scrolled through the computer screens again. "No," he said. "Nothing under that name." He handed the printout to Everett.

"Thanks," Burlacher said. "You've been helpful."

"Is this like a big deal?" the clerk leaned forward and asked, excitedly. "Will it be on tv?"

The waiting customers leaned in too. They were less amused.

45

Law abiding, speed limit minding citizen, Warren Eggle looked with horror in the rearview mirror of his shiny white rental car. Two—not one— California State Police SUVs were steaming toward his bumper with lights flashing and sirens blaring. They were approaching so quickly that he was afraid to brake sharply for fear he would be rammed. For no reason other than that it popped into his mind, he prudently clicked the emergency flashers button on the dash of the Land Rover and coasted to a stop on the right berm.

He was surprised that the troopers did not immediately leave their vehicles and walk to him. Instead, when the noise of the Land Rover's air conditioning blower faded, he heard the unfriendly voice coming through the bullhorn mounted to the closest cruiser.

"ROLL DOWN ALL YOUR WINDOWS AND STEP OUT SLOWLY WITH YOUR BACK TO US AND YOUR HANDS EMPTY! WE REPEAT, ROLL DOWN . . . ."

The repetition was unnecessary. The startled salesman from Omaha climbed out gingerly and raised his empty hands, forward facing as he'd been directed. He was fifty-six years old, short and materially overweight, made more evident by his Bermuda shorts, dark socks and leather loafers. Beneath a mostly bald head, he wore black-framed glasses with lenses excessively thick by current standards.

"Sure doesn't look like a marine," he heard one trooper say to the other as the two approached him. "Turn around," the same voice barked. "Keep your hands where they are." Oddly to the citizen, each trooper patted him down.

"Did I do something?" he asked, more timidly than obstinately.

"We want your ID and the car papers."

"It's a rental."

"We know that. Are the papers in the car?"

"Yes. In the glove box."

"Do you consent to our getting them out? Is there a weapon in there?"

"You mean a gun, or something? Of course not! Go ahead, get the rental papers. I rented it at LAX a few days ago."

"We know that too. Close the car door and stand against it. Facing it."

"Was I speeding?"

"No."

"Then what is this about?"

"The feds have a bulletin out for a white Land Rover with this license plate."

"The feds? What does that mean?"

"FBI and Homeland Security. A toll booth camera picked up the plate an hour ago."

"My God."

"Is your name Langley?"

"No."

"Wilton Goodbow?"

"Wilton *who*? No!" He reached to his rear pocket, retrieved his wallet, and held it out behind his back. "Here. Here's my wallet. Check my driver's license. My name is Eggle. Warren Eggle. I'm from Omaha. I never heard of those other guys."

"Just stay right there. Don't move."

One officer took the wallet and inspected the Nebraska driver's license. The other pulled the rental car folder from the glove compartment, then called his cohort over to his side of the Land Rover. They talked in low tones for two minutes, exchanging the wallet and rental papers. The frightened salesman leaned in to hear their susurrations, to no avail; the highway noise made it impossible.

"What are you doing in California?" they asked upon returning to him.

"I was attending a housewares trade show in Los Angeles. It ended this morning and I was driving up to see the wine country. I've never been there but I saw that movie *Sideways*. It looked fun. I'm going to Paso Robles."

"And you're telling us you don't know Huff Langley or Wilton Goodbow?"

"I don't. I don't. Were they in the movie?"

"We would like you to get in the first police vehicle, sir. Voluntarily. Will you do that? We need to check some things out."

It was embarrassing and he was still frightened, but at least sitting in the rear of the police SUV he could hear what they were saying.

"Run his driver's license and this California plate," one said. The citizen from Omaha was awed by the instrumentation on the SUV dashboard. It looked like an airplane cockpit with a computer screen; even a printer. "A single DUI three years ago," the other trooper said a minute later. "Nothing else on him. The plate is registered to the car rental company. And it's for a white Land Rover, same model, same year."

"Is there a VIN for it?"

"Yeah."

"Print it."

A thin white slip of paper sputtered out from the dash and the trooper ripped it off like a cash register receipt. He compared it to the vehicle identification number printed on the rental papers. "Shit," he said, then quickly left the SUV and walked to the white Land Rover on the berm, leaning down at the driver's side windshield.

"Shit," he said again, returning to the police SUV. "This plate doesn't belong to this car." Both troopers looked at trepid Warren Eggle in the back seat. "Did you change it?"

"No. Of course not! I told you, I didn't do anything!"

"Maybe you didn't, maybe you did. But you're not driving away in a car with a plate registered to a different one. It'd be the same as driving with no plate at all."

"You've got to be kidding!" the citizen said.

"There's a state police post thirty miles ahead. We're taking you there until we can straighten this out. We'll get your stuff from the car. A truck will come later to tow the vehicle."

"Am I under arrest?"

"Not yet," one trooper said. "Because we assume you'll come voluntarily. I mean, you wouldn't resist, would you, sir?"

"Well, if you put it that way, I guess I'll go."

"Buckle up," said the other trooper.

My word! the flummoxed citizen said to himself. *This didn't happen in the movie, did it?*

46

Whether the luckless Warren Eggle ever made it to Paso Robles was never reported, but it turned out in the end that his most severe consequence of the whole episode came not at the hands of the humorless California troopers but his even less humored wife in Omaha whom the police called to verify his trade show story. He'd never told her about the DUI—or the post-tradeshow escapade to wine country. You could say he achieved his "sideways" after all, just not in the manner he'd intended.

But the discovery of the switched plate was unfortunate for Goodbow too, though he had no way of knowing it had been made. Huff Langley acted as if it was inevitable. Every time Goodbow spoke with him on Sr. Hope Annie's burner phone, the marine asked if he'd been stopped yet.

"You seem worried about it," Goodbow said in their last call.

"I am. It's only a matter of time. Either the driver of that other Land Rover is going to return it, or he's going to be stopped. The changed plate is going to be found out eventually.

For all we know, it already has, and they've put it together. They could be looking for your Nevada plate right now."

"Well, Winnemucca's pretty out-of-the-way."

"Yeah, but you've got a lot of ground to cover, if you're still planning on driving to Minnesota. Maybe you shouldn't. Maybe you should just return it to Klamath Falls."

"Won't they know it then?"

"You could drop it after hours. It's a tiny airport there."

"And then rent my own car the next day?"

"No way. You'd have to show your driver's license and it would light up their screen. And even if it didn't, you'd be in the system and the FBI would have it in hours. You should just get out of Dodge. Fly back home and let the nuns do the rest."

"No, I'm going to Minnesota. I want to see them reunited. I want to see it through. See through my promise. And if I didn't, I'd feel like I left Sr. Hope Annie holding the bag. She'd be blamed alone if they find her there with the families."

"It's your hide, Goodbow," Huff said. "So far, you've done nothing wrong in the US. *I* changed those plates, and they can't even prove that I did. It could have been a screw up at the rental lot. But if you change cars in your own name—which I don't recommend—it's on you."

"I understand. I'm not going to do that. I'm driving this one to Breckenridge. I like driving it, by the way."

"Well, if you do, stay off toll roads. They've all got cameras. And there won't be a ton of Nevada plates to screen from. They'll pick it up fast. And never park with the plate showing, if you can."

"You sound like a professional fugitive."

"You're catching up with me," Huff Langley said.

* * *

Coincidentally, Burp Lebeau's ocean journey to San Diego with his new passengers, from their boarding in Amapala, was about the same distance in nautical miles as Goodbow's inland excursion from northern Nevada to Minnesota in land miles. About fifteen-hundred. But Lebeau's required twice as many days, sailing eighteen-hours each one. His course took him northwest along the coasts of El Salvador, Costa Rica and Guatemala, then more northerly for most of the length of Mexico, darting sharply west to the Pacific side of its Baja Peninsula, then due north to the U.S. border.

Goodbow called every night. The Honduran parents had been restless the first night, Burp reported, but seemed more relaxed the next, and even more the third. No one was ill and there were no objections to his cooking. The old sailor prepared simple dishes in large pots; stews and chowders and rice each night that he varied with different vegetables.

He found Mrs. Carrasco looking through the larder in the galley and, with Juan's help with English, she asked if she could cook dinner the fourth night.

"She says she likes to cook," Juan translated. "She says she could cook good food with what you have. Can she?"

"Sure she can," Burp said.

"She says, is spicy all right?"

"Fine by me," he said. Juan looked puzzled; he did not understand the expression.

"By *you*? But she wants to cook it."

"No, I mean that's fine. It's okay," Burp said. "Okay for her to cook, and spicy is okay."

"She says she will make Gloria's favorite dishes."

"Gloria?"

"Her child. She is very excited to be going to her."

About as excited, it turned out, as Burp and the parents were with her preparations. Her dishes were succulent. She saw the pleasure in the captain's face and smiled wildly. He didn't need Spanish to show his approval; she didn't need English to show her pride.

Soon after their departure from Amapala, the captain reminded them all that they could not come to the deck when boats were in sight or if airplanes were heard in the sky. He worried that staying below so much would cause sea sickness, but there wasn't any. Still, he watched for every opportunity to invite them up, and stayed far enough out to sea so that the starboard shore was below the horizon. All instantly welcomed the chance to come up each time Juan relayed the permission.

"When will you reach San Diego?" Goodbow asked in their nightly call.

"Before the whiskey runs out."

"Seriously."

"If these winds hold, four days. Do they know I'm coming at La Jolla Bay?"

The La Jolla Bay Sailing Club was the luxury sailing yacht marina where wealthy mariners could dock on call. Almost like a time share, a boat owner like Wilton Goodbow could, for a large one-time fee, enjoy mooring privileges at a dozen high-end boating clubs on the West Coast. Reservations could be made well in advance and adjusted on a moment's notice in the event of bad weather or unanticipated detours. Will, Grace and *Grace* had been there a half-dozen times.

"Yeah, but I gave them a range of days," Goodbow said. "Now, I'll tell them to expect you in four. But they told me there's weather brewing north in the Pacific."

"I saw that," Burp said.

"Expected to hit San Diego in five or six days."

"I saw that too. That's why I'll try to be in dock in four."

"You know you'll have to bring her in after dark."

"I figured."

"Way after dark. When the club staff is down to zero, or nearly."

"You mean they don't have a dozen Central American refugees and nuns on their piers every day of the week?"

"Not hardly. But remember that time we moored there a few years ago? We came in at midnight. There wasn't a soul there."

"I do."

"I didn't give them your name. Only mine. I told them we wouldn't need anybody to assist."

"Why would I? I've got a crew of twelve."

47

Even the finest sailor cannot anticipate everything the sea throws; even the most advanced technology will not always signal warning soon enough.

Burp Lebeau knew from his ocean charts that the seas surrounding the Baja were dotted with volcanic remnants. The largest ones were not the most dangerous. Their peaks rose above the water's surface in any tide, visible in daylight and invariably displayed on *Grace's* sonar screen in the helm console. Burp never relied only on the sonar; to him it was a redundant safeguard to his own eyes. He'd deliberately anchored the night before well in advance of darkness for this reason. Mooring early for one night would cost him four hours of progress toward San Diego, but he was confident time was ample. Goodbow wanted him to arrive late in the evening anyway. For safety, he could spare the sailing time.

The more nettlesome volcanic masses were the smaller ones that lay submerged, huge black boulders joined together in startling shapes with jagged edges often caused by collisions over the centuries. Usually, they laid near the larger peaks and

Burp set a course he judged safely distant from them. But at eleven in the morning, in full sun and moderate sea with nothing visible above the surface ahead, the console erupted in a warning siren and audible signal: "STRUCTURE AHEAD STARBOARD! STRUCTURE AHEAD STARBOARD!"

Had he not been standing at the helm at that instant, the result could have been disastrous. He spun the big wheel to turn *Grace's* rudder as left as it could go, trimmed the mainsails to the portside, and watched the sonar monitor as the boat approached the submerged rocks.

Left, Grace. Left, Grace. More!

The bow of the ship was only ninety feet from the rugged structure when he saw that the keel beneath the hull was angling just enough left to pass by cleanly. He breathed in relief. A fractured keel was irremediable at sea; the whole cause would be lost. But now he worried that the rudder below the aft was in harm's way. The maneuver had sent it to the starboard side, exposing it to the rocks that the keel would evade. He knew what he must do. He must time a turn of the rudder starboard—*toward* the danger—so that the rudder would move left for clean passage. But he must do it at just the right moment so that the bow and keel, which would then veer right, would do so only once the keel passed the rocks safely. It was the only way to save both the keel *and* the rudder.

He glared at the sonar monitor tracking his course toward the structure. Fifty feet. Thirty-five feet. The rudder was on a line for collision. At twenty-five feet he spun the wheel to the right as far as it would turn, until he heard the chain cables strain. His heart raced and he looked over the helm, his eyes closed. *Make it, Grace! Make it, Grace!* He heard the scraping from the aft, and then the metallic thud as the ship's hull bounced slightly. Contact, he knew; but not hard impact. He checked the console dials and the sonar ahead. All was clear.

He brought the mainsails back to full extension and reset his course according to his charts. He moved the helm wheel port and starboard. The rudder responded normally.

He knew the episode had frightened the passengers. A few of the couples had been on deck when the alarm first signaled and he had ordered them to get below, more sharply than he wished. He stepped halfway down the stairs and called to Juan Rodriguez.

"It's okay! We are fine. Come up if you want to. We are safe."

He thought it was true.

48

"Do you think my scar will go away?"

Little Gloria Carrasco wrenched herself against the car door so that she could extend her bare foot high toward Maria behind the wheel. The road sign read, "Fargo 220 Mi."

"I don't know. Probably."

"I hope it doesn't," Gloria said.

"Really? Why not?"

"It doesn't hurt anymore, and I want to remember it. It's how I got to America."

"Sr. Hope Annie says you were showing it to the boys."

"I was. They wanted me to. They said it was cool."

"Boys think a lot of things are cool."

"My mom was so scared when it was bad. She thought I was going to die. They didn't let her come to the hospital. Or my father. Sr. Hope Annie said they wanted to."

"She's right. Sr. Hope Annie was right."

"She's nice."

"She is."

"She's like a mom, but funnier."

"She is."

"She smokes!"

"She does."

"She found the family you are taking me to, didn't she?"

"Yes."

"How?"

"I really don't know, exactly. But she found out that some other children are there too."

"Did she tell them about my foot?"

"She told them you have a beautiful foot. And they said, 'Well, then, she can come!'"

"Do they have boys?"

"I'm not sure. Maybe."

"I hope so."

"Take a nap. We still have a long way to drive."

"How come I can go to this family in America, but my parents can't?"

"I wish they could. And maybe they can someday. I know it doesn't make sense. But good people are trying to change it, Gloria."

"Sr. Hope Annie said I should have faith."

"She would."

"Do you have faith?"

"I try to."

"I want to try to, too."

"We can try together. But now, try to sleep."

49

The Sails of Grace was only a hundred miles from San Diego when Burp Lebeau first noticed the sound rising from below the helm wheel. It was a squeak initially, so faint that the old captain thought it might be distant birdsong, frolicking gulls. But when he went to his knees and put his ear to the deck of the console it was clearly discernible whenever the wheel was turned more than thirty degrees. He put it down at first to a stretched cable, or maybe a stainless-steel pulley that disoriented in the hard, full turn he had forced on the rudder to avoid damaging it on the submerged boulders off the Baja. Nothing too serious, he reasoned. Once his passengers had disembarked at the yacht club, he could take apart the decking and readjust the parts.

He'd told Juan to keep all of the parents below deck as they sailed north in the afternoon sun. Navy ships of all manner dotted the horizon and the large coast guard station was not far ahead. He angled west and took a course thirty miles out from shore, beyond site of any vessels except a few deep-sea fishing cruisers. He wanted no one to observe anything unusual that might prompt a search or inquiry.

Grace sailed by the fleet and the station beyond the starboard horizon without incident. He began to relax. He could easily maintain his course until he was lateral to Lo Jolla, then turn directly into the yacht club under cover of night.

On the sea, a plan is always a plan until it isn't anymore.

At nine o'clock, just as his bearing was taking *Grace* on a straight line into the La Jolla Bay Club, a group of three coast guard vessels appeared ahead on the horizon line. He checked his GPS measurements, then moved up onto the deck to examine them through the telescope affixed near the bow. The boats were sitting only a mile at most offshore, he judged. And worse, they were *sitting*. Literally, *sitting*. Anchored for the night, he presumed.

Goodbow answered on the first ring.

"I didn't wait for you, Burp," he said. "I'm on number two already."

"I may need more than two," Burp said.

"Is something wrong?"

"I'm fifteen miles offshore of the club."

"Well, that sounds good. You can wait a little while and then take her in."

"Through the hulls of three big coast guard boats?"

"What?"

"Three coast guard boats. What the hell are they doing there so far north of Tijuana or their station?"

"Aren't they moving?" Goodbow asked. "They're probably heading down there."

"No, they're moored, Will. Fifty yards apart. They're not going anywhere tonight."

"Can you tell what kind of ships they are?"

"They look like search and rescue. I could see smaller boats and rafts hanging over their sides. It must be that storm out in the Pacific. They must be staging. In case they're needed."

"Well, you'd better wait then," Goodbow said. "You can't get around them if they're that close to the club."

"You really think they'd paid attention to a boat like *Grace?*"

"Maybe not. But I'd hate to risk it when you've brought them this far."

Lebeau dialed his radar monitor to see what it showed north and west in the Pacific.

"There is weather out there," he said. "Nasty, too. It's probably ten hours out from the LA port. There's always a lot of traffic in that water. They're probably waiting to go out there."

"Is it heading to you too?"

"Not right now. It shows it turning northward once it hits Los Angeles."

"Then let's delay the delivery until midnight tomorrow. Hope the coast guard is gone by then. I'll tell the nuns."

"Aye, aye," said the captain. If his words suggested sarcasm, it was not, in truth, intended and not received as such by his friend from New England as he poured his third and last bourbon in his Winnemucca motel room.

"I'll back out a few miles and anchor for the night," Lebeau said.

"Gloria's mother still cooking?" Goodbow asked.

"Yeah. I've lost that job."

50

Elation has a way of turning to deflation in an instant. And when it does, at the most inopportune times. The unanticipated harsh word of a spouse in a moment of presumed tenderness; a home run by the weak-hitting visiting foe on an 0-2 pitch from the star hurler, stunning the hometown fans. For Burlacher and Everett, it was the text message from the Santa Barbara post of the California State Police:

Isolated and stopped desired CA license plate on rental car from LAX. Driver in custody.

But the message went on:

Driver not, repeat not, H. Langley or Wilton Goodbow. Driver is salesman from Omaha; no criminal record. Plate did not match VIN of apprehended car, a new white Land Rover. CA plate belongs to different Land Rover, same color and model, from same LAX rental lot. Plates presumably swapped by undetermined person; possibly employee error.

At large plate: NV 168P14. New APB issued. Will advise. CSP.

"Employee error, my ass," Burlacher said.

"Maybe it was," Everett said. "They *were* the same model. Maybe there was a mix-up at the lot. But who cares? We've got the right plate now."

"They could be anywhere by now," Burlacher said, dejectedly. "It's been a week!"

"What makes you think Langley and Goodbow are still together?"

"Why wouldn't they be?" Burlacher asked.

"Maybe they are. But if that plate was swapped, one of them knows what he's doing. I doubt it's the rich guy."

"Why do you say that? If Langley's so smart, why did he take a plate from the same damn model?"

"To get out of the lot. A Chevy Malibu pulls up, the guy at the check-out gate sees the wrong paperwork right away. But when he looks down and reads 'Land Rover, White,' he probably doesn't look further."

"They teach you that at Quantico?"

"No, my kid brother pulled it once as a stunt. To see if he could get away with it."

"Did he?"

"He did from the rental car outfit, at least for a while. But he didn't from our dad. It was dad's credit card account and when the rental people eventually found out, they hit him with a big charge. That was the last 'additional user' card the old man ever gave any of us."

"The sins of your brother," Burlacher said.

"There's always somebody sinning."

51

The captain went below to find Juan Rodriguez. He needed him to explain to the others that the plan had changed; they could not sail into the port that night. The rendezvous with the nuns at the boat club had to be delayed by one day.

"But only one, right?" asked Juan. "Only one more night?" Lebeau saw that all of the other parents were looking at them talking, anxious to know what was being said. "I will want to tell them it is just one more night and day," Juan said.

"Yes," Lebeau said. "Only one more day. We will go into the docks tomorrow night at the same time."

He knew he shouldn't have been so definitive; he could not truly know that the coast guard vessels would leave by then. But he saw the concern leaping from Juan Rodriguez's eyes. He thought that if he said he didn't know with certainty that the attempt could be made the next night, nervousness would spread among them all. Quarters below were close enough, without nervousness.

He checked the radar and the projected sweep of the storm

to the northwest. The radio confirmed it was a large weather formation but not an extreme one. It was not yet a so-called "named storm", and not expected to turn into one. But with sustained winds of thirty miles per hour, heavy rain and lightning, he knew it was no storm to sail in voluntarily, even if an experienced crew was on board to help manage it. If he anchored *Grace* in place, most of the storm would pass to their north. But not all of it, he judged. The southern tip of the system would extend to them before sunrise. Better to move out further to sea.

The waves were picking up, normal ahead of weather approaching from the north. He set the electronic furling booms to a course due west by turning the helm wheel eighty degrees. The wheel spun roughly. He sensed danger. As the four mainsails unfurled and loaded with wind, he heard the rattle-whine-snap of the rudder chain and the immediate dull thumping of the chain swinging freely against the submerged hull. The helm wheel went limp, tensionless. He could spin it like a gyroscope.

"*Oh, fuck!*" he shouted.

There are some words that require no translation. Several of the men below rushed up the stairs to him, fear in their faces. Rudderless, *The Sails of Grace* rolled in the sea, listing severely.

"What is happening?" Juan asked.

Lebeau did not answer him, just burst past the men and down the stairs to the galley. He pulled a leather tool bag from under the sink and raced to the rear of the boat. Against the hallway near his own quarters, he unflapped a long compartment and pulled out the emergency tiller, an oar-like length of stainless steel, nine-feet long, with a flat square flange at one end drilled with four bolt holes and a series of grips leading to the other. *Goddamnit, I should have checked that tiller chain in Newport!*

He waved the frightened parents to the side and pulled the steel tiller through the galley and up to the helm console. On the floor beneath the wheel he unbolted a hatch to the rudder post and reached for the dismounted chain, pulling it up through the hatch-hole with both hands. It dropped with a thud to the console base and he fastened the square flange of the steel tiller handle to the emergency fitting with a socket wrench, giving each nut an extra tug for surety.

It had been years since he'd handled *Grace* with the emergency tiller, and then merely to see how it maneuvered the ship. Never in waves this firm. He was surprised how easily he was able to bring *Grace* about and trim the tall sails so that the boat leveled. He glanced down the stairs and smiled at Juan and the parents huddled with him; saw relief come into their faces. But he knew, knew somberly, that there was no true cause for enduring relief. He could manage the movement of the rudder in this wind, and for a short time. But it was like holding a basketball in your palm, waist high. For a minute or two, bearable. Try holding it for thirty. Inevitable collapse.

More than five minutes had lapsed during the rudder procedure and the wind had pushed *Grace* a mile inland, further into the path of the oncoming storm. Using the manual tiller, Lebeau directed the rudder and sails upwind to move the boat portside and west to what he hoped would be safer seas to sit out the storm, further from shore and the coast guard vessels that had come back into view, still motionless.

Juan and the others saw the dark sky to the north. "What will we do?" Juan asked.

"We're moving farther out," Lebeau said. "Most of the storm will pass closer to the shore. When we are out far enough, I will take down all the sails and we will ride out the winds that reach us."

"Wouldn't it be better to go now to the land?"

"It would. Yes. But we can't. You would be found. I have been in many storms when I could not sail into shore. With the sails down, we will be safe. The boat is big enough to sit through the wind."

"Okay," Juan said, tentatively.

"Go back down to the others. Tell them it will be all right. Tell Mrs. Carrasco to cook now, before the waves get worse. I'll eat mine up here so I can man this tiller."

"What should she cook?"

"Spicy is fine," the captain said.

52

When Goodbow reached Sr. Hope Annie he found her untroubled by the news that the offboarding of the parents was set back a night.

"Well," she said. "Everything can't go right on schedule. That would get boring. Besides, it will give me a day with the Dominican. She's here with us. With the van. It's like one of those airport shuttles. I can get used to driving it; we're going to take turns."

But Huff Langley was less accepting of Goodbow's insistence that he leave the mission and return home to El Paso. He'd grown comfortable around the nun. To the point of liking her and enjoying the banter between them. She reminded him of a female sergeant he'd been posted with in Iraq, he told Goodbow. "At first, I was surprised she was even there," he said to Goodbow about the soldier. "That she was in a goddamned battle group. So, I was skeptical, like most of us. But after a while, I saw she had guts as good as anybody else's." They'd become friends and comrades on many patrols, even asking to be assigned together. Huff felt the same way now about Sr. Hope Annie.

"Why can't I stay with her for the ride to Minnesota?" he asked. "I think I should."

"Well, I don't," said Goodbow. "You were with me in Tegus, you were with me in Los Angeles. You rented my car. You know they're looking for you just as much as they're looking for me. If the van is stopped with you in it, they'll have cause to hold everybody. If you're not in it, that nun may be able to talk her way out of it. You know how she is."

"And if they stop you in your car? What happens then?"

"If they do, they do. That won't keep the nuns from getting the parents to their kids. And don't worry, your name is not coming out of my mouth. Any more than the captain's. I can't help what they already know about what you've done for us, but they won't learn any more from me. You have my word."

"You're saying it's best for everybody if I step out."

"I am."

"Maybe I should trail them. Stay close enough so if they get in a jam they could call me."

"No. You need to go home. They can manage."

Silence came over the phone. Goodbow said no more; he knew better than to push further, and he was sure Huff understood the sense of his insistence.

"Okay," Huff said finally. "Okay. I'll stay in San Diego for a day after they leave. I won't fly from here because they'll know then that I was here. I'll take a bus to El Paso. The bus records are crap."

"At least eat and drink well," Goodbow said. "Just put it all on my bill."

"Oh, believe me. I will."

53

The Sails of Grace rocked wildly in the sea as the storm roared. Burp Lebeau struggled at the tiller, trying to find the rudder's most stable position in the thrusting waves. It was the worst kind of gale, with spinning gusts, pushing the water unpredictably. *No consistency,* Lebeau thought. *No goddamned consistency.* Old sailors called it "confused sea." If only the wind would begin driving in the same direction—any direction—he could lock the rudder with the hydraulic controls. He could get off the heavy tiller stick and settle down the parents cowering below. But when he tried to stabilize the rudder with the automatic lock, he had no sooner fixed the controls when the vessel heeled violently starboard or port, or fore or aft, answering a reverse ocean gust. If he had not completely downed the mainsails and the fore and aft jibs before the storm's intensity picked up— "laying ahull" as sailors put it—he knew the lurches might have killed them all.

He leaned toward the hatch and called as loudly as he could. "Juan! Juan! Come up here!"

Juan Rodriguez climbed up to the captain, holding both

side rails of the hatchway stairs to steady himself. He was a strong man. It was one reason Burp had summoned him. But there was another reason. He could talk to the other men to recruit more assistance.

"Yes, captain!" Juan said. "What is it you want? Everyone is frightened down there."

"I need two men who can understand me. You are one. Is there another who speaks some English?"

"Miguel."

"The small man?"

"He is small, but he is brave. He can say only a little English, but he understands more."

"Get him. And get a life jacket on. Him too."

Burp held the tiller in a death grip, waiting for Miguel and Juan to return to the deck. He wished he could leave it or lock it so that he could walk with the men to the slender jib sales at the front and the back of the boat and show them what he wanted them to do to steady the boat. But the crashing waves to the hull caused the rudder to bolt whenever he released pressure on the tiller even a little. The only way he could keep the boat relatively stable was to move the tiller constantly in response to the forces on the hull and keel. He was like a rodeo rider atop a bronco, managing the to-and-fro and back-and-forth purely with reflex, instinct and strength.

"Come close to me!" he shouted at the two men when they appeared at the top of the hatch. The wind and waves were deafening. "Bend over to me so you can listen!" Juan and Miguel leaned down to him, inches from his rough face. "We have to get control of the boat," he said. "With all the sails down, the water is taking us wherever it wants."

"But you put all the sails down to keep us from blowing over, didn't you?" Miguel asked.

"Yes, but the forces of the water below and at the sides of

the boat are too great now. With the sails down, the wind will not blow us over, but I am afraid the waves will." Burp knew as quickly as the word "afraid" left his lips that he should not have used it. *Afraid!* The eyes of the two fathers were filled already with enough fear for a dozen men. "But don't worry! See, I am holding it steady enough with the tiller. But this will not work if the waters rush much more." A high wave slammed the port side near the bow; the sudden force fired the tiller handle port-side too. The captain lost his footing momentarily as he struggled to keep both hands and wrists on it.

"What will you do?" Juan asked.

"*We,* Juan," the captain said. "What *we* will do. I have to stay here and ride this tiller. But I am going to tell you two what to do. What to do to help us." Miguel and Juan nodded seriously.

"We must get the boat moving under some wind. But not too much wind. And not with the big sails. That will be too much. It will pull the keel from the water and over we'll go. But look at the front of the deck and the back. Do you see those narrow sails? They are thin and not as tall as the main masts. Do you see them?"

Miguel and Juan peered to the bow and the stern through the whistling rain and the free-swinging chrome clips and ropes.

"Yes," Juan said. "There are two sails on each pole. They are skinny. I remember them from when we were sailing before the storm."

"Right. There are two separate sails at each end. They're the jib sails. You're right, they're skinny and not as tall. They catch some wind, but not too much. We need to raise only one jib at each end of the boat. In a special way."

"But before you raised them with the motor. With the switches. Are the motors broken?" Juan looked terrified.

"No, the motors are fine. But they will only raise *both* of the sails at the front and both of them at the back. We must raise only *one* of each, and at a special angle, not the angle they would usually go. So we have to raise them by hand. By *your* hands. Yours and Miguel's. One of you at the bow, the other at the back." Burp saw the two men look at each other and nod. "Does Miguel understand what I said, Juan?"

"I think so."

"I must know for sure that he understands. Tell him what I said."

Juan used his hands liberally, pointing to the bow and then to the stern, and to Burp and Burp's hands on the throbbing tiller. Miguel listened as Juan held up two fingers, then one, then two and one again. Miguel nodded.

"He understands," Juan said. "What is the special angle? How do we know to do it that way?"

"At the base of the gib masts, at the bottom of each of the skinny sails, there is a dial. The numbers go from 30 to 90. The first thing you each do is turn that dial to 90. *Nine zero.* There is a handle and clamp to lock it there. Lock it." Juan nodded. "Explain it to Miguel."

There was more of the talking hands.

"He understands."

"And there is one last thing you must understand. You and Miguel must raise the sails at the same time! So that you are pulling them up at the same speed and they reach the top of the masts at the same time. Or damned near the same time. You must be watching each other and listening to me as you pull. Unclip the rope of one sail and look to me for the signal to begin pulling. When the sail is all the way up there will be no more rope to pull. Put the clip back on the mast."

Burp Lebeau had used the maneuver only twice in his life on the seas, and then with experienced crew. The object was to get the craft moving in a direction—any direction—that could thereafter be predicted, and therefore managed by the tiller and rudder. As it now lay in the sea "out of irons" and unable to be anchored, *The Sails of Grace* was at the will and mercy of water movement alone. Violent, changing, swirling water movement. By raising one small sail at the bow and one at the stern, each held perpendicular to the hull, he hoped that within seconds the boat would "find wind," but not too much of it. He couldn't know until then whether it was pushing him or pulling him. But he didn't much care. Once he had manageable wind power—a fraction of the power the mainsail would throw—he could orient the vessel with the tiller and move slowly upwind —"tacking"—against its drag. Oh, it would not be smooth sailing, that he knew. But it wouldn't be this perilous thrashing left, right, up and down. And when finally the storm receded, he could reset all of the sails and make a plan to return to course.

Water crashed over the deck as the two Hondurans crouched and scrambled to opposite ends of the boat. Burp watched as they knelt over the gauges. Juan seemed to rise too quickly at the bow.

"Lock it in!" Burp screamed through the wind. "Did you lock it in!"

Juan turned and knelt again to secure the setting. At the stern, much closer to him, Burp could see that Miguel had secured his gauge. The captain could only hope he'd turned it to 90 degrees but knew he would see soon enough when the pulling began.

Burp threw his right hand up. "Now!" he cried. "Now! Watch each other!"

Miguel and Juan pulled on the ropes and the jibs began to rise. The hull rocked, as if puzzled, and Burp rode the tiller handle with all the strength he could muster, responding to its vibration. He was pleased that the men watched each other closely. Immediately it was clear that both sails were rising in the perpendicular position Burp wanted and—fortunately—not directly into or against the wind. Burp wrestled the tiller to keep the rudder and keel where it was, preventing them from finding much wind until the jibs were fully up and secured, and the men back to him safely. If a powerful gust found the jibs, slender as they were, the vessel might bolt or heel before he could stabilize it and turn it into the wind.

Miguel crawled back from the bow; Juan from the stern. They looked puzzled. The sails were flapping but the boat was not really moving. "Did we do it wrong?" Juan asked.

"No, No. You did it right. Hold on to the rail. Now I can see how to move into a safe wind."

He moved the tiller. A little left, then further left, then back a fraction. Even in the fierce noise, an audible swoosh sent *The Sails of Grace* upwind, into the waves as if in slow motion. The deck leveled and Burp locked the emergency tiller in place.

"Where are we going?" asked Juan.

"Out of the storm," Burp said. "Out of the storm with *Grace*."

* * *

On this, the captain was correct. An hour later, *The Sails of Grace* emerged from the winds and into calm dark seas beneath an umbrella of stars. As soon as he could find water suitably shallow, Lebeau dropped the bib sails and both anchors to moor for the night.

The old captain was exhausted. He had wrestled with the terror of the sea and, at last, subdued it to tranquility. For him, the struggle of the past hours was hardly a new experience. Far from it. His decades at sea were a scrapbook of such episodes and some had been worse. But the leather-skinned sailor knew the same could not be said for his frightened passengers below. Almost cruelly, the vicious storm had rolled in so near the end of their journey to the American *terra firma* they prayed for, prayed for so dearly. It was as if the storm was bent on dashing their hopes—and their very lives—just when they could finally believe that, yes, they might reach their children.

Lebeau knew the parents did not share his fatigue and his desire for sleep; he knew that fear invigorates and that sleep would come slowly to them. He could not retire to his quarters and leave them in their fear. He checked the mooring straps and descended. He found Juan first and asked him to translate for him. He spoke to each man and woman individually. At first, it was difficult for him to smile as he spoke, but when he saw the gratitude in their eyes returning his assuring words, it became easier.

"We are safe now," he said. "Go up and look. Look at the stars and see how clear the sky is now. How calm the sea is." They all did, except for little Gloria's mother and Juan. They waited below with Lebeau.

"Captain," she said with Juan's help. "I will cook you some beans and rice with scallop and chiles. You didn't eat very much."

"I couldn't. I wanted to."

"I will cook it for you. Spicy, yes? I will cook it. As soon as I go up and see the stars."

* * *

At daybreak, Lebeau spotted the three coast guard vessels on the horizon, moving out to sea. The path was cleared for the delivery that night. The parents would step from the dock to American soil in the deserted yacht club and begin their journey to the Upper Midwest.

But the storm was only beginning for Will Goodbow.

PART IV

54

The FBI Learjet taxied into a hangar at the Klamath Falls, Oregon airport with Burlacher and Everett aboard. It was the same place that Huff Langley had suggested Goodbow leave the rented Land Rover afterhours, the suggestion Goodbow had rejected a few days earlier. But the Bureau agents didn't fly to Klamath Falls to inquire about a rental car. They went there on account of the wonder of telecommunications technology. For Goodbow, the frightening wonder.

The agents' request for tracking of the Rhode Island cell phone number had been dispatched to the Bureau's Pittsburgh field office because one of the Bureau's national cyber command units was located there. A call from Breen Edwards pushed the request to the front of the line and a labyrinthian web of satellite tracers were launched almost immediately.

"Winnemucca, Nevada?" Burlacher said when he and Evcrett received the first report from Pittsburgh. "Where the hell is that?"

"Where we're going," Everett said.

Within hours they walked into the lobby of the *Mountain View Lodge and Resort*.

"We're looking for a man who made calls from a cell phone here," Burlacher announced abruptly to the elegant-looking woman at the registration desk. "A bunch of them over the past week." He thrust his credentials toward her and held it open over the counter.

"Would you keep your voice down," she said, displaying a decided lack of intimidation. "There's no need for a scene here."

"Well, it's urgent."

"Then you might start by telling me his name. Since it's urgent."

"Goodbow. G-O-O-D-B-O-W. Wilton Goodbow. Is he staying here?"

"Oh, Mr. Goodbow!" She seemed to soften. "Do you work for him? He's a very nice man."

"No, we don't work for him. We want to find him. He's a person of interest to the government."

"What kind of interest? He's a nice gentleman."

"Ma'am. Is he here?"

"He *was* here, but he checked out yesterday."

"When, yesterday?"

"After breakfast. He said he enjoyed it very much. And his whole stay here."

"Did he say where he was going?"

"Why would he say where he was going?"

"Please, ma'am. Can you please just answer the question?"

"No, he didn't. And I don't care for your tone, young man."

"I'm sorry," Burlacher lied. He wasn't in the least.

"I'm sorry too, ma'am," Everett said, more genuinely, stepping next to his partner. "You said Mr. Goodbow was a nice gentleman. Did you speak to him often when he was staying here?"

"Every day, I think."

"What did you talk about?"

"Just about the area. About family. He told me he'd lost his wife recently."

"How did that come up?"

"I asked if he was married. I'm not. I told you, I thought he was a nice man. Gentle. Handsome. Big."

"Did he say why he was here? In Winnemucca?"

"He said he'd heard from a friend that it was a good place to relax. Good views. Natural beauty. He drove around the area a lot, little excursions."

"Was he alone?"

"Well, nobody stayed with him, if that's what you mean. And I don't think he had any visitors or relatives around here. But he was sociable with us. Enjoyed the food and the bar. I heard he tipped very well. Not all tourists do. A lot of them think, 'I'm never going to see this person again, so why leave a big tip.' But he wasn't like that."

"His car," Everett said. "What was he driving?"

"It was like a big jeep. White." She went to a drawer and retrieved a folder. "Here it is," she said. "A Land Rover. License plate NV168P14."

"He gave you that plate number?"

"Why wouldn't he? It was his car! Why are you looking for him? Did he do something wrong?"

"We don't know."

"Well, that would be a surprise to me. He just seemed like a nice gentleman doing a little touring after he'd been through some things; after his wife had died."

"How many bartenders do you have?"

"One and a half. One full time, another on weekends."

"Are they both here?"

"Is this the weekend?" she asked dryly. It was Wednesday. *On TV they seem sharper than this!*

"All right. Is *he* here?"

"Comes in at four-thirty."

"We'll wait."

The two agents took seats at the far end of the rustic lobby. The bartender was due in an hour. Maybe by then there would be another ping report from the Pittsburgh monitors.

"Don't let it bother you, Burl," Everett teased the other agent. "You're probably just not her type."

"What are you talking about?"

"You had to notice. She liked Goodbow a lot more than she likes you."

* * *

It turned out to be an hour poorly spent by the agents. The bartender was cooperative—and easier to question than the lady at the front desk—but he offered nothing more than she. Goodbow hadn't talked about what he was doing in town or where he was headed next. "Just a nice old guy and a great tipper," was his report.

Goodbow remained at large.

55

In little Breckenridge, the mood was festive, anticipatory. Not only among the foster parents of the Honduran children but once word got out that another child was coming, the whole town, it seemed. The main street department store delivered a new bed frame, box spring mattress set, and fresh linens to the Swensen home—the largest of the houses in the church group of foster parents—and wouldn't be paid for them. The local clothing store sent six outfits for a nine-year old girl and sneakers in four sizes with a note that the pairs not fitting the newcomer should be given to others of the refugee children who could wear them. And the Lutheran minister, the Rev. Burton Leif, arranged a welcoming party in the church hall for anyone interested, complete with refreshments, baked goods and even a performance by Angelo Presti, an electronic accordion player who, though Catholic, was a fixture at town celebrations with his medleys of every ethnic music genre imaginable.

"Does he do Honduran?" the Lutheran minister had asked

his Catholic counterpart when he called asking him to arrange his parishioner's attendance.

"If there is such a thing, Angelo will know it," the priest said. "Count on him. He'll be there. And I will be too."

From the reactions of the children when the big Italian piped up his broad accordion upon the noon arrival of Maria Angeles with little Gloria, he surely knew music familiar to them. The crowd was gathered on the church lawn, the waving Honduran children stood in front, when Maria pulled up amid Angelo Presti's buoyant chords.

"Is this for *me?*" Gloria exclaimed.

"Why, who else would it be for?" Maria said. "They are so happy to see you come! See?"

While the children gathered around Gloria, the minister came to greet Maria. He was a demure man with white hair and perfectly round tortoise shell polo glasses. He extended his small hand and smiled.

"Thank you, Maria. It is Maria, right?"

"Yes. Maria Angeles."

"You have come a long way to bring Gloria."

"She is a delightful child."

"She seems to be fitting in already."

"You know that she was very ill when she came into the country. A foot wound that became seriously infected."

"Yes, Sister Hope Annie told us."

"She is worried about her parents."

"Yes, all of the children are. But they won't be for long."

"What?" Maria was startled. "What do you mean?"

"Their parents are on the way here. Gloria's too. Didn't you know?"

"*No!* How are they getting here? They were all sent back to Honduras. I know that for a fact."

"They were sent back, yes. A year ago. But now Sister

Hope Annie and a Dominican nun from California are driving them here. To reunite them with their children."

"Did Lane Williams arrange this? Do you know him?"

"I know Mr. Williams, yes. The aid worker from Texas. He is the one who called me about Gloria; could she stay with one of the families here watching the others? Of course, I said yes. But he didn't tell me anything about the parents coming. I don't think he knew."

"Who told you they are coming?"

"Sister Hope Annie. A couple of days ago. I asked her how in the world this could be, and she said a man named Goodbow had come to her and that he had arranged it. That he'd found a way to get the parents from Honduras to California and that she was then bringing them here. With the other nun. In the other nun's van. You didn't know this?"

"No, Reverend. I know Sister Hope Annie, of course. I work with the Red Cross in El Paso. We all know her. And I have met Mr. Goodbow. But I did not know the parents were coming, or how."

"I am glad we talked, then," the minister said. "Because the children don't know yet. Sister Hope Annie was clear about that. They mustn't be told because she said it was possible it would not work out. They might not make it here. But, of course, I had to tell the foster parents, and she said that was okay so long as they knew not to mention it to the children."

"So the foster parents know?"

"Yes. And they are overjoyed. They all said they will make room in their homes for the parents, one way or another."

"And when is this all to happen?"

"I don't know for sure. She said she will call a day ahead. I think it will be any day now. But there will not be a big welcoming like this. Sister Hope Annie said there must be nothing like this. They will come late at night when the children are in bed. No one is to know until they have arrived and are settled with their children. So I have told no one in the town except the foster parents. I wouldn't have told you, but I assumed you must know since you have brought the new one."

"And Sister Hope Annie didn't tell you how the parents got into the US?"

"No. Just that this man Goodbow found a way. That was it."

Maria turned and looked at the scene on the church lawn. The children were all introducing Gloria to their foster parents. Many of the townspeople were heading into the church hall. Maria seemed deep in thought.

"Are you heading back to Texas right away?" the minister asked.

"I had intended to," she said. "But now I'm not sure."

"Well, you are welcomed to stay at the church residence." He pointed to a small brick bungalow behind the church parking lot, surrounded by a tended flower garden. "My wife and I have a spare room. Two, in fact. You must be tired of motels and food on the road."

"That's very kind of you," she said. "I will take you up on it."

She walked to her car to retrieve her small suitcase. *What have that nun and Goodbow done?* she thought.

56

The falling sun swept over the green barley fields of Idaho as Goodbow merged onto Interstate 84 toward Blackfoot and Idaho Falls on his second day since leaving Winnemucca. He didn't know that Idaho was so important in barley production. But it was plainly a subject of state pride. *The Best Beer Starts HERE,* read the billboards.

He'd traveled only a hundred-fifty miles the first day, reasoning he did not want to arrive in Minnesota too much in advance of the nuns' transport of the parents. In fact, he hoped that they would arrive before he did. He knew he was risking detection by even going there—Huff had argued against it—and worried that if he *were* found at the site before the parents met their children, their reunification might not happen at all.

But he was relieved that one of Huff's concerns had *not* materialized. The route to Breckenridge did not present a single toll road in its entire fifteen-hundred mile length. Just a series of interstates and well-groomed US highways with mild to little traffic. He almost wished for more traffic. He felt exposed and conspicuous rambling along with hardly a vehicle in sight. He looked in the rearview mirror incessantly, as Huff had urged, trying to make out police cars or state troopers approaching from the distance. Once that morning, a few miles over the Idaho line, he'd spotted one behind him and quickly turned off at an opportune exit before the cruiser was close enough to read his license plate. He waited a few minutes and fetched coffee at a truck stop before getting back on the interstate.

"Where are you now?" he asked when Sister Hope Annie answered. "Is this a good time to talk?"

"It's fine, yes," she said. "Sister Marcus Marie is driving now. It's my turn in an hour. We are in Utah. I think in about the middle. Is that right, Sister?" she asked the Dominican. "She says, yes, about the middle of Utah. It is very beautiful here!"

"No problems?"

"No. Everyone is fine. Sister Marcus Marie kept me out of trouble. We went through Las Vegas last night. I said, 'Why don't we stop and gamble? I'm feeling lucky.' But she didn't think it was a good idea."

"She was right. It wasn't."

"You'd get along with these Dominicans, Goodbow. You're both party poopers." She shot a teasing glance at the nun behind the wheel.

"And you reached the minister up there in Minnesota?"

"Yes. Burton Leif. A very nice man. He said Maria arrived with little Gloria and they all love her. He said Gloria is staying with the Rodriguez children. Juan's children. The Swensen family has taken them in. That will be our first stop when we arrive. I'll text you the address. That's where you should go too."

"Good."

"By the way, he said Maria is staying to wait for us."

"What?"

"He said he didn't know Maria didn't know about the parents coming. He told her I was bringing them. She was very surprised."

"I imagine."

"Why? Is that a problem?"

"I promised her I would not tell anyone about her. She has her husband to think about."

"So, you *won't* tell anybody."

"Well, I don't like the thought of her getting into trouble."

"You should be worrying more about yourself and not the rest of us. Here I am, a nun. You are the businessman. But I have to ask. Have you thought about getting a lawyer? I think you should."

"I thought you said I needed to have faith. You never mentioned a lawyer."

"Sometimes faith needs a helper."

"I hear you."

"Good. Get one. We should pull in tomorrow night. And bless you, Goodbow."

* * *

Twenty minutes later, Burlacher and Everett simultaneously received the text from the cyber surveillance office in Pittsburgh.

401.346.5858 pinged cell tower at mile marker 149, I-84, near Idaho Falls, ID:

1603:48. Idaho State Patrol notified. Question from them: if found, what is basis for arrest?

Everett immediately did a map search on his cell phone.

"Shit, he's got seven hours on us," he said. "At least."

"And he's headed *east!*"

"Yeah."

"Why east? Do you think he's going home to Rhode Island?"

"Why would a guy like that drive all that way? He flew to Texas—and first class, at that."

"I don't know. None of this makes sense for a guy like him."

"What's our answer to the question? What do they tell him if they find him before we do?"

"Person of interest in federal investigation."

"Can they hold him on that?"

"That's for them to decide. But they could sure as hell put a tail on him."

They left their lunch—half finished—and raced to their car.

57

"I don't see it," said Elias Humphrey, the chief federal judge of the FISA court to his two judicial colleagues examining the application before them, delivered that evening. "Here is a man with no criminal record, without even *suspected* connections to any terrorist organization. An American citizen of apparent means. He travels to Honduras to the US embassy there, a visit sanctioned by a legitimate NGO and accepted by the consulate there. What is the factual basis to infiltrate his phone calls?"

"I see your concerns," said one of the other judges. "But shouldn't we show some deference to the statements of the DHS Secretary? The man's wife was a vocal activist. Writing to the president and all."

"All within her rights as a citizen," Judge Humphrey said. "Anyone can write the president. She never made a physical threat. Nothing even approaching one in any of these letters. How does that make her husband a 'suspected conspirator against the United States?' I think it's without substantial foundation. They don't even claim he has actually done anything illegal."

"But the purpose of the statute is to prevent acts before they occur."

"*What* acts?" Humphrey asked. "Bombings. Killings. Terror attacks. By foreign actors. What is this old guy from Rhode Island going to do? Harvey, how do you see it?" he asked the third jurist.

"I'm with you, Elias," he said. "The Fourth Amendment has to mean more than this. The FBI has other ways to find him if they really need to, without any warrant. They have his cell phone number, they'll eventually locate him. They can question him, if he wants to talk to them. And if he doesn't, and they have probable cause that he's committed any crime, they can go to any judge for a regular warrant. I'm surprised Justice even brought this to us under FISA. I think it's an end-around. It's overreach."

A stenographer was called in and five minutes later the two-line ruling on the application was entered:

APPLICATION DENIED. PRESENTED GROUNDS INSUFFICIENT.

All three judges signed the order.

58

After speaking with the nun, Goodbow had driven longer than he'd intended. He was surprised that he never felt sleepy as the miles rolled past. Normally, he would keep himself alert with talk radio to engage his brain, but his senses seemed so heightened that he didn't feel aid was needed. Looking back later, he would realize that his growing fear was probably the stimulant. He was on the run and nearing his destination, whatever that destination might bring. It was an excitement new to him. And unsettling.

He didn't stop until he crossed into North Dakota and found a small town ten miles off the interstate. He noticed the expressway sign for a Holiday Inn Express and dutifully parked in the rear before entering.

"Just for the night," he told the night manager.

"Long day on the road?" the young man asked.

"You could say that."

"License number and model?"

"I really don't remember. It's a Land Rover of some kind."

"That's okay," the manager said. "Rental?"

"It is, yes."

"Nobody knows the plate numbers on them. It's fine. Just leave that blank."

"Appreciate it. Is that place across the driveway still open for dinner?"

"Willie's?"

"If that's what it's called."

The manager checked the time. "Another half hour."

"They have a bar?"

"Oh yeah."

A lot of decisions are made at bar counters, and though he couldn't have known it at the time, the one Goodbow made as he nursed his bourbon at Willie's that night likely made all the difference in what would transpire over the next twenty-four hours. He decided to wait until morning to call his lawyer friend from Boston, Tom Brewster. Oh, the blessing of a pingless night in North Dakota.

The hamburger at Willie's was satisfying and the mattress and sheets in his room more comfortable than he'd expected when he lowered himself into bed. His apprehension, dulled by the bourbon, receded quickly and he drifted to a sound sleep in minutes.

* * *

Unlike Agents Burlacher and Everett, and half the force of the Idaho Falls Police Department. All through the night, they covered the streets and parking lots of the city like a blanket, sweeping flashlights over a thousand license plates before giving up just before sunrise.

"No more pings?" asked a patrol officer to Burlacher.

"Not a Goddamned one," he said.

"I don't think he's in Idaho Falls any longer," the patrolman said. "We've looked everywhere. Let's call this off."

59

"Is anything I say to you confidential?" Goodbow asked his friend, Tom Brewster when the Boston lawyer returned his call late the next afternoon. "You know, because you're a lawyer?" His Land Rover steamed across North Dakota; his GPS navigation projected an eight-thirty arrival in Breckenridge at the Minnesota border.

"Not unless I'm *your* lawyer," Brewster said.

"How do you become my lawyer?"

"Easiest way is to pay me." Goodbow could almost see his amiable friend smiling on the other end of the phone.

"That figures."

"Honestly. That's true," Brewster said. "Okay if I send you a bill for a hundred-dollar consultation?"

"Only a hundred dollars? I thought firms like yours billed that much for a doughnut in the office."

"A hundred will do. Will you pay it?"

"Sure."

"Then I'm your lawyer and you're my client. Talk away.

What the hell is going on? Your voice message said you're driving to Minnesota, for Pete's sake."

"I may have gotten myself into some legal trouble."

"Did you do something illegal?"

"I don't know for sure. But I think, probably."

"There can be a lot of room between 'probably' and 'for sure.'"

"Well, I think I can use all the room I can get."

Brewster listened in amazement at what Goodbow told him. On the one hand it seemed preposterous that his conservative, mild-mannered and—to Brewster's knowledge—largely apolitical friend could have done the things he told him he'd done. But, on the other hand, Brewster thought, there was probably nothing Will Goodbow wouldn't do for his late wife, Grace. He had known Grace well—most everybody in Newport did—and he, like many others revered her. But all, including Tom Brewster, knew that no one revered her the way Will did. Except, maybe, crusty old Burp Lebeau.

"So you're going to be with these smuggled parents tonight?"

"Do you have to use that word?"

"Okay. These elegantly transported parents."

"Yes."

"And you think you might be found by the FBI before you can get back to Newport?"

"I'm afraid so."

"Well, if they do catch up to you, I assume all hell will break loose."

"That's the advice I'm paying for?"

"Good. Keep your sense of humor. And here is some real advice. If you are caught and questioned *don't* lie to them. That itself is a crime."

"Of course, I wouldn't."

"The best thing is not to talk to them at all. You do not have to. It's your right to remain silent and it's my strong advice that you do. At least for now."

"Grace always said I was the silent type. Wanted me to talk more."

"Well, for everybody's sake, don't start now. If they charge you with anything, I assume it will be something under the immigration laws. That would be brought in a federal court. You said you went to Honduras from El Paso?"

"Yeah."

"Probably there, then. They'd probably charge you down near the border." Brewster paused. "You know, Will, I'm not a criminal lawyer."

"Do you have to use that word?"

"Okay, I don't work in matters of 'statutory non-compliance.'"

"Much better. But you can find me the right lawyer, can't you?"

"Yeah. We've got good friends in law firms all over the country. Someone will know who's the best down there. I'll get on it. Where's the boat now?"

"She dropped her helm chain. Burp is having her hauled back overland from San Diego."

"You two are something. I'll give you that."

"Grace was worth it," Goodbow said. "To both of us."

"I understand. I just hope a judge and jury will too. If it comes to that."

60

Will Goodbow was not the only one feeling anxious about what would become of him once the parents arrived in Breckenridge and their presence there with their children was known around town. Maria Angeles was well-aware that the parents' entry into the country could not be kept quiet for long. And she was convinced that the US immigration authorities—and Breen Edwards—would be incensed. From her room in the minister's residence, she struggled with what she should do, what she *could* do, not only for Goodbow, but for the parents. Would all of them, including the old industrialist, be detained immediately? Would the parents, having come all this way to find their children after having been turned back at the southern border many months earlier, be summarily deported again to face the Honduran gangs they had fled from?

Maria knew she could not call her husband with these questions; she could not involve him, even after the fact, with what Goodbow and Sister Hope Annie had done. But, she decided, there was one person she could safely call.

"Maria?" Lane Williams said. "I was wondering when

you'd call. Did you deliver Gloria Carrasco? Are you back already from Minnesota?"

"I delivered her, yes. The Swensens are wonderful people. Gloria is very happy there with the other children."

"Good."

"But maybe not so good for long. And no, I'm not back. I'm still up here. I'm worried."

"What do you mean? Are there problems in the town? They don't want the refugee children anymore?"

"No, no, the town is fine. The Lutherans and the Catholics up here have embraced the children. Half the town showed up to greet Gloria. A party and everything. The kids are like celebrities here. And the minister told me the townspeople are worried about their parents, too. They're very much against the separation."

"Then what is the problem?"

"The problem is that Goodbow and Sister Hope Annie somehow found these kids' parents in Honduras and now—God knows how—they've gotten them into the country to join their children! The minister told me this. Sister Hope Annie is supposedly driving them here right now. They'll be here tonight!"

Lane Williams gasped. "*All* of them?"

"All twelve, including the Carrascos. In some big van with another nun from California."

"Holy, holy shit," Lane Williams said.

"So, obviously, you didn't know about this either?" Maria asked.

"Of course, not!" Williams said. "I wondered if the nun was up to something with Goodbow, and I asked her if she was, but she wouldn't tell me anything. Neither would Huff Langley, Goodbow's security escort. I wondered, but I never thought she and Goodbow would go *this* far. My God! I don't know whether I should strangle them or hug them."

"Well," Maria said. "I want to hug them. And I don't want this to explode on them or the families. I want to help them, now that they're here."

"And just how can you do that?"

"I have no idea. That's why I called you. I thought you might have some. I can't get Manny to help. He'd want to, but it's out of the question."

"Just hold on the line. Let me think a minute."

The Human Rights First manager spun in his office chair and with one hand extracted a cigarette from a rumpled pack and lit it. He knew in his heart that what he had said to Maria about his reaction to this startling news was not really the truth. He held no anger toward either Goodbow or Sister Hope Annie. How could he? The whole purpose of his own work—his own devotion—was the humane treatment of immigrants and refugees, and what could be more humane than reuniting fleeing parents with fleeing children? Goodbow had come to him first, he remembered. He had cautioned the naïve widower not to get in over his head; that it was dangerous in all sorts of ways. He'd discouraged him from doing anything stupid. But apparently, he now knew, the old man could not be deterred. He'd somehow found a way, with the help of indefatigable Sister Hope Annie and perhaps the grace of God, to fulfill the promise he'd made in grief. No, he could not feel anger to him or to the nun. It wouldn't be right. It just wouldn't be right.

"You say the town is supportive of the children?" he asked when he returned to the phone.

"Very," Maria said.

"And this minister. He believes the town will welcome the parents too?"

"He does. He really does."

"Well, then, you've got one of the two things you need. Support of the local people."

"What's the other?"

"Publicity. Lots of publicity. You've got to take that town viral."

Lane Williams spoke to the Red Cross worker for a few more minutes. She made careful notes. When he signed off, she ran down the stairs to find the minister.

61

The Rev. Burton Leif peered through his round lenses and over his coffee cup as Maria Angeles explained what the Human Rights First manager in El Paso had urged. A modest and unselfish man committed only to the spiritual health of his congregants, he was loath to drawing attention to himself and averse to political assertion. What he heard ran counter to those deep inclinations. But he listened anyway.

"Tell me again how the parents and children benefit if the media gets involved?" he asked.

"If the press puts a spotlight on their presence, on their situation, it puts a spotlight on the government too," Maria said. "The parents cannot be swept away by ICE or the FBI in silence, without the public knowing. That's what happened when the family separations first began. They were going on for months, but nobody except the parents and the government knew it was happening. When it became known, there was an uproar. Remember?"

"I do," the minister said. "The separations were cut way back."

"Not before five-thousand kids were kept in the US without their parents. If it weren't for people like you, talking to your townspeople and finding foster homes for them, they'd still be in detention centers. And the same for others like little Gloria who was brought across more recently for medical care."

"But it was the right thing to bring Gloria in," he said. "She was very sick."

"Yes, it was. My husband and other border control agents are doing their best to protect these children. But they have to follow policy. It wasn't right to keep her parents from her, but that's the policy. If Lane Williams had not found you to take her in, she'd be stuck in one of those detention centers instead of the Swensen home."

"So, you're saying we need to engage the public about the parents. About their arrival tonight. Make it more difficult for the government to remove them."

Maria nodded and without further persuasion the minister lifted his phone. He called the Swensen's and repeated much of what Maria had told him, and that he too was concerned about what might happen to the parents and their benefactors, Goodbow and Sister Hope Annie, in consequence of their efforts. Were they okay with him trying to arrange for media presence that evening? It might be helpful to the parents and everyone else. As he listened, he nodded encouragingly to Maria sitting across from him; they promptly consented. He flipped through a contact list he kept in his drawer and started dialing another number.

"Lon Vensensen is the town's lawyer," he said as he punched the buttons. "He helped all the local families with the DHS papers when they wanted to take in the children. I asked him to. He's respected. The media has interviewed him."

"Lon," he said. "It's Burton Leif. Could you be at the Swensen house tonight about eight-thirty?" Maria listened, amazed that as far as it appeared, the town counsel didn't even inquire why. *He must hold this clergyman very dear.* "Oh, that's good," the minister said quickly. "There's something else, though. Could you call the *Daily News* and the television stations in Fargo and tell them something pretty big is going to happen there?"

The minister listened intently as Maria strained, unsuccessfully to hear what the lawyer was saying.

"No," he said, "I'd rather tell you all about it when you get there. There's kind of a lot to it. But it's only three hours from now, so I will be grateful if you call the press right away. To give them time to send people. Especially from Fargo. They've got a bit of a drive. I really need them to be there."

Another pause.

"You could tell them it involves the Honduran children," the minister said. "That there's been a big development about them and that I called you and asked you to notify them. They'll trust us, don't you think?"

A shorter silence.

"Ah, thank you, Lon. This means a lot to me. I'll be there to greet you."

It happened as easily as that. The even-tempered, humble minister with bookish glasses who never wanted attention, much less credit, fame, or their opposites, was about to become a national figure and receive all of those things. And be a shepherd to his little flock in northwestern Minnesota. And to a man from Rhode Island he'd never met—in a way as profound as it was unanticipated.

62

Like many others, it was a slow news day in Fargo. Until the town lawyer from Breckenridge called the tip line at WABC-TV with word that "something big is happening here tonight with the immigrant children. There will be a big crowd at 118 Bluebell Street."

As a border community to North Dakota and sister town to Wahpeton, North Dakota on the other side of the Red River, Breckenridge was well known to the news staff at the station. For years, sports reporters had grudgingly taken turns covering Friday night high school football games in the small towns. But word that something was about to happen to the refugee children living there sounded like *real* news to the station chief. WABC had covered the arrival of the children many months earlier and followed up with a feature story interviewing most of the host foster parents only a month ago. The station chief immediately dispatched his best reporter with a full camera and sound crew. "We'll hold the ten o'clock lead for you," he told her. "Get moving." And he told the news anchorwoman in the studio to modify her promotional spots that would air every twenty minutes until the newscast. The new broadcast headline:

DRAMATIC NEWS OUT OF BRECKENRIDGE, MINNESOTA
TONIGHT. WHAT IS HAPPENING TO THE SEPARATED
CHILDREN THERE? TONIGHT AT 10!

Every time the anchor's spot ran, more phones rang across the Minnesota town, and in neighboring Wahpeton too.

But trusty town counsel Lon Vensensen didn't take any chances. He also called the other two network affiliates in Fargo with the same tip, and they reacted with the same vigor. As it turned out, the media caravan streamed down Interstate 90 to the Swensen family home at the border only thirty minutes behind old, uninformed Will Goodbow driving the same highway in his still undetected white Land Rover.

It was probably best that Goodbow didn't know about the camera laden scene he was about to encounter. His heart was already racing, his senses afire. He'd known all along that he could not be a fugitive forever and didn't want to be one. What he'd done would become known soon enough, probably immediately. He'd accepted that. He would deal with the consequences. He wanted no one to lie for him. But, like Reverend Leif, attention had never been his aspiration. Seeking it was totally against his nature. Had he known as he completed the final few hours of his journey what awaited him at little Gloria's new home, he'd have exploded with anxiety. No, it was better this way. And, for whatever it might be worth, no one could ever say that he had planned it this way.

He pulled to the curb on Bluebell Street as sunset approached. Tall maple trees, a mixture of red and green, were spaced evenly along the trimmed tree lawns. Lutheran tidiness, he assumed. He squinted to read the first house number he could make out. *112. I'm only a few houses away.* He put the Land Rover in park mode and called Sister Hope Annie.

"I'm here in town," he said. "Waiting down the street. How far out are you?"

"What does the map thing say, Sister?" he heard Sister Hope Annie ask her cohort. "When do we get there? . . . Thirty minutes, she says."

"I'll wait for you."

"No! Go in there and meet the children!" the nun said. "See the little angels you've been working for! Gloria is there, and Juan's kids too! Meet his boy, Rigo. He is a sparkplug. Tell the minister we will be there in half an hour." He could hear the buoyant Spanish voices of the parents behind her in the van.

Lampposts lined the winding stone walkway from the sidewalk to the house's well-lit front porch. Inside, Burton Leif peered through a side pane and opened the front door before Goodbow reached the steps. Gene Swensen and Lon Vensensen stood beside him. All three were smiling.

"Mr. Goodbow?" the minister said. "Mr. Will Goodbow?"

"Yes. Are you Reverend Leif?" He climbed the porch stairs.

"Just call me Burt. This is Gene Swensen, father of the home. And this is Lon Vensensen. He is the lawyer for the town of Breckenridge."

Goodbow's expression turned serious. "The lawyer for the town? Is there a problem?"

"Oh, no," the minister said. "Far from it. Lon has helped us place the children in town. And helped us prepare for tonight."

"Prepare?"

"Yes. To welcome you and the parents. We are all very excited here."

"But won't that draw a lot of attention?" Goodbow asked.

"That's really the point," the reverend said. Goodbow, towering above the short minister, seemed startled. "You'll see," Leif said. "It will be better this way. But please come in. The children are still up. They love visitors; you know kids. And now they are very excited. We just told them their parents are coming tonight."

"Excited" didn't capture the half of it, as the old Rhode Islander saw when he walked into the living room. The children were literally jumping and dancing in undiluted joy. They were all very young; Goodbow judged the oldest, a boy, was perhaps ten years old. The foster father brought the boy forward and Goodbow knelt to meet him.

"And what is your name, little man?" he asked.

"Rigo," the boy said. "I am the boy of Juan Rodriguez. I can talk English and I have two little sisters and a little brother here with me. They can speak English better now, but not as good as me yet." Then immediately, "Our parents are really coming tonight?"

"Yes," Goodbow said. "I have met your parents in Honduras. And yes, they are coming tonight. Sister Hope Annie is driving them here now. You know her, don't you?"

"Sister Hope Annie!" he shouted. "The smoking nun! She loves us!"

Reverend Leif tapped at Goodbow's shoulder and drew him to the side. He could see that the large man had grown emotional.

"Maria Angeles has told me why you've done this," the minister said. "Lane Williams has too. He says you were warned against it."

"I was."

"But you did all this anyway?"

"I did."

"But how? How did you get them into the country?"

"On my boat. My sailboat."

"The parents *sailed* here?"

"To San Diego. With a brave captain with a good soul. And then Sister Hope Annie brought them—she's driving them—from there."

"But you were not that captain?"

"Oh, no. I just own the thing."

"Then who was the captain with the 'good soul?'"

"That will never be known, I hope."

"My God," said Burton Leif. "No wonder Maria and Lane are so concerned for you. The government must know something about this."

"More than I wished they did. The FBI was trying to question me in Honduras. I'm told they're probably trying to find me now."

"Well, we will protect you and the parents as best we can," the minister said. "Lon and I and the townspeople."

"By hiding me?" Goodbow's face wrinkled in disapproval, non-consent.

"No," Burton Leif said. "By *not* hiding you. By standing next to you. And next to the parents."

Goodbow did not understand fully what the minister meant and in that instant, truthfully, couldn't process it anyway. The emotion of the moment flooded his brain as the foster parents brought each child in turn to meet him, the ecstasy in each of their eyes piercing his. This was all that mattered to him now. The glee, the anticipation of the children. The arrival of their yearning parents any minute. *Yes, Grace! Yes, Grace! Are you pleased?*

63

The propitious order of the arrivals after Goodbow's on Bluebell Street provided maximum effectiveness for the hastily assembled plan launched by Maria Angeles and the Reverend Leif that afternoon. First, the three TV vans with their rooftop satellite dishes pulled to the curb in near unison. Technicians and mic holding reporters poured from them and onto the tree lawn. Gene Swensen hustled out and introduced himself as the property owner, inviting them warmly onto the lawn in front of the porch, asking only that they keep the stone walkway clear. "Important people are coming," he announced to nodding heads.

"*These* people?" one reporter asked him, pointing to the dozens of citizens coming up from both ends of Bluebell Street.

"No, not them," Swensen said. "Those are people from town. They heard about it. They're coming to be a part of what's happening."

Minutes later, a long passenger van turned into the driveway and sounded its horn twice. Goodbow, Reverend Leif, and Mrs. Swensen led a pack of five Honduran children, plus two of Swensens' own, through the crowd of media and townspeople to the passenger door of the van from which Sister Hope Annie jumped out in full habit and high-top sneakers, *sans* cigarette. Goodbow bent to receive the arms that she threw around him. She locked her smiling eyes on his less-smiling ones, then flung open the sliding door on the side of the van. The women came out first, all of them crying. The fathers followed.

The small minister turned to the cameras and shouted through cupped hands:

"THESE ARE OUR PARENTS! THEY'VE COME TO BE WITH THEIR CHILDREN! ALL OF OUR PARENTS ARE HERE! OUR OTHER CHILDREN WILL BE BROUGHT HERE SOON!"

Our parents. *Our* children, Goodbow thought. *Listen to him, Grace. Listen! Can you hear it?*

A station wagon, two SUVs, and a cramped compact sedan, all honking, soon pulled up to the curb behind the TV vans. Two foster fathers sprinted into the street to prevent their excited passengers from running the wrong way into it; the other foster parents guided—if you could call it that—the remaining Honduran children racing to their parents, standing with the nuns and Goodbow at the side of the van. The reporters shouted out questions:

"HOW DID THEY GET HERE?" "WHO BROUGHT THEM HERE?"

"WILL THEY STAY NOW WITH THE CHILDREN?"

"We hope they will stay," the minister shouted back. "We want them to stay."

But any chance that the small reverend could be heard above the joyous din was mooted when the parade of law enforcement vehicles pulled to a stop in the street, their flashing lights twirling. The largest of the officers waved to the others to turn off the sirens.

Still standing at the van with Sister Hope Annie and Lon Vensensen, Goodbow looked at the police with fear in his heart. But Lon put his arm on his shoulder and assured him.

"Don't worry," he said to Goodbow. "That's Woody Burns. Our local chief and his deputies. They are not going to give you any problems."

"How can you say that?"

"*Because* he's our local chief and those are his deputies. They are the law in this town, not the FBI or anyone else. You know that motto a lot of police departments have: *"To Protect and to Serve?"* Well, Woody and his people really mean it. They've been terrific with the kids since they came here. And Burton Leif's word is gold to them."

Goodbow was shocked to see the police chief take off his hat and wave to the gathered townspeople as he walked toward Vensensen.

"Evening, Chief," Lon said.

"Same, Lon. Where's Reverend Leif? Everybody doing all right here? Nobody giving you trouble? I see the kids' parents are here now."

The diminutive minister was standing there the whole

time, but the police chief didn't see him behind Goodbow's huge frame. He stepped in front of Goodbow.

"There's no trouble, Chief," Reverend Leif said. "Did somebody say there was?"

"Not really. But the Fargo TV stations are chirping about big doings here involving the refugee kids, so we wanted to come over and make sure you're all okay."

"That's wonderful of you."

"And I got a call from the FBI."

"The FBI?"

"Said they're looking for a fella named 'Goodbow.'" The Chief turned to Will. "That your Land Rover out there?"

"Yes, sir."

"Well, then, that would be you."

"It is."

"Nice to meet you, Mr. Goodbow."

Nice to meet me? This is crazy!

"You the fella behind the parents getting here?"

"Yes."

"Okay," the Chief said. "You probably shouldn't say anymore."

"Are you going to arrest me?"

"Now, why would I do that? You commit some crime in our nice little town?"

"Of course, he didn't," Burton Leif interjected. "He and these nuns have done something special for us. For our town."

"That's how I see it too," the Chief said. "Don't worry too much about the FBI, at least for tonight. This is *my* jurisdiction. Me and the deputies will stick around in case they show up."

The big policeman looked to the street. "Looky there," he said. "Angelo's here with his accordion."

Reverend Leif was surprised, but delighted. "Lon, did you call Angelo?"

"No, I did," said the chief. "Thought you could use a little music. But I did tell him he'd have to turn off the damn thing at eleven. Local ordinance."

Vensensen, the minister, and even Goodbow laughed.

The Chief did not have to wait long to protect and serve. A black sedan turned into the driveway and stopped uncomfortably close to the rear bumper of the Dominican van. Myles Burlacher and Robert Everett climbed out in their standard issue deep blue jackets emblazoned with the gold FBI insignia stitched on the back. The reporters and their camera people surged toward them. One of the reporters was heard talking to her studio on her cell phone. "Boss," she said. "Let the networks in on this in New York. You can't believe what's going down out here. The FBI has showed up and there must be hundreds of people here. The local police chief too."

Chief Burns waved over his deputies and the three of them walked in a vee formation through the crowd and toward the FBI agents, like a lead goose and two in his draft. All three put their hats back on.

"We're agents Burlacher and Everett," Burlacher said when the police officers reached them.

"Welcome to Brekenridge," the chief said. "Woody Burns. I'm the police chief." But he did not return his hand to Burlacher's outstretched one. "What can we do for you?"

"We're looking for Wilton Goodbow."

"The man you called about."

"Yes. Is he here? His phone pinged a cell tower down the block. We've driven all the way from Oregon trying to catch up with him."

"He done anything wrong?"

"We don't know yet."

"So you're not asking me to help you arrest someone charged with a crime?"

"Well, no. Not yet."

"'Cause if you were, I'd naturally help you. But if you're not saying he's a criminal, I have to consider him a guest in town and protect him like we protect any other visitor."

"You're kidding us."

"No, I am not kidding you. Besides, Reverend Leif has asked us to protect him, and these parents that have come to be with their children. Reverend Leif has requested that."

"What does that mean?"

"It means plenty to us. Here in Breckenridge, Minnesota."

Chief Woody Burns walked over to the minister and Goodbow, leaving his deputies with the agents.

"Reverend, why don't you go inside with Mr. Goodbow. I don't think these agents will be here long. I can't make 'em leave, but I doubt they'll be interested in talking to these reporters." The chief turned to Goodbow. "And I assume you're not interested in talking to them, are you?"

"No, I was advised I shouldn't."

"That's probably good advice." The chief started back through the crowd. "And, oh . . . I forgot," he called back. "Welcome to Breckenridge."

64

Who could have foreseen that a little town on the Red River in the American northland, two-hundred miles from the Canadian border, would be propelled—by a force so few could describe but so many would feel—into the national consciousness, literally overnight?

Apparently, Lane Williams. From his swivel chair in his bland El Paso office down the street from the border patrol station. The NGO worker had remotely directed the bulbs-popping, cameras-clicking spectacle that happened on the spacious front lawn of the Swensen family after Will Goodbow's arrival. The next day, Sister Hope Annie teased him over the phone.

"You missed your calling, Lane Williams," she told him. "Maria Angeles told me the news coverage was your idea. You should be a TV producer! But remember. You can't let people smoke on TV! You should be proud of me. I didn't!"

"I noticed," Lane Williams said. "I wish you could show that willpower in my office."

"If you can do more for the parents, maybe I will. I am afraid ICE or the border patrol will come for them."

"I doubt it. The border patrol can't come in more than 110 miles from a border and you're all further than that from Canada. Not by much, but you are. And with all this publicity, I doubt they'll send in ICE either. It'd be a spectacle. It's all over the networks and social media. Besides, the country is mostly against separating families. Even a lot of the people who want to restrict immigration think it's wrong. But New York has agreed to send a lawyer from Human Rights First to represent the parents on asylum petitions. She'll be there by tomorrow."

While Lane Williams mobilized in El Paso, Breen Edwards raged in Washington. Staffers for the DHS Secretary said they had never seen him so beside himself. The cable networks were running live coverage from the Minnesota town in a seemingly endless loop. There was interview after interview of the foster parents sitting in their homes with the Honduran children and their newly arrived, invariably smiling, biological parents. Most of the asylum seekers spoke through interpreters. "Your country is so wonderful!" they said. "You have been so kind to our children! We are all safe here! Thank you, America!"

Breen Edwards fumed as he watched them.

"Thank you, America for *goddamned what*?" he bellowed. "I want that sonofabitch Goodbow nailed to a goddamned wall!"

Even the Attorney General Ray Muncie did not escape his wrath.

"What the fuck is your FBI doing, anyway? Arrest the fucker!"

"It's more complicated than that, Breen," the AG said. "What are we going to charge him with? Right now, we don't even know how he brought them into the country, if he really did. We'll know before long, but right now we've got nothing specific."

"Nothing specific? The guy isn't even denying it!"

"He hasn't said anything one way or another. He's not giving interviews. We did hear from a lawyer from Boston who says he represents him for the time being."

"Well, he's not goddamned denied it."

"We'll get the evidence. Don't worry. And, hell, Breen, *you* run the immigration service. Why don't you send out ICE and pick up these parents? Put them in summary deportation."

"Oh, *sure.* Rip them from their kids a *second* time. On national TV! When they've got that little cherub of a minister and pretty little nun speaking for them and the whole town and most of the goddamned country supporting them! The President has no interest in that. He says the whole idea was Jeff Session's anyway. Says it wasn't his. Says he never really agreed with separating families, but Sessions insisted there was no other way."

"Are you saying he just wants to let it all go?" Muncie asked.

"Hell, no. But it's Goodbow's ass he wants. The rest is bad politics."

"Well, in that case, it could be a lot easier to nail him."

"How so?"

"We could talk to the parents and offer them asylum—they won't have to go back. They can stay with their kids permanently and they can work with the churches and whoever to situate themselves. So long as they cooperate with us on how they came in, and testify against Goodbow, if he is behind all this. Imagine it. The president can look gracious, letting them stay together and all. But still set an example by prosecuting the ringleader. In the name of law and order."

"Where would you charge him? Not up there in the woods, I hope."

"No, we'd have jurisdiction over him down at the border. If it turns out he cooked this up in El Paso. There are only three federal judges on the bench there now. The president appointed all of them. All tough conservatives."

"Then go for it. But get that Goodbow behind bars. Get the rich bastard."

65

Of course, the news cycle could not focus on the politically charged developments in northern Minnesota forever. As the weeks passed, and he remained in the town at Burton Leif's invitation, Will Goodbow's surreal euphoria had dissipated to sober realism. Not fear, not depression. But also not the tingling anticipation he had felt in the weeks leading up to the delivery of the parents in Minnesota. His soul was resolving, he knew, almost as in the stages of grief, into acceptance.

A lot had happened in just three weeks. The media frenzy continued, almost unabated, for the next two and half of them, though Goodbow himself stayed away from the cameras, eschewing all interview requests. And there were hundreds of them. Still, his face was watched all over the country and his name uttered everywhere. News video of the hysteria on Bluebell Street upon the parents' arrival clearly showed him standing next to Sister Hope Annie and the emotional parents, and even in conversation with Chief Woody Burns. The networks replayed the video feeds incessantly, often juxtaposing them with Goodbow's passport photo that Breen Edward had ordered released. For better or worse, the large-faced man from Rhode Island was soon nationally known. All without speaking a word.

But Sister Hope Annie and the Reverend Leif were not camera shy like Will Goodbow. Encouraged by the Human Rights First lawyer that Lane Williams arranged, the nun and the preacher sat for numerous interviews and were becoming veritable celebrities.

"The more the better," the lawyer told them, referring to their public appearances with the parents and children. "Publicity is our friend."

"Even the conservative outlets?" Burton Leif asked.

"Everybody," the lawyer answered. "DHS has already contacted me. They don't want a scene with either of you, and they don't want to tangle with Woody Burns, your local police chief. Apparently, he made quite the impression on them. They say they may consider a deal, rather than face the backlash of deporting the parents and hauling them out of town past Woody. They may agree to a grant of asylum to all of the parents and give legal status to their children too."

"Wonderful!" Sister Hope Annie said. "I saw something about that on the news, but I thought it was just a rumor."

"They *may* grant asylum, *if* the parents cooperate in the prosecution of Goodbow."

"Oh," the nun said, deflated. "You mean, they'll have to testify against him?"

"Yes. And give written statements. You know, as their lawyer, I have to recommend they accept the offer, if it's made. It's a remarkable offer."

"But only truthful statements?" Reverend Leif asked. "They would be asked to make only truthful statements, right?"

"Only truthful," the lawyer said. "I would be with them,

and I would be permitted to check any statement for accuracy before it is signed."

"Because they might try to get them to say things," the minister said. "Like, they had to pay him, or something. These parents are desperate to stay. They might be coerced into saying things. They're vulnerable."

"I could insist that you be there for the interviews too, Reverend. And you too, Sister. I think they'd allow it. They'd look terrible if they didn't."

"Could Sr. Marcus Marie be with them too?" asked Sister Hope Annie. "She is still here helping the parents settle in. And they like her very much."

"I'll arrange it for the Dominican nun too," the lawyer said.

And so it went. DOJ attorneys and a DHS interpreter from Minneapolis came to Brekenridge and interviewed all of the nervous parents under the careful brows of the two nuns and Reverend Leif, who wore a starched black clerical shirt and collar, rare for him. Sitting at the end of the table in Woody Burns' police station meeting room, the three looked like a gaggle of parent penguins protecting their young. Pair by pair, the parents listened, conferred with the Human Rights First lawyer, and signed the asylum papers. Each asylum grant was revocable immediately if that parent failed to cooperate with the government and testify if called at the trial of Wilton Goodbow.

Juan Rodriguez called to Sister Hope Annie as the parents left the police station and headed to the Dominican passenger van. He was crying.

"Sister, I did not want to do that," he said. "I did not want to agree. I do not want to hurt Mr. Goodbow."

"Mr. Goodbow will be pleased, Juan," she said. "He is still staying at Reverend Leif's house and I will tell him right away. He will think you did the right thing. That you did the right thing to stay here with your children. So that all of you can be safe in this country. It is why Mr. Goodbow did all that he did. So that you could be. He would want you to do anything you needed to do to stay here. He will be pleased, Juan."

"But will he go to prison?"

"He may. But he will have God on his side. And in the end, that is always the most important thing."

When Sister Hope Annie an hour later related to him her advice to Juan, Goodbow smiled. Of course, he'd been pleased—mightily—when it was reported earlier that the government might be contemplating an asylum deal with the parents. And he sensed that he *had* become more spiritual, more like Grace in that way, in the course of his mission. But now, uneasily waiting to hear from the FBI as he stayed at the comfortable little church residence, he was not convinced that having God on his side 'at the end' would make the next ten or twenty years before him more pleasant.

* * *

And then came his indictment and arrest. While the truth was that Breen Edwards' fury had caused them to occur in warp speed, when two and a half weeks had passed with no word from the FBI, Lane Williams and the nuns began to entertain the naïve notion that maybe, just maybe, the publicity was sufficient to deter the government's pursuit even of Goodbow. But Goodbow knew better; he could feel it in his stomach. He'd accepted Reverend Leif's invitation to stay at the church house to await his fate. He enjoyed the serenity there, which would never have been available in a hotel, and avoided the reporters who came every day to the church parking lot, which had become their gathering place, without objection of the reverend. But in the evenings he took long walks with the minister through the town, talking about books and their lives, and what might lie ahead for each of them. When they returned to the church house after their last walk together, Agents Burlacher and Everett were waiting in a black Chevy Tahoe with FBI license plates. Goodbow merely glanced at the arrest warrant Everett handed him.

"You've been indicted by a federal grand jury in El Paso," Burlacher said.

"That was fast," Goodbow said, but not in a flip tone.

"We can take you to the federal center in Minneapolis and ask to have you extradited to Texas, or you could choose to come with us voluntarily to El Paso for your arraignment."

"Tonight?" asked Reverend Leif. "It's getting late. Couldn't he stay here with me overnight and get his things together? I will vouch for him. You can take him in the morning."

"Take him *where* in the morning?" asked Burlacher, looking at Goodbow.

"To El Paso," Goodbow said. "Extradition won't be necessary. I'll go with you to El Paso. But it would be nice to sleep here tonight. Say my goodbyes. And arrange for a lawyer down there."

The agents huddled on the sidewalk. A red eye to Texas didn't sound appetizing to them either.

"Okay," Burlacher called from the sidewalk. "We'll be back at nine in the morning. But remember, if you're not here, you will both have serious problems."

* * *

Goodbow left with them in the morning, without incident. Handcuffs were not used. He was processed into the El Paso federal detention center that afternoon and told he would be arraigned before a judge the next morning.

66

Tom Brewster reached his incarcerated friend soon after he was booked in El Paso.

"How did it go down?" Brewster asked. "The arrest."

"Better than I thought it would. They weren't aggressive. Weren't rude. Just told me they'd come to arrest me and read me my rights. Even let me stay another night with the minister and picked me up this morning. Asked *me* if handcuffs were necessary. Asked *me!* I said no, and that I appreciated that. They said I'll be arraigned in the morning. Till then, I'm here."

"Where's 'here?'"

"The sign says, 'Detention Facility.' I think it's attached to the courthouse. There aren't any bars or those jail cells like you see on TV. At least where they have me. Just a door with a little narrow window in the middle. I've been in smaller hotel rooms."

"They're treating you okay?"

"Not badly, really. The towel looks clean. I hope I can sleep okay, though."

"And you haven't said anything? About the case."

"Of course not."

"Good."

"I found you a lawyer. His name is Gillen McCoy. He's older than dirt. In his nineties."

"Nineties?"

"Yeah. But still spry, everyone says. Sharp as a tack. It was obvious when I spoke to him. Been practicing in El Paso and the Rio Grande Valley his whole career. He's a legend down there in criminal defense."

"What else do you know about him?"

"That he's not cheap."

"Nothing about this has been cheap. How bad is it?"

"He wants a retainer of a hundred thousand. And when that's used up, another hundred thousand."

"Dollars?"

"No, *pesos*. Goddamnit, of course dollars. Just be glad you weren't indicted in New York. It'd be twice that."

"I understand. It's fine."

"Gillen is in San Antonio now for another case. He can't be back in time for your arraignment, so he's sending a young partner to cover it."

"Do we know who the judge is?"

"T. Creed Rockburn. I don't know much about him, but Gillen will. He said he's certain you'll be released on a reasonable bail. Call me if you need me for that. He'll see you tomorrow."

"Okay. And thanks for finding him."

"Thank me when you get back to Newport. I see *Grace* is back at her pier, by the way."

"Yeah. She did her job. I miss her."

* * *

Brewster's description of the old lawyer's background did not prepare Goodbow for the man's appearance when he met him the next afternoon following his arraignment and release—surprisingly to Goodbow—on his own recognizance.

Gillen McCoy looked 70 years old, tops. His build was slight but athletic, his gait lithe and effortless as he moved across his spacious office to greet Goodbow. He was strikingly handsome for a man of any age. His ruddy Scotch-Irish face was crowned with thick white hair perfectly coifed over piercing blue eyes and a kind smile. The two made quite a visual statement standing together in front of the lawyer's broad table desk on which legal treatises were piled at a corner. At six-foot four, Goodbow and his large frame dwarfed the short, trim lawyer. But there seemed to be chemistry between them right from the start.

If only chemistry solved legal problems.

"I've got to say," his first words to Goodbow were. "I've been doing this down here for sixty-five years. And I've never seen a case like yours."

"And they told me you were experienced!" Goodbow laughed. So did the lawyer.

"Your arraignment this morning," McCoy said. "Sorry I couldn't be there. I could have had it delayed, but I didn't want you locked up in that room any longer than necessary."

"I was surprised that Judge Rockburn didn't make me post bail. Only made me turn over my passport. Said I should stay in Texas, but that if I wanted to go home to Rhode Island, you could ask for it."

"I called him before the arraignment. He knows you're not a spring chicken. I pointed out that you stayed in that town up there the whole time without trying to go anywhere. Plainly, you're not a flight risk. It was smart of you to stay put."

"I never really thought about it that way," Goodbow said. "Everybody was just so friendly."

"Still, I'm sorry I couldn't be there this morning."

"Your young partner was fine," Goodbow said. "He said, 'Not guilty,' and I nodded. I don't suppose it's all that easy."

"No, I'm afraid it won't be. I wish I could say for sure that you'll be acquitted. But I can't."

"I wouldn't expect that."

"On what I know so far, it will be very tough for you. But if ever a case presented a conflict between the law and morality, it's yours." They sat down.

"I have felt very conflicted through all of this," Goodbow said. "I've always been a law-abiding citizen. As far as I know, I've never done anything before that was wrong in that way. You know, illegal. Against the law. Not any important one, at least."

"Well, it's not clear to me yet that you did anything this time that is actually—in every required way—against the law. At least any law that they will want to convict you of. One that would put you in prison for any length of time."

"I'm not following you."

"We'll be talking a lot. Eventually, you'll see what I mean. But for now, let me put it this way. Laws are imperfect. They always are. Because men make them. But morality—doing the right thing—is never imperfect. It may be messy. It may be heart-wrenching. And, unfortunately, it may not always be 'allowed'. But it is never imperfect the way laws are."

"How could that help me?"

"It's the truest beauty of a jury. Once in a while, you can get one to see the imperfection of the law—the wrongness of it applied to what happened to someone. To what someone did. If we can make the jury see and feel that what you did was right under imperfect laws, you have a chance. Just a chance."

"How could we do that? I did everything they say I did."

"Don't say that until I show you the words—all of them—in the statutes. But, whatever they say, they may mean something else when you tell the judge and the jury *why* you did this."

"But I won't be doing that."

"What do you mean, you won't."

"I won't testify."

"You have to testify."

"I won't. Because if I testified, I'd have to tell the truth about everything, right?"

"Of course."

"Well, then I can't testify. I would be asked about who helped me. Who I asked to help me and what they all did. And I won't do that. This all has to be on just me."

Gillen rose from his chair and looked at his client in silence.

"Do you drink?" He finally said. It seemed an inopportune question from the old lawyer.

"Sometimes too much," Goodbow said.

Gillen McCoy walked to a walnut cabinet against the wall and removed a bottle of expensive single-malt scotch and two crystal glasses.

"Don't worry, this comes with the retainer," he said, setting them on his desk. "I find that in conversations like this, when a bottle opens, sometimes a mind does too. Neat? If you want ice, I've got some in the kitchen nook."

"Neat's fine."

McCoy poured a finger and a half in each of the glasses. He held them up to his eye level and carefully checked the amount of his pour. "In moderation, of course," he said, handing one to Goodbow.

The two of them talked for nearly four hours in Gillen McCoy's office, even after the old counselor waived off his assistant and sent her home for the evening. Later Goodbow would say it was one of the deepest conversations of his life, rivaling his below-deck talks with Burp LeBeau and even his cherished ones with Grace. Gillen walked him through the formal charging document prepared by the US Attorney. The intimidating charge ran nearly twenty pages, loaded with references to numerous provisions of the federal criminal code, each of which the old lawyer explicated with care. Dryly, objectively, almost academically. But whether by design or merely because he needed occasional breaks from his tedious reading through the slim reading glasses that draped over his nose, he stopped periodically, talking about his life and asking Goodbow about his own. He asked about Grace and what she was like, where they'd traveled together, and listened attentively as the Rhode Island widower reminisced.

"So, do you want to stay down here a bit while we get started with your defense?" McCoy asked. "Or do you need to get home?"

"If the scotch is this good, I think I'll stay for a while."

"Where will you stay?"

"The Fine Sombrero, I think."

"*The Fine Sombrero Motor Inn?* By the border? You're not going broke on me, are you?"

"No, I like the place. I won't be bothered there. The bartender is good. It's close to Sister Hope Annie's center. And I've made some other friends near there too."

"Suit yourself. But we're not having any lawyer-client dinners there." McCoy looked through the papers on his desk. "You know, they're sending down a special prosecutor from the Justice Department in Washington to try your case. Some young firebrand."

"Is there something wrong with the guy here?" Goodbow asked.

"No. The US Attorney here is just fine. And he'll still be involved. They're just trying to make a statement. Sending down a heavyweight. His name is Preston Bell. Yale Law School. Funny, I went to Yale too, for my own law degree. And this guy did his regular college at Bowdoin. In Maine. I did too! I guess we'll see what difference fifty years makes."

"You're from New England?" Goodbow asked.

"Born in Boston. My father came from Ireland after WWI. Worked in a shoe factory. My mother was Scottish. I got into Bowdoin as an athlete. A baseball catcher. 'Course, you had to have the grades too. When I went to Yale for law school, my father told me, 'When you get your degree, you get the hell out of here.' The prejudice against the Irish was terrible in Boston."

"But Boston has always had a ton of Irish people."

"Yeah. Because we're so damned stubborn. Wouldn't get out. But back then they never got the best work, not the best paying jobs. Even if you loved the place, you had to get out to make it big. Why do you think the Kennedys made their money in Chicago?"

"I've lived close to Boston all my life," Goodbow said. "But I guess I never really knew."

"So my father told me he knew people who'd settled down here. Way down here! More opportunity for white immigrants, he said. We weren't looked down on. And he was right. A lot of Scotch-Irish have been living here ever since."

"Well, I'm glad you're one of them," Goodbow said. "I don't really understand all these charges against me. They seem pretty much the same, just different words."

"As usual, they're piling on," Gillen said. "But at least they didn't charge that you smuggled anyone in for a profit."

"Of course not! For *profit?* All this has cost me a small fortune. Or will, by the time I'm done paying you!"

"For which I thank you," Gillen said, his Irish eyes smiling.

"And I know that you didn't do anything for money. I'm just saying they wish you had. Because there are long prison terms for that. But because you didn't do it for financial gain, the only offense that really fits is this first one here." He slid the official document over to Goodbow and drew a mark in the column with a highlighter. "Basically it's smuggling undocumented persons into the country, but not for a profit." Goodbow read the language with a grim face.

"Sounds like what I did," he said, after reading it slowly.

"It is. But it could be just a fall back for them. I'm not sure they will even keep it in. They might drop it from the case if they think the jury might go for this one instead of the other charges, if they have the choice."

"Why? They'd have me dead to rights on it."

"But look at the penalty for it. Hardly any jail time and only a modest fine. And they know the judge may not sentence you to *any* time. Probably wouldn't against a first offender, much less one with your background. It's these other statutes—the other counts—that are more important to them. What they really want to get you on." He pointed to two sections on page fourteen of the document:

COUNT II

18 U.S.C. Section 1512 (k). <u>Conspiracy to Obstruct Justice in the Enforcement of Immigration Laws.</u>

The defendant Goodbow corruptly conspired with others, known and unknown, to obstruct and impede the administration of justice and the enforcement of the immigration laws of the United States by surreptitiously arranging for the transport and entry of persons from Honduras who were unauthorized to enter the United States, felonies in violation of 18 U.S.C. 1512(k).

COUNT III

18 U.S.C. Section 1512 (c)(2). Aiding and Abetting Obstruction of Justice.

The defendant Goodbow corruptly acted, alone and in concert with others, known and unknown, to aid and abet the illegal entry into the United States of persons from Honduras who were unauthorized to enter the United States, thereby obstructing and impeding the enforcement of the immigration laws of the United States, felonies in violation of18 U.S.C. 1512 (c) (2).

"These are much more serious crimes," McCoy said. "They carry mandatory and minimum prison sentences."

"How minimum?"

"At least three years, up to twenty."

"Why does it say felon*ies*? Plural?"

"Because, technically, it's a separate offense for each person you brought in."

Goodbow was visibly shaken.

"For *each*? For each of the twelve parents? My God, even *you'll* be dead before I get out."

Gillen McCoy laughed so uncontrollably that he started coughing. He was still giggling when he composed himself.

"You know, they say a good laugh every day is better for you than anything," he said. "But seriously, that's more of a technicality. It's not the most important thing. I don't think Judge Rockburn will multiply the sentence. But read those charges again carefully. Read them right now."

The old industrialist placed his wide forefinger on the page and read them slowly.

"Okay," he said. "I've read them."

"Read them again," Gillen McCoy said. Without resistance, Goodbow did. "There is one word used in each of them that's not in the first charge, not in the one for simple smuggling," the lawyer said. "See it?"

"'*Corruptly?*'" Goodbow said. "Is that the word?"

"Right. Those two counts say that you acted '*corruptly*' in conspiring against the laws of the United States and corruptly in aiding and abetting violations of the immigration laws. And that is the most important word for us. 'Corruptly.'"

"What does it mean?"

"Whatever the judge tells the jury it means."

"What do you think it means?"

"What I think it means doesn't matter. But I know what we want the judge to think it means and what we want him to tell the jury it means."

"And what's that?"

"Let me put it this way. When you planned and carried out this whole thing, do you think you acted 'corruptly?'"

"Well, I knew it was probably against the law."

"Not a great answer." McCoy frowned. "Think about it again. Did you think what you did was '*corrupt*?'"

"Well, I did think it was the right thing to do, even if it was against the law."

"Now, that's a better answer," McCoy said. "You thought it was right, not wrong."

"If you put it that way, I guess that's true."

"We have to convince the judge and the jury that when someone—namely, Will Goodbow—does something believing he is doing the right thing and not the wrong thing, he can't be acting 'corruptly.' And if you're not acting 'corruptly,' you can't be guilty of either of these crimes."

"Do you think we can do that?"

"With Judge Rockburn, it will be very hard, even though he likes me."

"He does?"

"I've known him since he first became a judge in the Texas state court thirty years ago. And before then, even. In the old days, you'd call him a 'hanging judge.' He hasn't changed much, and he's a Trump appointee. But he's always been honest and fair, at least to me. But this argument will be a tough one, even when you testify and you tell him and the jury all of the reasons you did this. What your wife believed. What she wanted you to do for her. What you saw when you went down there. How you came to believe you had to do it; had to do it because it was the right thing, the moral thing."

"I told you, I won't testify. I would have to name others. I'd be breaking my word."

"Then you're tying my hands! If you don't tell your story, we can't sell this. Especially with Rockburn."

The demure lawyer turned in his chair and gazed out the window to the El Paso street below. After a minute, he spun back and reached for the bottle of Scotch on the desk. He refilled the two tumblers, as carefully as he had the first time.

"What are you doing?" Goodbow asked.

"Seeing if two drinks will work," the old lawyer said.

When he walked Goodbow to the elevator an hour later, he knew it hadn't.

67

In no way was he expecting them, but Goodbow recognized instantly the sturdy shoulders atop the bar stool at The Fine Sombrero. Even on the wobbly stool, the ex-marine sat erect and muscular.

"Huff!" he called, as he walked into the lounge. "What are you doing here?"

"Thought you might need a hacksaw or something."

"Kind of you."

"But you look all right, old man. Good to see you."

"How'd you know I'd be here?"

"Sister Hope Annie told me. Your lawyer friend from Boston looked her up and called her to tell her who your lawyer is down here. So she called the lawyer and he told her you were staying here."

"Oh."

"Gillen McCoy is your lawyer? *The* Gillen McCoy?"

"You know him?"

"Hell, everybody knows him. He's outlived every lawyer and sheriff in Texas!"

"He seems very good."

"The best. But why are you going to stay here?"

"With him as my lawyer, it's what I can still afford."

"Bullshit."

"I just want to stay out of the limelight. I can't leave Texas without permission. And this way I'm close to Sister Hope Annie's center. I was thinking of helping her out over there. What else have I got to do?" Goodbow motioned to the bartender; he brought over two whiskeys.

"Well, you know we're all pulling for you."

"Just don't pull so hard you fall in too. And what did you do about the license plate thing?"

"It's not going to be a problem. I called the general manager of the rental car company. Offered to make restitution if I cost him anything. He's not pressing charges and said before I called him that he'd already told the FBI he doesn't know how the plates got mixed up. Said it's not the first time it's happened."

"Amazing," Goodbow said.

"It didn't hurt that he's a marine too."

"Semper Fi?"

"Semper Fi." Huff Langley raised his glass. "And since you're not really broke, I have your bill for you." He slid an envelope over the bar top. Goodbow opened it.

"It's a lot less than I figured," Goodbow said.

"I'm not taking any money for anything except your protection on the trip. Nothing for any time with the nun."

"Huff, you were helping her for days. You should be paid."

"I met the parents, though, and the priest. And all that. I don't want to be accused of doing anything for money. Because it's not why I did it." Goodbow remembered what Gillen McCoy had explained about the seriousness of smuggling undocumented persons for financial gain.

"I guess that's smart then," Goodbow said. "Maybe down the road I can make it up to you some way."

"A ride with you and your captain on that goddamned sailboat would be nice. I couldn't believe that thing."

"Consider it done. But I have to level with you. Can you wait twenty years?"

68

It didn't surprise Gillen McCoy that his client did not wish to waive his right to a speedy trial, the way most indicted persons did; when they waived, their trials were postponed for many months. But even though the old counselor saw one advantage in his client's preference, his desire for speed worried him a bit.

"Most people are happy to waive it," the lawyer told Goodbow. "Especially if they're free on bail and not sitting in jail. Most are in no rush for their trial. Mainly because they think they're headed to prison after it. But you're free on your own recognizance. And I told you, we have a chance here at trial. That is, if you'll come around and agree to testify for yourself."

"I just want to get it over with," Goodbow said. "If I have to go, I have to go."

"That's not a great way to look at it," the old lawyer said. "It sounds like a defeatist attitude. And if it is, it will show through to the jury. Especially if you don't take the stand. You can't sit there looking glum and guilty. Jurors always think that if a guy acts and looks like he's guilty as hell, he must be."

"It's not really that," Goodbow said. "I just don't like the waiting."

Gillen held a slim sheaf of papers in his hand.

"Well," he said. "As long as you feel that way, there is one good thing about having the trial quickly." Goodbow looked at him with interest. "You'll still be fairly fresh in the news, and so will your supporters," Gillen said.

"You mean the people from Minnesota?"

"I mean everybody involved. The parents. The minister up there. Sister Hope."

"Sister Hope *Annie,*" Goodbow corrected him. "She's touchy about that."

"She's a big plus for you."

"She's really been something, I know."

"And don't try to tell *her* not to testify."

"You don't tell Sister Hope Annie anything."

"Good. Because she wants to. I've already talked to her."

"Could she get in trouble?"

"They'll never touch her. And Judge Rockburn is a devout Catholic, anyway."

Goodbow appeared surprised by the comment. "Things like that matter?" he asked.

"Boy. You really *aren't* as old as I am, are you? *Everything* like that matters."

"What have you got in that folder?" Goodbow asked.

"The prosecution's documents. It's called 'pretrial discovery.' I asked for it, and they turned it over today."

"I've heard of it in lawsuits, but I didn't know it happened in criminal cases too."

"It's not like it is in civil cases. There aren't depositions or written questions answered by each side under oath, that sort of thing. And in a criminal case, the defendant doesn't have to turn over anything unless it's something he's going to bring into the trial. Like an expert's report, or documents or photographs he's going to rely on for his defense. But the prosecution has to give *us* what they've got on *you*. Anything they've written in the investigation. Police reports. Evidence list. Witness statements. The affidavits they wrote to get warrants, etcetera."

"That doesn't look very thick." Goodbow pointed to the folder in Gillen McCoy's hand.

"It isn't. I thought there'd be more. But maybe that's another reason to have the trial soon. Before they do get more. Here," Gillen said, handing the sheaf to Goodbow. "Look through it. Tell me if anything is wrong."

It took Goodbow only ten minutes to read everything in the folder. The largest document was an FBI investigative memo signed by Burlacher and Everett. It detailed Goodbow's travel to Tegucigalpa, his meeting and contacts with the consulate official, Leary Deen, and the meetings with Father Lopez at his church. Then it chronicled his travel with Huff Langley to Los Angeles and the Land Rover rental; the cyber work from Pittsburgh tracking his cell phone as he drove from Nevada to Minnesota and his arrival—and that of the Honduran parents—on Bluebell Street. Midway through, he began to chuckle.

"What's funny?" asked Gillen McCoy.

"Oh, the poor guy with the other Land Rover!"

"Yeah," McCoy smiled. "Don't expect a Christmas card from him."

By the end of his review, Goodbow looked somber.

"So? Is it correct?" McCoy asked. "All of it? We make our living on discrepancies. Usually, there's something inaccurate. We need something for cross-examination of the agents."

"I don't see anything wrong."

"What about the stuff about the official at the US embassy down there. Leary Deen. Is that part all true?"

"Yes."

"He's a good guy?"

"Oh, yeah."

"Well, you see that they say he told them the truth. When they went back to him and asked the right questions, he answered them truthfully."

"I'm glad he did. He stuck his neck out a long way. I'm sure they're not happy with him."

"In the embassy, the higher-ups are standing by him, according to young Mr. Preston Bell. In Washington, not so much."

"But they haven't fired him?"

"Not yet, at least. But he's on the government's witness list. They probably want to see if he plays ball at the trial."

"Leary Deen will tell the truth. You can bank on it."

"That's what I was afraid of," old Gillen McCoy said.

69

Judge T. Creed Rockburn sat in his chambers reading the morning's *New York Times* that his young law clerk, unrequested, had brought to his desk. He saw immediately why he had. A headline on the bottom half of page one read:

TRIAL OF INDUSTRIALIST SET IN EL PASO;
WILTON GOODBOW FACES IMMIGRATION
SMUGGLING AND CONSPIRACY CHARGES

The clerk had barely left when he returned with additional news.

"Judge," he said. "You have a call from Judge Elias Humphrey. From Washington. He's holding for you."

Rockburn was surprised. *What does Elias want?* He knew and liked his federal colleague from Washington. They had met three years earlier at a gathering of the federal judicial conference in Philadelphia, shortly after Rockburn's investiture. Both were staunch conservatives, though Elias Humphrey had been appointed decades earlier by the first President Bush. The senior judge was an icon in the federal judiciary but his manner was unassuming, modest, friendly. Rockburn recalled how warmly Elias treated him on first meeting, as if they had been trusted brothers of the bench for years.

"Elias," he greeted him on the phone. "I'm pleased to hear from you, but I have to wonder why? Are you well?"

"I'm fine, Creed. I see you're front page news today."

"Oh, the Goodbow case. I've set it for trial next week."

"It's why I'm calling. I wanted to check on something."

"About this case?"

"Sort of. A related issue. Are you aware of the application for a FISA warrant to intercept and record this man Goodbow's phone?"

"No. A pending application? He's been indicted. That would be completely improper."

"Nothing is pending. The application was denied three months ago. By my panel. The government didn't disclose this to you?"

"No. I know nothing about it."

"Then, neither does Wilton Goodbow or his lawyer."

"No doubt."

"I had a hunch they hadn't disclosed it. We thought it was an improper application in the first place. FISA warrants are for terrorism-related investigations, as you know. The application from the FBI and DOJ didn't even allege probable cause of a violation of *any* law, much less a terrorism charge. It was an overreach. We thought it amounted to FISA abuse, and we told that to DOJ after we denied the warrant. And in any event, it should have been turned over by the prosecutors in your case with the other discovery. That would be my view, at least. But it's your case, of course, Creed. I'm not suggesting anything to you, I just wanted to be sure you were aware of it."

"Well, I'm grateful, Elias. I will deal with it. I'm not sure how, but I will. Could you fax me down the application you denied?"

"You'll have it minutes. Good luck with the trial. I'm sure the media will be all over it."

Judge Rockburn strode to the door of his chambers and called for his law clerk.

"Get ahold of Gillen McCoy and Special Prosecutor Bell. Tell 'em I want them over here right away," he said.

"You set the pretrial conference for tomorrow," the law clerk said. "Remember?"

"I'm moving it up. Get them in here."

* * *

The defense lawyer and the federal prosecutor arrived at the courthouse at nearly the same time. They followed each other through the security check and rode the elevator together to the fourth-floor courtroom and chambers of T. Creed Rockburn.

"Odd that he moved up the pretrial," Preston Bell said. "He do this kind of thing often?"

"Only when he gets a last-minute invitation to go quail hunting," Gillen said.

But when the two lawyers were ushered into Rockburn's private chambers and saw the look on his face, each knew there was no recreational reason behind the summoning. Rockburn appeared livid.

"I just received a call from the chief judge of the FISA court in Washington!" he boomed, glaring at Preston Bell. "Now *why* would I get a call from him, mister special prosecutor?"

Preston Bell's face went crimson. He said nothing.

"Do you have something to tell the court and defense counsel? And, more to the point, why haven't you told us already? Why didn't you disclose it in your discovery?"

"Disclose what?" asked Gillen.

"Tell him, goddamn it!" Judge Rockburn barked. The prosecutor turned toward Gillen.

"An application for a FISA warrant was filed on Goodbow," he said. "The FBI asked for it three months ago. To monitor and record his phone calls."

"Who in the FBI?" Gillen asked.

"Agents Burlacher and Everett. And Breen Edwards vouched for it."

"It was denied out of hand!" Judge Rockburn said. "And you didn't disclose it to McCoy or to me!"

"It wasn't relevant," Bell said. Gillen had to admire his composure under the circumstances. "It was denied and not used to collect any evidence the government will present against the defendant," Bell said calmly. "It has no place in this trial."

"Oh, for Pete's sake," the judge said. "You know goddamned well that if it *had* been granted, you'd blow it up the size of a billboard and parade it back and forth in front of the jury. 'Even the terrorist court wanted this guy investigated.' That's what you'd say."

"Well, that's not going to happen, your honor."

"You're goddamned right it's not going to happen. I'm not sure now that *anything* is going to happen. This is serious prosecutorial misconduct. Don't you agree, Gillen?"

"I do, your honor. Are you inviting a motion to dismiss the indictment?"

"Oh my God!" said Preston Bell. "That is way out of bounds."

"You shut up!" the judge said. "Prepare your motion, Gillen. I want you both to brief it within forty-eight hours." He handed a copy of the paperwork Judge Humphrey had sent him to Gillen. "Here's the application they filed and the denial order, Gillen," he said. "*You've* already got the goddamned thing," he said to shell-shocked Preston Bell. "This came to me under seal and it will stay that way. The motion to dismiss and your briefs too. This absolutely does not get out to the press, at least until I've ruled. I don't want a circus out there or anything that could prejudice the jury panel, one way or another. If there is one. Am I understood?"

Preston Bell nodded grimly. Gillen McCoy fought back a smile. Successfully. But his heart leaped.

70

"Does that nun of yours have a direct line to God, or something?" Gillen said to his client that night over drinks at The Fine Sombrero. "I mean, this thing has just fallen right from heaven! I would never have expected anything like this to happen."

"You really think the judge will throw out the case over this?"

"He could. It would be extraordinary, that's for sure. When something like this does happen, it's usually *after* a trial, after a conviction. The police screwed up some blood test and knew it or didn't reveal they had a witness who corroborated the defendant, that kind of thing. And nine times out of ten, the court says it wouldn't have mattered anyway. So called "non-prejudicial error." But this is coming out *before* the trial. I've never seen Rocky that angry. He really lost it with Bell."

"What about the local U.S. Attorney? You said he's a good guy. Do you think he knew?"

"Oh, I just can't believe that," Gillen said. "Herb Morales is as straight as a Nebraska highway. Total integrity. If he'd known about it and knew it hadn't been turned over with the other stuff, he'd have called me and Rockburn and told the guy from DC to go to hell."

"If they had given it to you?" Goodbow asked. "What could you do with it in the trial anyway?"

"I'd use it in cross-examining Burlacher and Everett. *'This isn't the first time you went to a court against this citizen, is it? You singled out this citizen and wanted to listen in on his phone calls, didn't you? And what did those judges—three of them!—think about your investigation?'* "

"You lawyers think of everything," Goodbow said. "I'm just happy they didn't get that warrant. They'd know about Burp. They'd know about Maria Angeles."

The old lawyer sipped his whiskey and looked intently, but kindly, at Goodbow across the table.

"You told me the nun said you should stop worrying about the others and worry more about yourself."

"She did, yes."

"I hope you take her advice more than you've been taking mine."

71

T. Creed Rockburn worked through the night studying the legal authorities cited by Gillen and Preston Bell in their briefs and issued his eight-page decision just two days later.

It was like so many judicial opinions; powerfully written and music to the ears of the old Texas lawyer. Until its conclusion. Judge Rockburn castigated the government for its nondisclosure of the FISA warrant application, calling it "an appalling violation of the federal rules of criminal procedure intended to protect the rights of a defendant to a fair trial." He called the prosecution's decision to withhold the information "inexcusable" and a "legitimate basis for the court, in its discretion, to void the indictment as a remedy." But, and in such matters there is so often a *but,* the conservative judge ultimately concluded:

> But while the Court finds the government's action and inaction deplorable, it cannot say that the undisclosed application produced material evidence probative to

the merits of the offenses charged in the indictment. At most, the government's unsuccessful attempt to obtain the FISA warrant bears on the credibility of the FBI agents and the Department of Homeland Security and their motives in pursuing the defendant. It may be used for such purposes at the trial of this case. The Motion to Dismiss is denied. Trial will begin as scheduled by prior Order.

SO ORDERED.

T. Creed Rockburn
United States District Judge
Western District of Texas, El Paso Division

"Rocky couldn't bring himself to do it," lamented Gillen McCoy after reading the decision to Goodbow over the phone. The Rhode Islander was at the Place of Angels Respite Center where he'd been running errands for Sister Hope Annie. He'd been coming every day that Gillen didn't need him in his office. He enjoyed seeing the children and it kept his mind off the upcoming trial.

"You really think he should have granted the motion?" Goodbow asked.

"Honestly, no. They had the better argument."

"So, I've got the only honest lawyer in Texas? Just kidding, Gillen. I suppose there are a lot of them."

"There are. And Rockburn is an honest judge. We lost the motion, but who knows, maybe it will help us win the war. Preston Bell has put Rocky on his bad side. And the judge will make a hundred decisions before your trial is finished. Objections granted or overruled. Testimony allowed in or excluded. And the jury instructions that could make or break it for you.

Most of them will be on-the-spot judgment calls for him. Maybe what happened these last few days will linger in his attitude. When he's making them. And he's letting us use the FISA business in the trial. They were going to try to keep it out. It was abusive. It doesn't make the government look good."

"I didn't know there was so much involved in a trial," Goodbow said. "I can see why it took you ninety-four years to learn it all."

"How's Sister Hope Annie?"

"Her usual. Tireless."

"Remember not to talk to her about the trial or her testimony."

"I haven't and I won't."

"I mean it. She'll be asked on the stand if she's been talking to you down there. It won't look good."

"I got it. And she knows too. She hasn't brought up anything. But I think she's happy that I'm volunteering. She sends me out for what she needs. A lot of diapers and washing detergent, paper towels and stuff. I can't believe these Walmart stores! They've got everything. You ever been in one?"

"Oh my God, Goodbow," Gillen laughed. "Where the hell have you been living?"

"They don't have one in Newport."

"We'll leave that out of your testimony. Oh, I forgot. You're not testifying. Or will you now? Make my day. Tell me you've changed your mind."

"That's not going to happen," Goodbow said. "We've been over it enough."

"I know. But I have to keep trying. I'm your lawyer. Besides, you're growing on me."

"Really," Goodbow said. "Enough to hold back on that next retainer payment?"

"Not that much."

72

When the United States Federal Building in El Paso opened in 1938, it housed only two large courtrooms on the fourth of five floors in the original design of architects Percy McGhee, Guy L. Frazer, and Thomas P. Lippincott. But as demands on the building grew over the decades, most of the interior was radically re-configured to allow for numerous new federal offices and many additional, smaller courtrooms, mostly for immigration hearings. The proud architects surely would have disapproved of the sledgehammers taken to their exquisite structure and the modern drywall that replaced the rich dark hardwoods that burnished every wall in the original building. But they could take some solace in knowing that two aspects of their masterwork remained untarnished: The neo-classical exterior of sanded white limestone and fluted columns; and the two original illustrious courtrooms on the fourth floor. One of which was now appreciatively occupied by Judge T. Creed Rockburn.

When Goodbow walked into that courtroom on the first day of his trial, nothing that Gillen McCoy had told him—and he had told him plenty—prepared him for the heavy grandeur of the huge room or the weight of worry that it placed on his shoulders. At the front of the room a raised bench long enough to hold a dozen chairs featured only one, in the center, its leather back stretching higher than any person could ever require. It was unoccupied under the massive medallion of the United States of America that hung behind it. The molded ceiling loomed at least thirty feet above the shiny marble floor and deep walnut seating, fifteen long rows on each side of the wide center aisle. In comparison to the expansive elevated bench at the front of the courtroom, and the two-tiered jury box positioned on the left, at an angle facing the judge's chair, the two small desks sitting left and right on the main floor in front of the observer pews seemed oddly tiny.

"Are those little tables for us?" Goodbow asked as they walked up the aisle.

"The one on the right is ours," he said. "The prosecution gets the one closer to the jury." He saw Goodbow's curled brow. "Just the way it is," the lawyer said.

"Why are we so early?" Goodbow asked. They were the only ones in the courtroom, though they had passed reporters gathered on the outside steps. "The order said nine o'clock. It's not even eight yet."

"Just something I do. Especially with a first-time defendant. Give you a chance to settle down. Take in the place. You feeling okay?"

"Well, it is a little intimidating."

"You're doing fine, believe me. I've had clients throw up by now."

"Well, I'm not going to do that, for God's sake."

"Just so it doesn't happen in front of the prospective jury panel. The judge is going to call them all in—the whole pool, a hundred and fifty people—and have them sit in those rows back there. They're all going to be in here until they're either excused or selected. I've never had a client acquitted who puked in front of them."

"My God, you have seen it all, haven't you?"

"Whenever I think that, a guy like you comes along."

* * *

An hour later a door opened at the front of the room behind the elevated bench and out stepped black robed T. Creed Rockburn, climbing to his perch.

"All rise," announced the bailiff.

But the only persons in the vast courtroom, other than the stenographer, were Gillen McCoy, Wilton Goodbow, Preston Bell and the junior Assistant U.S. Attorney sent by Herbert Morales to accompany him.

"Before I bring in the prospective jurors, is there anything from counsel?" the judge said.

Preston Bell shook his head. "No, your honor."

"Mr. McCoy?"

"Yes, Judge," Gillen said. "The defendant has been informed that a church event—a vigil of some kind—will occur tonight in Minnesota involving the immigrant parents and their children there. Mr. Goodbow had nothing to do with organizing it and he has committed to me that he will make no statements or appear before the press for the entirety of his trial. But I feel obliged to bring tonight's event to your attention. There will likely be media coverage on site there, perhaps even live coverage on national cable networks. It may be difficult to prevent the jurors who are seated today from seeing it tonight. Though the media attention may favor the defendant's cause, we feel we should bring it to the court's attention in the event the court might choose to sequester the jury once it is selected.

As you can imagine, my client is not looking forward to being on trial. We don't want to have to do it a second time."

"Understood. Thank you for telling me, Mr. McCoy," the judge said. "The marshal says a flock of reporters will be outside the courthouse, too. Probably throughout the trial. Coming in this morning, I saw a couple of TV vans setting up already. So, I've been considering sequester. With what you've told me about Minnesota, it's clear to me I need to do it. Is there a hotel that either of you recommend?"

"Anyplace but the Fine Sombrero Motor Inn, your honor," Gillen said. "Mr. Goodbow is staying there."

"The *Fine Sombrero?*" The judge was clearly surprised. "What's he doing there?" He looked down for the first time directly into Goodbow's eyes. "Is he *that* expensive?" Gillen and the judge laughed; Preston Bell was unamused.

For some of the jurors, a hotel room in El Paso would likely be welcomed. The El Paso division of the Western District of Texas covered only two of the fifty-four Texas counties comprising the Western District as a whole, El Paso County and Hudspeth County. But Hudspeth was the third largest county in all of Texas, sprawling northeast toward New Mexico. The jury pool would be randomly selected from the voter rolls of both counties, including their furthest stretches from El Paso. At least a few of those ultimately impaneled for the trial of Wilton Goodbow would face a round trip drive of two-hundred miles each day.

But they might not appreciate the restrictions that would be placed on them in sequester. Judge Rockburn instructed his bailiff to secure rooms at a quality hotel with twenty-four-hour room service, but to have all televisions disconnected before the jurors checked in. He ordered the federal marshal to arrange overnight staffing to prevent any juror from leaving his or her room except to walk in the hallways, and even then, accompanied by a marshal. And he instructed the federal watchmen to collect all of the jurors' cell phones before they were transported from the courthouse. Jurors could ask for their phones to make personal calls from their rooms, but for only that purpose, after which the phones would be recollected. No media streaming or internet surfing would be permitted.

"In view of these rules, your honor, could I suggest that the jurors be permitted unrestricted access to the menu at no cost to them?" Gillen said. "Including alcoholic beverages?"

"Including *alcohol*?" the judge said. He motioned to the stenographer to go off the record.

"Well, I'm sure some of them will be accustomed to an evening cocktail or two," Gillen said. "And they may be sequestered for a week."

"Do you object, Mr. Bell?" the judge asked. The prosecutor nodded that he didn't.

"All right, then," the judge said. "We don't normally pay for liquor, but I guess this is an unusual circumstance. But I better not see anything about it in an appeal brief!"

* * *

Jury selection—*voir dire*—as it was called, was laborious. Goodbow looked every prospective juror in the eye as the lawyers questioned them, as Gillen had instructed him.

"Don't smile at them, but look them in the eye. Just look pleasant. Friendly."

"Pleasantly serious," Goodbow said.

"Right. And very attentive. Nothing turns off a jury more than a bored defendant."

Goodbow was impressed by the judge's demeanor and apparent fairness as the jury was selected. One prospective juror took his seat when called, holding a red ball cap in his lap.

Before Preston Bell could ask even his first question, Rockburn leaned down and interjected his own.

"Sir, would you hold up that hat for me?" the judge asked. "MAGA" was stitched above its bill. "You're excused, sir," the judge said, immediately.

"Your honor!" the prosecutor objected. "He hasn't even been asked whether he can be objective!"

The gavel came down instantly. "Thank you, sir. You're excused," the judge said matter-of-factly.

So many jurors were excused because they acknowledged they had formed an opinion about the case—or because they *didn't* admit it but clearly had—that it took until five o'clock to seat the twelfth juror, plus two alternates. To select those 14, 142 were considered. Though he had merely listened, looking pleasantly serious all day, Will Goodbow was mentally exhausted when he left the courthouse with Gillen McCoy, by the rear door.

Opening statements would be made in the morning.

73

The idea for the *Vigil for Justice* was Lutheran minister Burton Leif's alone, intended in his mind as prayerful support for the reunification of the Honduran families in his town. But when an idea resonates in enough hearts and minds, it can take on a life separate from its originator. And as the event took shape that evening in Breckenridge, no one could rightly call it anymore a simply Lutheran devotional. It became as ecumenical as such a gathering could be in the deep upper northland.

As the calls came in from clergy as far away as Minneapolis and Fargo, asking to participate, the small, articulate minister with the gentle face soon knew the small candlelight service he'd envisioned in his modest church sanctuary was emerging as something much bigger. And when Police Chief Woody Burns reached him two days before the scheduled service, urging that he move the vigil out of doors to the expansive church lawn, the reverend readily agreed.

"But you may want to keep it from getting too political," the chief said. "As best you can."

"My thinking, exactly," Burton Leif said. "It's not meant to be a protest. It's meant to be a prayer. A prayer for thoughtfulness and tolerance."

The crowd that appeared as the sun set that evening surpassed any expectation, even of the police chief. The priest from the Breckenridge Catholic parish, together with the ministers from the local Methodist and Presbyterian congregations, flanked Reverend Leif on a makeshift platform at the edge of his church parking lot. The rabbi from the synagogue in Fargo and the Unitarian minister from St. Paul came too, followed on the highways by cars filled with congregants.

Woody Burns and all but one of his patrolmen, who the chief left on duty at the police station, stood in the front row of the crowd, in full uniform. They weren't there for security; they came unarmed. The closest thing to security guards were the six lanky ushers from the Catholic parish, loaned by the priest to make sure children did not run into the street from the rear of the crowd.

Burton Leif's posters around town had said that vigil candles and wax holders would be distributed to all who wanted them. "Signs and loud talking are discouraged," the poster said diplomatically. "Hymns will be sung," the poster further said, implicitly conveying hoped-for solemnity. As solemn as you could hope for, that is, with accompaniment by Angelo Presti on his electronic accordion.

Gillen McCoy came to Goodbow's room at the Fine Sombrero to watch the news coverage.

"This place isn't as bad as I thought," the lawyer said as they sat on the couch with the whiskey he'd brought up from the bar. "But that TV is almost as old as me. Is there even a remote?" The heavy big box with the eighteen-inch screen sat on a wobbly wire TV stand, with manual knobs.

"No, but it works fine," Goodbow said, almost defensively,

rising to turn it on. "They jerry-rigged it for cable and everything."

The images on the screen shook them both. Reverend Leif looked to the side of the gathered crowd and motioned, calling someone to come forward. Sister Marcus Marie led the children and all six mothers from Tegus in single file to the front of the platform. All of them stood and faced their gathered supporters, most of the younger children held any part of their mothers' legs they could find.

"There's little Gloria," Goodbow said. "Third girl from the left. Gloria Carrasco."

"She looks very happy," Gillen said.

"Where are the fathers?" Goodbow asked. "Only the mothers are there."

"Bell brought them all down *here*. They're all on his witness list. Only the mothers are up there with the kids. Run through the channels for a minute. See if they're all covering this." Goodbow did. "My, God," the old lawyer said, "Even *Fox News* has it on!"

They settled on CNN and watched quietly. The network showed live the whole of Burton Leif's understated, reverent remarks, without interruption. Many in the crowd listened with bowed heads, including the big police chief and his men. Maybe others could tell that Angelo Presti's music came from an accordion, and not a church organ, but neither Gillen nor Goodbow could. The singing voices of the multifaith crowd rose beautifully above his expert accompaniment.

Wilton Goodbow's name was never uttered from the platform, and when the TV reporters cornered Burton Leif after the vigil, not even then, at least by him.

"Reverend Leif," one asked, "When you called this 'a Vigil for Justice,' did you mean 'Justice for Wilton Goodbow?' His trial began today in El Paso."

"Tonight was not about politics," he said. "It was not even about changing the legal system, though I wish it would change for the cause of immigrants and refugees. Tonight was about prayer. Prayer for understanding. Prayer for these reunited families. They have now received justice. We celebrated it. I pray that the gentleman from Rhode Island receives justice too. Whatever that justice is."

Goodbow turned off the television and walked with Gillen to the door of the motel room. The lawyer could see how moved his client had been by what they watched.

"What kind of justice do *you* think I will get, Gillen?"

"I will tell you the truth, Will." He reached up to the much taller man's shoulder. "I fear the wrong kind. But whatever happens, you'll always have what you saw tonight."

74

T. Creed Rockburn dropped with a thud into his chair behind the high bench and glared down at Gillen McCoy as the fourth day of the trial began. Will looked to the jury box. He saw what he feared he would see. The jurors were all rivetted on the judge's impatient expression.

"So," the judge said. "Is Mr. McCoy prepared to continue his examination of this witness?"

"I am, your honor." The small old lawyer rose before he said it. Then he turned to the jurors and paused, smiling as a grandfather might when looking upon his progeny.

"Well, then proceed," the judge said. "You will have our complete attention, I am sure."

"I will try not to test it, your honor."

"Oh, you test it all the time, Mr. McCoy. But go ahead." A weak smile was discernible on the judge's face.

If there had been one exchange of this kind in the trial so far, there had been a dozen, Will thought. Whenever Judge Rockburn showed irritation—and displeasure seemed his default countenance—Gillen unflappably countered with some courtesy or other that invited a witty response from the judge. After the second day of testimony, Will had raised the practice with Gillen over their nightly drink.

"He's such a grump," Will had said of the stern judge. "He stares at you and makes sharp comments, right in front of the jury."

"Oh, that's Rocky."

"And you react so kindly every time he does."

"I do."

"And then you set him up to say something clever."

"I do that too."

"Why?"

"Because he's doing his job, which in his mind is to show he's running the place with a whip. And my job is to take his medicine willingly. Show respect no matter what, and make the judge look smart. Which 'ole Rocky is, by the way."

"Will that help me with the jury?"

"Probably not. But at least they'll like your lawyer."

"Very comforting."

"Well, Will, they're not going to get much chance to like *you*, are they? Seeing that you won't talk to them yourself. And all they're hearing is that you did just what the government says you did. And deliberately as hell."

Daily—without fail—Gillen had urged Will to reconsider his insistence against testifying in his own defense. "I have got to give them *somebody* to like on our side of the room," he'd said. "It's looking like that comes down to me and the nun, you poor bastard. But I can say this: we need that judge to smile at me as often as opportunity and heaven allow. As far as the jurors go, if he's smiling at me, he's smiling at you. There's never been a jury in the world that didn't ask themselves, 'What does the judge want us to do?' It doesn't mean they'll go for you if they think the judge likes us. But if they believe the judge *doesn't* like us ... well, you might as well order that orange suit right now."

Since the first day when the jury was seated, it seemed to Goodbow that everything, other than Gillen's opening statement, was going against him. Gillen told him it was always that way; trials were like rollercoasters. The prosecution was always climbing at first. It went first with its case, normally convincingly. But then, Gillen assured, there would be ups and downs and, inevitably, sudden turns. "Some nights you'll feel devastated," he said. "Some nights you'll feel hopeful. It's just the way it is. Enjoy the hopeful ones."

But Goodbow had yet to have an evening to be hopeful. On the first day and a half of testimony, the jury heard from the two FBI agents, Burlacher and Everett. To Goodbow, they seemed as impressive and credible as the actors on television. *And why shouldn't they! They're just telling what happened, as it happened!* Answering the questions of fit-looking, impeccably attired Special Prosecutor Preston Bell, they described their posting in the US Embassy in Tegucigalpa; how their principal assignment was the interdiction of narcotics on their way to the US border and chasing the money that came back in return; how the visit of Wilton Goodbow to Honduras had drawn the attention of the Department of Homeland Security; and all the rest.

The only hint of optimism for the senior citizen industrialist came during Gillen's cross-examination of Agent Everett. The wise lawyer had made only a slight reference to the FISA warrant application when crossing the first of the agent witnesses—Burlacher—whispering to Goodbow that this was intentional. He wanted the jury to receive the impact of the episode when the second agent testified. "Juries don't like repetition any more than anyone does," he'd explained to Goodbow at the defense table. "I don't want to get after both of them on this. I'm only planting the seed with Burlacher so they understand what I'm talking about when I unload on Everett."

"So, Agent Everett," Gillen asked when the second agent finished his direct testimony. "When you wanted to find Mr. Goodbow after his visit to the embassy, you were not prepared to accuse him of any crime, were you."

"No, we didn't have anything on him at that time."

"So you had no basis for seeking an ordinary warrant for his phone records, isn't that correct?"

"That's correct. We knew his cell phone number because he had called the embassy in Honduras, so we could look for his phone when it pinged cell towers."

"But you didn't need a warrant to do that, right?"

"No. We do that in every investigation when we're trying to locate a person.

All it tells us is that his location was near that ping at the time a call was made."

"It doesn't tell you anything about what was said, or even the number dialed, does it?"

"That's right. But we didn't have probable cause for a regular warrant to listen in. It was the best we could do. That's why it took us so long to find him. He was moving quickly and not using the phone much."

"When you concluded that an ordinary criminal investigation warrant could not be obtained—because, as you said, there was no probable cause to support it—you and Agent Burlacher filed an application to a special court for another kind of warrant, didn't you?"

"We did. Yes."

"You tried to get a very special warrant that allows the tapping of the phone of a United States citizen who is believed to be involved in terrorism, or is believed to be involved in an imminent threat to the national security of our country, did you not?"

It was clear that all of the jurors were struck by the question. Goodbow saw the heightened attention in their faces as they looked at the witness.

"It's called a FISA warrant—F-I-S-A—for Federal Intelligence Surveillance Act," Gillen said.

"You wanted one of those, correct?"

"We did. Yes. I just said we did."

"What grounds did you state in that application?"

"That his wife—his deceased wife—had written letters to the president. And she had encouraged others to write letters to him."

"About what?"

"About the separation of parents and children at the border."

"Did Mr. Goodbow send any of these letters?"

"No."

"Were his late wife's letters threatening?"

"What do you mean?"

"Did they threaten the president or anyone else with violence?"

"I wouldn't say 'violence,' but she was pretty angry."

"She wanted the president to stop the separations and she wanted him to reunite the parents with their children. She wanted him to do that. Isn't that all that she said in her letters?"

"Yes."

"And the same thing was demanded in letters from others that she solicited?"

"Yes."

"But none of the letters came from Mr. Goodbow, here?"

"They did not."

"Did the special FISA court give you the warrant you asked for?"

"No."

"It was denied?"

"Correct."

"Unanimously?"

"Correct."

"So, here we are in the federal district court of the Western District of Texas, El Paso Division. And this is not the first court in which you have pursued Wilton Goodbow, is it?"

"Objection!" screamed Special Prosecutor Preston Bell.

"Overruled," said Judge Rockburn, calmly, but with his gavel's punctuation.

"We wanted his phone calls," the witness said. "The FISA court said no."

"Because a private citizen is entitled to the privacy of his own phone calls, correct?"

"I guess that's true."

"You guess?"

"That's true."

"Just to be clear, you do not contend that Mr. Goodbow has or has ever had a relationship to any terrorist organization, isn't that correct?"

"No, he doesn't. He never has."

"And yet the Department of Homeland Security pushed you to seek the terrorism warrant, did it not?"

"They wanted it, yes."

"In fact, the Secretary of DHS himself, Breen Edwards, told you to do it, didn't he?"

"He did."

"So, is it fair to say, Agent, that a member of the president's cabinet was personally targeting Mr. Goodbow here because he thought he was interested in the separation of parents and children at the border?"

"Objection!"

"Basis?" Judge Rockburn asked Preston Bell, calmly.

"Breen Edwards is not on trial here, your honor. His interest in the case is irrelevant."

"I'll allow it," the judge said. He looked down to the stenographer. "Repeat the question to the witness." She re-read Gillen's question in a choppy, nasal, monotone.

"He may have been, I don't know for sure what his motivations were. But he did want that FISA wire-tapping."

Goodbow stared at the witness. *Thank God, he didn't get it. Thank God they don't have Burp.*

"Nothing further, your honor."

* * *

"So then," Judge Rockburn said again. "Please continue with your examination of Mr. Rodriguez. Remember, Mr. Rodriguez, you remain under the oath you swore when you began your testimony before the lunch recess."

Juan Rodriguez nodded, unenthusiastically, and took his seat in the witness chair below and left of the judge on the side of the courtroom nearer the jury box.

The father's testimony that morning on behalf of the government was expected, but still hard to hear for Goodbow. Prosecutor Bell's questions elicited methodically the whole journey. The meeting at St. Antonio's church where the parents learned of Goodbow's plan. The trip in the vans to the harbor at Amapala. The boarding of the massive sailboat. The quiet, firm captain whose name was never spoken. The storm at sea endured to avoid the coast guard ships. The midnight disembarkment at the deserted boating club near San Diego. And finally, the long drive across the mountains and plains to Minnesota and their children.

Listening to it all next to his lawyer at the small table in the courtroom, the old industrialist knew that but for him the refugee on the stand and his wife would still not be with their children and would never have been granted the asylum they and the others were awarded under their immunity agreements. But Juan's testimony did not make Goodbow feel turned upon or unappreciated. Indeed, he had fully agreed with Sister Hope Annie that the parents should accept the offered asylum in return for their assistance in convicting him, and he was pleased that his work to bring them would not be made for naught by their deportation. But though he would never be able to explain why—even to himself—he felt *sorry* even now for the position he had put them in; the emotional conflict, the pain of publicly stating that they knew it was illegal to board his boat and be secreted into the country, and all through the effort and suggestion of Wilton Goodbow who had come to meet them in the little church in Tegus, by no invitation of their own.

"Mr. Rodriguez, when did you first encounter a federal enforcement officer when you came into the United States?" Gillen began.

"You mean when they found me in Minnesota with my family?"

"No, the first time at the border. When you tried to get in to apply for asylum more than a year ago."

"You mean when they took my children away?"

"Objection, your honor!" Preston Bell jumped to his feet. "Move to strike!"

"Basis?" the judge asked.

"It's non-responsive. He was only asked when he first encountered a border agent."

"And he said 'When they took my children away'" the judge said, expressionlessly.

"What would you expect him say?"

"But it makes it sound like his kids were dragged off, or something."

"Overruled. Sit down."

Gillen walked slowly around the defendant's table before he stepped back toward the witness chair. The silver-haired lawyer stood directly beneath Judge Rockburn, to the right of the witness so that the jury's view of Rodriguez was unimpaired.

"Mr. Rodriguez," Gillen asked, "when you met that first enforcement officer, did he know you were the father of the children?"

"Yes. He had forms that said it. He read us some of it. That we were a family. But I told him anyway. He believed us, that we were a family coming together."

"You and your children had come to the border station together, hadn't you?"

"Yes. They were always with me until then. And with their mother too."

"Your English is good, Mr. Rodriguez. Did you speak in English to the officer?"

"Yes. And I told my oldest boy, Rigo, to address him in English too. And to be polite. He speaks well. The school in Honduras taught him and we practiced it at home before we came."

"Why did you do that?"

"We were told we would have a better chance if we spoke like Americans."

"A chance for what?"

"For asylum."

"Yes, it says that here on the immigration form from the

border station," Gillen said. "That you asked for asylum, that is." He held the two-page record in his hand and looked up to the judge. "Defendant's exhibit 22, your honor. May I show it to the witness?"

"Of course, Mr. McCoy."

"Well thank you, your honor. That's kind of you."

Preston Bell leapt to his feet. "What is that supposed to mean?"

Gillen turned to him dead on.

"I said it's kind of the judge to show it to him. The enforcement officer wouldn't."

Judge Rockburn slammed his gavel and motioned Gillen and Bell to the far side of the bench.

"Gillen, you know goddammed well how to try a case," the judge said, unhappily. He leaned close to both lawyers, spoke in a low tone, and flipped a switch that flooded the main courtroom with white noise. "You've tried a thousand of them. You don't have to use *me* to try this one. And, Mr. Bell, knock off the histrionics. You have a beef, ask to approach. You're not claiming the border agents *did* show him this form, are you?" Bell nodded that no, he wasn't. "What I thought," the judge said. "Go ahead, Gillen. But no more of that 'judge' stuff."

"Mr. Rodriguez, Exhibit 22 is the record of your asylum interview by the first border agent. As you testified, it reflects that when you reached the border point you stated that you were seeking asylum for your family and for yourself."

"I did, yes. That's why we came."

"But look at the part of the second page, where it says, 'Agent Comments.'"

The witness turned to the page and read for only a few moments. He became visibly shaken.

"What's the matter, Mr. Rodriguez?" Gillen asked.

"It says here, 'Family does not speak English!'"

"And you and your son both spoke English to the agent, didn't you?"

"We did, yes! Rigo even introduced his brother and sisters to the man in English. Told him what grade each of them was in school!"

"Did you ask the agent to let you see what he had written on his report?"

"Yes."

"Why?"

"The people helping us in Honduras, the aid workers, they told us always to ask. There might be something wrong. Our names could be misspelled, or something else."

"Did the agent show you the form when you asked to see it?"

"No. He wouldn't give it to me."

"Did you object or complain?"

"No."

"Did you ask to speak with another agent or his superior?"

"No."

"Why not?"

"I did not think he liked us. I did not want to make him more angry. I thought this would not be good."

"What happened next?"

"The agent said the children had to go somewhere else, without us. Without me or their mother. She and I had to stay there for more things. We might be sent back. He didn't know about the children. This scared me. All of us, it scared. My daughters and Rigo's younger brother started crying. They all could understand, even though their English is not as good as Rigo's."

"And Rigo. Did Rigo cry?"

"No, Rigo is brave. He said, 'Papa, I will be *you*.' He pointed at me. 'I will watch them for you, Papa,' he told me."

"And then?"

"Another agent came and took the children from us."

"From you and your wife?"

"Yes. My wife was crying hard. I did not know what I could do. For them or for her."

Gillen stepped to the witness and reached for the immigration record in his hand.

"This all happened," Gillen looked at the form, "on June 5, 2018. When did you next see your children, Mr. Rodriguez?"

"When Mr. Goodbow's boat took us to America and the nuns drove us to them in Minnesota."

"In July 2019."

"Yes."

"And that's when you met Mr. Goodbow again, wasn't it?"

"Yes. He was there in Minnesota at the house with the children when we arrived."

"Did you speak with him that night?"

"Yes, he said he had met Rigo already. That he had told Rigo he had met me in Tegus and that it was true that we were coming that night. And he told me I should be proud of Rigo."

"And you knew that Will Goodbow was the man behind your trip back to America, back to your children?"

"Yes, I knew. Everyone on the boat knew. And he met with us before at the church with Father Lopez when he told us what he could try to do and asked us if we wanted to go on his boat to America. And the captain told us some about him."

"The captain that never said his own name?"

"Yes, him."

"When you met Mr. Goodbow again in Minnesota, did you ask him why he did all this?"

"I never did. I thanked him, we all thanked him. But I never asked him why he did it. Maybe I should have, but we were together again with our children. It didn't seem to matter why he did it."

For the first time, Mr. Rodriguez looked from his chair to Will sitting alone at the defense table. Juan did not smile. He looked penitent, sad to have named his benefactor. He nodded, measurably, to Will. Will nodded back, less measurably.

"Oh," Gillen McCoy said, walking back to his seat next to Will. "One last question. How old is Rigo?"

"He is eleven now. He was ten, then."

75

"I'm ready for one of those good days you said we'd have," Goodbow said that night to Gillen.

"Today *was* a good day," the lawyer said. "Everyone liked Juan Rodriguez. Everyone could see his feelings for you. His gratitude."

"What does that get me?"

"Gratitude." Gillen ordered a second scotch. "Look, you need to be realistic. There's not going to be some silver bullet that saves you. It's more of a mosaic. Little things here and there, but all of them fit together."

"To form what? Sympathy?"

"No. Rich people don't get sympathy. You don't qualify for sympathy. But just maybe, you can get *empathy*. I won't give you malarkey. A lot of empathy only goes a little way. But it's better than the opposite."

"Which is?"

"When they think you're a lying scoundrel."

Goodbow did not smile as widely as Gillen did.

"But really," the lawyer said. "I think tomorrow may be a

lot better. They're going to rest their case and it's our turn. You've got a good leadoff hitter."

"Sister Hope Annie?"

"Right. We'll call her first. I know Preston Bell is worried about her."

"How do you know that?"

"Because he filed a motion asking the judge to tell us how he is going to instruct the jury on the meaning of 'corrupt intent.' Says he needs to know for purposes of his cross-examination of our witnesses. But mainly, it's the nun he's thinking about. How badly does she hurt his case? To weigh that, he needs to know how Rocky is going to define 'corruptly' in the criminal statutes when he gives his jury instructions. I told Rocky he shouldn't decide on the instruction until he's heard all the witnesses testify. Not till the end."

"When will he rule, then?" Goodbow asked.

"I don't know. He wouldn't say when. Or give me any idea how he will define the word when he does announce his jury instruction. And the prosecutor also filed a motion for an order preventing me from asking anyone, including Sister Hope Annie, what you told them about your reasons for doing this."

"He can do that?"

"Yes, because it's all hearsay, unless it comes out of your own mouth in that courtroom. It's the whole point of the 'hearsay rule.' I told you that. Bell said you shouldn't be able to have it both ways. If you don't want to take the stand in your own defense, you absolutely do not have to, and they can't talk about the fact that you're not testifying. But you can't *not* testify, avoid cross-examination, and have somebody else tell your story for you."

"I guess I can understand that."

"Enough to change your mind about taking the stand?"

"You know I won't do that."

"Well, you should know that Rocky granted his motion on that point. Now I can't ask her what you said to her. Or Lane Williams, either." The lawyer sounded displeased with his client. "That isn't going to help."

The two of them sat without speaking for several minutes. It may have been that the old trial lawyer regretted his tone. "It's all right, though," he said. "That nun will do fine anyway."

"You seem confident."

"I am. I've been getting around that hearsay rule for fifty years."

"I thought you said you've been practicing for *sixty-five* years."

"Took me fifteen to learn it."

76

You might think that a forty-year old nun who had never been in a courtroom in her life would be unnerved walking with a bailiff to the witness stand in the ostentatious room of justice. If she was, Sister Hope Annie disguised it well. She walked briskly and erectly to the chair, smiled up at Judge T. Creed Blackburn, and said her 'I do' to the oath in a strong, clear voice. Goodbow noticed that she had chosen a longer pure white veil than she normally wore. Perhaps to add additional decorum for the occasion, he thought. But if that were her purpose, it was likely offset by the ankle-high black sneakers into which her white hose descended beneath her long skirt. She looked her usual pretty self; her complexion rich and smooth, her dark hair tucked into her white coif above friendly deep brown eyes.

The only awkwardness in her arrival before the jury came when she seemed to have discomfort settling into the padded witness chair, as if she were sitting on her wallet or other object in her skirting. She squirmed visibly, finally leaning to one side and removing an even more visible pack of cigarettes that she moved to another pocket. Goodbow saw the brows raise on the judge's face, and several of the jurors smile.

"Are you prepared now, Sister?" the judge finally asked.

"Oh yes, sir. Is that what I should call you? *Sir?*"

"That's fine."

"Don't worry, I know I can't smoke in here."

Rockburn answered with only a constrained smile. "Please begin, Mr. McCoy."

Gillen spent ten minutes with questions about her life and work in the Rio Grande Valley. She'd entered the sisterhood when she was twenty-three, the jury learned. She had already been educated as an elementary school teacher. She was the youngest child in a big family, an aunt to fourteen nieces and nephews. Surprising everyone—the nun probably more than anyone—Gillen asked her if she had ever been married.

"No, but I almost was," she said, smiling. "Those were the days!"

The bailiff and several jurors laughed aloud. Rockburn lowered his gavel, but not sharply.

"When did you first meet Wilton Goodbow?"

"When I picked him up at The Fine Sombrero Motor Inn about eight months ago."

"Why did you go there to pick him up?"

"Because he called me the night before. He said Lane Williams had referred him to me. He said he wanted to learn about the problems of the families at the border here."

"Who is Lane Williams?"

"He is the manager in El Paso for Human Rights First. It is a nonprofit organization. It is headquartered in New York City. We work together often, finding shelter for the children who are allowed in. And for their parents when they are too. He is a fine man."

"*Objection!*" said prosecutor Bell.

"Sustained."

The nun turned and looked up at Judge Rockburn, puzzled.

"What is wrong with that?" she asked. "It's the truth. He *is* a fine man."

Rockburn leaned toward her. "Nothing is wrong, Sister. But a witness can only state facts, not opinions."

"But it *is* a fact. Everybody knows Lane is a good man!"

Wisely, Rockburn simply looked at Gillen. "Just proceed, Mr. McCoy," he said.

For an hour and a half, Sister Hope Annie responded to Gillen's deftly worded questions. She described in detail the perilous arrival of little Gloria Carrasco, her near-comatose state from the infection that had started in her cut foot and raced through her body as she walked with her parents in the caravan all the way to the US border. How Goodbow himself had witnessed her emergency entrance at the border patrol station and seen her weeping parents turned away as their daughter was rushed to an El Paso hospital. She told how Gloria came to live at the *Place of Angels Respite Center* when she had recovered and how the nun had worked with Lane Williams to place her in the home of the Swensen family in Minnesota.

But the crafty lawyer astutely refrained from ever asking the nun to repeat anything that Goodbow himself had said to her.

"Is Mr. Goodbow a widower?" he asked.

"Yes, his wife died shortly before he came down to learn about the border. Her name was Grace."

"Are you aware that his wife wrote letters to the president protesting the separation of parents from their children at the border?"

"Yes."

"If you know, Sister, what did Mr. Goodbow think about the government policy?"

"He was not sure that he agreed with his wife. He was not an activist like her."

"Did he miss his wife?"

"Very much."

"Without relating anything he said to you, how do you know that?"

"He didn't have to say anything. I could see it in him. Every time I saw him, I could see it in him."

"Was he always sad?"

"Oh, no. Not sad. But very determined. The more he learned about the border, the more determined he seemed to be."

"Did you go to Honduras at his request? Did he ask you to go there?"

"I offered to go. I wanted to go."

"He was happy that you went?"

"Yes. He was happy. He was determined to go through with his plan once he learned that the parents wanted him to."

She testified about the blessing they had all received from Father Lopez before they left for Amapala. But before Gillen McCoy could stop her, she blurted out that an ex-marine had protected her and the parents.

"I'm sorry, your Honor," Gillen quickly said. "I ask that the witness's last comment about a marine be stricken."

"You want to strike what your own witness said?"

"I did not ask her about any such thing. It should not be in the record."

Sister Hope Annie looked repentant.

"Granted," the judge said, looking down at the stenographer. "Strike it."

Gillen resumed. "When Mr. Goodbow's boat came into the harbor in Honduras, did you meet the man who sailed it?"

"Yes, I met the captain. I walked the parents onto the boat and introduced them to him."

"But you never learned his name?"

"No."

"Can you describe him?"

Goodbow rustled in his chair. *What's he doing? Why is he asking about Burp?*

"He was very handsome." A few jurors giggled. "Strong."

"How old was he?"

"I don't know. I'm not good at guessing ages. Like you for instance. I'd say you're maybe 70."

Judge Rockburn tried—and failed—to repress a hearty laugh.

"The sailboat, Sister. Did you see its name?"

"*The Sails of Grace.* It was called *The Sails of Grace.*"

"Grace?"

"Yes, that was the name of Mr. Goodbow's wife. I think the parents were sailing for her. Sailing for Grace. She wanted it. And he did it."

Purposely, Gillen walked to the defense table and shuffled through his notes. He wasn't looking for anything in them. He was letting the nun's last words sink in.

"I am almost finished, Sister," he said, finally. "I want to ask if you were interviewed by the FBI after Mr. Goodbow's actions were discovered. Were you?"

"Yes."

"Did you cooperate?"

"Fully."

"Is there anything more you would like to say before you are cross-examined?"

"Can I ask a question?" She looked up sincerely to the judge.

"Of course, Sister." Rockburn said, smiling. "What is it?"

"Could we have a break? I would like a cigarette outside."

The gavel came down immediately, this time with authority.

"The court is in recess," Rockburn boomed. "We'll resume in thirty minutes, Sister."

* * *

Gillen and Goodbow would never know which of the two things that happened in the next half hour before T. Creed Rockburn brought the jury back to his courtroom was the more critical. It didn't truly matter. All that mattered was that they changed everything that came thereafter in the case of the United States v. Wilton Goodbow.

The first was the phone call Preston Bell made from the courthouse lobby to Attorney General Ray Muncie in Washington.

"What is it?" Muncie asked. "How's it going?"

He listened grimly to the special prosecutor's report. "Ahumm . . . ahumm . . . ahumm."

Bell told him he believed a defense verdict was a distinct possibility, notwithstanding the uncontroverted evidence that Goodbow had planned and purposefully carried out the entire extrication of the "illegals" from Central America and their secretive landing in the US.

"I'm not sure this was the way to go," Bell said. "He's the wrong defendant with the right nun. It's all coming down to good people versus bad policy. And this ancient lawyer down here has Judge Rockburn eating right out of his hand. The FISA thing didn't help."

"I never should have let Breen Edwards talk me into that," Muncie said. "What do you suggest?"

"We don't know yet how Rockburn will instruct the jury on the 'corrupt' intent wording of the statute and the conspiracy charges. We need him to simply tell them that as long as Goodbow knew he was breaking the law, and did it anyway, he was acting 'corruptly.' But if he tells them he's not acting with corrupt intent unless he's doing something he thinks is just 'wrong'—I think they'll acquit."

"On everything?"

"On everything that will get him time in prison. And they may even acquit him on the smaller charge, the way it's going. The nun was unbelievable. They loved her."

"What are you saying?"

"I think if we find out Rockburn's going to give them a favorable jury charge, we have to decide whether it's better to have a not guilty verdict or just dismiss the indictment altogether before verdict. At least put a decent public relations face on this."

"Breen Edwards isn't good at public relations," Ray Muncie said. "But the president hates to lose. And he never really wanted this goddamned policy anyway. I'll talk to both of them. In the meantime, find out what the judge is going to do with that jury instruction."

* * *

It didn't take Special Prosecutor Bell long to find that out. When Judge Rockburn walked up to his bench after the recess, he motioned to the bailiff to hold the jurors in their waiting room. He told the stenographer to go on the record. He read from a prepared statement.

"The government has moved the court for clarity on how

the jury will be instructed at the close of the evidence on the meaning of the word 'corruptly' in each of the two conspiracy counts of the indictment. Defendant's counsel has objected to an early ruling on the jury instruction on the ground that all of the evidence is not yet in; however, defendant's counsel has submitted an alternative proposed instruction in the event the court agreed with Mr. Bell that an early ruling from the court was appropriate. Mr. McCoy is overruled on his objection to a ruling at this time. I am making my decision on the instruction now."

"Your honor, may I be heard?" Gillen said, jumping to his feet.

"No," T. Creed Rockburn said, sternly. "Sit down, Mr. McCoy."

"I think the government's request for an early ruling on this element of the charges is reasonable," he went on. "So that the cross-examination of the defense's witnesses can be reconciled with the court's charge. The government has proposed that the jury should be instructed that, quote,

> 'If you find that the defendant knew or should have known that his actions in arranging for the entry of the undocumented parents were in violation of a law or laws, and that he acted deliberately nonetheless, you should find him guilty on Counts II and III of the indictment, even if he believed he was acting morally, or if you as jurors think he was acting morally.'"

Goodbow froze at the judge's words. Rockburn stopped and looked down at Preston Bell.

"Did I get that right, Mr. Bell?" the judge said. "That is the charge you want?"

"It is, your honor. We think it's the correct charge."

The judge turned over the page and put another in his hands.

"Well, I don't," the judge said. Goodbow felt Gillen's hand on his wrist. "I don't see how it can be that when a law requires a corrupt mind to offend it, you offend it anyway by acting morally and in good conscience," the judge said. "You can square *immoral* behavior with corruption, but you can't square *moral* acts with corruption."

"Your honor!" Bell protested. "The law cannot be permitted to be intentionally broken!"

"These laws don't say 'intentionally broken.'" The judge said, evenly. "They say '*corruptly* broken.' I've read your argument; I've heard your argument. But I am going to go with Mr. McCoy's proposed instruction."

He read from the second paper he'd picked up. "Quote,

> 'Counts I and II of the indictment require that the defendant must have acted 'corruptly' in devising and carrying out his plan to bring the undocumented parents from Central America into the United States. If you find that the defendant acted in belief that his actions were morally correct and not 'wrong' or 'corrupt' in the normal sense of those words as you know them, you should find him not guilty under Counts II and III of the indictment.'

That will be my instruction on that element of the offenses at the close of the evidence. Now, let's move on."

He waved for the bailiff and the jury took its place in its box. Sister Hope Annie was escorted in and took her seat in the witness chair.

"Mr. Bell, you may proceed with your cross-examination."

The prosecutor rose, ashen faced.

"The government has no questions of the Sister," he said.

Goodbow looked into the piercing eyes of Gillen McCoy. Whether purposely in the name of judicial demeanor or simply because he was not surprised, T. Creed Rockburn simply looked down matter-of-factly at Sister Hope Annie.

"You are excused then, Sister," he said.

Sister Hope Annie rose, looked at the jury, then at Goodbow, and walked down the center aisle and out of the courtroom. Judge Rockburn looked down at the lawyers.

"All right, then," he said. "Next witness."

"The defense calls Lane Williams," Gillen declared.

Before the bailiff could retrieve the witness from the waiting room, Preston Bell rose and took one step toward the judge.

"Your honor?" he asked. "May we approach the bench?" With one hand Rockburn signaled the lawyers to walk up; with the other he turned on the white noise. Leaning low over the bench in his billowy gown to be near the ears of short Gillen McCoy and Preston Bell beside him, his elbows out, the judge looked like a massive eagle bending over the young in his nest.

"What is it now?" he asked Bell.

"In light of your ruling on the jury instruction, your honor, the government wonders if you would entertain a recess for the day so that I could confer with my superiors in Washington. To inform them of what has happened."

"What are you saying? That you may dismiss the charges?"

"It will be my recommendation, your honor."

"Well," said Judge T. Creed Rockburn. "Tell them they'd be wise to accept it."

EPILOGUE

Though he'd never been one to complain about the Atlantic coast winters in Rhode Island, Goodbow allowed himself that as long as he had to go through what he had, at least his timing was acceptable. He'd been away for the hard months. When he returned at last from Texas the crisp spring mornings were giving way to mild afternoons in Newport Harbor.

Sitting on the deck of *Grace* with Burp Lebeau, he relished the sailor's retelling of the long sail through the gulf and the Panama Canal, the pick-up at Amapala where he first met Sister Hope Annie, and the midnight drop in La Jolla where he met her again. Goodbow was not surprised that his old friend remembered the names of all of the parents. He was like that, Goodbow knew, always paying more attention than given credit for; caring and sensitive, even gentle, under his sun-crusted skin.

They were waiting for Gillen McCoy.

Only three weeks had passed since the abrupt end of the trial and Goodbow's walk from the courthouse as a free man, the old lawyer at his side. When Goodbow called him the next week to thank him—and tease him for sending the bill for his second retainer payment so promptly—he was surprised that Gillen was receptive to his invitation to visit him in New England for a cruise, and so soon.

"I would like that very much. How about week after next?"

"Really? You can get away that quickly?"

"People say I shouldn't put anything off for long."

Goodbow had hoped that Huff Langley could come too, but the marine asked for a rain check; he was planning a trip back to Amapala with a new girlfriend. "I like the place; what can I say?" he'd told Will.

"What time was Ben getting him at the airport?" Burp asked on the deck. Goodbow saw he was fidgety.

"About now. But we don't have to wait, Burp. I'll go down now and get the bottle. Is there enough Wild Turkey for both of us?"

"You know goddamned well there is. I made sure there's good scotch for the lawyer, too."

The single big cubes in their glasses had barely melted when Ben Goodbow strode up the ramp with Gillen. It was the first time Goodbow had seen the old lawyer dressed in anything other than a pressed suit and tie; he was wearing well-fitted khaki slacks and a black linen short-sleeved shirt. His trim, muscled arms looked like Burp's.

"Fine son you've got here," he said.

"He is."

"Don't outlive him."

Gillen often had a way of merging the serious with the light, but Goodbow knew this was a case of the former. The old lawyer had buried his own two sons and had told Goodbow that their deaths before his own were the most painful times of his life.

"Ready for scotch?" Goodbow asked. It seemed like a proper response.

"Sure, but first, could Burp take me around this thing? I want to see *The Sails of Grace*."

The captain and the lawyer went below. The father and son sat atop. They could hear Burp explaining the helm and all the dials on the monitor, and Gillen's many questions, interrupted by frequent laughter.

"I'm glad it worked out, Dad," Ben said. "I was afraid it wouldn't."

"You weren't the only one."

"I'm still getting calls from people wanting me to talk to them. About you."

"So is Gillen."

"You still want me to tell them 'no?'"

"Yeah. I don't want any attention. Gillen is sending them away too. It'll die down eventually."

"When are we setting sail?"

"After drinks. We'll eat at sea when we stop for the night. Burp's got something he wants to cook. Says it's something your mom liked."

"She liked everything he cooked. And everything they cooked together."

"So true."

Burp and Gillen returned to the deck and the lawyer lowered himself limberly into a chair at the rail, his drink in hand.

"It's like a fine hotel down there," he said.

"You like your state room?" Goodbow asked.

"Like it? What's not to like?"

"The ocean's gentle tonight," Burp said. "Really, there's good weather for the whole trip down and back."

"Where are we going, anyway? You said we'll be gone five

nights." Gillen said. He gazed out to the ocean beyond the array of high masts.

"Charleston," Goodbow said. "Charleston Harbor. South Carolina."

Why Charleston? Gillen wondered. But he remembered what Juan Rodriguez had said on the stand that he'd never asked the man from Rhode Island why he'd done what he'd done for the parents and their children. It seemed an obvious question. But in the moment, the father from Honduras had told the jury, it didn't seem to matter *why* he'd done it. All that mattered was that he and the other parents were with their children again. And now, after all that had happened, Gillen McCoy reasoned, it didn't much matter why Goodbow and his captain had chosen Charleston Harbor for their trip.

A few hours later, after the boat was anchored for the night in calm waters, they sat for dinner at the galley table. Goodbow took his glass and gestured to them all; a toast.

"To Grace," he said. "And to Sister Hope Annie. Two who did so much together without ever meeting."

The clinking of glasses was interrupted by Gillen McCoy.

"No, no!" he said with conviction. "That's not true, Will."

Goodbow was taken aback. He looked at the old lawyer, puzzled.

"Oh, they met, Will," McCoy said. "They met through you. You and Burp. Huff Langley. And Leary Deen, God love him. Through the little minister!"

"Burton Lief," Goodbow said.

"Yeah, through him Grace and the nun met. And that police chief in Minnesota. What was his name?"

"Woody Burns," Goodbow said.

"And the others too. Even Judge Rockburn. But especially, through *you*, Will. You did right by Grace. You did. You did right by everybody."

Though unintended, the old lawyer's summation brought objectionless quiet, near solemnity, to the table. Little was spoken as they ate Burp Lebeau's good meal or even when they rose to the deck for last call under the stars.

There was nothing more to say.